For My Beautiful Wife and Daughter

Laura and Mya

My Inspiration
My Engine
My Life

Chapter 1

God this job sucks!

The sun crept through the slats in the Venetian blinds, and particles of dust floated through the uniform streams of light which projected across the room. An alarm clock radio clicks into action. *"Good morning, you're listening to three two four in the morning, it's a miserable and cold morning in the west, but let's brighten it up with some classic rock. It's seven thirty five, I'm Tunebox Charlie and this is Creedence with Bad Moon rising."* The room was filled with a loud and tiresome groan, it was the sound made by a man who had no interest in moving from his pit, never mind surfacing and facing a day's work. Michael Cameron stretched his arm towards the alarm clock and like he did every morning, struck the snooze button with exaggerated force. He hoped today would be the day that he would not have to get up and make the daily commute. The sun grew gradually brighter and the light through the blinds caught his eyes for a brief moment, he retracted immediately, disgusted at the abrupt wakeup call and pulled the duvet up and over his eyes. It was a large double bed, and was lavishly draped in various layers of quilts and blankets which matched each other. The room was decorated by a woman, scatter cushions and pastel colours covered every wall and Michael's nose was filled with the same aroma of chemicals from the air freshener. It was battery powered and each morning automatically filled the room with a sickly sweet smell of vanilla which he had grown to despise. Michael's eyes were heavy and he began to drift back to sleep. *"Three two four in the Morning!"* A suitably cheesy Jingle played and Michael swung his hand in frustration towards the radio once again. *"Hey there, I'm Tunebox........"*. Smash! His hand came down and the radio alarm clock was silent for a second time. "Shut it Tunebox... same crap every morning..... Arsehole!" He grabbed a thick white pillow, wrapped it around his head in frustration and lay defiant. *"I'm not getting up today"* he thought. The bed frame rattled, he slowly removed the pillow from his face and glanced towards the end of the bed. The sunlight was casting long elongated shadows across the room and one of the streams of light perfectly lit the face of a young woman, she was pretty, in her mid to late twenties with long dirty blond hair. She peered at Michael with a look of disapproval. *"Mind your language Michael, Joseph is just next door getting ready for school"*

1

"Sorry sweetheart, I just hate that clown, every morning it's the same old shite". He grimaced as he swore again. *"Michael, I won't tell you again".*

"Oh come on, I only said shite".

"Now you're pushing it". Michael smirked as he reached out and grabbed his wife Kaitlin by her waist and pulled her down to bed tumbling on top of him, she smiled and pecked him on the cheek *"Come on, we need to get going....no time"* Michael pinned Kaitlin to the bed, and restricted her arms and began to tickle her ribs *"Shut it you ya wee shite"*

"Stop it" she said as she tried to wriggle free while giggling uncontrollably, Michael continued to wind her up *"Shite, Shite, Shite....say it!"* Kaitlin Struggled to speak through her giggling *"I will not"*

"What are you?, say it and I'll let ye go" not conforming to his demands, she struggled on, laughing and wrestling until Michael leaned towards her face and kissed her softly on the lips. Without warning an item struck Michael square on the forehead, sending him off balance and crashing to the floor. It was a miniature spider-man. A plastic figurine and it left a small lump. In the doorway stood a small boy about three foot tall with jet black shoulder length hair, he had on spider-man pyjamas and he stood staring at his father with a mischievous glint in his eye. *"Don't you call my mum a wee shite"* Michael grimaced again, knowing what was coming. *"Joseph Cameron!"* Kaitlin's face turned from laughter to a far more serious expression that only a mother is able to produce. *"Don't let me hear you use that word again"* Joseph stood still with his head bowed and glanced at his father for support. Realising that he was in just as much trouble as his son, Michael averted his eyes from Kaitlin's steely gaze and tried his hardest not to laugh. *"Your daddy should know better than to use bad words. Now promise that you won't use that bad word again"* Joseph responded like a typically scolded child *"I promise"*

"Now go and get ready for school" The little boy shuffled off as his mother turned to Michael, raising her eyebrow. He knew the look, although she was not normally proven to be right quite this quickly. *"I told you, he's like a sponge, imagine if he goes to school and speaks like that?"* Michael smiled

"It's not funny Michael!" Kaitlin turned away and began to collect various bits and pieces from the around the bedroom. *"O.K honey, I promise to try harder when he is in earshot, I don't mean it"* She ignored him and he made his way over to her, putting his arms around her. *"I'm sorry"* Kaitlin turned and kissed him on the end of the nose

2

"No more"

"O.K. O.K."

"Right then its five past, you're going to be late again"

"Do I have to go?"

"I know you hate it, but a job is a job, and the money isn't bad" Michael sighed and began to collect his uniform from a heap on the floor. *"I just thought that I would have got somewhere by now"* Kaitlin stopped what she was doing and moved over and embraced him *"You've got me and the little one"*

"I know, I want to be out discovering them and digging them up, not standing guard to make sure nobody tries to nick them!"

"You never know, another opening could come again soon" Michael was working as a security guard at the local art gallery and museum. He had previously studied for a degree in archaeology and wanted nothing more than to be out in the field, quite literally. *"Now that Joseph is in school, I can find a part time job and you can finish your degree"*

"We can't afford it Kaitlin!"

"We've survived until now, we can cope. I can't bear to see you hate your job so much"

"Maybe". Michael continued to get himself dressed as Kaitlin disappeared downstairs to continue with the morning rush. After a few moments he started down the stairs and made his way to the kitchen. The house was small; two bedrooms and not the most luxurious, but it was home and Michael was grateful for what he had. It could have been much worse. He had a beautiful wife who loved him very much, and a perfect little son who would make him gasp with amazement every single day. He could not help feeling that he could have been so much more and wished he could have provided a far more comfortable life for Kaitlin and Joseph. He walked into the kitchenette, the space was maximised and every part of the area was utilised in some way. Standing on a chair, Joseph reached out towards a cupboard door and grabbed a large box filled with frosted flakes, they were not the branded type advertised on television which he would sing along with, but the supermarkets own budget version, a sign of the times in the Cameron household. Michael stood and watched his son for a while, he was already dressed for school and was reading a comic book while eating his cereal. *"Who is it this morning Chief? Spider-man?"*

"I've read all my Spider-man ones Daddy, Mummy got me a new one"

"Is it good? Who is this one about?"

"Batman, it's dead good, but it's a bit scary"

3

"Not too scary I hope"

"No, not for me daddy, just a bit scarier than Spidey, that's all" Joseph loved superheroes and read comic books at such a rate that he had read them all a dozen times or so before Michael could afford to buy him some new ones. "Right you two, fingers out!" Kaitlin had now moved into the kitchen and had started directing the morning rush. The family had done the same every day of the week. Michael would work six days out of seven and if offered the overtime on a Sunday, he could not really afford to knock it back. "Right you little man, teeth, shoes, satchel, jacket, door, seatbelt, school. And as for you Daddy, five mins till we need to be out the door." Michael and Joseph glanced across the table and smiled in perfect unison with each other. They stood up poker straight and saluted "Yes Sir! Thank you Sir!"

"Come here you!" Kaitlin chased Joseph around the table and he scarpered upstairs giggling as he went. "He's just like you, you know" Michael smiled as Kaitlin likened him to his son. "I hope he's happy, do you think he's happy?" he asked. Kaitlin smiled

"As long as we stay together here as a family, and we don't keep wishing we had more than we need, we will always be happy"

"I just can't help thinking that there is something missing" Kaitlin cut him off and continued to emphasise how their life was more than sufficient. "You're a good man, with a wife who loves you so very much, and a perfect little boy, what else do you need Michael?" " I know you're right, I'm sorry" Kaitlin reached her arms around Michael and squeezed him tight, he could feel how much she really wanted him to be satisfied with their life. No matter how humble it was. He embraced her and kissed her softly on the forehead, trying to reassure her that he was satisfied, although the doubt was still there at the back of his mind. They continued to busy themselves getting ready to leave and were soon reassembled in the kitchenette. "Give him a shout, watch this" Michael Buttoned up his jacket and placed a towel over his arm. His jacket was a typical blazer with large shiny brass buttons. He stood up straight with the towel over his arm and grabbed a tea try from the side like a waiter in a restaurant. Kaitlin called Joseph downstairs and the house rattled as he thundered down the stairs at full pelt. He screeched to a halt as he entered the kitchenette. Michael tilted his head back slightly and pointed his nose upwards with towel and tray on display. " Good morning Master Bruce, would it suit Sir to travel in the Bentley and leave the 'other car' at home today" Michael winked at Joseph who recognised his character straight away "Excellent idea Alfred" Joseph giggled and he ran out the front door and jumped into the back seat of the car. " He loves you, he's your

4

double" Kaitlin laughed then kissed her husband and waved them off as Michael drove off down the street to drop Joseph off at school and make his way to work. The car was not a Bentley; in fact, it was a nine year old Vauxhall Corsa, which had seen better days. But to Michael and his son it could have been a Rolls Royce or even a NASA space shuttle. They always created an imaginary world, were they would fantasise that they inhabited different characters, today it was Batman and Alfred the butler, tomorrow it could be anything from Egyptian Mummies to astronauts. Michael's mind wandered as he pulled up outside the school. *"Daddy?"* Joseph looked puzzled as Michael continued to stare blankly into space. *"Daddy?"* The louder shout from Joseph startled him and he turned to face him *"Sorry Sir, I was thinking about butler stuff"* Joseph chuckled and opened the back door of the car. *"You have a good day wee man"* Joseph jumped out the car and started walking up the path towards the school entrance. *"Love you son"* Joseph turned and saluted like they had done that morning to Kaitlin, he waved goodbye and disappeared into the main door. Michael pulled out and headed for the main road. The traffic lights turned to green and he crossed into the junction. From nowhere a car zoomed past the front of his car and just missed the front end. Michael's eyes were transfixed on the vehicle, it was a bright red Porsche 911, a car that he had always dreamed about owning. The seriousness of the incident that had just occurred was lost on him, he had been so mesmerised by the car that he did not even break a sweat at the chance of being flattened by the oncoming vehicle. The car behind him began to honk its horn, the noise helped to bring Michael back from the fantasy land he had slipped into dragging his consciousness back to the real world. *"Alright mate, Give us a break"* Michael restarted the engine and gave the impatient driver behind him a dismissive flick of the wrist and resumed the usual route towards his work. Not being important enough for his own parking space, Michael parked on the street outside the museum and paid for a ticket to cover his twelve hour shift. He placed the ticket on the dashboard behind the steering wheel and locked the doors. Turning to face the museum, he took a long deep breath and made his way through the entrance wondering whether this would be the shift when he finally cracked up with the monotony. The museum was old, sandstone and its exterior was very gothic in style. The main entrance was grand and had large solid wooden doors which had been heavily polished and treated with great care. The interior was generic like any museum. It could have been situated anywhere and had exhibits dotted about the main entrance that you could have seen in any museum around the world.

5

The large wooden doors swung slowly shut behind Michael, they creaked with a shrill and uncomfortable wail which made him squirm with displeasure. The main desk was large and central in the entrance hall, stairs and corridors went in every direction. Michael noticed that the temperature was a lot cooler than usual. *"Jesus Christ Pat! It's Baltic in here!"* Behind the desk sat a middle aged man around fifty years old, he was bald on the top with grey shaved hair on the sides and back, he was absolutely huge. The desk chair that he sat in looked as if at any moment it could explode into its component parts and sent it's occupant to the earth with an almighty crash. *"Where the hell have you been?"* Pat barked at Michael while eating a pasty which he lifted from a plate which contained another two upon it. Flakes of pastry flew from his mouth in every direction. *"What you talking about? I'm not late am I?"* Pat blew air through his nostrils and replied *"Yeah for once"*. The fat guard turned in his chair and reached for a leaflet which he threw in Michael's direction. The desk chair groaned like a caged animal which was being subjected to constant torture. "AMAZING ARTEFACT ADVENTURE". The leaflet detailed a special day at the museum which involved a special tour of "MYSTICAL AND UNIDENTIFIED OBJECTS". The open day was an attempt to lure the next generation of budding school children to visit the museum and spend their pocket money in the gift shop. *"Yeah? So? What about it?"* Michael looked at Pat with a puzzled expression and stood patiently for the next instalment of his regular morning abuse session. *"Well if you were in early like you said you would be, you would know"* *"Listen Pat, I said I might be able to come in early, I never......."* Pat cut him short and barked at him again *"If you ever want to get anywhere in this company then your attitude really needs to change"* Michael sighed and tried to make his disinterest in what Pat had to say as obvious as possible. *"I never made it to supervisor by lying in my bed, or sitting on my arse".* Michael sniggered at the irony of Pat's comment and quickly covered it up with a tactical clearing of the throat. *"Alright Pat, what's the deal?"*

" Had you come in early............................... then you would have known what happened with this morning's delivery" Michael looked at him blankly and intentionally did not speak to him, having decided that he would not waste any further brain cells on museum security's answer to Jabba the Hut. *"It's in the basement and it's a massive delivery"* Michael continued to stare blankly at Pat, knowing full well that he was trying his hardest to break his temper. *" We have been asked to help bring it up to the exhibition space, cordon the area off and get the display ready for public consumption"* Michael raised his

eyebrow with confusion at what Pat was saying to him. *"Bring it, and set it up?"*

"That's what I said didn't I?"

"Since when do we do the curator's job?"

"Since I said to the manager that I would help as they are short staffed today, and since I am sitting here, that means that you are going to be a busy boy" Pat sniggered as he could see the rage building up in Michael's face. He held his temper, even though he was completely seething at what he was being subjected to. *"What's the matter Cameron? Bit of manual labour too lowly for the university dropout? Come on, chop, chop"* Michael's face was now bright red and if he had been a cartoon, steam would have been coming out of his ears. He took a deep breath and tried to focus on the bigger picture, it would have given him the greatest amount of pleasure to physically and verbally destroy Pat where he sat but he remembered Joseph and Kaitlin and how important his wage was, no matter how measly and insufficient it was. For now at least he would have to accept the horrific abuse of power that he was the victim of. Exhaling slowly, Michael looked Pat straight in the eye and nodded. Although the nod confirmed his obedience, Pat looked uneasy as it was the sort of nod that gave the connotation that his card was marked. Michael walked away towards the service elevator, safe in the knowledge that he had given Pat a stare which had unsettled him. He allowed himself a private snigger as he imagined himself being a mafia don who had just stapled a price tag to a wise guys forehead. The service elevator was large and had a wrought iron gate which had to be shut manually. It was old and occasionally it would stick but Michael knew just the right way to pull at it and slammed it shut, pressing the button to start the descent to the museum basement. The descent lasted less than a minute and the whirr of the lifts mechanism was loud and industrial, it stopped suddenly and Michael pulled at the handle a few times until it finally opened with a loud creak from metal which needed some overdue lubrication. The Basement was in total darkness and Michael reached for his torch which was dangling from his holster attached to the belt which was part of his uniform. The basement was even colder than the foyer upstairs and Michael could see his breath bellowing up towards the ceiling when he shone the torchlight in front of his face. He walked up the centre, between two large racks which ran the entire length of the basement until he reached the wall at the far end. He shone the torchlight onto the wall and located the switch to turn on the main lights and flicked the switch. The large sodium bulbs began to hum and flicker as they grew gradually brighter. They lit in order

7

from one side of the basement to the other. Michael left the lights to fully illuminate as he always did and headed to the back corner of the basement where a small corner office was situated, he opened the door and flicked on a small lamp which lit instantly, quickly shutting the door behind him. He lit a small gas fire in the corner of the office and flicked the switch on his little kettle making himself a cup of coffee. Sitting down he shut his eyes and tried to relax, putting the last five minutes spent with Pat behind him. Pat was always on Michael's back. He lived alone and had no family of his own, Michael had guessed that was why he was so mean to him. Pat never really had anything to look forward to in his life and it seemed he had made a decision to fill his time with making his subordinates suffer more than he was, filling the rest of his spare time eating pies, cakes and torturing furniture. Michael finished making his coffee and sat back in his chair, putting his feet up on the desk. He didn't have to worry about Pat down here, he very rarely left his desk and it was unthinkable that he would drag himself all the way down to the basement. He spent the next ten minutes or so relaxing and enjoying his coffee before he stood up and groaned, stretching his arms high above his head and got his days' work under-way. The delivery was enormous, box after box of the weird and wonderful. It was a large collection of wooden crates and containers and Michael had to prise each of them open with a crowbar and a claw hammer. The exhibit was based around the unexplained and unidentified, and it was to be made as much fun for the kids as possible. So each exhibit was supported by a back story. A myth or legend which would suitably get the cogs turning in the children's minds, letting their imagination run away with them and inspiring them to part with theirs and their accompanying guardian's money. Michael got a certain degree of satisfaction from getting involved with the objects, although it was mainly just fetching and carrying. Amongst all the items was a Scottish Claymore which was enormous and he struggled to lift it from the shredded paper which it lay in. It was encased in a glass box and he only just managed to shunt it onto his trolley and push it into the service elevator. As he pushed it towards the exhibition area he took the time to read the description card which was attached to the front of its glass case "16TH CENTURY SCOTTISH CLAYMORE BROADSWORD. *A TWO HANDED WEAPON FROM THE HIGHLANDS OF SCOTLAND, THIS PARTICULAR SWORD IS SAID TO HAVE BEEN USED BY GENERATIONS OF THE SAME CLAN, BRINGING ITS WEILDER UNRIVALLED STRENGTH AND STAMINA".* Michael smiled as he read the inscription, he could see how the author had hammed up the description in order to catch the imagination of

8

the visiting children. The next exhibit was large and was easily the heaviest of all the items that Michael had to carry to the exhibition space. The sarcophagus was large, about 6 feet long and made of solid stone. Michael had to utilise a pulley and a flatbed trolley to get it into position. He had used the equipment on many occasions before, he was always called upon when a particularly large item was delivered to the museum. The description read *"EGYPTIAN SARCOPHAGUS:CIRCA 1200 B.C. THIS LARGE STONE OUTER SHELL WOULD HAVE BEEN THE FINAL RESTING PLACE OF SOMEONE OF GREAT IMPORTANCE, THE IDENTITY OF THE MUMMY INSIDE STILL REMAINS A MYSTERY TO THIS DAY"* Michael spent the entire morning and well into the afternoon moving items to and from the exhibit area. The final few items consisted of various ceramics from around the world and about a dozen stuffed creatures. The biggest of them all was a model of a woolly mammoth, it was not life size, but it only just made it into the service elevator. There was a mock-up of an abominable snowman and an interpretation of the missing link. Michael took great care not to damage any of them as he strategically placed them around the exhibit, taking his time to select the best viewing area with regards to era and place of origin. The last few boxes were in the miscellaneous category and included items which had no real solid identification, they could have been anything and were too obscure in the main to make a definitive claim as to their origin or purpose, the aim of their inclusion in the exhibit was to engage with the children's imagination and encourage them to invent what each of the items could have been for. Michael carried the first box of unexplainable oddities up to the exhibition room and began to carefully unpack them. They had all been carefully wrapped and stored with the same care as the items which had identification, after all they could have been the rarest objects on earth, simply awaiting a great thinker of our time to categorise them. Michael began to lay the items out on the table, the first item was a sort of spoon with two thin parts which came from its end which made it look like antennae. Michael spent five minutes attempting to identify it before moving onto the next object. It was made of bone and was very fragile, it had five small holes in it which seemed to be ideally spaced for the fingers of one hand to fit into. Michael imagined it was some sort of primitive weapon, from a bygone era where it was not unusual for the tribe leaders to match their fittest and prized children in a fight to the death over territory or even marriage rights. He was guilty of drifting off into his own little world, regularly doing it at work, because unlike today he was always at his most bored while wandering back and forth watching the punters ogle

9

the artefacts. Recently though he had started to drift away even when he was at home with Joseph and Kaitlin. Kaitlin had noticed his distant and fragile demeanour and suggested that he go to see a doctor. After a few weeks of deliberation, he decided that it was the right thing to do and made an appointment. The doctor advised that *"Due to the pressures of modern living he was stressed and bordering on a depressed state"* Michael felt that the doctor's prescription and diagnosis were way off the mark; no pills would help him get a grip on what was going on, something was missing. The disappointment of his failed career as an archaeologist generated most of his resentment and unhappiness, he felt he had so much more to offer and was being chained down by his acceptance of reality and his desire to just make do with what life had given him. He would sometimes wake in the night and blurt out incoherent babble which Kaitlin jokingly likened to the *"Cuckoo's Nest Syndrome"*. She used humour to divert his and her own attention from the actual severity of the problem. Michael would wake at times in a state of absolute hysteria and it would take Kaitlin as much as an hour to calm him down. It was always the same feeling of fear and dread, but he was never able to remember what the nightmare had been about. Michael stood staring blankly into space as he examined the various objects and slipped between one little fantasy and the next, his imagination kept him sane for the most part. The tiresome and familiar sound of Pat's voice was the next assault on his senses *"Hey professor Cameron……. You've only got an hour to finish that"* Pat's sarcastic remark had fallen on deaf ears, Michael was having a great time working with all the interesting objects and he wasn't going to let Pat get him down. Making his way back to the basement, Michael continued to complete his task. Although it had been a lot of hard work, he had really enjoyed getting to touch and work with the artefacts. The added bonus was he had been that busy that the day had disappeared and I wouldn't be long until he was able to go home to see Kaitlin and Joseph. It certainly beat spending the day marching up and down and reprimanding people for getting too close or directing old ladies to the bathroom. There were a final few crates to empty and Michael had been bringing them up one by one so as not to drop or damage any of them. The last thing he needed was an excuse for Pat to get on his case for something else. The service elevator descended for what felt like the hundredth time and Michael made his way through the basement towards the final few crates of the delivery. As he approached, he was stopped in his tracks by an unusual and alien noise, it was unlike anything he had ever heard before. A loud buzzing and crackling emanated from the freshly

10

delivered crates. The sound got louder and louder until it was so loud that Michael had to cover his ears and winced with pain, it rang out for a few seconds more then stopped as abruptly as it had started. It was accompanied by a basement wide power failure. The entire area was in complete darkness and Michael began to breathe quicker, his heart pumped more vigorously and the beat was more pronounced with every extra moment spent in the darkness. He fumbled at his belt for his torch and it crashed to the floor, it rolled across the floor in the darkness and Michael could have sworn he heard someone moving in the aisles of the basement *"Who's there?"* Panic had sent his mind wandering, noises rang out through the basement, creaks and groans echoed throughout the old building and for a moment he could have sworn he heard the sound of a woman's voice. He took a deep breath and made his way in a straight line towards the light switches. He was only a few feet away when he was once again stopped dead in his tracks. The lights came back on in the basement. The brightness of the lights was overpowering as his eyes attempted to adjust to them. They had come on all at once which was unusual as they always came on in the same sequential order. The noise of the elevator kicking into action grabbed his attention and he opened his eyes. The elevator had started to head back up the main floor, it had been called by someone upstairs. Michael was concerned at who it could have been, no one ever came down to the basement on his shift, it could only have been one person and it had to be an emergency or a really big problem to get Pat out of his chair. The elevator started to make its descent and Michael made his way across the basement to greet whoever had made the effort to come for a visit. His good intentions were soon doused by the acceptance that it was indeed Pat who had prised himself from reception to make an unscheduled visit. His brow was soaked with sweat and he struggled to get the breath to speak *"What's wrong Pat?"*

"*You.........*" Pat took a long deep breath and continued *"What did you do?"* Michael thought for a second and then he realised that Pat was quizzing him about the power cut. *"Oh the power"*

"The whole building went out, what did you do Cameron?" Michael was straight on the defensive *"I never touched anything, there must be a problem with the circuit board"* Pat snorted with distaste at Michael's explanation *"So now you're an electrician eh?"* Pat hit the button in the elevator and it started to head back up to the main floor *" And hurry up with the rest of that gear, the boss will be here in a half an hour and it better be ready"* Michael made his way back to the office and picked up his coffee, he was overcome with anger and

frustration at the way in which Pat had treated him and launched his cup at the wall, it bounced back landing on the desk the right way up, leaving no evidence that he had even thrown it in the first place " *Can't even smash a fuckin' cup!*". He took another long and deep breath and composed himself. *"Rise above it Michael"* he said aloud. Turning to the delivery, he began to collect the remaining boxes fitting them onto the flatbed trolley, there was no time left for individual delivery, he had to make this deadline or he would be harassed by Pat. The trolley filled with relative ease until he reached the last box, Michael tried every way he could to get the last box to stay on the trolley securely. The box would not fit and he slid it onto a shelf and turned to push the rest of the items to the elevator, he could run down at the last minute and grab the final one he thought. The trolley was heavy and he struggled to get it moving and just as it released and started moving, Michael stopped and turned to face the last box, he was drawn to it and approached to study it with more care. The description read *"CATEGORY: MISCELLANEOUS, ORIGIN UNSPECIFIED, ERA UNSPECIFIED (CARBON FREE)"* Michael entered the office and opened the folder which new deliveries were recorded in, he thought he better store it correctly, just in case it went missing. That would result in him losing his job for sure. Michael scanned the folder for the first available position on the racks *"Row D, position 324"* Michael noted the position in the folder and carried the box to the shelf space. The elevator clunked into motion and Michael wheeled the remaining items to the exhibition room and set them up, he cordoned off the valuable items with metal stands and embroidered rope finishing with a few moments to spare. *"About time as well Cameron"* Pat was just about to deliver the next insult when he jumped up from his chair like a coiled spring and his demeanour changed from the big unfriendly giant to a far more practiced and professional manner. The front doors had slipped open and a middle aged lady in a dress suit had entered, she was making her way straight to the exhibition room. The woman caught Pat and shouted across the foyer to him *"Pat, how did we get on with the staff issue?"*

   "We managed Mrs Coleridge, I hope it's to your liking" Michael stood back and watched as Pat grovelled to the museum manager. She walked around the exhibit and Pat followed like a man servant awaiting her judgement. *"Pat........come here"* Pat scurried over to her side and Michael was repulsed by the blatant ass kissing he was witnessing. Mrs Coleridge took a sharp intake of breath and abruptly asked *"Who's responsible for this?"*

"Oh I'm sorry Mrs Coleridge, I had no choice, I got Cameron to do it"

"Get him" Pat turned and looked at Michael

"Michael, could you come over here please?" Pat's pretence was hilarious to Michael, *"What a complete brown nose"* he thought.

"Michael is it?"

"Michael Cameron, Mrs Coleridge" interrupted Pat.

"Pat, go and get me some tea"

"Right away Mrs Coleridge" the Manager sighed with relief as Pat left for her tea

"So again, Michael is it?"

"That's me"

"Alison Coleridge, Area Manager.......you set up this display?" Michael nodded in agreement. *"Hardly the work of a security guard is it? Have you done this sort of stuff before?"* Michael cleared his throat, anticipating his next words

"I studied a bit and then my son came along, you know?"

"Listen Michael, can I call you Michael?"

"Sure"

"This is excellent work, you're wasted in that uniform. A position just became available upstairs within artefact selection and procurement, I think you would be perfect" Michael stood silent and struggled to find anything slightly intelligent to reply with, he could have kissed her right where she stood *"So are you interested?"* He gathered his thoughts for a second and considered the ramifications of his reply. *"It is the opportunity I have been looking for, but due to my commitments, unfortunately it would come down to the wage, I couldn't take a cut, we couldn't afford it"* Mrs Coleridge looked unfazed by the deeply personal details Michael had revealed to her. *"How much do you make now?"*

"About eighteen including overtime"

"O.K, how about thirty with no overtime, unless you want to work it that is" Michael's excitement was impossible to hide *"I don't know what to say?"*

"Say yes Michael Cameron, you could go a long way with us"

"Yes, definitely yes"

"Excellent, O.K. Monday morning, suit and tie, don't be late". Mrs Coleridge turned to face the reception desk and shouted to Pat *"Pat put the word out, we need a new security guard"* Pat watched on as Michael shook hands with Mrs Coleridge and then made his way over to the reception desk. Michael remained emotionless and busied himself sorting the exhibition leaflets which were piled up on the desk

13

front. *"So what was all that about?"* Michael played dumb *"What's that Pat?"* Pat became irate and barked in his usual fashion *"Spit it out Cameron"* Michael took a long deep breath of fresh air and looked Pat direct and menacingly in his eyes *"You better get your fat arse out of that poor chair and check that circuit board, protocol dictates that I bring in cakes to celebrate my promotion, you'll like that"* Pat's face drooped with disappointment at the realisation of the situation *"And Pat.......from Monday it's Mr Cameron......O.K?"*

Chapter 2

Stop, look and listen

The alarm clock was just as piercing and irritating as it always was, and was just about to be given the same treatment it received on a daily basis. An outstretched arm reaches over to it and flicks the snooze button with no hesitation. It was another morning spent in the same vein as always for Michael Cameron, he tried as ever to put the inevitable on hold. The snooze button was pressed so much that the lettering had started to fade and the white plastic casing had started to show through the paint. *"Michael! You are going to be late!"* Kaitlin had hollered again, it was at least the third or fourth time this morning. Michael groaned loudly, the tone of his voice made it obvious that he was in no mood to be getting out of bed and he retracted his feet immediately once they had slipped from the comfort of the duck down duvet cover and planted on the icy cold floor. A beautiful hardwood polished finish, shone under the cracks of light which broke through the curtains and lit the room with a dim yellow light. Michael stood up and stretched, his back cracked as he circled his arms by the side of his body and he let out a satisfied groan. He walked towards the window and opened the blinds, it was a miserable and cold day. It was one of those mornings that could have been dusk. Grey, wet and lifeless, Michael let out a snort of disapproval after inspecting todays attempt at weather. The street was quiet and was lined with lots of well-maintained and architecturally attractive homes with well-kept gardens. Across the street a white van was parked in the road and painted across the side of the van was the company's name, printed in red and black lettering "J PARKES AND SON QUALITY HOME IMPROVEMENTS" Michael watched as a few bodies scurried back and forth from the van, going about their business. The men carrying various tools and materials for a job which was being carried out around the back of the neighbouring house. Michael was well aware what was being constructed as he had been subject to a detailed verbal description from the site manager. Mrs Wallace was his over-friendly and somewhat locally despised neighbour. It was a conservatory and not just any old conservatory, the biggest and best conservatory that money could buy. Michael found it hard not to dislike the Wallaces, they were the sort of people who would not have spoken to him or his family just a short while ago when he was a lowly security guard. Mr Wallace was not quite so bad, but he was still no

15

stranger to bragging to anyone he could about their latest upgrade or extension. Mrs Wallace had emerged from the background and was now standing, inspecting like a Nazi overseer. She stood stony faced and glared at the workers as they darted back and forth like prisoners in a concentration camp. Michael watched how the men avoided making eye contact with her, scared that she would scold their performance or even issue them with yet another task to carry out. Or worst of all get stuck in one of her pointless, yet lengthy conversations which Michael had been caught with on a few dire occasions. If Mrs Wallace could do anything it was talk for long periods about anything, regularly herself. Michael stood for a short while and watched the latest grand project continue while he slipped away into his own little world. Gazing blankly out the bedroom window. *"Michael! Michael!"* He shook his head, to bring himself round from his dazed condition and answered his wife *"O.K I'm up!"*

*"Twenty minutes and then we need to go "*Michael turned back to the window for a second and a feeling of dread came over him as he was caught in Mrs Wallace's gaze from across the street. She was immediately buoyant with excitement as she had caught Michael watching her empire grow. Michael was caught and it would have been too obvious now to simply ignore her as she looked right at him and started to wave while mouthing *"Hello Neighbour"*. Michael tried to be as convincing as he possibly could with his forced smile and reciprocated wave. He stepped back from the window out of her site again *"Hello Neighbour.....pah!"* Michael mimicked Mrs Wallace in a particularly nasal tone of voice and crossed the bedroom into his bathroom. There were two solid oak doors, side by side and Michael entered the left hand side one. There was an ornate bathroom set, including a sink, toilet pan, bidet and a shower cubicle which was a decent size, tiled from the floor to the ceiling. Michael filled the sink with hot water and began to wash his face. The next stage was the deliberation over whether he had to shave or not. He stood massaging his chin, getting an idea of the current state of growth *"You ready yet?"* Michael winced at the sound of Kaitlin's voice, his patience was being sorely tested. He took a long and slow breath and replied *"Nearly, I've just got to shave.......ten mins"* Michael sighed and picked up his razor. It was rough on his skin and he grimaced as it cut its way through the short stubbly hair with a staggered and stunted motion. He was in a rush, as he always seemed to be and never had the time to prepare his skin correctly to allow a nice smooth and clean shave. He was nearly finished and had just one small area of unshaven skin just

under his right nostril. The razor pressed against his face and he was sure to tilt his head back to ensure that he got the last of the stubble in one easy stroke. *"Five mins"* Kaitlin's sudden outburst made him jump and he let out a little yelp of pain. *"For fuck's sake!"* Michael threw the razor into the sink and rinsed the remaining foam from off his face. Kaitlin came storming up the stairs and Michael could hear the clip clop of her heels on the hard wood steps. Her approaching stride was laboured and Michael could tell that she was coming to his aide with a degree of reluctance. *"What's wrong with you?"* Michael never answered and let the action of dabbing his top lip with some toilet paper demonstrate exactly where his outburst had come from. *"What? Is that it? I thought there was something wrong!"*

"It's your god damn timing, I'm sure you do it for badness sometimes" Kaitlin stood at the bathroom door and displayed a look of bemusement at Michael's ridiculous claim. *"What the hell are you talking about?"*

"You!, with your fuckin' cockerel impression every morning, it's eight o clock, it's half eight……..five mins, now I've got to look like a teenager in front of the board" until now Kaitlin had remained calm, but was now red in the face and looked ready to explode any second. *"Just get a move on, I've got loads to get done this morning…..no time for tantrums"* Michael had also become fired up and was lining up his next insult, ready for retaliation when he stopped himself and decided to concentrate on getting out the door as quickly as possible. *"You're slowing me down with your crap, I will be ready on time, just like I am every morning"*

"Great! I'll be downstairs waiting, the kitchen is gleaming and there's some fresh cookies in the oven" Kaitlin left the bedroom and slammed the door angrily, the wall shook and Michael winced again, feeling that one of these days the door would fly from its hinges. Kaitlin's sarcasm was not lost on him and he even allowed himself a wry smile, he could appreciate a bit of aggressive humour even if it was directed at him. A lot had changed in the last few years. Little Joseph was now a young man and had just spent his first semester at St Cuthbert's private school for boys, a perk of being more financially stable. Kaitlin's life could not have changed much more, her previous existence as the perfect housewife and mother, had now been replaced by a far more career focused one. She was now the sole owner and Manager of a chain of hair and beauty salons. Soon after Michael was promoted and they began to see the monetary benefits of

his new position, they decided to employ an Au Pair. While the paid addition to the family dealt with many of Joseph's needs and wants, Kaitlin was able to focus her time, building her own little empire. Unfortunately with success and progression there comes a downside and the increased bank balance had a detrimental effect on the family unit, which suffered some lasting damage. The first step which led to the massive shift in the Cameron household's happiness was when Michael gained his first promotion. Within a year he was transferred to head office in the city and it was not long until he was flying high in the world of antiquities acquisition. The office block was massive, all glass and shiny stainless steel. It was the sort of building that once they had finished cleaning the windows they just packed up their stuff and started all over again. Michael's office was the third corner office on the twenty fourth floor and it was larger than his house when he was still working security at the museum. Michael moved across the bedroom to Kaitlin's side of the bed which had unwrinkled bed clothes and was generally uninhabited in recent months. He slid open a large door which revealed a plethora of suits in many shades and designs, there was an array of shoes, all Italian and the smell of leather was almost overpowering. At the back of the wardrobe was a large solid iron safe, it was very old and had been an item which Michael acquired through his contacts at work. He kept important documents and a small amount of cash for emergencies. He threw on a shirt and tie and picked a suit with suitably matching shoes *"Kaitlin"*

"Yes dear?" Kaitlin continued with the sarcasm which Michael chose to ignore again *"That's me right.....where's my case?"*

"I've just finished polishing it" Michael held his tongue and proceeded to head downstairs. Kaitlin stood in the hallway and was fixing her hair and make-up in the large mirror which took up most of the wall. *"Thought you were ready?"* Michael couldn't help getting his own little dig back at her and her replied exasperated *"Just move will you"*. Both of them had become long sick and tired of the constant bickering at each other, their success in their working lives had come at a price. They now passed each other like ships in the night, and the longest conversation that they had this weather was usually an argument. They lived in a mansion in comparison to the little house that Joseph had been born in. Five bedrooms, double en suite and a son in a prestigious private school had replaced, two bedrooms, non-branded cereal but an altogether far happier existence. Michael felt at times that the relationship was too far gone to even bother attempting to remedy it. *"Right, let's go"* Kaitlin Pointed to the front door and

18

they both exited and headed around the side of the house over the top of the chipped marble driveway towards the large double garage. Michael pressed the button on his keys and the garage door lifted, revealing a space big enough for four family cars. On one side of the garage there were two cars parked nose to tail. A large BMW estate car blocked in a little soft top sports car which Kaitlin had been given as a birthday present a few years earlier from Michael. The other side of the garage was piled high with all sort of stuff. Lawnmowers, cardboard boxes full of paint pots and old photo frames, along with various other bric a brac which was in no sort of order. *"I know I'll get it at the weekend"* Michael was quick to get in there before Kaitlin who was primed and ready to get on his back about a recurring issue. *"If it was clear, then I could use my side and you wouldn't need to block me in every night."* Michael sighed again

"Alright, I'll get to it" Michael snapped impatiently and stormed around the garage placing his briefcase in the back seat and prepared to leave, he turned to Kaitlin. *"I'm working late and then I'll go and pick up Joseph?"* Kaitlin failed to register Michael's question and he coughed to get her attention. *"What?!"* The impatient look was one that Michael had been accustomed to. He repeated himself *"Working late, and then pick up Joseph?"* Kaitlin nodded her acceptance and muttered unenthusiastically

"Right, see you later". Kaitlin sat down in her car behind Michael's and peered through the windscreen at him with a look of expectancy on her face, he sighed for what felt like the hundredth time and made his disappointment at their morning repertoire as obvious as he could. He was worn down and yearned for some sort of common ground in their relationship. The spark had left their partnership a long time ago and they both had suffered, through their pursuit of perfection and financial security in their careers. Their affection, love and respect for each other had almost completely dissipated and their hope of any sort of revival had become as empty as one side of the Queen sized bed from which Michael had awoken that morning. He looked through the windscreen at her again and shrugged his shoulders. Opening the door of his car, he was met by the pungent smell of stale cigar smoke. One of the pitfalls of success was the need to socialise with potential business partners and buyers, and with them came golf, casinos and countless cigars. The large diesel engine kicked into action and Michael slowly crept out the garage and down the driveway. The marble chips displaced and a few pinged across the garden like low flying bullets, gently coming to rest on the finely

19

packed artificial grass. Kaitlin swung her little soft top, around the right hand side of Michael, did a quick check and shot off down the road, leaving Michael without a goodbye. She was on her way to her first meeting of the day at one of the salons. She had to meet a few suppliers and mingle with the upper class wives and partners who frequented her highbrow establishments. Not unlike Mrs Wallace, Kaitlin understood the importance of providing lip service as she knew it massaged their ego which ultimately led to their continued patronage. Some of her high end custom had been generated through colleagues and business associates of Michael, it worked out mutually beneficial to both parties and in turn helped to grow the Cameron Empire. Michael pulled up outside an enormous tower block and reversed into his parking space which was now reserved especially for him, no more parking meters and long walks in the rain. *"Morning Mr Cameron"*

"Morning sir". A chorus of greetings rang out as Michael made his way to the front doors of the building, never once lifting his head in acknowledgement. Michael Cameron had become one of *'them'*. He remembered how he used to despise them when he worked in the museum. Too high level to even have the good manners to greet the lowly dogsbodies. His excuses were flimsy to say the least and he constantly remind himself of them in order to douse the burning feeling of guilt. He could not be seen fraternising with the workforce, not in his position. The front doors were on an automated sensor, about ten feet tall and made completely of glass. They hummed with a quiet whirr as they opened.

"Morning Mr Cameron"

"Morning Eddie...you good today?"

"I'm great Mr Cameron and you?" Michael leaned into Eddie and whispered into his ear *"You know how it is Eddie, same shit, different day"* Eddie laughed

"That's right sir" Michael continued on his way to the office and was trumpeted on his way by Eddie's voice *"You have a good day, Mr Cameron"* Michael turned and smiled, then continued his way to the elevator. Eddie was an old man who was way past retirement age. He had been given special permission to work on from upper management. Eddie was regimental with his work ethic, being an ex-forces man he was disciplined and reliable and was well known and

popular with all the staff. His wife had passed away the year previous to his retirement and he had hinted that he would have nothing else to do but grow old and die had he been forced to take his retirement. Michael had always stayed friendly with him. He gave him some sort of connection to his roots that he had lost touch with and he was the one who sanctioned Eddie's request to continue in his position. Eddie was the head of security and Michael always looked out for him, secretly taking pleasure, knowing that he had not been totally consumed by his new executive lifestyle. The elevator clicked at the twenty fourth floor and he headed down the corridor towards his office. A few others greeted him as they passed and they were subject to the same disinterest that Eddie was exempt from. A young woman approached and handed him a pile of papers *"Morning sir...........the Mayan expert at eleven thirty and the distribution committee will be here at two p.m.......board meeting in half an hour as usual"*

"Thanks Carol"

"Will there be anything else sir?"

"Coffee please" Carol disappeared and Michael entered his office. It was incredibly modern and clinical in style. A large glass desk was accompanied by a trio of leather chairs. The office was on the corner of the building and three of the four walls were glass from the floor to the ceiling. The view was magnificent. Michael sat in his chair at his desk and was completely oblivious to the plush surroundings that had become normality for him. The office door opened and Carol entered carrying a small tray with some cups and a steaming hot pot of coffee. There were also some small accompaniments on a little side plate, mini cakes and biscuits. She proceeded to start to pour a cup and Michael stopped her *"I'll get it Carol"* Carol smiled

"O.K. Sir, you have twenty three minutes"

"Roger" Michael smiled and saluted Carol jokingly, who giggled a little and left. Michael finished pouring the cup of Coffee and then sat staring into the freshly poured cup, watching the hot steam rise and disappear into the atmosphere. It wasn't long before his mind began to wander again. Although life had changed considerably in the last few years, Michael still drifted off and thought about the same things he had when he worked at the museum. He always got lost in his thoughts, always with the underlying feeling that something was missing from his life or that something just didn't fit. The view from

21

his office was unbelievable and he sat staring into the distance trying to contemplate exactly what it could be that preyed on his mind for so long. What else could he need out of life? He had the big house with the top of the range luxuries and the fancy car. He had the Job he had always dreamed about. His family was still there, at least he had managed to keep them together, no matter how fragile it had become. Michael knew that his inadequate relationship with Kaitlin needed some serious attention, but he never sought to give the problem the correct amount of attention because deep down inside his soul he knew that the root cause of his distress was not a matter of the heart. Whatever it was, he never made any progress on determining what it could be, no amount of money or power or domestic happiness and wellbeing would satisfy his thirst to understand what was missing from his life *"Mr Cameron?"* Michael Jumped out of his skin as Carol broke him out of the deep train of thought which he had been consumed by again. *"That's the gentlemen on their way up"* Michael did some facial exercises and woke himself up and was soon joined by five other men. They all sat around the large desk at the far end of Michael's office. They were all similar in appearance and demeanour, flash suits and middle age spread. The next few hours were spent crunching numbers and debating the various ins and outs of antiquity sourcing, buying and selling. Michael was glad to see the door shut behind them as they headed off, satisfied with their mornings work. The door had only just clunked shut as it opened again and Carol popped her head through *"Five minutes boss"*

      "Mayans already?"

      "I'm afraid so, coffee?"

      "Three Carol" before he even got a chance to catch his breath Michael was joined by a South American woman and a young man in his early twenties. They both sat down at Michael's desk, he liked to keep the external customers a little closer to him and would regularly have them at his smaller desk, giving the impression of a more intimate and personal touch. Generally this type of associate was the barrier between the company and the retrieval of certain objects, so it made sense to get on more friendly status with them. *"Coffee?"* Michael reached out and poured the two visitors a fresh cup of coffee

      "Ah, Colombian?"

"I know you well" The visitors were pleased at the little personal touch and soon Michael was immersed in business again. The expert was recommending possible artefacts that the company could procure and the young man had accompanied as an apprentice who was learning the nuances of international trading, although he was also serving as a translator due to the woman's limited capacity with the English language. The meeting was long and a few hours passed by in a heartbeat. Michael breathed easily once more as he closed the door behind them. *"Oh fuck off"* Michael lost his temper as the telephone on his desk started to ring. He reached out and grabbed it. *"Phone call"*

"Oh Carol fob them off for me"

"It's Mrs Cameron and it's urgent she said sir"

"O.K carol, put her through" the receiver made a clicking noise as the line switched to Kaitlin. *"Michael, we need to go to the school"*

"What the hell has he done now?"

"They wouldn't say, but they said that they needed to see us" Michael had no desire to go to the school again. It was becoming more regular that they would have to go and apologise for Joseph's behaviour and he tried to wangle his way out of attending. *"I'm really swamped here, can you go on your own?"*

"Oh surprise, surprise, do you not think that our son is more important than that office? Michael groaned

"Don't start"

"Anyway they have insisted that we both attend anyway, so it's just tough" Michael accepted the inevitable and began to collect up his bits and pieces *"Jesus Kaitlin, this is getting out of control, I wonder what he has done this time?"*

"I don't know do I? No point in both of us driving, pick me up?" Michael got his back up and snapped back uncontrollably *"Why do I have to drive?"* Kaitlin laughed and replied smugly *"O.K so will we put Joseph in the boot,* no in fact you take him on your knee" He knew when he was beaten. *"Fair play, see you in twenty minutes"* The conversation came to an abrupt end and Michael dialled through to

23

Carol. *"Need an excuse to miss the distribution meeting Carol, family emergency"*

"But sir they are coming to discuss the specialised research items for the U.S"

"Just rearrange it Carol, I need to go into Joseph's school"

"O.K then, I will explain as best I can, hope everything works out". The screech from Michael's tyres generated a plume of smoke from the burning rubber. Kaitlin was stood, arms crossed smoking a cigarette, she quickly finished it off and threw it to the pavement, stomping her high heels into the tarmac as she extinguished it fully. She slumped heavily into the passenger seat and sat silent for the remainder of the journey. Michael focused on the road and on a few occasions was ready to begin a conversation, but he stopped short every time as he realised that everything he thought of to say was antagonistic. He remained focused on the road and in just under an hour they approached the gates of St Cuthbert's. The chips on the vast driveway crunched and cracked under the weight of Michael's car and he pulled into a free space outside the main entrance to the school. The school was really old and beautifully designed. It had been at the top of the exam result tables in that area for over 100 years and it was only the wealthy who could afford to send their children there. Michael had managed to organise a meeting with the headmaster through one of the executives at the office and Joseph was pulled from the local comprehensive and integrated with the upper crust of education. Michael still felt out of place mixed in with the wealthy and privileged, even though he probably earned more than most of them, he still had reservations about the ones who had inherited wealth and had never worked a day in their entire lives. Kaitlin led the way down the long wooden panelled corridors, they wound their way through groups of children and hopped over the cable from a vacuum cleaner that a little old janitor was busy using. They reached the headmaster's office and outside to their horror stood two policemen who were taking notes and in conversation with the head master. He was tall and thin and made his way over to them as soon as he had finished speaking with the police officers. *"Mr, Mrs Cameron.......please"* the headmaster beckoned Michael and Kaitlin to his office and closed the door behind them *"Please take a seat".* At the opposite side of the room there was a boy sitting looking out of the window, he had a shaved head and sat casually flicking a zippo lighter open and shut repeatedly. *"About Joseph"*

"Is he O.K?" Kaitlin asked and her enquiry was met by a snigger from the boy in the chair *"I can assure you that he is in perfect health Mrs Cameron"* Kaitlin looked relieved and Michael found himself directing a comforting look in her direction which unsettled him. *"When it comes to the rules and regulations of this ancient establishment, then no, he is far from all right, in fact he is uncontrollable"* The skinhead sniggered again and Michael lost his cool. *"Do you think it is appropriate that we be discussing our son while this boy eavesdrops on our conversation?"* The headmaster sat back in his chair defiantly and glanced towards the boy who had now stood up and turned to face Michael and Kaitlin. *"What's the matter olds? Not recognise your own son?"* It was indeed Joseph, he had a black eye and was out of uniform *"Joseph Cameron! What have you done to your hair?"* Kaitlin broke down at the sight of her little boy, who although was only twelve years old had the look of a much older youth and was unrecognisable. *"I told you I didn't want to come here, just take me home"* Michael watched his family slowly crumbling before his eyes before his eyes. Both Joseph and Kaitlin were reduced to tears, he had to do something. He handed Kaitlin the keys to the car *"Kaitlin, here take him out to the car"* She took the car keys and headed out quickly, wiping the running mascara from her eyes. Joseph followed obediently leaving Michael to deal with the headmaster. He spent over an hour with the headmaster and he had explained how over the last few months, Joseph's attendance to class was becoming more infrequent and his general behaviour was unruly and argumentative. The headmaster continued and explained that today he had pushed the boundaries too far. His Chemistry teacher had noticed his non-attendance and after searching the school grounds he was found smoking pot behind the janitor's building. The Teacher confronted him and he proceeded to steal his car from the car park and go on a joy ride, which had resulted in the police involvement. The headmaster explained that the car had been returned undamaged and no charges had been pressed in an attempt to protect the good name of the school. Michael made his apologies and headed outside, heading down the gravel drive to the parked car, Both Kaitlin and Joseph were sobbing and Joseph looked up sheepishly at his father *"I'm sorry dad"* Michael paused and looked at both of their faces, they were so sad and lost, he felt a lump grow in his throat as he wondered how things could have gotten so bad. *"What happened to us?"* Kaitlin was surprised by Michael's reaction and was lost for a reply to his question, so he continued *"Right, out of the car"* Michael opened the back and front doors at the same time, Joseph quickly jumped out and Kaitlin

followed straight after, both with unsure expressions. *"Phones, watches, tablets, get it all in the glove box"*

"Michael, what are you doing?"

"Just do it, both of you" Michael locked the glove box and in turn locked the car

"Come with me" Michael led his family into the grounds which surrounded the school and they walked for a short while until Michael stopped and tuned to face them. *"This is all wrong, who are we? It stops today, I'm putting in for a month off, so are you Kaitlin, no arguments. Joseph, I'm sorry son, I've forgot about you. My work has taken over everything"* Michael turned to face his wife *"Kaitlin, I'm sorry….."* Kaitlin interrupted

"No Michael, I'm sorry, we need this"

"What are we going to do for a month?" Joseph looked confused and Michael put him at ease *"We will go on holiday anywhere you like and sort out this mess once and for all, things are going to change for us and it starts today"* The family spent the next few hours talking and laughing, making plans for their months break, they smiled and laughed and Michael thought to himself that he had gone some way to filling the unidentified void that had been looming over him for as long as he could remember. The car journey was far more representative of a normal family, the conversation was full of hope and laughter and they enjoyed each other's company more than they could remember ever having done. *"Will we stop for something to eat?"* Kaitlin asked and father and son answered in unison

"Yes sir!" the little roadside café that they stopped at was much more basic than they had been used to recently. But they drank and laughed like they had not done for years, with every mouthful of burger or swig of carbonated cola washing away their trouble for a short while at least. *"Time to go"* Michael directed the family back to the car and they set off towards home with a renewed boost of hope and enthusiasm for their future together as a family. The motorway was quiet and Michael flicked the radio through the stations until they found something that was suitable for all their tastes. *"Oh, this is minted!"* Joseph got really excited while hearing the song which began to play on the radio and started to attempt some body popping along the back seat of the car. "How do you know this one son?" Michael asked

26

"This is a classic dad, everyone knows this". It was MC Hammer with "U Can't Touch This" and before long all three of them were singing and badly imitating the original artist. Joseph was laughing his head off and dancing around in the back seat just as he was interrupted by a loud scream from Kaitlin *"Watch that tire!"* the front wheel of Michaels car clipped a wheel which was left in the middle of the road from a previous accident and Michael swerved to avoid it, he applied the brakes to try and steady the car. It was too late and the momentum sent the car into the air, clipping the central reservation on its way sending the vehicle into a series of rolls. Time seemed to slow down and Michael became more and more disorientated. The car collided with a large truck and bounced down to the verge at the side of the road. His vision was blurred and he could only make out parts of Kaitlin's and Joseph's faces. His ears popped with the loud smash from the initial collision. The car grew silent and Michael was engulfed in light. He heard voices as he slipped into unconsciousness *"Where are you?"*

"He's under" the voices stopped and the light faded, he was alone and cold and finally lost consciousness altogether. *"Hello, hello, can you hear me?"*

"His eyes are open"

"R.T.A doctor"

"Alright get him to crash" Michael could hear again, he was in a hospital *"Can you hear me? What's your name?"* a doctor shone a torch in his eyes but he was unable to respond and began to drift out of consciousness again *"Stay with me"*

"O.K, stay with him, keep him monitored" Michael grew sleepier really quickly and again became incapable of comprehending his surroundings. The medical staff wheeled him away and two doctors stood speaking about the accident. *"How Many?"*

"Just one vehicle, a BMW"

"Not the cars, the people!"

"Sorry three there was, a family, a mother and an adolescent boy"

"Condition?"

"DOA, both of them, looks like daddy's got a rough time if he survives"

"Horrific, if it was me I would just hope they let me go"

"We are not in the business of letting our patients expire"

"Still though, poor bastard"

"O.K, contact the relatives and speak to the blues and twos"

"I'll get the coffees, milk and two is it?"

Chapter 3

The show must go on.

The radio alarm clock makes the same old tone that it has since it was first plugged in all those years ago. The lettering on the snooze button was almost completely gone and the white plastic casing was showing through, it was fast becoming the main colour of the old worn appliance which was in dire need of replacing. The alarm continued for another minute and then it automatically clicked onto radio mode. A classical composition replaced the robotic and industrial tone of the alarm, it was beautifully soft and calming with gentle violin being the prominent instrument. The digital display on the front of the alarm reads six forty five and the bed next to it lay empty. It is still made and appears to be untouched from the night before. At the end of the bed lies a man's suit, it is laid out on the bed with great attention to every detail, an obsessive amount of effort had been put into its preparation. Michael Cameron was already up, he was in the bathroom flossing his teeth. His life recently had become far more organised. He would get up early every morning and would be washed and shaved and dressed long before he had to be anywhere. He had real trouble sleeping at night and regularly filled his nights by doing all the mundane tasks which he would normally have been rushing around mad in the morning trying to fit in before the commute to work. Doing all the tasks well in advance had resulted in Michael being miles ahead of schedule almost every single day. The cold tap shut off with a light thud as it cut the supply of water, Michael slipped his toothbrush back through the little hole on the glass plate where it was kept leaving a small drop of minty white foam on the polished glass surface. He grabbed a piece of toilet paper and wiped it off immediately, leaving it clean and unspoiled. Wiping his face with a towel Michael neglected to glance at himself in the mirror, most mornings he would get stuck for what felt like hours staring blankly at his reflection in deep thought and he could not afford any delays this morning. His suit was completely dust and bobble free, it had been pressed within an inch of its life and the matching shoes he had left out had been similarly buffed to a military shine, he could have seen his face in them. He avoided getting trapped in a staring match with his reflection in the shiny black leather, *"Must not be late"*. Michael had spent the last six months in limbo. Long days blurred into long weeks and at times, time seemed to stand still. Michael's brain had begun to hurt with the

29

constant deliberation over the tragedy which he had endured. He constantly recounted the events of that day and regularly sunk deeper into the bottom of a bottle of single malt. His employers at the office had been more than accommodating. They had given him as much time as he needed to get himself to a "controlled emotional state". Michael laughed at himself as he pondered that statement, two out of three was not bad. He was emotional and in a state, anything but controlled. Today was the day when he had agreed to return and make the first step towards reintegration with normal society. Michael was dreading having to deal with other people. He had tried his hardest to avoid them at all costs since the accident. Having to pretend that everything was O.K was going to be nothing short of an impossible task. It was clear to Michael that no matter what, he would never be the same again for the rest of his days. All the old clichés seemed to apply in situations like this "Give yourself a shake", "Brush yourself down and get back on the horse", although they sounded like good and simple advice, Michael knew he had a mountain to climb. The kitchen was now obviously only inhabited by an individual and was similarly spotless like the rest of the house. Michael sat down at the table and took a little sip from a cup of coffee, visibly wincing at its taste. The coffee had been lying for hours since it was first poured and the icy cold film on top caught his taste buds and he quickly rejected it. He placed it back on the table beside a slice of toast on a plate which had a couple of small bites from it. Recently Michaels appetite had been another casualty of his mental state and he ate little and infrequently, replacing the missing calories with whiskey. Recently most nights in the Cameron household were spent with a bottle close at hand, around twelve hours in bed, tossing and turning for most of that and getting small bursts of sleep. Some nights would be spent watching various ridiculous programmes on the television. Michael could now explain in great detail the various processes in the assembly of a spark plug and had an extensive knowledge of the various indigenous tribes which lived on the banks of the Amazon River. The days were spent with more active tasks as the television would only help to mask his thoughts when accompanied with a bottle of liquor. He would clean, tidy and reorganise every area of the house and garden with obsessive attention to detail. The accident was only past two weeks when he took on the pile of junk that had accumulated in the garage. Shadow boards had been created and hung throughout to give all his tools a home, loft ladders had been installed, the attic had been floored and a whole new area for storage had been created. All the junk had been collated and organised only to be worked through on multiple occasions and reordered. Michael had worked through all his belongings countless times now, but he never dared touch anything of Kaitlin's or Joseph's. He had recovered to a certain extent, but was still in no fit mental state to start sifting through the memories that surrounded him, and could never considering packing away or removing any of them permanently. As long as he kept things just as they were it allowed him to slip into a fantasy for a moment, pretending that they had just popped out for a moment. Kaitlin had gone to pick up a pizza and Joseph would be back from school any minute. Those little episodes of make believe helped in the short term and at least contributed to combatting his loneliness. Pouring the remainder of the stale coffee down the sink, Michael stood up from the table, he took the remainder of his breakfast items to the sink, washed, dried and returned them to their place in his meticulously organised kitchen cabinets. He wiped all the surfaces clean, scanned the entire area for anything that was out of place and a few moments later was satisfied that he had captured everything. He headed through the house and into the garage. Kaitlin's little car was parked where the large pile of junk had previously laid, it had a thick film of dust over its entire surface. Michael's car sat in its usual position, cold and silent with a similar coating of particles upon its sparkling new paint. The cars had sat and literally gathered dust, Michael had not left the house much and in his recent mental condition would not have been fit to drive, and certainly not under the limit. The insurance company had dropped off the company's replacement and backed it into the garage. Michael had come out to inspect it but had avoided driving since the accident. The cold aluminium handle sent a shiver down his spine as he pulled at it to open the door, he placed his case on the back seat as he always did and then sat down in the driver's seat shutting his eyes as he slumped into position. The flashback was instantaneous and graphic. He could hear Kaitlin screaming in the back of his head along with a blast of sirens. He could almost smell the distinctive odour of burning rubber. Placing his head on the steering wheel he broke down and started to wail uncontrollably, the windscreen had begun to steam up as his hot and wet breath filled the cockpit of the car. After a short while he lifted his head from the steering wheel, his reluctance had made his head feel as if it weighed twice as much as normal and he struggled to remove it from its fixed position. A long deep breath followed by a snort of the nose was accompanied by a glance in the wing mirror of the brand new vehicle. *"Keep it together"* he said aloud. A few more deep breaths and Michael peered into the rear view mirror at his puffy and tearful eyes.

31

He looked tired and had lost a lot of weight over the last six months. He stared blankly into his own lifeless eyes for a while and then nodded silently as if to agree with a thought he had had *"Right, I can do this"*. The garage doors whirred as the automatic mechanism kicked into action, lifting the doors and letting the bright morning light through. Michael's eyes took time to adjust and the light only fuelled his desire to escape back inside to his comfortable, controlled haven. The sun had already began its ascent and the morning sky was clear and blue. Michael slipped on his shades to help combat the brightness and to soothe the pain in his whiskey addled eye sockets. He had stayed relatively sober the previous night but was suffering from a hangover which seemed to have lasted for months. He slipped on his seatbelt, checking it a couple of times to ensure it was fastened correctly. The engine roared as it sparked into life and the brakes made a little cracking noise as the car began to role to the edge of the driveway, they had accumulated some surface rust in the six months dormancy. Michael checked one way then the other, and then he checked again. The road was clear of any potential hazards, but Michael continued to check and then check again. He shut his eyes for a split second and he was instantly overcome with fear. Screams and sirens filled his ears again, the smell of rubber filled his nose, and a feeling of panic overcame his senses as the confinement made it seem that he was still trapped within the mangled remains of the old car. Blind panic took over and Michael failed in his efforts to slip the car into reverse on three separate attempts, grinding the gear stick and crunching the metalwork hidden below. Finally the stick slotted into place and Michael's foot slipped from the brake to the accelerator, sending the car hurtling backwards. The car roared with excessive revs and careered relentlessly towards the back wall of the garage. Snapping out of his panic he slammed on the brakes, stopping the car with inches to spare. *"Fuck this shit"* Michael jumped out of the car and grabbed his briefcase from the back seat, slamming the doors shut in disgust. He stepped outside and the garage doors came down behind him. Taking yet another long, deep gulp of fresh air, Michael removed his mobile phone from his pocket and began to key in a number. It rang two or three times. *"Can I have a taxi please?.........Cameron"* The journey to the office seemed to last for an age and Michael became even more anxious as the driver spoke to him like he was the first human being he had seen in a month. Ironically it was Michael who had had no human interaction for such a long time. The last thing he felt like doing was discussing the weather or current politics with the driver so he just nodded occasionally and looked out the window. The taxi came to a halt in the car park just outside the main entrance to the office block and Michael quickly paid the driver and exited the vehicle. The driver never let up gibbering the entire journey *"Have a good day mate"* The taxi driver sped off in search of his next hire and a more responsive passenger. Michael stood oblivious to its departure with his gaze fixed onto the main doors of the building. People came and went like they always did, all different shapes and sizes. Couriers weaved their way through the crowds of office workers, trying to make their way through the main doors. Michael watched on and they seemed to slow down in front of his eyes as he pushed himself to take the first step towards the rest of his life. He lifted his foot and it felt like a ton weight as he moved at the same laboured pace his mind was creating around him. His feet planted on the ground and the surrounding environment burst into the normal hectic pace and it wasn't long before the morning chorus began to ring out all around him. It was earlier than Michael had ever made it to work before but it did not stop his colleagues from engaging him in the same way they had always done *"Good morning Mr Cameron"* and similar greetings built steadily as he made his way to the main entrance. The large glass doors slid with the familiar electronic whirring noise and Michael stepped through the opening into the lobby. Everything seemed the same as it had the last time he attended and the realisation that life had just carried on without him, unaffected by his own personal trauma was unusual for him to accept. A familiar voice greeted him and he winced as he realised that he was being forced into conversation. It was the first time for months that he had to contemplate social interaction and he turned to face the instigator. He mentally prepared himself with a deep and calming breath of air. *"Morning Mr Cameron"* Eddie was visibly nervous upon approach and Michael noted his sheepish tone as he engaged him in light conversation. Eddie avoided asking how he was and tried to focus on generics *"Cracking result last night sir"* Michael was not even aware that there was a game on and was just desperate to make his way through the morning rush and hide in his office. *"Sure was Eddie"* Eddie noticed immediately that Michael was in no fit state to stand and be engaged in small talk *"O.K Mr Cameron, you have a good day"*

　　　"Thanks Eddie"

　　　"We've missed you around here Sir" Michael never replied and kept his stride steady as he crossed the lobby and entered the elevator. The elevator doors shut and he breathed easier for a moment, he walked the short distance to his office and unusually was

not greeted by Carol. It was too early. His office was cold and empty, it had been kept clean and tidy and other than the low temperature it appeared as if it was still being used on a daily basis, Carol had been keeping herself busy he thought. Overwhelmed by the magnitude of the occasion, he slumped into his leather bound desk chair which was equally if not colder than the rest of the office. He sat shivering as he waited for the office to heat up. The building began to steadily fill with more and more employees, as it got closer to the regular starting time. Michael made himself a cup of coffee, not able to rely on Carol who had not yet arrived ready to service his every need. The view from his office was exquisite and as the sun rose, it beat down through the glass onto his desk. He sat silently and stared blankly into space yet again. He felt physically and mentally exhausted already, all those late, whiskey filled nights had taken their toll on him. He tried to remain focused on his work. There must have been a lot to get through, having been off for six months, the backlog of paperwork must have been quite substantial. Soon enough the office door opened and Carol entered holding a large pile of papers, she had not noticed Michael as her view had been obscured by the bright morning sun. Michael pushed a button on a small remote which was lying on his desk and the electronically activated window blinds began to descend to the floor, blocking out the bright sun *"Hi Carol"* Carol let out a yelp of surprise and the large pile of papers were soon raining down on the floor all around her, Michael got down on the floor beside her and started to help to clean up the mess that he helped to create. *"Oh! Mr Cameron, you gave me such a fright, no one said you would be back today Sir."*

"I know Carol it's been a long six months"

"Tell me about it" Carol stood up and pointed towards her midriff, she was sporting a well-developed bump and was beaming with excitement *"Seems I've missed quite a bit then? You and Dave must be really happy"* Carol sensed the pain in his voice as he forced himself to conduct the expected congratulatory pleasantries. The happiness of such an event only served as a painful reminder of what he had lost. *"Boy or Girl?"*

"Oh, a wee surprise Sir"

"That's the best way". Michael took some relief from speaking with Carol. It had been too long since he had just conversed with someone, and due to the circumstances which surrounded the conversation, he was forced to be positive. A new baby on the horizon

was without hesitation a happy topic of discussion and it allowed Michael to push his personal dismay to the back of his mind for the time being. *"Would you like some coffee then?"*

"Let me Carol, you take a seat" Carol waved her hands in a derisory fashion and cut Michael off.*" No, no, no, I'm not on maternity leave yet"* She pushed him out of her way and before too long returned with a fresh pot of coffee. *"I haven't got anything booked on for you today"*

"It's O.K Carol, I've got to go see the boss anyway"

"O.K, I'll be in my usual place if you need me for anything"

"Thanks Carol" Carol nodded and left Michael to return to his desk and his coffee. He sat and sipped it, smiling with satisfaction at the far more agreeable taste of Carol's version. The Telephone on the desk rang and startled him, the light upon it indicated it was carol buzzing through. *"Yes Carol?"*

"Mr Ferguson is on his way down"

"Thanks" Mr Ferguson was the top man and Michael was confused with his unannounced visitation, surely he could have waited for the meeting later that morning. He composed himself the best he could and sat waiting in silence until the office door swung open again. An elderly man entered. He was in no way a frail man for his age, short and stout with a full head of wiry grey hair and a thick moustache in the same colour. He beamed with a large grin and stuck his hand towards Michael with exaggerated excitement *"Michael, it's great to see you son!"*

"Likewise Mr Ferguson" Michael stood up from his chair as he greeted his visitor

"Sit down son, and call me Bob" Michael smiled and sat back down in his chair *"Coffee sir?"*

"Please Michael" Both men sat in silence for a few seconds and after a slurp of his freshly poured coffee Mr Ferguson began the unenviable task of breaking the ice and trying to re-integrate his employee *"Before we get started, I need to ask you how you are son?"* Michael hesitated and was quickly given respite from his response by his boss *"There is no need for details Michael, just let me know, are you ready to come back?"*

35

"I think so ......Bob"

"If you need more time off, it's not a problem, take as much time as you need son" Michael considered a possible extended holiday and then quickly dismissed the idea from his mind. The thought of spending another minute in that house was enough to put him off the idea altogether. *"No, I'm ready, I need to get on with it, stay busy"*

"O.K son, we will leave it there then, they have just about managed to keep the old ship afloat without you. Carol has been a godsend."

"She is an excellent assistant sir" Mr Ferguson sipped his coffee again and Michael could see that he was priming himself to breach an important subject. He sat patiently until he spoke again *"So here it is son, everything here is ticking over nicely, Carol has held the fort and we have managed to get our affairs in order"* Michael sensed he was not going to like the next part. *"I think, due to the circumstances, that you could be doing with getting away for a bit?"*

"I'm fine…..honestly Mr Ferguson….Bob" Michael panicked, the thought of being moved to another office or another position was too much for him to handle. *"Just hear me out son, remember before………….well you know, six months ago, you had that meeting, regards the research artefacts with the yanks"* Michael breathed a little easier

"Sure, I remember"

"Well we informed them of the circumstances surrounding yourself at the time and they advised that you were the only person they felt suitable to continue with the project and insisted that they wait till you were ready" Michael gasped

"They waited for six months?"

"They insisted"

"You must have impressed" Michael sat back in his chair and shook his head in disbelief *"Well I suppose it's a compliment, when are they coming?"*

"Well, that's the thing" Mr Ferguson again braced for an announcement. *"The meeting has been rescheduled for the day after tomorrow"*

"That's not too bad, shouldn't be too complicated sir"
Michael supped his coffee and relaxed a little until he nearly spat the contents of his mouth all over his boss upon hearing his next revelation *"It's in the U.S"* Michael sat down slowly, flabbergasted at what lay ahead of him. He had only just began to get settled out with the confines of his housebound solitude and was just about to be flown halfway across the world. *"I take it there is no point in arguing with you?"* Mr Ferguson nodded in agreement

"You can stay on for a while see the sights…..get your head sorted"

"Looks like I better get off home and pack then eh?" Mr Ferguson smiled and thrust the same enthusiastic hand towards Michael, sealing the deal with a firm shake *"Great stuff Michael, I knew we could rely on you"* Michael had been made an offer which he could not refuse. Although *"Bob"* had tried his hardest to butter it up, it was obvious to Michael that he was being sent away for his own good and that his boss had his best interests at heart. The meeting itself would only have consisted of the mechanics of transferring some items which were being investigated in a cross Atlantic research project. It was a joint venture and any data which Michael and his team had collated would be passed over to their American counterparts, with Michael remaining on site to provide any further consultation. It was basically a trans-Atlantic delivery service he was to provide, being used as an excuse to send him away for a while. Michael was aware of this and let his gratitude be known *"Thanks Bob"*

"No, no thank you Michael………..and take as long as you need" The pair said their goodbyes and the door swung shut behind Mr Ferguson as he left the office. The door opened slightly and he popped his head back through momentarily *"It's good to see you back son"* Michael buzzed Carol who was quickly in attendance. He begun to explain the new turn of events and was quickly stopped as she handed him a brown envelope *"He has filled me in sir, here is your itinerary"* Carol smiled mischievously as she handed him the envelope with everything that he needed *"You knew all about this didn't you?"*

"I don't know what you are talking about?"

"Yeah whatever"

"Just get yourself home and get ready, your first flight leaves at three in the morning" Carol smiled and headed back to continue

with her duties. Michael collected everything he needed from his desk and said his goodbyes, he spotted Eddie waving just as he sat in his taxi and waved back much too the old man's delight. Most of that night was spent cleaning and tidying. He rearranged his travel bag about a dozen times and by eleven o'clock he was ready to leave for the airport. Opening the fridge he poured some coke, half filling a large pint glass, he then grabbed a bottle of cheap bourbon and proceeded to fill the glass until it was nearly at its brim. He sat again in deep thought at the kitchen table and tried to remember Kaitlin and Joseph. Whenever he thought of them, he was always brought back to a particular occasion. It was before he had had his first big promotion. A family barbecue, he remembered that Kaitlin had looked so beautiful that day, perfect. The smell of burnt meat was alive in his nostrils as if the scent had been preserved and he had unlocked it from deep within his unconscious mind. The glass got emptier and Michael sat studying old photographs as he slipped deeper into his alcohol fuelled depression. He was leaving for a while and would not be able to engage in his sad and lonely ritual. He suddenly felt the need to do something that he had been avoiding for months, the impending journey had encouraged him to stand up from the table, take a large swig of his drink and climb the stairs until he stood on the landing outside Joseph's bedroom door. The room had lay untouched since the accident and the brass handle was still smudged with finger-marks, he turned the handle and attempted to minimise the removal of any of the smudging. The door creaked and the dry metal on metal from the hinges unnerved him. The room was cold and stale and the air was dank and heavy. It was exactly as he remembered, you could not move for figurines, all superheroes and villains. Joseph's love for comic books had grown with him as he got older and he had amassed quite a collection. Michael sat at the end of the bed and placed his drink on the floor, he couldn't contemplate disturbing the bedside table with an alien object. Placing his head in his hands Michael sobbed until he was crying uncontrollably. The feeling of guilt was ripping him apart and he muttered to himself *"What did I do wrong?"* Michael clutched a picture of them close to his chest and lay down with his head on the pillow. The grief he felt was still so heavy and visiting Joseph's room had drained him, he wept softly as he drifted into unconsciousness. *"Daddy........Daddy...........Where are you?"* Michael jumped up from the pillow, startled by the very real sound of Joseph's voice, although he did sound about four years old again, the realism of his voice had woken him and completely freaked him out. He checked his watch, it was twenty past one in the morning

"Shit……….Can I have a taxi please? Cameron………The Airport".
Rushing around like mad, Michael quickly pulled on his jacket and carried his luggage to the front door, he carefully placed a small photo of Kaitlin and Joseph in his wallet and looked around for his whiskey. He had left it in Joseph's room and quickly darted upstairs and grabbed it from the floor. He took one last big swig and downed the rest of the glass, looking around the room for what felt like the last time *"See you when I get back son"* the door creaked with the same unmaintained groan and clicked shut. Just as his mobile phone rang to alert him of the taxi's imminent arrival, it pulled up outside the house. The driver was less talkative and this was far more to Michael's liking. The journey dragged on and his head dipped with fatigue numerous times on the way to the airport. It was reasonably quiet at the terminal and Michael made his way quickly to the desk, it was five past two and the girl behind the check in made her disapproval known *"Mr Cameron, cutting a bit fine are we not?"* Michael chose not to comment, grabbed his documentation a d headed straight to the bar in the departure lounge *"Single malt please"*

"Bit of Dutch courage is it sir?"

"Something like that" The barman poured his drink and he swallowed it like it was the first drink he had had in years *"Again"* the barman poured another and Michael listened as an announcement came over the loudspeakers "*Passengers for flight BA324 to Philadelphia, please make your way to gate 36"* The departure lounge sparked into life and Michael paid for his drinks and made his way through the crowds to the front of the queue. Before long he was storing his luggage in the overhead locker and taking his seat. It was a window seat and was of course first class. The plane filled up with passengers and soon the engines roared into life and they were airborne. A large American woman had sat next to him and had begun to explain that she had just finished her trip to the U.K. Michael tried to remain as friendly as he could but wanted nothing more than to fall asleep. The flight was going to be long enough without the running commentary from a third generation Jacobite, explaining how she was a direct descendant of Robert the Bruce. After around an hour Michael managed to slip into a deep uncomfortable sleep. The same old dreams plagued his unconscious mind. Joseph and Kaitlin's voices rang out eerily like echoes and flashing images of items from his past shot through his mind. Memories of arguments and celebrations appeared and disappeared frantically and without any order. Another voice rang out *"Where are you?"*

"Mr Cameron" Michael stirred and struggled to focus on what was real *"Mr Cameron"* The flight attendant woke him with an abrupt shove and he came out of his deep sleep and snapped at her *"What is it?"*

"Sorry to wake you sir, could you please fasten your seatbelt, we are experiencing a bit of light turbulence"

"O.K, O.K, I'm sorry, you surprised me" The flight attendant did not wait around for his apology and quickly made her way to her own seat. The plane shunted and shifted around from the heavy weather outside and Michael could sense the atmosphere in the cabin had ascended into light panic from the other passengers *"Please remain calm, there is nothing to be concerned about"* The attendant struggled to hide her own feeling of panic as the turbulence grew stronger by the second. The Cabin grew increasingly unstable as it swayed to and fro and Michael was now wide awake and sharing in his fellow passengers' concern. He peered out of his window. The night sky was dark and lifeless until a massive flash of light filled the sky for a fraction of a second. It was brighter than anything he had ever seen before and seemed to emanate from the underside of the aircraft and flash outwards away from them until it vanished just as quick and the sky was left dark and empty again. The plane rocked violently and the cabin began to fill with the sounds of mass hysteria and uncontrollable shrieking from panicked passengers. A buzzing noise grew louder and louder and it too seemed to be originating from the bowels of the plane. It continued to increase in volume and the turbulence had grown so much that people were now being thrown around the like rag dolls in their seats. From above, oxygen masks dropped and people scrambled to utilise them as quickly as possible. Michael's knuckles were white, as he gripped his seat with all his might. This was it, they were going down. People all around braced for impact, it was a time like this that Michael wished he had paid more attention to the flight attendant as she performed her well-rehearsed emergency drill. With a loud whistling sound the plane began to hurtle into a nose dive and articles of luggage began to land all over the cabin. The plane creaked and the metal hull stressed under the sheer force of the uncontrolled descent. Michael's ears and the shift of fluid in his inner ear had come as a welcome relief as it replaced the buzzing noise that was deafening him. A loud crack rang out as the fuselage was twisted and reshaped under the extreme pressure. The buzzing returned and Michael felt as if his eardrums were going to explode. The plane cracked for one last time and the fuselage buckled under the stress.

Michael watched as the nose of the plane severed from the rest of it. Time seemed to slow and he watched as the flight attendant who had woken him was sucked out into the darkness. The American woman who had sat next to him had gone also, Michael sat frozen in position, struggling to keep his eyes open, hoping he would wake up any moment. There was a light in the distance and it grew closer until it became obvious that it was fire, more specifically the reflection of fire. Within seconds they were under, the plane was going as such a speed that the remainder of it submerged in the ocean like a diving heron and then slowly began to rise to the surface. The sound of chaos and terror was replaced by the muffled silence that being submerged in icy cold ocean water brought. Michael was able to reach his belt and release it, he rocketed from his position and was launched out into the depths of the ocean through the severed opening that the nose of the plane had left behind. The jolt had knocked him clean out and he began to sink unconscious to the depths. Around him bodies of other victims rose and sank. Luggage was sprawled everywhere and the ocean was filled was debris. The containers from the cargo hold had begun to rise the quickest, the wooden crates had improved their buoyancy. Michael continued to sink until the darkness engulfed every last piece of light. The water had come become bitterly cold and the change in temperature forced him back into consciousness. He was surprisingly calm and held his breath while he decided on a course of action. A crate from the cargo hold descended in front on him and Michael attention was drawn to it immediately. It was the only crate which was not ascending to the surface. He could only just about make it out in the darkness, it seemed to be glowing on the inside with light breaking through the gaps in the wood. He reached out to grab it. Before he could touch it, the buzzing in his ears returned to deafen him as it had on the plane. The light from within the crate grew brighter and the buzzing increased in rate and volume until the two combined, shattering the crate into a thousand pieces. An object glowed brightly in the darkness and Michael was transfixed on it, a spherical core with twelve uniformly placed cylindrical rods protruding from it. He was compelled to touch it and he reached out until his finger rested on its surface. His body tingled with an electrical charge and he was engulfed in its light. Michael slipped into unconsciousness again. Was it death? Was he awake? Whatever it was it had taken him.

Chapter 4

The Samaritan and the Samurai

The temperature was almost freezing. Michael awoke and was so cold he felt as solid as stone, he took a massive breath of icy air like a patient who had just been revived on an operating table. He was alive. He lay face down on a pebble shore, the tide must have washed him inland. He let out a loud groan of pain as he struggled to stand up. His body ached and resembled the strength and posture of a man at least twice his age. The crash had taken it out of him and he was aching over his entire body. The cold only made the pain worsen, and the numbing effect of the temperature increased with every extra flake of snow that landed on his wet body. The snowstorm grew into a blizzard and Michael struggled to see through it as it swirled all around him, making his attempts to stand up ever more difficult. He straightened his left arm and planted his frozen fingers on the river bed. Shifting his weight he tried to push himself up. He crumpled to the ground and let out a sharp shriek of agony. He had broken it and the artic temperature had hidden the extent of the damage, he tried to straighten it again and let out another cry of pain, finally resting it close to his chest and rolling his body until he managed to get up onto his feet. The blizzard had reduced the visibility almost completely and Michael shuffled up the beach, hoping to at least get out of the water. He managed a few steps and collapsed to his knees with no energy, becoming drowsier at an alarming rate. *"C'mon"* Michael urged himself to his feet, knowing the graveness of his predicament, he would surely freeze to death if he didn't find shelter soon. His eyes strained as he scanned the shoreline. Snowflakes clung to his face, nipping his skin as they touched it. Through the snow he could just make out a vertical surface nearby. It looked like a rock face and he stumbled, dragging his body slowly towards it, until he rested against the sharp and craggy surface. There was a small opening in the rocks which he could just about fit through and he felt his way carefully along the rock face until he managed to slip through the gap. The dramatic assault on his senses as he entered the dark cave was too much for his fragile state, the wind ceased and was replaced by a ringing in his ears which pierced through his skull sending him to the hard dusty ground with a thud. As he lay shivering, he began to drift out of consciousness. Peering through the gap in the rock face he watched as the sky cleared for a moment revealing a beautiful vista. A blue sky and the top of a large snow-capped mountain in the not too far distance. Michael's mind raced with confusion as he lost consciousness all together, where could he be? How could the flight have crashed thousands of feet above sea level? It must have been a dream. He lay motionless on the cold, dark cave floor and the muffled whistle of the wind blew through the crack on the cave wall. Michael's head was banging as he is awoken by the frantic chatter of an old man. He lay still on a wooden framed bed which has been lined with straw trying to make out the somewhat incoherent babble which is coming from the old man who was currently out with his visual range. There was very little else in the small room where he lay, he was under a thick blanket which was bristly and only partially covered his body, next to the bed was a small table. Upon the table was a jug of water and a pile of small cloth towels. Michael's eyes slowly adjusted, bringing his surroundings a step closer to clarity. The old man had approached and was now kneeling at his side tending to the wound on his arm. He was changing the dressing on a bandage, only moving the arm as little as required, careful not to cause any further damage. The old man turned to look him and Michael, now with almost normal vision scanned his face, he was oriental in and had big bushy eyebrows which almost covered his eyes. He had a beard which was tied in knot and clasped with a little red coloured band at its base. He started to speak in a dialect which was definitely of the far east Michael thought. The fast gibbering of the old man was incoherent. Michael had no clue what he was trying to communicate to him. He opened his mouth to explain that he did not understand and he quickly interrupted him *"Shh shh shh"* He insisted that Michael remain silent. Michael did not attempt to argue with him, he was exhausted. The old man it seemed was a friend to him, he had tended his wounds and was caring for him. As he began to tire again he caught a glimpse of the old man, his eyes shut and quickly opened again as he tried to prevent the inevitable slumber which was upon him. The old man was signalling him. He pointed at himself and spoke *"Noritomo, No-ri-to-mo"* he repeated himself again as he split the word up into its syllables, trying to stress its meaning to his patient. Michael fell asleep, satisfied that he had learned the name of the old man who had been so kind, he was indeed a Good Samaritan. As he wakes he notices that he is much warmer, the sun was beating through a nearby window and Michael felt much stronger and was able to stand up. The wound on his left arm ached a little, but the feeling had returned and he was able to move it freely without too much pain. There was a small door which Michael headed towards and he was soon standing outside. His eyes adjusted to the

43

bright sunlight and he stood in awe at the mind-blowing scene which surrounded him. Lush green trees of unparalleled variety lined a softly flowing river of the clearest fresh water which was lined with banks of pebbles which were perfectly rounded and almost all completely uniform in size and shape. It was soon quite obvious to him that he was a long way from home and unless he was still concussed from his injuries he was sure that he was nowhere near to his original destination either. Michael stood, trying to make sense of where he was, the breeze on his face felt real and he was satisfied that he was awake. *"Where am I?"* He muttered. Maybe the old man would hold some answers. Michael turned to face the house from which he emerged hoping to spot the old man who had been his saviour. He stopped dead in his tracks, startled by a frightening sight. Glaring at him was a menacing and ferocious beast. It was an enormous wolf, covered with thick bushy fur. A mouth full of large sharp white teeth, dripping with saliva, glistened, as it eyed Michael with obvious and dreadful intentions. Michael was easy prey he was slow and injured. The wolf started to pace around, assessing its best possible attack plan. A few yards away, the remnants of a fire which had burnt through the night lay smouldering and Michael made his move. He moved as quickly as he could until he pulled out a charred branch, thrusting the smouldering embers towards the beast *"Yah!"* The beast backed of temporarily, but it was hungry and its mind had been made up, Michael was to be the next item on the menu. It slowly crept towards him with its back arched and its head close to the ground. Its shoulders moved up and down in rhythmic motion as it pushed him ever closer to the water's edge. The pebbles displaced beneath his feet and soon he was faced with a decision. Did he retreat into the depths of the river? Hoping his attacker would not follow or did he make a run for it and maybe make the house. The decision was taken out of his hands as without warning the wolf pounced towards him. It launched itself from the ground around eight feet from Michael's position and he shut his eyes with fear swinging his branch blindly in its path. The branch flew through the air and swung all the way around, clipping him on the opposite shoulder. He opened his eyes as he heard the high pitch squeals of pain coming from his fearsome adversary. It was the old man, he flew through the air as if he was floating on the mountain breeze. In his hand he clutched a long wooden staff which was basic in design but looked well used. He struck the wolf with blinding speed and accuracy, every move performed with immense skill and agility. Michael watched with gaping mouth as the frail old man finished the beast off. Striking the beast he sent it straight up in the air with his staff as if it was made of paper. As it fell to the ground, he extended his leg and broke the beast's back over his knee, killing it instantly. Michael's chin dropped even further as he looked on in amazement. The old man's skill and technique was mesmerising enough, but his apparent defiance of old age left him dumbfounded. He placed his hand on the head of the wolf and bowed his head, shutting his eyes. He muttered some words which Michael had thought to be a prayer of some sort. His respect for the beast which he had just slain was obvious. He lifted his head and turned to face him. Michael nodded with appreciation and pointed towards the old man *"Noritomo"* The old man nodded his head and pointed to the house and then back to the wolf, Michael understood his meaning and helped to drag the carcass through the door and into the house. Noritomo sat on a bench at a wooden table and began to furnish it with various vegetables and some dried meat. He urged Michael to eat, and it was not until now that he realised his hunger was overwhelming. Michael ate with hurried desperation and pondered how close he had come to being a meal himself for the wolf which now lay on the floor ready to be skinned and gutted. For a short while, why or what was going on had seemed unimportant. Noritomo left and returned with a canvas sack which he handed to him, indicating that the contents contained within were intended for him. Michael took the sack and started removing its contents. It contained the uniform of a warrior, a samurai in particular. Confused but not wanting to look ungrateful, Michael smiled and nodded in acceptance. Noritomo sat by the wolf's carcass and began to expertly skin the hide from its body, he sang to himself as he carried out his task. It was the same in descript language that he had spoken before. At the bottom of the bag lay a solitary item, it was a spherical glass orb and he recognised it immediately. His head buzzed with pain as he had a flash back of sinking to the depths and his death. The sphere was different from before. Michael noticed that it was black and shiny, like onyx and now it had twelve holes in it where it previously had the protruding cylindrical parts. As he held the sphere up to his face it started to flicker with a blue light and it buzzed with an electrical charge. His body tingled all over and his attention was diverted to the singing of Noritomo. The old man continued, unaware of the unusual antics of his guest who was now listening intently. The buzzing became loud and unbearable until they stopped altogether replaced by the now far more familiar utterings of Noritomo *"Oh wolf, how honourable you are, The mountain feels your pain"* Michael dropped the sphere and backed off, *"What the fuck is going on?"*. Noritomo jumped as the sphere bounced on the wooden floor. *"I may still be quick and strong my friend, but I have an old man's heart! Would you see fit to scare me to my grave?"* Michael retreated to a wooden stool and sat quietly with his head in his hands, his body was shaking and his mind raced trying to create a reasonable explanation for the events he was witnessing. Noritomo watched him with great interest and Michael decided he would have to speak to him *"Sorry if I frightened you"*

"Ah, you have arisen from your stupor, for a time I thought you to be a mute or a simpleton, speak now boy, I have wondered of your tale" Michael was numbed by the whole ordeal and began to tell his host of the events leading up to their meeting. He was quickly interrupted by Noritomo who laughed raucously *"You truly have taken a knock to the head, flying over oceans indeed?"* Michael ceased his explanation. *"You have come from afar my boy, the next village is thirty miles over Mount Tsurugidake. Ha, not as far as your dream would have us believe"* His throat began to dry up and his chest tightened, he shook his head in disbelief and struggled to catch a breath. What was going on? Was any of this real? The pain in his arm certainly felt real. Noritomo watched him with concern, his visitor was acting in a bizarre manner and Michael had noticed how the old man peered at him with concerned interest. Michael began to feel a little anxious as the man stared at him and began checking his body for any unsightly additions from the crash. He studied his hands and arms, they had a slight yellowish tint and the hairs seemed to be thicker and far darker than usual. Searching through the bag of belongings that he had been given, he noticed that there was a dagger hidden within the armour. Unsheathing it he looked into the shiny steel surface at his reflection *"Ah your family's blade perhaps, maybe some answers for you my friend"* Noritomo sniggered and continued *"It may help your mind to return"* The dagger fell from his hands as he caught a glimpse of the vessel which he possessed, eyes with the darkest brown colour and a distinct oriental shaping. Michael's breath grew quicker and he began to hyperventilate. The whole situation had become too much for him to take and he grew dizzier and more disorientated as each second passed. Weird glowing orbs and learning a new language in a matter of seconds was enough for him to take already, but he was inside the body of someone else. *"Who are you, what is going on?"*

"Be at peace my son, you are safe here" Noritomo tried to calm him and approach with his hand outstretched. *"Stay away from me, what is this?"* Michael's ears filled with the same loud buzzing and he fell to the floor, his body and mind overloaded. Noritomo lifted his

head and placed a small folded towel underneath it, protecting him from the hard floor. *"Faints like a little girl this one"*. Noritomo giggled and busied himself, leaving Michael to sleep it off. *"Wake now, time is of the essence my friend"* He was quickly aware that the voice was Noritomo and his predicament was unchanged. He closed his eyes tight in the hope that upon opening them again he would awake in more familiar surroundings. It was an attempt which ended in disappointment and he sat up, rubbing his face while stretching his neck and shoulders. The blade caught the light of the sun and Michael reached out to take it. The blade was clean and very sharp and on its side some writing was etched into the highly polished surface. *"Minamoto Nakamura"*. Michael studied his hands with great detail as he tried to fathom the reality of his situation *"Japan"* he said aloud *"Must be Japan"*. Noritomo was bustling around the house with urgency, there was something going on which had him very animated. There were two bags on the table and he was filling them with a number of items, including some food, it become obvious that the old man had some sort of journey planned. He stopped short of the table and turned to look at Michael, noticing that he had re-joined the land of the living. *"You only have two days, the transport will be here in less than an hour"* The old man seemed to know a lot more than Michael could even begin to take in, and he reluctantly played along in the hope of finding out as much as he could. *"Where are we going?"* Noritomo stopped what he was doing and approached him, he looked concerned. *"As you slept, I have taken some time to think my son, your blade has told us your name, Nakamura"* Michael nodded in agreement and looked at his host with expectancy. Noritomo grimaced *"You must awake from this slumber in which you are hiding, if you do not focus and resume your training you will never be ready, and if you are not focused, it will surely result in your death, the champion will show no mercy"* Michael was now completely lost, whatever the old man was describing, it did not sound appealing and he had to find out as much as he could *"Noritomo, I have lost my way and my memory is broken, please explain, who am I, what must I do?"* Noritomo scoffs impatiently

"We have little time for tales my boy, but you are in luck, I too am going your way. I need supplies and have some skins to trade at the market." Michael smiled and sighed with relief, Noritomo was proving to be a real asset. Without any benefit to himself, he seemed genuinely interested in helping him *"On the way to the city, I will try and help you to find your way again, although I hope you can*

remember to use a sword, that my friend will be very useful" The old man chuckled and smiled at him. Michael's heart was beating twice as fast as normal and he tried not to show his fear, having just learned of his impending fate. He smiled back at him and thanked his new found friend *"Somehow, I will repay you for everything"*

"Rubbish, rubbish" Noritomo shrugged his shoulders and dismissed Michael's gratitude, although it was plain to see that he had appreciated the gratitude that his bizarre lodger had shown him. *"O.K if you assist me with the preparations, we can be sure to make the transport and be in the city by the morning".* Michael nodded in agreement and asked what he could do to help. He had nothing else to go on, the situation was out with his control and it seemed sensible to go with the flow. *"Well my friend, you look nothing like a warrior with that growth on your face, go to the river and get yourself ready, I will continue here".* Approaching the river Michael carried a small bar of soap and an old towel, not having his modern razor at hand he brought his new blade with him. He had to go with what he had, both practically and mentally, it did not look like he was waking up anywhere else anytime soon. He stopped about six feet from the water's edge and soaked up his surroundings. It truly was how he would have imagined rural Japan. Fresh air, a sea of green, with dramatic rolling hills and craggy mountain tops. The sky was as blue as he had ever seen it. Moving towards the water he braced himself, breathing deep and long he stepped forward and looked into the clear river. Looking back at him was a young Japanese man in his early twenties, he was in desperate need of a wash and shave. Michael stood staring at his reflection for about five minutes, inspecting his shell with disbelief. The water was cold and the soap did not lather as much as he expected or would have liked. He was glad as he removed the final overgrown stubble. Staring blankly at his reflection, he questioned what was happening to him, would he wake up soon, would he ever wake up? He wracked his brain, thinking about the sphere, what could it be? It definitely had something to do with what was happening, the situation was alien and the sphere also suited that description. The possibilities were endless, he could be in a coma in a hospital bed, he could be dead and this could be his afterlife. But it was so real, he felt pain and cold as well as hunger. He bled, which was apparent by the numerous nicks on his face from shaving. Michaels daydream continued until he was interrupted by Noritomo's voice once more *"Come now my friend, we must hurry"* Michael went into autopilot and helped Noritomo to pack, he placed his dagger in his

bag with the uniform which he had inherited, he picked up the sphere and it buzzed and hummed as it contacted with his skin. It seemed alive, aware somehow and Michael felt it was also attuned to their imminent departure. He decided to study it more while on the road. The sphere had some part to play in all this, it seemed it was what helped him to understand Noritomo. He made a mental note *"I must keep it safe"*. Ten minutes passed like ten seconds and the travelling partners were outside, they had reached a point on the dirt road about five minutes from Noritomo's house. It was a further five minutes from the Mountain and stuck in the ground was a signpost, Michael likened it to one he had seen in a movie, the writing was in Japanese, but again just like the blade, his mind translated the letters and he could read them instantly. The sign pointed back to the mountain and read *"Ogamichi 30 miles"*, the other side of the signpost read *"Tagoya City 83 miles"*. *"Ah ha, it comes"* Noritomo pointed to a horse drawn wagon approaching. It was basic in design, but looked comfortable enough. It soon reached them and they had soon boarded and taken their seat, before long the light dimmed and the long dark journey through the night had begun. After around an hour the weather had returned to bitterly cold and the travellers sat silent in the darkness. Broken only by Noritomo who snored with the volume of an overweight elephant. There was no light and the sky shone with stars, it was how Michael imagine it would look like from outer space. He spent a while studying the sphere with great detail, it felt almost alive. Michael could not help feeling that it had some sort of consciousness and felt that it was yearning for something. It definitely seemed to connect with him, buzzing and flickering whenever he touched or even thought about it. It was important, that was something he was sure of and he told himself that he must protect it at all costs, it could be the key to getting some answers or even finding his way home. *"What is that orb which you covet so dearly my friend?"* Noritomo had awoken and was watching his companion with his strange sphere. *"At last, I have been waiting for you to wake"* Michael slipped the sphere back into its bag and turned to face the old man. *"Tell me, what do you know about me? You spoke of sword fighting?"* Noritomo screwed his eyes up as he noticed Michael's obvious attempts at diverting the attention from the sphere, but he soon started to explain what he knew as he had promised. It felt like he spoke for hours and Michael listened intently. *"You my friend are a warrior, from the moment your mother knew of your arrival, the preparations began"* Noritomo went on to explain in great detail, a life of servitude which was all focused on one goal. The city of Tagoya holds a tournament once every five years. Each village within the city's jurisdiction would train a child from birth to compete for an ancient and worshipped item. "The Staff of Fortune". Noritomo spoke of the staff as if it was a gift from the gods, he bowed his head with respect each time he mentioned its name. *"The village which has the staff is blessed with the luck and good fortune that it holds. People come from afar just to see it, bringing trade and custom, some even say that the staff brings a bigger harvest and keeps the lands safe from the wrath of Mother Nature."* Michael had a little smile and Noritomo noticed how he dismissed his tale as a simple fable. *"You laugh, and yet you have spent your life training for this, do you really think you are ready?"* He shook his head in agreement

"No, I am not ready, I have to fight against people with a sword, who have trained their whole life? I cannot even shave my face without looking like I have taken a beating, I cannot do this." Noritomo looked nervous

"Tonight you should sleep my friend, perhaps by the time the sun rises you will have your memory, here this will help you sleep" He handed Michael a small leather bottle and urged him to drink. It was strong and burned his chest on its way down, he wheezed *"Ha, get some sleep my friend"* The burning sensation turned to a warm glow which helped him drift slowly off to sleep. He awoke in another strange bed, Noritomo must have lifted him into the small inn that they had rented for the night, his head was banging and he struggled to his feet. Searching for his bag, he found it at the base of the bed. It was open and he rushed to check its contents only to find the sphere was missing. Michael was overcome with panic, separation from the sphere made his stomach churn. *"Noritomo……where are you?"* There was no answer. Michael stood in silence and his attention was grabbed by a familiar humming and a slight vibration through the wooden floorboards of the inn. It was coming from a small door at the back of the room. Michael darted to the door and opened it, before him lay Noritomo on the floor of the bathroom. He was sat with his back against the wall with an outstretched arm. In his hand was the sphere which hummed and flickered with bright blue light. Noritomo was in some sort of trance. Two ribbons of the same bright blue light, snaked from the sphere into the eyes of his companion. Michael watched as it seemed to be draining the life force from Noritomo, he moved forward to intercept and aid his friend. The sphere lost all its life and fell to the floor silent and as black as he had seen it. Noritomo slumped to the ground in a heap. Michael tended to him immediately,

he lifted him back to the bedroom and placed his body on the bed, quickly checking him over. He was still alive, and appeared to be asleep. Michael turned and looked at the sphere, it appeared inert and lifeless. He approached it with a renewed caution, grabbing an old broom and knocking it back into its bag. He was fearful of touching it, having seen what it was capable of. He returned to Noritomo's side and watched the old man sleep for a while. The day passed slowly and Noritomo remained silent until that evening. Michael had spent the day worrying about the ever nearing tournament and studying the sphere at arm's length. *"Minamoto son"* Noritomo had awakened and was groggy, he beckoned Michael to his side *"I am sorry my son, you must think me a nosy old fool"* Michael was quick to respond

"Never my friend, how do you feel? Can you stand?" Noritomo struggled to his feet. *"The orb, it called to me, I could not resist its song, and it engulfed my thoughts."* Michael listened to Noritomo with great interest, he had to know what the old man had experienced *"Can you remember anything? What did it do to you?"* He urged him to explain in as much detail as possible, hoping for some snippet of information which might help to piece together an explanation. *"It read my memories like the pages of a book, I seen my father and my mother as if they stood before me, Akari.........she was there, beautiful and as fair as the first day I laid my eyes upon her"* Michael listened as Noritomo explained his experience. Akari it seemed was his late wife and Michael could tell that he missed her completely. He sighed as he thought of Kaitlin and Joseph, the talk of Noritomo's loss brought them fresh into his mind and he struggled to remain in control of his emotions. He missed them more with every minute that passed. Noritomo continued *"I was a passenger as the tales of my life were travelled, watching as the days of my childhood were studied. A time when my father taught me to handle a blade, it burned brighter as it drank the details from my mind, and then I woke, just a few moments ago"* Michael could see that the old man was still exhausted and tried his hardest to comfort him *"Rest now, after a sleep you will feel better"* Noritomo slipped off to sleep and Michael returned to his attempted analysis of the strange glowing sphere. The excitement had taken it out of him, and soon he had fallen asleep. The tournament was now only hours away and Michael was physically and mentally unprepared for what lay ahead of him. He was lost and alone in a strange world, he inhabited the shell of another and everything seemed to be connected to the strange artefact. His mind was burned out and he had now started to focus on his immediate surroundings.

51

The question of where, and why he was experiencing what he was had now become painful and tiresome. It was easier to focus on the here and now. *"My friend, my friend!"* Noritomo was in a panic and shook Michael vigorously *"My friend!"*

"O.K I hear you" Michael groaned as he awoke abruptly, his head banging and still ringing as he surfaced from his deep slumber. *"It is the morning, the tournament is upon us"* Noritomo urged Michael to make haste and was met with a less than enthusiastic response *"My memory has still not returned Noritomo, I cannot take part in any tournament"* Noritomo looked exasperated, took a deep breath and looked him dead in the eyes *"Minamoto son, your memory it seems has also denied you of your senses, you cannot withdraw or you will be hunted down like a cowardice dog, only for your village to be disgraced for three generations!.... Are you not able to remember? You must remember!"* Michael bowed his head, he could not explain the truth to the old man and he sat helpless and devoid of any idea what his next move could be. *"Come now, we will go to the arena, the sights and smells of the preparations may help to jog your memory."* Michael took a deep breath and stood from his position, he had no idea what was happening to him, it seemed inevitable that he take part in the tournament, perhaps this adventure would spell the end of this dream he was forcibly involved in. Was it a dream? His new life? Was it even reality? Whatever it was his mind had been made up for him, pushed towards the tournament by an unconscious force he decided to play along. Michael packed up his things and followed his old friend to the arena. *"Ladies and gentlemen, the tournament will commence in fifteen minutes"* A town crier had been counting down the minutes until Michael's demise for the past hour and the feeling of impending doom grew heavier with every update. Michael sat on a small wooden bench with Noritomo at his side, just around the perimeter of the large arena. Enormous men with strong leather bound armour circulated the vicinity, while other competitors engaged in ritualistic preparations. Michael watched them and wondered how he would fair against such dedicated and practised opponents. The arena area was filled with many traders, stalls selling all manner of different items bustled with clientele. The area was filled with people, it was a big occasion and the attendance reflected its popularity, with each person there to cheer on their chosen warrior. Noritomo had spent all morning trying to help reboot Michael's memory, while Michael had wracked his brain to try and decipher a way of avoiding having to take part at all. He was in an alien place with no-one to turn to or confide

in, the truth of who he was, was so fantastical that he questioned just how believable it was. Soon he accepted that he had to take whatever came his way. Kaitlin and Joseph filled his thoughts and he felt that at least he would be with them soon enough. Perhaps he was in purgatory and it was now just a matter of time until he could feel the soft touch of Kaitlin's lips and hear the sound of his little boy's laughter. He felt happy. It was death, but just not how he had imagined it. *"Last call for the Tournament!... Combatants proceed to the arena!"* Michael turned to Noritomo *"Oh well, thank you for all you have done for me my friend, it seems my time is up"*

"You seem too ready, too calm, do you wish to be killed my son?" Michael shook Noritomo's hand and smiled *"There are ones that I wish to see again, death I hope is my passage to them"* Noritomo gripped his hand tightly and Michael could see the tears building in his eyes. *"Then I hope your journey is quick and painless…..but at least allow me a parting gift."* Noritomo reached into his bag and removed a sword wrapped in a piece of black silken cloth. It was very old and the detail on the handle was exquisite. *"May it bring you the knowledge you need and guide you safely to your journeys end"* Michael smiled with gratitude and bowed his head like a man who had been born and bred in Japan. He was getting more into character and felt more comfortable playing his part. *"If only I could learn how to use it in five minutes"* Michael jumped to his feet and his back bend under the weight of the armour which he had been wearing in preparation for the main event. *"That's it Noritomo…Where is my bag?"* Noritomo handed Michael his bag and he checked that its contents were still intact. *"Minamoto Nakamura, this is your final call"*

"I am here" A pair of large armoured guards approached Michael and silently beckoned him to follow, he followed then to the now fully populated arena, the other warriors were dressed in their fighting armour and awaiting the missing contestant's arrival. The sound of the crowd was deafening and Michael struggled to hear the Armed Guard as he spoke to him *"You have one minute to prepare yourself, do not make us search for you again"* The guard smirked, able to smell the fear which Michael reeked of and he left him to his final preparations. Michael took his chance and reached into the bag and grabbed the sphere, removing the cloth it was wrapped in. It buzzed and flickered and Michael felt the same shiver as he had back at Noritomo's home. He closed his eyes and felt his entire body shudder with electricity. In what felt like a few seconds Michael absorbed the knowledge and memories of his aged companion, the old man's life

flashed passed and Michael's brain consumed it completely.
"Combatant, combatant" Michaels eyes opened and his mind
resurfaced, he replaced the sphere and took his place among the
others in a robotic trance, with no care or attention to his
surroundings, he was focused, ready and completely calm. The crier
made a final announcement *"Commence"* and it began. Michael
remained still and silent. The samurai flew through the air before him,
swords clashed and rung out like the clattering metal parts or a vast
machine. They performed what seem to be a balanced and
choreographed dance and demonstrated how highly skilled and
merciless they were. Michael stood motionless and waited. A young
warrior came at Michael from his right, he sidestepped with one swift
movement and thrust the butt of his sword into his assailant's throat.
The warrior crumpled like a piece of paper and fell to the dirt. Michael
remained still and another soon approached only to join the first
attacker in the dirt, this time with a broken jaw. After each attack
Michael returned to a meditative state, dispatching each warrior
without even breaking a sweat. Soon only Michael and two others
remained, it was quickly Michael and one other. A giant of a man, he
turned to face Michael while removing his sword from the skull of his
penultimate victim. Michael had fought with honour, he had showed
respect to his opponents and only sought to incapacitate them.
Noritomo had been a just and noble warrior and Michael had absorbed
his morality as well as his superb skill as a martial artist. He dodged
right then left, avoiding every strike thrown at him by his hulking
opponent until he took his chance. Flying through the air he
pummelled the final warrior until he shrieked with pain *"I surrender"*
The arena erupted with applause *"Ladies and gentleman, Minamoto
Nakamura of Ogamichi, our three hundredth and twenty fourth
champion and winner of the staff of fortune"* Michael looked around
him and soaked up the atmosphere, beaming like a victorious
gladiator. The giant warrior pounced from the ground with no warning
and sunk his sword deep into Michael's back. Michael grimaced with
pain and looked upon his own chest just as the sword burst through
covering the presentation party with the contents of his rib cage.
Michael's body reacted without his control, instinct took over as he
spun on the spot and turned to face the giant man. He swung his
sword as he turned leaving the giant slightly shorter as his head rolled
through the dirt, detached from the rest of his body. Michael slumped
to the floor and Noritomo came rushing to his side. *"You remembered
my son! Help me with him"* The entourage of the other competitors
helped Noritomo without hesitation, moving Michael's failing body to

the side of the arena. *"Here it is my friend"* Noritomo held out the staff, It was made of two parts, a carved wooden base with a glass fixture attached at its upper end. It was cylindrical and a deep shining black. Michael recognised it as he drifted slowly in and out of consciousness, he was haemorrhaging blood rapidly. It was about an inch in diameter and looked like onyx, Michael struggled to speak *" Nor......it...omo, my bag"* Noritomo handed it to him instantly *"Anything my son"* Michael reached into the bag and removed the sphere, it was glowing bright blue, just like it had when it consumed him in the depths of the ocean and when it snaked from the eyes of Noritomo. The onyx cylinder from the staff shone bright and both parts hummed and buzzed in unison with each other. Michael removed it from the wooden base and gripped both parts in his hands, they yearned for each other and he knew that whatever the outcome would be he had to unite them. Looking Noritomo in the eye he thanked him for a final time. The old man smiled and a tear ran down his face. Michael moved the two parts together and they clicked into place almost magnetically. The Light shone brighter and brighter and the sphere vibrated and hummed with increased ferocity until he was once again completely engulfed in its light, once again it had taken him.

Chapter 5

The bad man of Baker Street.

"The morning sun when it's in your face really shows your age" Michael is woken abruptly by the sound of a radio alarm clock, quickly followed by the sound of a man singing. His voice was deep and raspy and Michael recognised it immediately. He was reminded of his mother, cooking homemade soup and dancing around the kitchen to the songs of Rod Stewart. Still stirring from his slumber, Michael flipped the pillow over to the far more satisfying colder side and repositioned his body *"Another five minutes won't hurt"* he thought. The song on the radio faded out and was replaced by the voice of an over-excited radio presenter who for Michaels liking was far too buoyant and awake for that time of the morning. *"It's seven fifty six on the tenth of September, not many have been spared the cold and soggy morning. That was Rod Stewart with Maggie May. News from around the world coming up, but first some Bill Withers"* Michael stirred again, he could not be bothered with work today, another classic song played on the radio and he lay disregarding his need to get out of his bed and get ready for the day with the rest of the family. Kaitlin must have woken earlier as he was sprawled over her side of the bed leaving no room for another occupant. He flipped over again, the thought of today's chores had made getting comfortable again an impossible task. *"It's eight a.m., let's head over to the news desk for today's headlines and weather report".* A particularly cheesy jingle followed. Michael was now wide awake and he lay on his back with his eyes forcibly shut, still neglecting to accept the inevitable. He listened to the news report which included various stories, mostly crime and a little uplifting story at the latter end to cheer up the early morning commuters and insomniacs. Michael never really paid attention to any of the reports. Until the newscaster began to report on the sport which perked his interest considerably. *"And to today's sport, in football, local boys Chelsea take on Coventry City, Liverpool are visiting Spurs, and Arsenal are in Birmingham taking on West Bromwich Albion, hoping to retain last season's good form and retain the league championship."* Michael's eyes opened and widened instantly *"Man City won the league last year?"* He listened with much more purpose and interest than he had been *"A high of fourteen in London today, slightly higher*

than the seasonal average, and it's been the wettest September in five years, it's 8:07 on September the tenth 1971 and this is The Who with Won't Be Fooled Again". Michael started to wheeze, the feeling of fear and dread which was overcoming his senses almost caused him to pass out. He scanned the room for some verification of the nightmare which was unfolding around him, why did he not notice sooner? The carpet was about six inches thick and was made with what looked like a woollen material, it was emerald green in colour. The wallpaper was again a greenish colour, but much paler than the carpet and it had a heavy print all over it in a dark brown colour. The evidence was building but the décor was not enough to convince him that he had not just woken in a random location after a heavy session on the whisky. Although it had been quite a while since he had been out with the lads. Kaitlin had been on his back lately, she had commanded that he spend more time with her and Joseph. Michael stood up and felt his legs stiffen, they ached and he hobbled across the thick carpet towards the bathroom. His head spun as he tried to fathom what was going on, the weird dream he experienced where he was in another place, inhabiting the body of another man couldn't actually be happening, could it? There was only one way to find out, he staggered towards the bathroom door, taking in his surroundings as he went. He passed a black ash telephone table, placed upon it was a large plastic telephone, it was an upright with the receiver resting on top attached with a thick spiral cable. Michael glared at it with wonder, if it was two thousand and twelve, then the flat he had crashed out drunk in was an excellent example of how to waste your money on retro accessories. Michael reached for the handle of the bathroom door, the only way to know the truth of his situation was to face up to it man to mirror. He pushed the door open and before he could get through, it swung open and he was met by a mass of red hair. He stumbled backwards and tripped over the black ash table. He landed with a thud and the telephone rang like a bell as it crashed beside him on the floor. *"What's up love?"* The semi-naked girl spoke to Michael while concentrating in the mirror she had hopped over Michael to return to. *"You look like you've seen a ghost, you need to calm down on the weed"* Michael could not take his eyes of her as he struggled back to his feet, she was young and vibrant and very attractive. He listened intently to her as she continued *"I need to run, I'm so late"* Michael stared at her as she got dressed with accelerated pace and lit a cigarette all at once. *"O.K that's me off, I'll see you tonight. Remember Mario's at seven O.K?"* The girl approached him and leaned up to his face, her cold lips touched his and he could taste the fresh smell of smoke on her breath *"Seven*

O.K?" She looked at him expectantly and repeated herself again
"Wake up you! O.K for seven?" Michael replied eventually "O.K seven"

"Bye, got to go" The girl rushed out the door and slammed it
shut behind her. Michael rushed to the window and watched her with
great interest as she crossed the road and got into a bright blue Mini
Cooper, he watched as she faded into the distance. Michael was
mesmerised by the street scene below, it reminded him of a television
set, and it was so perfectly dated and stereotypical of a bygone era.
The Mini Cooper disappeared down the road closely followed by
another car, Michael eyes followed it until his attention was instantly
grabbed by something that he recognised immediately. It was another
vehicle parked further up the street. Michael's face was filled with a
wide grin as he stared longingly at its bodywork. It was a Porsche 911
in fire engine red and he had always wished he could have had one.
This particular model was a 2.2 litre Targa, the exact model that he
usually perused on the internet when he felt like imagining he could
actually afford to buy one, it was in immaculate condition. A man and
a woman crossed the street and Michael's eyes were immediately
drawn to the figure hugging top and tight hot pants that the woman
was wearing. Her hair was cut short, almost like a male's cut and he
likened her to a photograph he had seen in a magazine of a young Cilla
Black. The man's trousers were enormous at the heel and he wore a
tight fitting knitted tank top. Michael stood for another thirty or forty
minutes soaking up the unbelievable view which appeared before him
like a snapshot from the past. He was not home as he had hoped and
his mind cast back to Japan and his previous unusual episode. Had he
dreamt the entire episode? There was no evidence to suggest that he
had been there at all. Moving to the bathroom door, he stopped short
of the mirror and composed himself, he took a long deep breath and
gazed into the glass. Another man gazed back at him, just like before
he inhabited the body of a stranger. This time he was a far closer
match to Michael. A young man, white with neck length silky black
hair which reminded him of George Best, a favourite footballer of his
from that era. It was a style that was actually pretty generic for most
young white males around that time. Upon further inspection Michael
was impressed by the spectacular moustache that he was sporting, he
was amazed by the hours of effort that must have gone into
maintaining its volume and shine. Michael turned away from the
mirror after the bizarre experience of studying the face of his new
shell. Michael's thoughts focused on the sphere which had played
such a large part during his time with Noritomo. The sphere had to be

protected. It was such a powerful and obviously significant element. His heart began to race and almost as if the sphere felt his presence it began to buzz violently and he was drawn to its location like a moth to a light bulb. It was near, not so near that he could see it, but it compelled him to its location, it was calling for him. Michael grabbed a pair of jeans which were discarded at the bottom of the bed and pulled them on. They seemed to fit well, they had large bell bottoms and Michael smirked as he buttoned them up *"Retro"* he thought whilst grabbing a white t-shirt from a chest of drawers next to the bed. The drawers were typical of the seventies, faux wood effect, functional and mass produced. The top drawer opened with a squeak as it was a bit stiff and it took a few tugs to open it fully. The plastic veneer had seen better days. He reached into the drawer and retracted his hand like it had been bitten by a venomous snake. He could not see the item his hand had touched but it was obvious what it was, even to Michael who had no experience with weapons. It was the cold steel of a handgun. He reached in again, this time removing the piece and holding it nervously between his thumb and fore finger as though it could go off at any minute. He placed it down on the bed and sat down next to it. What did he need a gun for? The possibilities unnerved him. Reaching into the drawer again he removed a wallet, it was leather and filled with a considerable amount of cash, it was joined with a shiny metal badge and Michael realised immediately that it was a Metropolitan police officer's badge. Michael sighed nervously, the enormity of his new surroundings were taking their toll already and the picture was beginning to slowly piece together of who he could be this time. There was no accompanying name on the badge and Michael delved into the drawer in the hope of finding a more definitive clue to the identity of his current possession. Excitement had replaced the feelings of trepidation, he was becoming more intrigued by each little revelation revealed by his deductions. Michael removed a set of keys from the drawer, there was no key ring and four keys. A large mortise dead lock key and smaller door key was accompanied by a much smaller silver key, it must have been for a padlock he thought, it was too small to be for a door lock. On the circular part there was a silver embellished number, it read "324". The next few moments were particularly unusual. Michael forgot the enormity of the supernatural conundrum that he was experiencing, he had no clue where he was or what he was involved in yet he let out an excited giggle like a teenager *"Oh yes!, You little beauty"* He leaped to his feet and darted across the room to the window and peered down the street again *"Jackpot"*. It was the fourth key, black and sleek with a little shiny badge which he

59

recognised immediately. The little horse in the middle of the design rearing up on its hind legs set his pulse racing. Michael quickly pulled on a pair of tan leather boots he found discarded on the bedroom floor and headed straight for the front door, he lifted his hand to open the door, and his palms were sweaty with anticipation. The madness of his situation had taken a back seat, he felt full of life and was ready to be part of whatever was thrown his way. Unlike his previous experience in Japan, he was injury free, warm and comfortable. The disassociation from his memories also came as a welcome relief, they had recently plagued his dreams for what had felt like an eternity. Being separated from his real life was becoming far more comfortable and Michael was becoming ever more accepting of his new symbiotic habitation. He had engaged with his new body and without noticing was being absorbed by his new persona, everything felt so real and normal to him that he momentarily forgot reality. He reached for the door and without warning as he turned the handle he was shoved backwards as a large middle aged balding man pushed his way through. *"Alright Dickhead?"* The man chuckled and Michael stared at him dumbfounded, his little bit of escapism was over and he came back to reality with an almighty crash. *'Who was this visitor and how did he know him?'* He thought. The man was tall, over six feet with a bulky frame. Not all muscle, but he looked strong and menacing. *"C'mon Alfie, we ain't got all day guvnor"* Alfie? What sort of name was that? Michael thought for a second, then he realised he had left the contents of the drawer strewn over the bed. *"Yeah, you'd better put that stuff back….I see the handcuffs are still missing"* The man chuckled again and Michael smiled nervously. *"What's up? You seem a bit tense…….is it the meeting? Less than a week to go now boss"* Michael nodded as if to agree with his visitor's insinuation. He was wary of too much interaction while he remained a passenger in his new predicament *"O.K let's go then, if we leave now we can grab some scran on the way."* Michael grabbed a leather jacket from the back of the front door, it was a little worn looking, but it stank of the most expensive kind of leather. He pulled on the bomber jacket and he followed the man through the door, slamming it behind him. Michael was conscious that his lack of information could potentially land him in trouble, so he stayed behind his newest friend, hoping he would lead him to his destination, picking up fragments of information as he went. The autumn wind cut through him as he left the building, it was in no way as unforgiving as the last climate he had experienced, but he tensed up his shoulders to try and curb some of its effect. *"You got your keys boss?"* Michael reached into his jeans pocket and pulled out

60

the keys. *"You want to drive?"* Michael held the keys out towards him *"Yeah whatever, good one boss"* the man sniggered and continued over to the other side of the road and turned to face Michael again. *"Go on, I'm still half asleep anyway"* His face lit up with excitement *"Wow, cheers boss......sure you're feeling O.K?"* Michael smiled and tossed him the keys. *"Boss"* he thought, that was a couple times he had said that now, his companion seemed to be addressing him with a level of respect, almost as if he was Alfie's subordinate in some way. The thought that he could be the boss of this large hulk of a man unnerved him and Michael had decided that it was maybe local dialect or a bit of friendly banter. *"C'mon then, the boys will never believe me when I tell them their old dad was driving a brand new 911"*. The man's excitement was impossible to contain and Michael watched him as he bounced around the car opened the door and jumped in. Michael's plan had worked, he had only offered the keys to him as he had absolutely no idea where they were going, he had to rely on the guidance of another. Just as he had in Japan, he could only hope that his companion would know the way to his destination, wherever that could have been. Reaching out to open the passenger side door, Michael felt a rush of electro-static tingle over his body. It was not your normal little snap, you would get from a woollen jumper or freshly laid bed sheets. It stopped him in his tracks and his ears popped, the sphere was nearby and its power was becoming ever easier for him to identify. The large man sat quivering with nerves *"I will be careful"*

"Relax and enjoy it" Michael portrayed his character with confidence on the surface, but he was nervous, if not completely terrified underneath. The key turned in the ignition and the engine purred with great ferocity and bass *"Listen to that boss.........Right then, full English is it?"*

"Sounds good"

"Rita's then?" Michael nodded and the car took off at a snail's pace, due to his chauffeur's dread at damaging it. *"Get the foot down, enjoy it I said"*. Michael had realised that in reality the Porsche was not his, in fact nothing was his at all, not even the body he was inhabiting and he was just as keen to see the car put through its paces. *"You're the boss"* The car sped off and Michael was pushed back in his seat by the acceleration. They shot passed the bustling life of the London suburb, with buildings and people obscured by their speed, heads turned as the roar of the engine passed them by, it was an

unusual sight to see a vehicle of such expense and style in what was a generally working class area of the city. Michael pondered his new surroundings *"You're the boss?"* he thought again. It was becoming more obvious to him, that his companion was either his business partner or due to his subservient nature possibly his employee. The car screeched to a halt outside a little café, which could only be described as a greasy spoon. Both men jumped from the vehicle and his companion turned to face Michael *"Cheers for that boss, see no scratches"* He threw the Keys over the roof of the car and Michael caught them, then moved quickly to catch him up as he headed towards the glass fronted façade of the café. *"Right boss, this is on me, I owe you one for that anyway"* Michael nodded in agreement, the awkwardness of not knowing the man's name was becoming increasingly difficult to contend with. The door swung open and they moved inside, the smell of bacon, coffee and cigarettes was overwhelming and Michael gasped for a mouthful of uncontaminated air, followed with a coughing fit. *"Alright Sweetheart"* He watched on as the large and thick fingered hand of his companion slapped the backside of a waitress who was clearing the remnants of a previous customer's breakfast away. She retaliated with a high pitched voice which seemed to be originating from her nose. *"I swear it, one of these mornings my arse will bite you back, Bernie Castleford"* Michael's coughing fit subsided as a feeling of relief cured him instantly, he finally had learned the man's name and sniggered to himself, proud of his patience paying off. *"And don't you be laughing either Alfie Charles, you're not too old for a clip round the ear you know"* The waitress, around mid-forties approached him and leaned in for a kiss *"How are you my love?..... Seen your mam the other day, she's looking well"* Bernie pushed in *"Alright Rita, put him down, we're starving"*

"Always thinking of that gut you are....two specials then?"

"Nice one Rita" Michael answered, he found himself beginning to relax and get right into his new persona. He felt like an actor and this was his latest role. Bernie and Michael sat at a table by the window, the table and chairs were made of cheap white plastic and had a blue gingham tablecloth over its surface. In the centre of the table was a selection of various condiments. HP sauce, salt, vinegar and the required elements for a good old fashioned cup of English tea. Michael's eye was drawn to the little tomato sauce bottle, it was a novelty tomato shape and the green stalk acted as the cap.

Michael smiled while he studied it. *"Something funny?"* Bernie asked, confused at Michaels behaviour

"No Bernie, just thinking......anyway what's on today's agenda" Bernie raised another confused eyebrow *"Agenda?....Ha, do I look like a fuckin' secretary.....agenda, you're losing it"* Michael didn't reply, his mind was now actively aware that his choice of words or behaviour could easily be construed as odd, he had to try harder to blend in. Bernie now was looking really uncomfortable, and he sat with his head bowed fiddling with a sachet of sugar until he plucked the courage to speak again. *"Sorry boss, it was just a joke"* Michael could see that Bernie was in fear of what his reaction could have been, Alfie Charles must have been a person of importance or at least a person in a position of power. If a man of Bernie's stature was quivering before him then there must have been a good reason. Michael felt uncomfortable with his companion's uneasiness and attempted to dissolve the atmosphere *"Don't sweat it big chap, my head is buzzing this morning, just give me a quick reminder"* The relief on his face was obvious

"Cheers boss, when we are done here, we are off to meet our four boys, I still think you should drop by the yard after we've finished with them?" Michael nodded in agreement *"Where are we meeting the boys again?"*

"Thought it would be safer if we just met them in the crown, it's your turf, less dodgy than the yard and nowhere near baker street" Bernie whispered the last few words of his sentence which made Michael feel really on edge, there was definitely something untoward transpiring. Bernie was not keen to advertise his information to the other patrons in Rita's café. Safe locations? And Baker Street, why did that ring a bell? *"Here you go boys, tea's on its way"* Rita had served up a typically English fry up accompanied with two rounds of toast for each of them. Bernie was silent as he began to devour his plate, the only sounds being that of a sausage being mashed between his teeth or the cutlery tapping on his plate. Michael slipped into a daydream as he worked his way through his breakfast also. Kaitlin was at the forefront of his mind and he remembered how she used to surprise him with a full English after he had been out late the night before. That was well before Joseph was born, he was lucky if he got a cup of tea in bed once he had arrived. The deeper he got engulfed in his daydream the more withdrawn he became and a pained look came over his face, his eyes distant and glazed. He remembered what his

63

reality had in store for him, if and when he returned to it and the thought of it cut him deep. There was no guarantee he would be returned anyway he thought and the past few days had been so obscure and uncontrolled that anything was possible. He had to keep faith that there was an end to it all and it would seem the only thing that had any answers for him was the mysterious spherical object. Michael's face turned from fear to concern, where was the sphere? He closed his eyes momentarily and he felt its power inside his mind, buzzing and humming, constantly drawing him to it. *"Back in two minutes Bernie"*

"O.K Boss" Michael stood up from his chair and left the café, he took a massive inhale of clean air as he exited, he had forgotten how the twenty first century smoking ban had really improved dining out. He headed across the road and approached the boot of the car, his body tingled with the same electro-static feeling. The boot popped open, it was in pristine condition, not a spec of dirt on the plush black upholstery. Inside was a holdall, not unlike one he had had when he was in school, basic and functional. Opening it he began to remove the contents. There was a large roll of fifty pound notes, in fact he removed several of them, and he stuck one of them into his jacket pocket. Included in the holdall was a brown envelope with "FOR WOLFE" written on its side, a brochure filled with various pictures of vehicles of that era, it read "A.C LUXURY MOTORS". At the bottom of the bag it lay quiet and only flickered slightly with its signature blue light, one of the twelve holes had now been sealed shut with the cylindrical fragment from the staff of fortune he had obtained in the tournament. Michael remembered how useful it had been in Japan and he picked it up and waited to be injected with some new knowledge or power just as it had before. It remained cold and dark. *"Alright Dickhead"* Michael dropped the sphere into the bag as Bernie startled him *"You alright guv? You're looking as bit pasty"*

"I'm good Bernie, time to go is it?" Michael shut the boot of the Porsche *"Give me those, you drive"*

"Cheers guv" Bernie didn't hesitate this time and grabbed the keys, Michael took two polystyrene cups filled with tea and carefully slipped into the passenger seat, ready to go to their next destination. After a short while, Bernie pulled up outside a typical London pub. It was a quiet and reasonably remote location for being in the heart of the city. *"Crown should be quiet today boss"* Bernie held the door open and put on a far more professional manner, he was

purposefully displaying his servant hood in their new surroundings. As they entered the barman immediately acknowledged their arrival *"The room is ready Mr Charles....usual is it?"* Michael nodded towards the barman, who went about his preparations with great care and attention, Alfie Charles it seemed was an important customer. *"I'll bring them through Mr Charles"* Michael acknowledged Bernie who had now completely lost all his personality and had it replaced with a practiced and deliberate behaviour. The pieces of this particular puzzle had started to come together, Alfie Charles was not your run of the mill successful businessman, he demanded respect, he was a player, a gangster of some sort and Bernie was his number one, bodyguard and token hard case. Michael felt weird as people in the bar avoided direct eye contact with him and was glad to be beckoned to follow the barman through the back of the bar *"your room is ready Mr Charles".* Michael followed the barman to a little back room, there was a mahogany table and chairs which was polished to a gloss shine and at one end of the table there was a large padded comfortable armchair, he removed his jacket and sat down. The barman sat a glass of whisky on a small paper place mat and offered him a cigar. *"Anything else Mr Charles?"* The barman winced as he waited for a reply, he was obviously fearful of Alfie Charles. *"Lovely all good"* Michael answered him as he took the first puff on the large cigar and could see the relief on the barman's face. He stood silent for a short while and Michael began to feel quite awkward when he realised that he was waiting to be dismissed. Michael wasn't a gangster, but as far as everyone else in this place thought, he was Alfie Charles. He decided to go for it and get right into character *"Alright son, off you go"* The barman moved off towards the door *"What's your name son?"*

"Billy, Mr Charles"

"You got a bird?"

"Wife and Little Billy, Mr Charles" Michael's mind drifted back to Kaitlin and Joseph for a second and then quickly faded *"Here you go, get them something nice"* He leaned forward and offered him two crisp fifty pound notes. The bar man looked at the money with wide eyes, but hesitated to take them, wondering what their receipt could leave him owing. *"No tricks son, you're doing a good job"* the bar man swiftly picked up the money and hid it away *"Thank you Mr Charles sir"*

"Get going then" Michael nodded towards the door and Billy left, shutting the door behind him. Michael roared with laughter *"What am I doing?"* he said aloud. The amusement of playing his part, had become a game for him and he was beginning to enjoy it *"Cockney geezer"* he laughed again and was stopped by the door opening. Bernie popped his head through the door *"That's them here, Mr Charles sir"*

"Send them in Bernie" Michael continued to play his part, becoming more adventurous and daring with each new interaction. Bernie returned and introduced the visitors in turn *"This is Tony, Thomas, Tucker and Wolfy"* the four men came in and sat at the opposite end of the table from Michael. *"Shout Billy in Bernie"* Billy rushed into the room with great haste and stood to attention awaiting instruction. *"Do the honours Billy son"* Billy distributed drinks and cigars to the guests then slipped away through the open door, Bernie followed him *"I'll be outside guv"* The door closed behind Bernie and Michael took a long drag on his Cigar while the four men sat patiently waiting on him to talk. He tilted his head back and blew the smoke towards the ceiling relaxed and casual. He really was beginning to enjoy being Alfie Charles. *"O.K, fill me in"* Michael started with an open question, as he still had no clue what was going on. *"Will I go lads?"* The oldest of the four which Bernie had introduced as Wolfy gained the permission of the group to do the talking. *"Well Mr Charles, the shop we have in mind is ideal, it's two doors up from the Lloyds, it sell bags and shoes"* the freshest face of the four interrupted *"Leather stuff"* Wolfy continued after casting a disapproving eye in the interrupters direction. *"We've been digging at the weekend to cover up the noise, nearly there now, about fifty feet to go until we reach the vault"* Michael's heart went into overdrive, if what he was piecing together in his mind was true then he was the man at the head of a bank robbery. He tried to remain focused and encouraged Wolfy to dispense with as much information as possible *"We should be ready to go tomorrow night as planned"*

"Good" Michael was lost for words and could only muster a one word answer. *"Did you get the envelope Mr Charles?"* Michael remembers the envelope in the boot of the Porsche *"I signed the lease just like you asked"*

"Good" Michael again breathed slowly and tried to remain calm, he was majorly freaked out by what he was finding himself to be a part of. *"So if there is nothing else Mr Charles, we will see you when*

the dust settles" Michael took a sharp intake of breath, his cigar sat in the ashtray and had a long ash due to a lack of use. *"Agreed"* The door opened and Bernie came in *"Sorted then guv?"*

"Yes Bernie, thank you" Bernie threw the car keys across the table at Michael and his eyes widened as if to remind him of something, Michael failed to notice Bernie's attempts and the big man took the initiative *"Mr Charles sir, you asked me to remind you of the change in arrangements"* Michael looked longingly at Bernie, if he knew the sign language for "Throw me a bone here" it would have helped him immensely

"Regards to box three two four sir?" Michael remembered the small silver key from before and began to sweat again, what the hell did it mean? Mr Wolfe interrupted *"Ah Mr Charles, you did mention this when you gave me the lease, rest assured deposit box three two four will be brought to you unopened as you requested"*

"Excellent, then we are done here gentlemen" Michael's pulse raced, he had managed to fumble blindly through the conversation. The group started to disband and Michael was left on his own for a while which was a welcome relief. Bernie escorted the four men off the premises. The magnitude of the situation he found himself in was totally overwhelming, Japan had its challenges, but this was something completely different, the language barrier had served to be beneficial compared to the possibility of being committed to an insane asylum for simply gibbering away like a crazy man, trying to decipher each new interaction. Japan had also been forthcoming with a detailed indication of what was expected of him. Seventies London had so far given him a detailed description of the events, but his particular role was still in the dark. He was the boss man, which he understood, did the Japanese events and the currents events have anything in common? The only constant was the existence of the sphere. Michael thought of how it had absorbed Noritomo's knowledge and skills and transferred them to him so easily, allowing him to complete the task. Unlike Noritomo, there were no likely candidates. Who would know about a crime which had not yet been committed? Michael supped on his whiskey that he had hardly touched and drifted into deep thought, his mind was absolutely buzzing and before he knew it Bernie had returned. *"Righto Boss, you still want to go down the motor yard? You look tired, I'll deal with it today if you want"* Michael was relieved at the offer of Bernie's assistance. *"Sure you can cope with it?"*

"I'm pretty sure that A.C Luxury Motors won't miss it's captain for one day.....c'mon, I'll take you home"

"Cheers Bernie".

Bernie locked up the Porsche and threw him the keys. *"O.K boss I'll get you in the morning, big day tomorrow"*

"Thanks again Bernie" Michael watched as Bernie crossed the road and flagged down a taxi, he opened the front door of the flat and it slammed behind him, he leaned backwards onto the door, physically and mentally drained. He placed the holdall on the floor, this time remembering to keep it close by. Sitting on the end of the bed he grasped the sphere and stared at its shiny surface for a few hours, it gave him no new information, no marks or indication as to its origin. It wasn't long till he collapsed on the bed fully clothed and fell into a deep sleep. The dream he had was just like how he remembered dreams, it only sought to reinforce that his reincarnations were in every way a real physical experience. Surely you did not dream while in a dream he thought. Michael began to wake and sat up quickly *"No Fuckin' way....it can't be"* He had realised where he was and what he was part of. It was nineteen seventy one and he was in London. He was involved in a robbery of a bank on Baker Street. It wasn't just any old bank robbery, it was probably the most famous one in British history and he was a part of it. Michael took the time to run over the details in his head once more. The four men had mentioned a tunnel, it was a Lloyds bank. "Oh shit" he exclaimed aloud. He had given the lease to the shop to Wolfy to sign, Alfie Charles was covering his tracks and putting everything in place to implicate Wolfy and the others in case the plan failed and the police caught up with them. Michael sat with a piece of paper and a pen which he had found in the bedside cabinet, he wrote down as much as he could remember about the robbery. A HAM radio enthusiast had overheard the robbers discussing the details of the robbery, there was a big police and media cover up, they escaped with millions of pounds. After a long time writing furiously Michael fell asleep feeling no closer to understanding what his next move should be, he had exhausted himself just thinking about it. The morning came round and Michael was awoken by the ringing of the large plastic telephone, he struggled towards it and missed it just before it stopped ringing and sat back down. It rang again and he answered it, it was the girl from yesterday *"Mario's at seven you said?"* Michael stuttered and was interrupted before he could get a word in *"So fuck you Alfie Charles, you and me are finished"* Michael listened to the tone of the dead line and lay down on the bed staring at the ceiling *"Give me a break"* he said aloud. The sphere sparked into life and he rushed to remove it from the holdall. It seemed to lose all its activity on his touch and he stood with it, lifeless in his hand for a few seconds until with a deafening buzzing sound and a flash of bright blue light, Michael's jacket flew across the room and the contents of the pocket stuck to side of the sphere with a powerful magnetic force. The keys dangled as he held the sphere up high in front of his face, studying the flashes of blue light which travelled across its surface like fluorescent veins. One key in particular was attached, the small silver one with the number on it. The sphere fell silent again and the keys fell to the floor. *"What, that's it?"* Michael was unmoved by the considerably less informative interaction. All he could do now was wait until Wolfy brought him box three two four. Exhausted by the events of the previous day, Michael had slept passed lunch time, he reached over to the alarm clock radio and switched it on. A song faded and was replaced by the voice of a female news reporter *"And now the weather Michael"* His attention was immediately drawn to her, he was sure she had just addressed him personally, he was becoming more accustomed to the unusual and a conversation with the radio was not so hard to contemplate. He turned the volume knob and tried to listen over the noise from the busy street below. *"There will be a strong westerly breeze which will make it seem a few degrees colder today"* A jingle played and the news report was over, Michael had conceded that he imagined it, he stood up and stretched, his back cracked loudly and he let out a massive tired yawn. The radio buzzed with interference *"The next message is dedicated to Michael in London 'Miss you lots daddy, let the light of Viera lead you to us, all our love Kaitlin and Joseph'"* Michael grabbed the radio and was rabid with excitement, he was definitely awake and that message was undoubtedly for him, more interference was followed by a final announcement *"This is Oasis with Wonderwall"*, the radio buzzed and clicked and turned itself off, Michael shook it vigorously and tried to switch it on, he reached down to the socket and stopped short, the hairs on his neck stood on end as he realised that the radio was not even plugged into the socket. Michael removed the small black cover on its base, there were no batteries either. It was all too much and he launched the radio at the wall in despair, it bounced off and landed on the heavy shag carpet. Michael rushed to it and picked it up, holding it close to his chest. He had made contact, to what end or for what reason he had no clue. He began to sob uncontrollably, he had heard her voice, was she alive? The uncertainty

69

was tearing him apart, what was he supposed to do? Why was he stuck in London? Michael screamed out at the top of his voice, why was he being tortured like this. He launched the Alarm clock for a second time and this time it missed the wall and flew straight through the window and plummeted to the street below. Michael moved to the window to see where it had landed. An old lady lay on the pavement with a gash on her forehead, he had cracked her on the head due to his substandard throwing skills. A passer-by had stopped to help the old lady and glanced up at the window where Michael stood still and guilty, he jumped back after noticing he had been spotted and rushed to pull on his boots. He returned to the window again. Another person had joined the old lady and had sat her up, tending her wound, the first passer-by was pointing towards Michael's window, directing a police officer, he was a stereotypical London Bobby, complete with bell shaped hat. Within a few minutes the front door rattled as a clenched fist beat on it. Michael considered climbing out the window, but the drop was a deadly one for sure, he swallowed down a large lump in his throat and opened the door. Rugby tackled by two officers, he was quick to try and explain his innocence *"It was an accide……."* Waiting for no explanation, one of the officers cracked Michael over the head with his truncheon and as he faded to unconsciousness he heard the voices of the officers *"Alfie Charles, now that's a collar".* The clang of metal on metal awoke Michael from his uncomfortable slumber, the turn key had opened his cell door, as he stood up the cell spun around him and his head ached with a different pain, usually associated with a blunt force trauma. Reaching for his head he pulled away as he touched the gash on his head, it was relatively small but it was accompanied by an enormous lump which felt like it was trying to push its way through his forehead. Michael turned to face who was coming through the cell door. His vision was still returning to normal and Michael screwed up his eyes as he tried to make out the attending officer's face. Without warning Michael received a stinging slap across his face. He staggered and the lump on his head throbbed even more from the impact. *"Bastard".* Michael recognised the voice *"So where was it? The crown? Or were you with that bitch again?"* In front of Michael stood a uniformed officer, she was fumbling in her pocket and removed a pack of cigarettes and a lighter. She lifted the cigarette up to her face and took a long drag. She was young and had a pale complexion And Michael noticed she was quite pretty, he watched as she lifted her other hand and removed her hat revealing a clearer view of the girl underneath, Michael gasped as he realised who she was, under the hat was a very neat and tightly slicked back mass of red hair, tied up in a bun on top of her head. *"Sorry about the other night"* Michael coughed and the sudden jolt of movement sent a fresh pain through the lump on his forehead. *"You could have called, you don't think about me"* Aware of the likelihood of another slap, Michael decided to try and win her over *"I was really busy, I promise I'll make it up to you"*

"You better". The girl moved towards him and landed a passionate kiss on his lips. Michael retracted with pain as she brushed over his injury in the process. *"Oh sorry, poor baby"* He relaxed for a second, happy that he had won her over. The confidence soon disappeared from his mind as he realised that he had no clue what her name was and he tensed up *"So what's to happen to me then?"* The girl exhaled a large cloud of smoke *"Same old shit, the old lady got a visit from Bernie, her purse got a little fatter and she dropped the charges"* Michael sighed with relief *"Anyway, Bernie is outside, you better get going"* Michael followed the girl out the station after signing the obligatory forms and collecting his personal effects. The Girl slipped to the side of the main entrance, out of her colleague's view and whispered *"See you tonight then?"* Michael was stunned, it was still dark outside *"Tonight? What time is it?"*

"It's half six in the morning Alfie, you've been banged up since yesterday" The couple moved towards Bernie who stood patiently outside awaiting their attendance *"Hope ye don't mind boss, the flat door was lying open, so I just grabbed your keys"* Bernie had brought the Porsche and Michael just smiled, still sore and tender. *"O.K, I'm off, remember Mario's at eight."* The girl glanced around to see if anyone was watching and pecked Michael on the cheek *"See you later Bernie"*

"Righto Serena sweetheart" Michael waved her off and considered the newly revealed name *"Never would have guessed that"* he muttered under his breath

"What's that guv?"

"Nothing Bernie, nothing" He opened the door of the Porsche and sat in the passenger seat, Bernie joined him and started it up. The engine roared with the same power and bass like before. *"To the flat is it boss?"* Michael nodded and before long they were pulling up across the street from the flat. The engine purred and then cut out *"O.K boss I'm heading, just like we arranged. I'll speak to you in a few*

71

weeks once the dust settles." Bernie put out his hand and shook Michael's hand firmly *" Remember that shit you wanted is in the boot boss, Oh and no more granny bashing, see you later"* Bernie laughed as he got out and headed down the street, lighting a cigar as he went. Michael was mesmerized by his swagger, he was such a stereotypical English hard case. His daydream swiftly dissipated as he realised what Bernie had said. While he was locked in the cells, the most notorious robbery in British history had taken place and by luck he had given himself the ultimate alibi. *"Priceless"* He thought. *"Banged up for assaulting a pensioner".* He got out of the car and opened the boot, his black bag was still there and it was accompanied with a black metal box. On the front of the box, the numbers three, two and four where depressed into the metal. He decided to forget the flat and he sat back down in the car with his bag and the newly obtained case. The sphere was still there and Michael grasped it, he felt immediately relaxed, knowing it was safe. He grabbed the keys and the sphere increased in activity, vibrating and buzzing slightly. He placed the small silver key in the lock and the metal box clicked open. Inside was a brown envelope and a small black box which was similar to the sort which expensive jewellery would be kept in. Michael flicked the small brass catch and opened the box, it was another segment, just like the piece that he had obtained in Japan. It began to glow and buzz with increasing intensity and the sphere reacted to it, as if it was aware of its presence. Michael knew what he had to do, he had no other ideas. The pieces clicked together with the same magnetism as before. The light began to engulf him and this time he was fully awake and prepared. Glancing to the box, he read the envelope in his last few moments *"CONFIDENTIAL"* In large red lettering. It was accompanied by what he recognised as a royal seal. He reached for the envelope and before he could take it he was completely engulfed by the light. Once again it had taken him. His thoughts turned to his family, hopefully this time he would be taken to them.

Chapter 6

Long Live the King

The light was blinding and the buzzing emanating from the sphere was almost deafening. His vision started to return and Michael became more aware of his surroundings. Being awake during the transportation sequence had proven more stressful than he had anticipated. The light engulfed everything around him as the sphere continued to crackle with interference. It was similar to standing too close to a speaker with a mobile phone, and it drowned out all the noise from the surrounding landscape which was slowly materialising. The process was disorientating even though it seemed to be a stationary one, but it did not stop the nausea that Michael likened to the sickness he felt while travelling in his parents' car as a child. As the static began to dissipate he could hear voices breaking through. First he could hear Kaitlin, then a giggle from Joseph, he could hear the songs sung by Noritomo and the hearty chuckle of Bernie who both seemed like a lifetime away now. The light continued to fade and more recognisable sounds and shapes began to appear at an ever increasing rate. Buildings, trees, a rabbit which one moment was miles away and the next moment only a few feet, he could hear his heartbeat, it was strong, calm and very distinctive and his breathing was measured and deliberate. With one final blast of light and sound, the pain forced Michael to close his eyes and when he opened his eyes a new landscape had been forged all around him. Michael's eye peered down the scope of a heavy rifle, in the distance a rabbit popped its head out of the long grass. The transportation had left him limp, fragile and a bit on edge. He shuddered with fright at the sight of the rabbit and pulled the trigger. The crack and fizzle of the bullet punished his already fragile eardrum and the rifle was thrown from his hands, several yards in the air, the rabbit disappeared into the long grass, Michael's inadequacy had proven to be its saviour. Sitting up, he massaged his shoulder, it had taken the full force of the recoil, he stayed in the long grass hidden, after all he might not have been the only person in these parts who was carrying a gun, and likely that person would have been a far better shot than him. From his hidden vantage point he looked around and began to assess the terrain, he

73

was on the outskirts of a small suburb. There were buildings about half a mile up ahead, not massive in height, about tenement size, there were nine in a row which he could see and the furthest away one seemed to be still under construction. It must have been autumn or early winter he thought, the trees had no leaves, large patches of the surrounding grass had succumbed to the cold. It felt remote and quite lifeless. In the distance a fire was burning and white smoke bellowed up, snaking towards the clear blue sky above. Michael retreated to the long grass, he was cold again *"must be winter"* he muttered to himself. Upon the ground lay a pack which was typical of a hill walker, or a survival pack that a student may have used while setting off on an adventure to the Far East. There were small pots and pans, cutlery, a few tins of condensed soup, lentil, chicken and rice and tomato. This was only obvious to Michael due to the pictures on the packaging as the writing on the tins was not in English. Eastern Europe he thought, maybe Russian. Emptying his pack he noticed the items removed were varied and well considered by the person who had sorted them. There was ammo which was presumably for the rifle which he had just failed to use miserably trying to kill the rabbit. There were some plastic containers which had some sort of stew in them. Michael's mind began to wander as he tried to think about where he could be, tin cans and Tupperware, he thought *"That's post 1950's I think"* he had become accustomed to speaking out aloud to himself, although he was surrounded by people in Japan and London, he was always alone and had started to assess his situation by questioning aims and stating facts out aloud, what harm could it do? He had already experienced events which any sane person would question anyway. It seemed logical to analyse and deconstruct before making any potentially dangerous or important decisions. From the pack he pulled one item after another, it seemed that whoever he was, he had packed what seemed like an entire person's life into one transportable package. At the base of the pack was a small canvas bag, it was square in shape a bit like a bowling ball bag and Michael knew what it was immediately. The sphere hummed gently and the magnetic force from which Michael had come to rely upon as his guide gently moved in his hands towards the town in the distance. He replaced the sphere in its bag and began to pack all the other items back into the large pack. Decision had been made, he was going to head for the smoke, maybe there were some people who could help him discover his next move. A menacing and raspy bark sparked Michael's attention, he remembered the wolf in Japan and grabbed the rifle, which had landed a few feet from his pack. It was getting closer. The openness of the terrain caused the barks to echo all around him and it cast doubts in Michael's mind as to the direction of its origin. The weight of the rifle was immense, it seemed old and well used. He shook with fear as the barks were replaced by the rustling of nearby dry grass. His breathing got shorter, and he was poised and ready to face the approaching beast. The long grass split behind Michael and from the opening a large dog pounced toward him. It was carrying something in its jaws. He pointed the rifle, his arms were heavy and he struggled to pull the trigger. The rifle clicked with a tame snap, the barrel was empty. Dropping the rifle, his heart pumped and he stumbled as he tried to move from the beast's path, it was too late the dog pinned Michael to the ground, a few stones stuck in Michael's back while he reached for a large rock to strike his assailant. Turning face to face with it, he stopped short of smashing the dog's skull with the sharp rock he had grabbed, the animal was not menacing at all. It leaned past Michael's head and placed the contents of its jaws on the grass. It was the freshly killed carcasses of two rabbits. As soon as the dog had dropped the carcasses, Michael became its next target. The dog let out a submissive whine which was accompanied by an uncontrollable onslaught of licking. Michael's face was soon soaked with the saliva of the beast, which had now won his affection. Around its neck hung a small brass disc, the name on the front was obscured and Michael was unable to make out its name. On the reverse side, there was an address, it read, 324 Stringer Ave. The features of the dog were very familiar to Michael, it was a German shepherd. When he was younger his father had kept them as guard dogs. The most impressive of all was King, he was strong. Michael remembered him as being big like a lion, a mass of long hair with large sharp, white teeth. King combined this menacing strength with loyalty and subservience, especially to his father, all he encountered were treated as hostile strangers, until they were given the all clear, by his master. The dog was not a pure breed like King, it was less brown in colour, blacker with grey splashes and had a resemblance to a wild dog like a Dingo. He was still strong and had an obvious love for the body, which Michael inhabited. Sitting up he reached out towards the dog "what's your name? Eh, boy?" He stroked the dog's long bristly coat and it rolled on its back and beckoned Michael to rub its belly. Kneeling on the dirt, next to his new friend he rubbed the underside of the dog with enthusiasm. It lay and lapped up the attention, with no sign of it ever becoming old. It would have lay there all day. Leaning on the ground, he pushed himself to his feet, a sharp twig snapped and pierced the skin on the palm of his right hand. Upon inspection, Michael studied his hand with great care. It was a new sight, the fingers were long and slender, the nails were short, but well maintained. On the left hand there were two rings upon the wedding finger, a simple gold wedding band, accompanied with a small diamond engagement ring. His eyebrow rose with concerned curiosity, "Surely not?" he thought. Hurriedly fumbling through the bag, Michael found a small case. Within it there was a toothbrush, a bar of soap and a small fragment of mirrored glass. It was once a circle and had been snapped quite neatly and was now a semi-circle with faded edges. It would be useful enough to help him satisfy his concerns. Nervously, Michael held the mirror at arm's length and looked into it, "What the fuck!" He shut his eyes in disbelief and then again gazed into the mirror. He was indeed a she, thirtyish, blue eyes, gaunt in appearance, malnourished, Michael thought. He peered at his new face for a few minutes and removed the woollen hat, he was wearing. His head was bare, with clumpy patches of hair, which was dark and fragile looking. After replacing his hat, he then felt around his body, he had all the appropriate lumps and bumps, in all the correct places, but he was thin, too thin. The dog whined with a comforting tone and brushed against Michael's leg. "Hello boy" "What's your name, eh?" He sat down on the grass, his body was numbed be the latest revelation and he stroked the dog again. "Since I am to be a Queen, then you can be my King". The dog dipped his head to the side and barked, as if to acknowledge his satisfaction. "That'll do then, King it is". "Good boy". Michael began to pack the bag up again, it was time to move. Who knows what awaited the couple in the town up ahead? Collecting the two rabbits, he strung them together with some string from his pack and slung them over his shoulder. The walk to the town seemed to take an age and would have been challenging for the strong and experienced. The body in which he inhabited was weary and tired and he routinely stopped to rest. King was sure to stay close by, straying off occasionally but returning regularly to check on his master. The terrain raised steadily and there was a small ridge overlooking the town below. He stood up from his resting point and began the final climb, it was tough and felt like it was never ending. About ten feet from the top, the end of the climb was in sight. He took a deep breath and moved toward the summit. A gunshot exploded and echoed from the other side of the ridge, Michael dropped instinctively and scrambled for the undergrowth. He could hear the rowdy laughter of a group of men, hoping that they had not seen him. As if he was used to this sort of occurrence, King cowered close to Michael's back and stayed low and out of sight. Unclipping his pack, he grabbed his rifle and headed up to the summit of the ridge. Peeking from his hidden

76

position he tried to catch a glimpse of the crowd in the distance. The first thing he noticed was the desolation of the area, the town looked destroyed and he likened it to the aftermath of a hurricane. At a distance it had looked like any other little suburb, but upon closer inspection the buildings had appeared to be deserted and not one of the windows still had glass within their frames. They were either smashed, boarded up or removed completely, frame and all. There were large weeds growing from the gutters. The main entrance to the area had been barricaded with burnt out vehicles and there was a large barb wire archway which had two men guarding it. They were dressed similarly to Michael, with extra layers and what seemed like some sort of makeshift leather armour. Michael's head turned quickly as his attention had been grabbed by the manic screaming of a female. She was kneeling in the dusty road, crouched over the body of a man who had been the recipient of the initial gunshot that he had heard. Reaching for his rifle, he peered through the scope at the body of the man lying still in the dirt. A single bullet hole in the forehead had produced a large pool of blood, which was seeping slowly into the dirt and creating a thick paste from the mixture of the gruesome ingredients. The executioner approached the woman and her dead companion, he was saying something to two of the other men in the group. They were too far away for Michael to make out what was being said. The man definitely looked in charge he thought, his garments were better maintained and the others in the group were quick to carry out his instructions. The two men grabbed the woman from the dead man's side, he had presumed that it was her husband or maybe her brother. She screamed and spat in their faces like a savage animal. One of the men let out a yelp of pain as she sunk her teeth deep into his hand, pulling his arm away quickly he raised it above his head, intending to strike her. The executioner moved towards him with great urgency and without any hesitation rattled him square in the face with the butt of his gun. It was smaller than the one Michael had, but clearly just as effective. The man picked himself up, bloodied and dazed from the blow and was quickly replaced with another of the men. The executioner pointed at a transit van which was parked nearby and the woman who was fighting to the last was put in the back. Michael leaned on a large rock, his hand had gone numb with leaning on it for too long. The rock tumbled down the ridge towards the gang below, he ducked down and kept as silent as he could. After about thirty seconds he heard the sound of a clapped out engine being fired up, he peered over the ridge once more. The executioner had his arm in the air and was circling it to indicate to the others that it was time to move out. The transit van was joined with an old four by four which six of the men bundled into. Two motorbikes pulled up in front of the van with a pair of men on each of them. The executioner stood alone in the dirt road, he turned and took a final long stare at the ridge. Michael retreated back into his hidden position, a few seconds passed and he heard the door of the van slam shut and crept back to his vantage point. The dust climbed high above the road as the vehicles accelerated into the distance. Michael sighed with relief, this was no ordinary town. Given the way these men had treated the woman, he would have to be extra careful while he inhabited his current shell. Collecting all his belongings again, Michael had a final check and started down the other side of the ridge. King stayed closer this time, he was nervous and was sniffing the air with more frequency than usual. The body was only a few feet away now. The man's face was unrecognisable, and it had been battered and was swollen badly. The gunshot wound had blown half his skull off at the back. King approached the corpse and began to sniff around it. Michael imagined that his new companion would start to gnaw on the carcass, but he ignored and actively avoided the blood stained areas, as if he knew that it was not an acceptable meal for him. King stopped suddenly and his head stuck up with his ears at full length, he had spotted something in the undergrowth. There was a derelict building nearby and Michael caught a glimpse of something moving. King was poised and ready to chase the prey down as soon as he was directed. Another flash of movement, too big to be a rabbit he thought. From behind a bit of corrugated iron came a missile in their direction, it was a rock, he sidestepped and avoided it. The attacker remained hidden, and was trying to scare him off, whatever it was it was capable of throwing with some degree of accuracy as the next rock came flying towards them, this time just narrowly missing King. Michael looked at King and gave him a nod, without hesitation King took off at great pace and honed in on his prey, the attacker made for the long grass and Michael was able to get enough of a look to determine that it was a small girl about seven or eight years old. King was on her tail and was catching her with ease. Panicking, Michael put his fingers up to his mouth and let out a whistle, King stopped dead in his tracks and turned his head to face his master. *"Stay"*, King lay down in the long grass. Approaching the undergrowth, he could see the skip of a scruffy baseball cap, just above the height of the grass. *"Hello?"* he whispered so as not to scare the girl off again, *"Hello?"* The girl pounced from the grass and started to swing her arms and legs towards him. She was shouting in a language which was alien to him and he could make out just one word

78

which she seemed to repeat a few times *"Papa"*. Grabbing the girl he tried to calm her down *"No, Not me! It's o.k..............shh"*. The child looked at him with a bemused expression and it was quickly replaced by a look of relief. She squeezed his leg and did not leg go until he peeled her off. *"Papa"* the girl darted to the body of her father and wept at the side of his lifeless carcass. Before he could approach and console the girl, she had stood up and removed a pendant from around his neck and was heading back towards Michael. She looked at him and started to speak to him in the same alien language that she had before, she seemed confused at his silence. At a loss as to what to say he tried to respond *"What is your name?"*

"Agnieska", Michael was stunned, she could understand him. As far as he could make out, what came out his mouth was English in his head, this child was bilingual or he was speaking in her native tongue, yet he was unable to understand her. *"Agnieska, I am ....Michelle and this is King"* King approached the girl and Licked her face, she giggled and patted his head. Michael smiled at her and she smiled back, both clearly relieved. Agnieska began to speak now at great pace and he was completely lost, there was nothing else for it he had to try the sphere. Removing his pack was a great relief, he was exhausted again. It flickered with blue light as he removed it from the pack. Agnieska's eyes widened with amazement and looked at the sphere with great interest. It was now fixed with two solid segments. Michael held it out towards the child and she backed off initially, but then approached and reached out to grab one of the cylindrical segments, the blue light snaked out from the sphere and attached itself just as it did with Noritomo. Both Michael and Agnieska were connected to it and during the process Michael saw a life flashing through his mind. Running, always running, hungry so hungry, violence and fear. Not the life of a child by any means. The blue light faded and the sphere grew dark and they both slumped to the ground unconscious. Michael's eyes opened slowly, King had decided it was time to wake him as he licked his face. His coarse tongue and warm breath proved to be an adequate alarm clock. It was dark and much colder than earlier. Agnieska had gone, he scanned the surrounding area, but it was too dark to see if she was nearby. His pack had gone and he was left with only his rifle which was lying beside him. A bright light beamed towards him from the distance, he could just make out the oncoming headlights of a vehicle, so he stumbled towards the edge of the road to take cover. Stranded and freezing, he hoped that the approaching people would be more agreeable than the men from

before. As the vehicle drew closer, he decided to flag it down. A night spent in the current climate would surely mean freezing to death. Raising his hand, he quickly retracted it, startled by the sound of Agnieska's voice *"No....bad men!"* Agnieska had appeared from the darkness, she was carrying a pile of sticks that she had been collecting. *"Come, quick, hide"*. He followed her to a large cement pipe hidden in the grass and they both climbed inside. The vehicle's brakes screeched as it stopped quickly and Michael listened for the sound of the door opening. An electronic whirr of the vehicles window sent his mind racing, it must have been at least the nineties he thought. The deep echo of a man's voice cut short his deliberation and replaced it with fear *"Nothing here"*

"Must have been nothing, the dark plays tricks on you". It was two men, Agnieska buried her head in her jacket and tried desperately to muffle and sounds which could have given their hiding place away. King must have slipped away in the darkness and was nowhere to be seen. He leaned on one of the sticks which Agnieska had collected and it snapped under his weight. The crack of the brittle wood echoed through the black silence of the night. *"You hear that?*

"Over there..... No left!" the sound of footsteps brushing through the dry dirt and grass grew louder as one of the men made his way towards them. The panic in Agnieska's eyes made Michael stiffen with fear, he took a deep breath and prepared to defend himself and the little girl. From nowhere King darted across the path of the man and then slipped away from their sight as quick as he had appeared. *"Ha ha.... what's the matter? The big doggie give you a fright?"* The man in the car had taken great pleasure in his companion's reaction. *"O.k. very funny! Just a stray, let's move out"*. He returned to the vehicle and it sped off into the distance. Agnieska exhaled and Michael smiled nervously, both just as glad at the men's departure. The grass rustled again, Agnieska let out a sharp squeal of fright and was quickly relieved as King returned to their side and immediately comforted the little girl by rubbing his long coat against her face. *"Good boy King....good boy"* Michael patted King's head with gratitude, he knew that he had just saved them both from an unknown but probably terrible fate, his companionship was becoming invaluable. After a short while Michael felt it was safe enough to make a move for more suitable shelter for the night. Agnieska gathered up her firewood and beckoned Michael to follow her. Making their way through the darkness, he stayed as close to her as he could, they approached a

derelict building which she had chosen as their camp for the night. It was the tenement building that he had viewed through his rifle scope earlier in the day. The windows had been boarded up and there was an old barrel which was black with charred ash in the corner of the room. Underneath one of the boarded windows lay his pack, the little girl must have carried it here by herself, he watched as she started to fill the barrel with the sticks. Michael was amazed at the ease in which the little girl started a fire, she had obviously done it many times before. In a matter of minutes she had fixed some paper for kindling and produced a box of matches from the pocket of her jacket. Before long the flames had risen and then settled to a far more manageable size. The smoke escaped through a small gap in the ceiling and it alerted him to the lack of structural integrity of their safe haven. Agnieska approached and offered him a drink of what looked like water, it was contained in a plastic bottle which had been recycled many times before. *"I have no food....daddy was taking us to find some"*, her eyes filled up at the mention of her father

"Where will they take your mother?" sniffling, she wiped her tears and answered

"To the big camp, where they take all the girls ......apart from the sick ones". For a short while he sat and comforted the little girl, occasionally asking questions to help him piece together a picture of what was going on. The woman whom he inhabited was sick, that was obvious by her appearance and Agnieska explained that it had been some sort of epidemic or plague. The people in this place were desperate and struggling to survive. Agnieska described a lawless place with no organised government or authorities. It was a sparsely populated area and other than the men and her parents, she did not talk of anyone else. King let out a big sigh and sat eagerly staring in his master's direction. *"O.k., food then?"* Agnieska's eyes widened with anticipation. Placing one of the pans from his pack on the makeshift stove, Michael delved deep into his pack and removed two tubs of the stew he had discovered earlier. The open flame cooked the stew rapidly and before long the three sat down to a long overdue meal. Agnieska scoffed the stew and it appeared she had not eaten for quite a while. Only a few mouthfuls passed his lips before he began to feel quite dizzy and tired. *"Hungry girl eh?"* He slipped his share over to her and she did not hesitate to scoff her second helpings. King had been given a fair share of the stew and he ate slowly with great care, being sure not to waste a single morsel. Periodically he would raise his

head at the slightest disturbance from outside before returning to his bowl. The little girl let out a weary yawn and Michael produced a blanket from his pack, it was woollen, an old fashioned red tartan and had clearly been used many times before. She moved over to King and pressed herself close to his warm coat. The blanket barely covered the two of them, but it was not long before she was fast asleep. He sat for a while and watched her sleep. What a life for a child he thought? His mind turned to thoughts of Joseph, everyone always commented on how alike they were *"It's like you just spat him out"* his father would say that almost every time they went to visit. He spent a while trying to remember. He was aware that he was becoming more and more detached from it. There had to be more clues as to what was happening to him, the sphere was the key to it all, it was the only constant in everywhere that he had been. Returning it to its original complete state seemed like the only plausible course of action. *"There was nothing else for it"* he thought. The next fragment had proven a mystery so far, there was no indication as to its location. He grew increasingly sleepy as he deliberated over what to do next. He made a conscious decision, that without knowledge of the fragment, as long as he was in this awful place he would make it his duty to protect the little girl who had fallen into his lap. The memory of his son only fuelled his determination to protect Agnieska from harm. In the morning he would make for the camp and try to re-unite her with her mother, and then he could concentrate on finding the missing fragment. His head slumped and he fell into a deep sleep. His dreams were erratic and merged memories of his real life with visions of his present circumstance. The sleep was disturbed and broken and he was woken still tired and sore by an unfamiliar sound he had not yet heard in this place, an Air Horn. It blasted three times, Agnieska and King had gone. He stood up peering through a small crack in the wood which covered the window. King barked and snarled and a man let out a shriek of pain as he sunk his teeth into his hand. *"Don't shoot it! A Dog that strong could be handy…..cage him".* It was the man from earlier and Michael watched as King was locked in a cage by three men who were glad to be rid of him. He never stopped howling and snarling till he was locked away. A gunshot rung out which was enough to calm his howling to a distressed whimper. The small gap limited what he could see, but he was sure that there was no sign of Agnieska. They must have her he thought, his mind started to race with thoughts of what she could be going through, at least she would be protected, the executioner had reacted furiously to the mistreatment of her mother. The convoy began to move out, it was still quite dark. Michael began to panic at the thought of losing his companions and left all his belongings and grabbed the sphere, throwing the bag over his shoulder like a satchel. He moved as quickly as he could out the building towards the convoy, wary of alerting them to his presence. The convoy was bigger this time, a few vehicles had joined, one of which was a pick up. It had a selection of random objects within it, an old armchair and some car tires, he surmised it was a collection of potentially useful items. With a large uncomfortable gulp of air, it was now or never, he crawled along the dirt path and moved towards the pickup. King spotted his master and he moved his finger to his lips to signal for his silence, the clever dog understood and kept a close eye on Michael without alerting the men. One of the men moved toward the pickup and Michael froze, he was too easy to spot if someone had gotten too close, until now the pickup had shielded him from view. King howled and drew the man's attention for a second and Michael took his chance. He sprung from ground and slipped into the pickup. Grabbing a tarpaulin and pulling it over his head, he held his breath for as long as possible. A few seconds passed and King stopped barking. The pickup spluttered into life and they began to move away. Michael began to think he had made a big mistake, he only had the sphere and no rifle. Hope was all he had, that he had made the right decision. The journey in the back of the pickup was uncomfortable and soon Michael's weary body ached all over. He reached into his bag and removed the sphere, it glowed only slightly, but seemed to be getting brighter gradually. The pickup stopped suddenly and he replaced the sphere carefully back in its bag. *"O.k....take them out and get them to the wash house"*

"Scud, you put the pickup in the compound and start emptying it, get Algie to help you". The blood began to rush to Michael's head, he had to get out quick without being seen. *"And you"* the executioner pointed towards the man who King had bitten before *"You can get a bit more familiar with your new friend"* he chuckled as he watched the man sheepishly move off towards the van containing King. As he approached, he signalled two others, who reluctantly came to offer their assistance. King was subdued, he did not snarl or bark and the men removed him from the cage, happy they had broken him. *"See what a little solitary confinement, does boss?"* The executioner turned to face them

"Watch him, he's a clever one". The pickup started and before Michael had a chance to react he was in the compound. The

83

rattle of a large metal shutter being pulled to the ground and locking into place signalled he was trapped. Inside the two men chatted between themselves and Michael struggled to hear what was being said over the pounding sound of his own pulse pumping inside his head. He slowed his breathing and tried to concentrate.

"Right….what's first?" One of the men made his way to the rear of the pickup, he reached out for the tarpaulin and Michael primed himself ready to fight his way out *"Scud! Scud! Come and help me with this psycho, it's going mental again!"* The men remaining in the yard had begun to unload the vans and King had seen Agnieska, and tried to escape, drawing the attention of the two men emptying the pickup. Yet again King had had been his saviour, although this time it seemed more like blind luck. A short while passed and Michael plucked up the courage to make his move, he jumped from the pickup and crept to a nearby window, it was thick with dust and grime, his eyes strained as he tried to make out his surroundings. The camp was surrounded by armed guards and barb wire seemed to be attached everywhere possible, no-one was getting in or out easily. The sphere began to buzz with the same familiar ferocity, indicating that the next fragment had to be close by. Looking out the window, Michael watched as a line of a dozen or so girls emerged from one of the buildings, they were no more than around twelve years old. Agnieska was one of them, her hair was wet and like all the girls she had an all in one set of overalls on, they were all exactly the same, a dark blue colour. Michael drew comparisons in his mind with images he had seen on television of the concentration camps during the Second World War. An old bespectacled man accompanied them and directed his speech towards the executioner *"These are all ready for the breeding program sir, I will put them with the others"* Michael's worst fear had been realised, the girls were being herded like cattle. It had looked to him that this place, which was devoid of any reasonable moral or ethical structure had descended into madness. Agnieska had been captured and was now being introduced to some sort of repopulation programme against her will. The welfare of these girls was not high on the agenda of the Executioner and his followers, it would seem that the protection he had displayed with Agnieska's mother was not out of compassion but purely to ensure that their precious incubator was not damaged. A light flickered from a pile of junk in the corner of the compound and it caught Michael's eye, removing some random items from the pile, his eyes widened with amazement. Discarded like a useless piece of nothing, the next fragment lay unguarded. *W*as there no pattern to all this? It was far too easy, especially when the last two fragments had

proven so difficult to obtain. Removing the sphere from the bag, it buzzed and glowed as bright as ever, now within touching distance of the third fragment. All he had to do was to join the pieces and he would leave this awful place behind him. He placed the sphere back into the bag and was careful not to accidently join it with the new fragment. He had two friends to help, he could not abandon them. There was nothing he would like more than to re-assemble the sphere as quickly as possible so he could discover the purpose of this whole adventure and hope he would be returned to his own body. To leave the little girl to this fate was unthinkable. It was dark outside and the yard was lit by large stationary floodlights like a sports arena. Agnieska was rounded up with the others and put into a building with an armed guard at the entrance. Michael searched the workshop for anything that could be of use to him, he found an old rusty kitchen knife amongst a collection of tools on one of the benches, it was weathered but still reasonably sharp, and he slipped it into his pocket. Moving slowly he kept low and crept to the passenger side door. He opened the door of the pickup, and reached inside the glove box. He felt cold steel, this time he did not retract as he had in London and removed the Gun. He checked the barrel and it was fully loaded with six golden coloured bullets. He slipped it into another one of his pockets. The workshop exit led straight out into the openness of the yard. Michael studied the movement of the guards for a few minutes, the executioner and the other men had left the yard empty and the guards were now keeping watch on the various buildings. He would have liked more time plan what to do next, but the fear of being discovered propelled him to act with limited knowledge of what he was about to face. Reasonably confident he had learned the sequence of movements that they were making, he made his move. He slipped across the yard, avoiding the floodlights and made his way towards the guard on the door of the building from where the girls had emerged earlier. He was on autopilot, the fear of being caught spurred him into reacting without thinking. The guard turned his back and Michael pounced from the darkness. Silently the guard dropped to the ground after a few muffled gurgles. The knife created a deep gaping slit across his throat and Michael's arm ached from the effort required to inflict the deadly wound. The door creaked a little as Michael opened it, it was a dormitory with beds lining each of the walls, and the girls were huddled in a corner of the room, protected by the older ones at the front of the bunch. From the looks on their faces, when the dormitory door opened it was time to be worried. *"Agnieska!"* the little girl emerged from the back of the huddle and flung herself at him, closely followed by her mother. *"Thank you…..Agnieska has told me how you have cared for her"*,

       "No time….we must leave now" Michael was sure to stress the urgency of the situation *"leave everything"*. Raising his finger to his mouth, Michael signalled to the woman to stay quiet and they proceeded to creep out the building and made their way towards the main gate. A solitary guard stood smoking a cigarette and his cold breath mixed with the smoke bellowed up into the darkness. Michael approached him from behind and dispatched him silently, he was better prepared having done it once already and the knife seemed to slice far easier. The group sneaked out one by one and gathered in the long grass a few yards from the compound. After the last woman had escaped, Michael made his way out the main gate and joined them. *"Make for the woods"* Agnieska's mother had assumed the command and directed the rest of the group who began to disperse into the darkness *"Thank you stranger….I will never be able to repay you for what you have done"*. Agnieska gripped Michael's leg with all her strength and wept *"Go now"*. He directed her to join the others and she slipped away into the darkness, he felt relieved, but sad that he would not see his little friend again. Agnieska's mother embraced him and smiled before leaving him standing alone once more. Reaching for his bag Michael prepared to reunite the third fragment with the sphere. He stopped suddenly and spoke aloud "King!" In all the commotion he had forgotten about his loyal friend. Sneaking back in the main gate, he made his way toward the large steel cage that King was being held in, he could not see him. Without warning the air horn from before sounded and Michael backed off to the centre of the yard, the men appeared form everywhere and he was surrounded with no hope of an easy escape. *"There's another one here boss!"* The men had discovered the two bodies *"all the females have gone!"* The executioner turned to face him and forced him to his knees *"you have one chance"*. The executioner removed his hat and revealed the patchy remnants of his balding head *"Where are they?"* Michael remained silent *"Where are they?"* He slapped Michael hard across the face and he fell towards the ground, he reached into his pocket and pulled out the gun he got from the glove box. He was exhausted, the exertions of the escape attempt had taken it out the fragile body he inhabited and he dropped the gun to the dirt. The executioner slapped him again and picked up the gun *"Last time bitch! Where are they?"* Michael looked up at him

"Fuck you" the man raised the gun to his forehead and cocked it, Michael closed his eyes awaiting the noise of the trigger clicking. A different noise came instead, a noise that had at one time seemed so menacing to him, the loud and fearsome bark of King rang out through the compound. King leaped over a six foot high fence that surrounded his containment area and headed straight towards the executioner. He moved fast as lightning and the gun was turned on him, the executioners hand shook with fear and fired the first bullet, it flew passed king and penetrated the fuel tank of one of the motorbikes which had been parked up for the night. King pounced through the air and pinned the executioner to the ground. The motorbike exploded with a deafening bang and the flames quickly spread to the adjacent buildings. Battered and bleeding Michael reached for his bag and removed the sphere, he had to get out now. King had saved him yet again, this time giving him enough time to reunite the third fragment. The fragment clicked into place and soon he was engulfed in light. A gunshot echoed all around him as he began to be taken by the sphere's power, it was followed by a pained yelp from King. Michael screamed out in anguish as he realised what had happened. Had he not gone back to save King, then his friend would not have tried to save him and therefore would have been no need for the men to kill him. King had made the ultimate sacrifice for his master and for sure, he would not be waking up. As he began to lose consciousness his mind began to wonder about the next place he would wake up. It was time to move on. "The King is dead, long live the king".

Chapter 7

Time to wake up daddy.

Michael's eyes ached with the exposure to the bright light emanating from the strange sphere. He was groggy and he drifted in and out of consciousness, gradually regaining focus after his latest transportation. His mind relived the events of the past few days, and he questioned just how accurate a description 'a couple of days' could have been. The rollercoaster of events he had been involved in had completely thrown off his concept of time. What felt like a blink of an eye could have been a few weeks or even longer? He was not yet awake and the possibility that it could all have been a dream came to the forefront of his mind again. Hoping more than anything that it was just as explainable as a really vivid dream and he would wake up no worse off for the experience. Kaitlin and Joseph filled his thoughts and the realisation that maybe the dream was a far better alternative than returning to the dark and lonely existence that awaited him. Michael felt increasingly more disconnected from them, the recent events had only widened the gap, and he became weary and confused when trying to remember them. He missed them so much and although it hurt him deeply to think about them he still tried to remember each little aspect of their appearance and personality. *"Never forget them"*. He repeated the words over and over inside his head. After considerably longer than the previous transports had been, the present circumstance became a far more pressing matter. He still had not resurfaced and was still in a state of limbo. Unable to move his body, he still had yet to regain his sense of sight and hearing, making identification of his surroundings an impossible task. Perhaps this was it. He was dead and suspended in purgatory or some other place between life and death. The possibilities raced through his head along with a rush of panic, an eternity in this state would be unbearable. The light got brighter and brighter and the buzzing increased in volume until it bordered on painful. Then darkness. Still, quiet and eerie nothingness had replaced the painful light and sound. Michael could feel his body but was unable to move it, although his hearing had returned. Traffic through an open window was accompanied with birds singing, his hearing was highly attuned to his surroundings but he lay still motionless and in complete darkness. Michael tried to lift his eyelids but like the rest of his body he could not move them. The feeling of being completely powerless was too much for him to handle and he attempted to let out a scream through utter frustration. He could not scream, any sort of human ability or sense apart from his hearing was completely lost and out with his control. He lay still and lifeless and assessed the possibilities of his latest incarnation *"I'm blind"* he said to himself *"I'm blind...I'm paralysed".* The worst outcome, that he had rematerialized as some sort of vegetable was now a distinct and plausible possibility. Maybe there was no real pattern of events or continuity. The sphere could be a random device with no controlled purpose which had transported him into an impossible to escape situation. Finding the next fragment with no control over his body would prove difficult. The sphere, now complete with the first three parts could be anywhere, it could be within touching distance of his current position, but might as well have been at the other side of the world. Michael's heart sank as he realised that this could be the end of everything, he could only hope that through some power, separate from his influence would come to his rescue. He lay for a while and tried to test the severity of his condition, his body felt like it was set hard in a concrete block. A great weight, like the G-Force from a jet fighter held his body and prevented even the slightest movement. *"I can hear, at least that's something to go on"* he thought. Michael turned his focus to the only stimulation he was able to control, he listened hard to all the little noises that rang out around him in the hope of deciphering some details of his current environment. He could be at home for all he knew and until some proper evidence suggested that he was stuck inside the body of a poor unfortunate, he was not oblivious to the chance that he had been returned. Traffic outside the window was generally light with the occasional siren ringing out. There were lots of chirpy birds, interrupted by the sharp, raspy bark of a dog. King came to the forefront of Michael's thoughts. Maybe he should have stayed behind and suffered the same fate as his loyal companion had. For to be stuck in his current state was worse than death itself. An elongated creaking noise awoke him from his deep thought. It was the sound of a hinge which was in dire need of some oil. Someone had entered his domain. Michael painted the picture in his mind, a small room with a window and a door. *"Shut that window, that's some draft coming in".* Michael listened as the window clicked shut and the background noise from outside became muffled, he focused on the voices with great interest. *"Thank you nurse"* It had been a male voice so far and he determined that he was in some sort of medical facility as there seemed to be a nurse in attendance. Michael reassessed his environment once more

"Room, door, window, nurse......town or city maybe?" The male voice spoke again *"So, fill me in on Mr?"*

"Doe, Doctor"

"Another J.D eh?"

"Yes doctor, this one was found washed up on the beach, large gash on the back of his head, non-responsive to all stimuli". Both the doctor and the nurse were speaking English as far as Michael could tell, but he did not take it for granted as languages had recently been a little unpredictable. They both spoke with an accent, American or Canadian and this was enough to convince him that they had not been Japanese or Eastern European. Michael's mind raced into overdrive as he began to put the small snippets of information together into a possible scenario. Could he be back? The plane had come down over the ocean, he was found washed up on a beach and he was on the right side of the world if the accents were anything to go on. It all made sense to him now, he was home, he had to be. Michael chuckled to himself *"Home"* thousands of miles away, but to him it was home. The tournament in Japan along with the bank job and the awful life of Agnieska were all too fantastical to be anything more than the overactive mind of his recovering body. He must have been in a deep unconscious state and his body now had begun to regain its grip on reality. *"How long has he been here?"*

"This is the third week doctor" Michael roughly counted up the days in his head, three weeks seemed like a plausible amount of time, the signs were all pointing to what he hoped was his release from the spiral of chaos he had been involved in. *"O.K give him 48 hours more stimulation therapy, all senses. If we don't get a response then we'll call it, can't have him taking up a bed any longer"*

"Yes doctor" The door creaked again with the same ear popping screech and the room grew silent. Michael contemplated the doctor's instructions. Two days till they switched his life support off, no-one has come to claim him *"John Doe"* he said to himself. The doctor could make the decision to clear him out as he had lay for three weeks and still no-one had been to claim him. Where was his mother? Or even his older brother? Surely they had heard the news of the plane crash by now. Michael was angry with the non- attendance of any, friends or family and even more his company, they must have known he was missing by now. He lay lifeless, unable to influence the current

90

run of events, he could only hope that by some miracle he could wake up in time and prevent his impending fate. The creaky hinge drilled through his eardrum and into his skull once more as the nurse returned to the room. *"Righto Miguel...let's get on with this"* Michael listened hard *"Miguel"* she said, *"We will start with the feet today"* the nurse lifted the blankets which covered Michael and began to squeeze and massage his feet. Michael could feel her hands touching him but was unable to respond. *"Oh come on Miguel"* the nurse seemed frustrated as Michael gave no reaction. His heart sank as he she addressed him again, it may have been a close translation of his name but she had called him Miguel. *"Nothing from the feet, let's try the hands then"* the nurse carried out similar methods on Michael's hands and he tried with all his might to give her the reaction that they both desperately wanted. He even attempted to flutter his eyelids but he was unable to move a single part of his entire body. Michael was now exhausted and struggled to understand how he could have become so out of energy, when he had not moved a single muscle, he had only thought above moving. *"Nurse Canning"* the door creaked again as another voice called to the nurse who was attending Michael *"You're needed in room fourteen.........I'll take over here"*

"O.K I'm just finishing off the hands" the door shut and the new voice was a far higher pitch than before, younger he thought, still North American. He pictured a student nurse. *"O.K hands then"* the nurse begun to work on Michael's hand much in the same fashion as before. Her hands were slightly softer to the touch and a little colder. Michael was almost completely out of energy trying to react to the nurse's stimulation but he continued, desperate to give a sign of any sort to prevent the doctor's instructions being carried out. *"Oh Daniel! You've not got long left now, you need to snap out of it"* the door creaked for what felt like the hundredth time, the noise was really beginning to annoy him *"How's Miguel? Anything?"*

"Daniel... is the same quiet and uninterested way he always is. Miguel? Honestly your pet names get worse by the day" Michael was reinvigorated. They did not know his real name, the nurses had called him whatever they had thought suited him. There was still a good chance that he was himself again. The latest revelation had made his attempts at movement all the more determined and he could feel something swelling up inside of him *"If Daniel does not react soon, he'll end up....."* The nurse was interrupted by the culmination of Michael's attempts at reaction. Her sentence was cut short by the almightiest of farts. Michael could have screamed if he could, he had

91

managed to get his body to do something. Surely they would know he was still in there. *"Jesus…..bloody hell Daniel, Miguel, whatever your name is. You're not dead yet but that certainly smells like you are"*

"Ha, your turn this time". The door creaked shut and the nurse proceeded to check Michael for any new arrivals *"Good boy, Danny…..no solids".* The nurse breathed a sigh of relief and started to speak to him in a far softer and sympathetic tone *"Well as I was saying Danny, you need to wake up, even a dead body let's one go every now and then"* Michael's disappointment deflated him, what did he have left to do? The nurse leaned over to the bedside table and switched on the radio *"Let's try some auditory stimulation instead, you like this stuff Danny?"* The nurse continued to tune the radio until she settled on what Michael could only have described as cheesy classic rock. *"My son, he loves all this stuff. Me, I love the greats, Sinatra or Elvis"* Michael tried to listen and pay as much attention as he could, although the conversation was anything but interesting he thought. He appreciated that the nurse was just doing her job and that the conversation content was pretty irrelevant, the continuous stimulation was the most important issue. Five or so minutes passed of the nurse chatting about various mundane topics and Michael had recuperated enough to try again. He concentrated hard and pushed. The feeling was like being wrapped up tight like an Egyptian mummy or being inside a coffin. The uselessness was beginning to really frustrate him and he was already beginning to run low on energy again. With one last big push Michael strained to get some sort of reaction from his lifeless shell he inhabited. He managed it again. The loudest and most disappointing fart he had ever done in his life, nothing to signify that he was still inside, desperate to break out. He could have broken down in tears if he had any control over anything but his bowel movements. *"In the name of god…..that's not right Danny"* The nurse stood up and opened the window. Michael listened to the mechanical click of the latch followed by the traffic and the same ambient background noise he had heard upon his initial awakening. *"O.K Danny if you're quite finished, we will see if a bath will spark you into life"* The nurse proceeded to remove his hospital gown from under the bed sheets. She was highly professional and Michael had noticed how she still maintained treating her patient with due care for his modesty, even though as far as anyone on the outside world knew, Danny, Miguel or whatever his name was had been completely unresponsive to what was happening to him. The bed bath was a weird sensation, Michael thought. As the warm cloth touched his skin, he could feel it

wiping the outer layer of his shell, it did not feel at all normal. It was a muted, an almost half sensation. The highly irritating door creaked once again and Michael counted to ten in his head. The noise was really beginning to piss him off. If only he had a can of oil or some grease. Michael chuckled inside as he rethought his desire for some oil or grease. Would not be much use without a functioning body to apply it with. *"Anything Jill?"* *"Other than the flatulence, Miguel is much the same"*

"What a shame too, look at that body" Michael had a weird sensation come over him, he felt embarrassed even though his state should have made any such reference to his body be completely insignificant, he was a vegetable. The nurses stood peering at his body and Michael listened intently for any clues to whether it was actually the lifeless carcass of Michael Cameron. *"I wonder how he ended up on the beach."*

"Maybe he was swimming and caught his head on the rocks"

"Doc said it was a clean wound, rocks would have left more of a mess"

"Sure is a waste though, I wonder if he is married?"

"The Sheriff's office and the missing persons have had his stats for weeks now, if someone is missing him, they would have come forward by now" Michael listened hard, drawn in by the juicy information. Had they informed anyone back home? The local authorities would have no record of a man from out of town. *"Oh well, let's finish up"* the two nurses promptly tidied Michaels room and he listened as the window clicked shut. *"Should we feed him?"*

"I got him earlier, we do need a sterile tube for the morning though" The young nurse fumbled around in the cabinet next to Michael's bed and pulled out a thin rubber tube *"I'll just leave it here on the side, is it you who's in, in the morning?"*

"Nope, got the day off....I think it's Cathy". The young nurse turned to walk away from Michael's bedside and stopped quickly and turned back, *"On second thoughts, I'll just change his water"* She removed the saline bag from the drip stand and efficiently clicked one in its place, like she had done it a thousand times before, with her eyes shut. *"You've really taken to this one eh?"* The young nurse neglected to respond to her colleague and carried on preparing to leave Michael

for the night. *"Right that's us let go....Goodnight Danny boy, sleep tight, same time tomorrow?"*

"You listen to me Miguel, no parties in here tonight, could be your big day tomorrow" the nurses chuckled as they left the room and the door creaked for the last time that evening. The room was still and quiet and the nurses had left the light on for him. In his state the need for a light was pointless unless he woke during the night and he would not be met by more darkness. Michael was a little anxious as he lay there still and lifeless, the occasional noise startled him. The noise of a passing siren on route to pick up the latest unlucky passenger twinned with the hurried scuffling of staff in the adjoining rooms and corridors. He was exhausted and found it hard to accept his lack of energy. The body he inhabited had not been engaged in physical exercise for the past few weeks. It was not long until he slipped off to sleep. *"Daddy! Daddy!"*

"I'm outside Joseph" The smell of burnt meat filled Michaels nostrils *"Oh shite! I mean shoot!"* Michael rushed across the patio towards a large gas barbeque. The patio was unmistakable, it was solid Indian stone slabs and Michael was mesmerised by the slabs which had been soaked by the water from the garden hose. It was why he had bought them in the first place, even when it rained the patio would sparkle with a rainbow of swirls from the exotic rock. Michael continued to run towards the barbeque and it never got any closer, he grew increasingly breathless and with every step he took trying to save the burning meat the distance seemed to grow farther and farther away. *"Daddy! Daddy!"*

"I'm out in the garden Joseph!" Michael became engulfed in darkness momentarily and quickly from the darkness a small green spot rushed towards him instantly placing him at the side-lines of a football pitch *"Go on Joseph! That's it son!"* A small figure was blurred in the distance, the colours that the figure wore, were so familiar to Michael but his eyes were kept just slightly out of focus, preventing him from deciphering it. Every time he tried to catch a glimpse of the face of the child he begun to lose focus of the figure in the distance *"That's it wee man. Ref, that's never a penalty...Boooooooooooo, Boooooooooooo"*

"Michael Cameron, behave yourself" The woman's voice cut through Michael's senses like a freight train, it was so powerful and strong in his mind. Kaitlin's voice was beautiful and he would have

94

recognised her anywhere. *"Remember he is only five you know!"* Michael turned to look at her, the anticipation was overwhelming. Dream or not, the opportunity to look upon her was too big a chance to pass up. Breathless, he turned his head towards hers, he felt an unnatural force making even the slightest movement intensely difficult. His head turned and just as it had before he became engulfed in darkness only to be reawaken by a loud bang. Michael's eyes focused on a black night sky filled with a multi-coloured display of fireworks. His arms embraced a shorter person in front of him who was watching the fireworks with him. He stood aside a galvanised steel fence and the woman in front of him pressed her back close into him, shielding from the early winter temperature. *"I love you Michael Cameron"* Michael dipped his head and sniffed her hair, the aroma was so strong and familiar to him and he inhaled another long and satisfying breath. The chance to gaze upon her face overcame him and he nudged her shoulder and beckoned her to turn and face him. As she started to turn the motion slowed and it seemed to take an eternity as she crept gradually into vision. Desire was replaced by fear as the face he hoped to see did not appear, a horrific featureless blank canvas replaced her face and Michael screamed out with terror as once more he was surrounded by darkness. The darkness stayed for a while this time and he felt alone and lost in a cold and lifeless place *"Where are you?"* a ghostly voice from the blackness sent shivers through Michael's body and woke him from the nightmare. The body which he inhabited erupted with a massive involuntary spasm which threw him from the hospital bed, sending him face first into the linoleum below. His face smashed into the floor and knocked him out cold, returning him to back his previous unconscious condition. *"Joseph! Where is Joseph?"* People shot passed Michael blurred and disjointed in every direction, their presence seemed unimportant and it looked like he was in the middle of a large shopping centre. *"He was just here"*

"Well where is he now?" Kaitlin's voice sounded abrasive *"Honest to god, you can't be trusted to watch him for five minutes".* The surrounding blurred crowd seemed to grow bigger and bigger as Michael frantically scanned through them to try and catch a glimpse of his son. *"Hi Mummy"*

"Joseph Cameron, where have you been?"

"I just got some ice cream"

95

"Come on, we're going" Michael watched as Kaitlin and Joseph began to walk away, their faces still obscured from his sight, *"Hey wait up, I'm sorry"* Michael rushed to follow them, but just like it had before, with every step he took towards them, they got farther and farther from his reach *"Wait!"*. The darkness engulfed Michael until the flickering of uniform moving lights replaced the cold silence *"Pay attention Michael!"* the darkness had been replaced by the night time glow of street lamps and fluorescent road signs *"I am paying attention, you're a pain in the arse"* Kaitlin snapped back.

"O.K, have a go, I'm only concerned for our lives you know"

"You would think I had just passed my test the way you go on"

"Red Light…..Red Light!" The car screamed to a halt and Michael sighed with relief *"Daddy, what happened?"*

"Nothing son, go back to sleep" Kaitlin did not waste any time

"I swear to god, one of these days you are going to kill us"

"You know what I'm sick of this same crappy journey anyway, why don't you drive if you're so fucking perfect?"

"O.K next time you can just stay at home them"

"Fine"

"Yes Fine!"

"Beep………..beep……….beep" Michael's ear was drawn to the sound of a heart monitor then a voice spoke *"No idea doctor….. The orderly came in at 5:30 and found him like this on the floor, nose broken with blood everywhere"*

"And his status?"

"Other than his nose he seems the same"

"No response?"

"No doctor"

"Keep a close eye on him today, if there is no change, then we go ahead as planned, also check reception, find out if anyone came in here through the night"

"But doctor, surely he must have moved"

"Nurse……with no explanation available, what choice do we have, he is still in a vegetative state"

"Yes doctor". The door creaked again which confirmed to Michael that he had awoken from one nightmare and returned to one that was only slightly less surreal. *"God, that's a mind-fuck"* He thought to himself. Michael spent the rest of the morning thinking about the vivid dream, it was definitely freaky, but even the chance to be anywhere near them was welcome. It helped him to focus on any memories that still existed in his bruised and tired mind. He thought hard about the car journey and questioned why his subconscious mind had focused on such a turbulent and painful memory to torture him further. *"Right Danny, explain yourself?"* The older of the two nurses had returned, she sat next to Michael and begun to massage his hands again. *"Did you have a bad dream son? I was thinking about you last night, you only have today left, you need to let us know if you're in there?"* Michael strained with all his might and was soon overcome by a similar feeling *"Oh Jesus Christ Danny, do you ever let up".* The window clicked open and the room filled with the sounds of the outside world again. *"Ha, maybe you blew yourself out of bed"* Michael stopped short of a little chuckle at the nurses joke, he was exhausted with effort again and was beginning to lose hope that he was ever going to resurface. *"O.K that's us done….don't you worry Miguel, your fancy woman will be here shortly."* Michael was left alone for what felt like hours until the noise of the creaking door came as a relief. It was the young nurse *"Hey there, good looking. How's my favourite boy today? I hear you took a tumble last night?"* Michael was soothed by the soft sound of the young nurse's voice. She was nice and he never felt quite as lost and alone when she was around him. *"Listen now buddy",* the nurse had sat down and was softly caressing Michaels hand, *"I sense you in there, my grandmother had the same thing you know. I can't explain it, it's a sort of six sense"* Michael was intrigued, not only by the young nurse's supernatural claim but the obvious sadness in her voice. She cared, really cared. *"Try and think about last night, what were you thinking about? What made you move?"* Michael focused really hard and tried again to react using the young nurse's technique. Dreaming of Kaitlin and Little Joseph was

97

what send him crashing to the floor. The young nurse moved to the window and stood peering out into the street. The door creaked as it always did and the second nurse joined them *"Hey Lovebirds!"* The young nurse stood silent at the window *"You O.K?"*

"It's just such a waste you know?"

"There is nothing we can do"

"Oh...I know"

"I'll go get his lunch, try not to think about it too much" The young nurse came back to Michael's side and touched her palm on his forehead. She sighed and Michael felt the warmth of her blood through the skin on his brow. *"Where are you?"* The young nurse spoke the three words and Michael's mind immediately fired with energy, the voice in his dream had spoken the same three words to him and his body started to tingle all over. The same involuntary jolt which had sent him to the floor sent his limbs firing out in all directions. The young nurse sprang into action and pulled the cord which alerted her colleagues. Within seconds the doctor and the second nurse rushed into the room *"He moved doctor!"*

"You're sure now?"

"He almost fell out of the bed"

"O.K stand aside". Michael lay as the doctor examined him. He felt like he was thawing out, more and more his body lost its numbness, and soon he felt much stronger *"Can you hear me? Hello....can you hear me?"* The doctor continued to stimulate his senses and the two nurses watched on, both ready to explode with excitement, ready to see their boy come around. *"Can you wriggle your toes?"* Michael moved each of his big toes with ease compared to the effort he had put into his disappointing flatulence. The young nurse squealed with joy *"that's my boy!"*

"Quiet now"

"Sorry Doctor" The doctor tried to keep a professional head while the two nurses could not contain their joy. *"Now your fingers"* Michael clenched his fist on his right hand which made the nurses hug and giggle with happiness. The doctor moved to Michael's head and was joined with the young nurse at the opposite side of the bed. *"O.K slowly now....try and open your eyes"* Michael's eyes opened like two

98

envelopes which had been stuck down with thick and stringy glue that had long since dried out. The crunch of weeks of sleep separating was loud and quite painful. The nurse dimmed light knowing it would help him to adjust. The doctor was an Afro-American, bald with a well groomed moustache. He stared into Michael's eyes with great interest. The young nurse was as pretty as he had imagined her, with blue eyes and jet black hair. She smiled from ear to ear *"Hello there mister"* Michael's mouth was as dry as he had ever felt before and the young nurse gave him a drink from a small glass almost telepathically. *"How do you feel?"* The doctor asked. Michael swallowed down the water and croaked as he tried to reply, the nurse gave him another sip of water and awaited his response *"Will somebody please oil that fucking door"* the two nurses giggled, so happy to hear him speak and the doctor smiled a big grin of shiny white teeth. *"Welcome back…..don't try and move just yet"*. Michael lay still while the doctor gave him the once over, checking reflexes and reaction times. He felt great and tried to sit up. Letting out a sharp yelp of pain he quickly lay down again. *"No, no not yet…it will be a long recovery process"*

"Where am I?"

"You are in a hospital, you've been in a coma for just over three weeks" The young nurse continued *"Do you know your name?"* Michael stopped himself before he spoke, as far as he knew he was Michael Cameron. *"Don't worry, it'll come back to you soon enough"* Michael so hoped that he was himself, but he did not dare take the chance until he knew for sure *"Do you have a mirror?"* The young nurse reached into the cabinet and produced a small rectangle mirror, similar to the ones which a barber would use to show you the back of your head. *"O.K are you ready?"* Michael took a large intake of breath and nodded to the nurse to indicate he was ready. The nurse put the mirror into position and Michael peered at the face of a young man of no particular significance, other than it was definitely not him. He was early twenties, handsome, but his face looked strained and tired with large bags under his eyes. The disappointment was too much for Michael to bear and he began to sob uncontrollably turning his gaze from the mirror *"O.K that's quite enough for now"* the doctor ushered everyone out of the room and closed the creaky door behind them. *"Would you like or need anything?"* Michael thought for a second and replied

"Do I have any belongings?"

"The student nurse is fetching it now, there was no identification, and unfortunately we do not know how you came to be here"

"I was found on the beach?"

"Found by a local dog walker who alerted the authorities"

"And no-one has come to visit?"

"No-one in three weeks", the doctor seemed anxious and was being cautious not to further damage an already fragile brain, by causing a relapse with too much stimulation. *"I think I want to try a sit up doctor"* The doctor supported him as he tried to sit on the side of the bed *"Easy now, take your time"* the door creaked again and the pair shared a smile, remembering Michaels outburst over the unmaintained hinge. *"Hey that's quick progress"* The young nurse entered with a large white sack containing Michael's belongings. *"I'll leave you to your belongings, nothing sudden, and rest, recovery is a big effort for your body"* Michael appreciated the help *"Thank you Doctor?"*

"Pope, Lawrence Pope" The doctor opened the door and turned to speak to him just as the hinge did its usual squeak *"Oh and I will find some oil too"* he chuckled and headed down the corridor. The young nurse tilted her head and caught Michael's eye *"Nothing yet then…? Well I'm pretty sure it's not Miguel anyway"* the young nurse giggled

"Well I'm Nurse Cartwright……Jenni"

"Thank you" Michael smiled and she appreciated his sentiment.

"Let's see what's in here then" Nurse Jenni produced a tailored suit, *"Expensive taste I see, a wallet with no I.D, of course"*

"That would have been too easy" Michael sighed

"There are some shoes, size nine, a set of keys and hold on……there's something in the bottom here" Michael prayed it could be some clue as to his origins or his next move. *"It looks like a piece of glass"*

"Give it here" Michael abruptly demanded the piece and it flickered slightly as it touched his hand *"What is it?"*

"I don't know, but I know it is something that I need"

"Would you like me to go through your wallet with you?"

"No thank you, in fact, I'd like to be alone for a bit"

"Oh O.K, I'll be back in an hour, pull the cord if you need me" Jenni left the room and he began to empty the wallet, there were lots of receipts and about one hundred dollars in cash. The receipts were for various items. Food, cigarettes, alcohol. Lots of alcohol. Underneath all the receipts was a train ticket, which Michael studied with great interest. It had *"Booth 3"* hand written on it in red ink. He presumed the station could have been close by *"As good a place as any I suppose"* Standing up slowly he dressed himself and slipping on his shoes, There were no socks, they must have been lost somehow and seemed unimportant in the current circumstance. He replaced the wallet into his trouser pocket and the fragment into the inside pocket of his jacket to keep it safe. Michael silently left his room and sneaked down the corridor, following the signs for the exit. No-one had suspected him and he made it out into the street without any hassle. The outside world was moving at a far quicker pace and the adjustment made him stagger with dizziness as he attempted to process all the new information. After a few moments he refocused and made his way to the edge of the road and flagged a passing taxi. He jumped in the back and showed the train ticket to the cabbie. *"No problem man, I get you there pronto"* The Cabbie was a stereotypical Jamaican man. A head full of dreadlocks and a multi coloured tea cosy style hat. *"So what goes down?"*

"Not much"

"You relax man, we get you there in five minutes" Michael did not know why he had got up and left the hospital and taken his current path, he was on autopilot again, it just felt right. If he had learned anything from his journey so far, it was to follow his gut. He pulled out the set of keys and studied them, he was none the wiser to their origin, and they seemed like just a generic set of keys. *"Here we are, and here is your ticket"* The cabbie pulled into the side of the road and returned Michael's ticket, he reached out and took it from him, studying the additional writing on its back. *"Six Fifty"*

"Here you go, keep the change"

"Thanks Man, peace" Michael gave the cabbie ten dollars, being a bit more frugal with the cash he had, he did not have the unlimited funds of Alfie Charles this time. The station was ornate and magnificent. Michael wasted no time getting inside. The station was buzzing with life. Commuters made their way to and from work and home oblivious to their surroundings. Michael stood still and studied his ticket, it was a weekly pass and was for something called *"ZONE 7"*. He flipped it over to the red ink again "Booth 3" He scanned the interior for anything that might give him an idea and spotted a bank of telephones about twenty yards from his current position attached to the wall of the station. The booths were not numbered, but there were three of them and he approached the one on the far right. The decision which one to choose was made easier as the left hand side booth had an out of order sign placed over the receiver. Picking up the receiver in the third booth, it rattled. The mouthpiece had seen better days and its innards were damaged, the line was not dead or engaged, it was silent and of no use to anyone. Michael replace the receiver and it rattled as it settled into position. He began to back off and stopped dead in his tracks, his gut drew him back to the booth, he was missing something for sure he thought. He picked up the receiver and without hesitation shielded himself from view and started to unscrew the mouthpiece. Inside was a small key with an orange cylindrical, plastic handle. Upon it in black plastic coated paint was that same recurring number again *"324 again, this has to mean something"* he said aloud. Causing a passer-by to glance at him with concerned confusion, he was talking to himself again. He hung up the receiver and made his way to a large bank of plate steel lockers which he had passed on his way to the bank of telephone booths. It did not take him long to find the locker and the key clicked and popped open to reveal a cardboard box within. Michael grabbed the box and headed across the station floor to the men's room just by the entrance to the station and locked himself within a cubical. In the relative privacy of the cubical Michael cut through the tape that held box shut with one of the keys. Inside was the sphere and Michael grasped it with relief, he was getting out of here. The three previous fragments were fused in place and he felt for the fourth piece which was still safe in his jacket. The only other item within the box was a piece of plain white paper which Michael removed and turned over. It read "V.I.E.R.A" in a large capital font along the top. Michael tried to work it out "V.I.E.R.A" he said aloud". the sphere started to buzz and hum violently and soon the cubical

102

started to vibrate until the door almost broke from its hinges, someone had entered the men's room and noticed the unusual light and sound coming from his cubical. *"Hey, you in there? I'm getting security"* Michael knew this time had lapsed and reached for the fourth fragment and slotted it into place, the cubical was engulfed in the brilliant brightness once more and soon he was drifting slowly into oblivion again. This time his thoughts were focused on working out the meaning of the recurring number and the newer, but just as unexplained acronym. V.I.E.R.A.

Chapter 8

Sun, Sand and Saddam

The bright light and buzzing had become par for the course, like a cow stretching for the luscious grass on the other side of an electrified fence, the pain was now acceptably bearable. He had become sensitised to it. Michael's disorientation lasted only minutes and he was in a new place. The bright midday sun was hampering his eyes in their attempt to return to a normal focus, in addition the temperature was sweltering and he began to sweat almost instantly. In his immediate vicinity stood around fifty men, they were all Middle Eastern in origin and were dressed completely in black. They were soldiers and they stood absolutely still and to attention, awaiting their next instructions from their commanding officer. *"Shit"* Michael checked his body, he was wearing similarly regimental apparel, his were far grander than the others and he realised that the soldiers stood awaiting his instruction. The sweat lashed down his neck and back. A combination of the sweltering sun and the realisation that yet again he was trapped like a rabbit in the headlights. An uncomfortable few moments passed with Michael standing with no clue as what to do next. One of the attending soldiers moved his head slightly and glanced in Michael's direction, he was trying to ascertain what the holdup was. Immediately one of two officers who had been standing just behind Michael's position stepped forward and began to hurl abuse in the face of the soldier. Michael watched as the little man's face grew scarlet as he bawled at the unfortunate subordinate, little bits of spittle landed on his face and it seemed he was being scolded for raising his head and breaking formation. Possibly just for looking in Michael's direction without prior permission. The language was Arabic in origin. He was in Libya or Iran, somewhere in that region of the world anyway and unfortunately he was not privy to his usual supernatural translation. The officer fell back into line and dismissed the soldiers. They all returned to various duties around the camp which was makeshift. The desert was bleak and the small collection of tents was the only civilisation for miles around. Michael turned to face the little officer, who had been respectfully trying to gain his attention. He began to speak at length and Michael had no clue as to what he was trying to communicate. The officer finished with an exaggerated and serious salute and Michael instinctively mimicked him. Standing alone in the middle of the camp, it gave him time to try and find some sort of direction to take. There were several small tents and no buildings to be seen. In the centre of the camp was a larger and far sturdier looking tent which had two armed guards outside its entrance. Michael had determined that he had status of some sort and presumed that this may have been his quarters. Trying to make himself seem purposeful he made for the two guards. As he reached them they both stood poker straight and saluted him instantly, again not making eye contact. Pushing the canvas veil to one side, Michael entered the tent. There was a camp bed which had been lavishly adorned with extra blankets and cushions, a desk covered in papers with an in descript language upon them. There was also a large wooden chest with a padlock on its front and a small table which had a selection of fruits and vegetables along with some dried meat. Two ceramic jugs were perched on the edge of the table, one filled with a white substance which he had guessed was milk and the other with fresh, cold water. Michael snatched the jug and gulped the water, quenching his thirst. The sun and his predicament had made his throat very dry. There were no reflective surfaces to be found and he spent a few minutes inspecting his body more thoroughly, after a little while the only definitive he could be sure of was his gender and ethnicity. He was a Middle Eastern male. His hands were dry and scuffed which made it difficult to accurately gauge the age of his the newest shell. He was Arabic, male and a soldier of significant rank, for now that was all he had to go on. The noise of the outside wind disturbed him as the canvas veil drew back and he was joined by the irate officer from before. He stood in the same attentive fashion, saluted and spoke again. Michael's thoughts turned to the sphere, he really needed to find it and hope it performed the same wizardry as it had in Japan. The officer handed him an envelope which was sealed and stamped with wax to prevent any unauthorised eyes from perusing its contents. The little officer stood upright and awaited Michael's instruction. He was an aide or right hand man and Michael sniggered as he realised he had his very own little gopher. The Envelope was useless in its current state but Michael was unwilling to let on that he was temporarily illiterate, just yet. He looked over at the opening of the tent and beckoned the little man to leave with a nod of his head. Following a quick salute and a few in descript but obviously military words. The short deputy left Michael alone. He looked at the envelope and let out a tired sigh. Shuffling unenthusiastically, he moved over to the large wooden chest and sat upon it. His mind wandered and he started to draw comparisons with the little man and his real life back home; *"Yes Mr Cameron"*. He was being revered in some way back home too, not to the same extent but it made him feel uncomfortable to compare his position to a military one. The thoughts of home had only served to bring emotions of what felt like a far gone and distant past. He shut his eyes and began to feel dizzy. Flashes of the car crash which had taken his world from him, jolted in and out of his conscious mind. He could hear the voices of Kaitlin and Joseph, although they sounded muted and out of reach. Images of the cold and empty rooms which he had left behind along with the clinically hygienic kitchen sent his heart racing. Another flash and he was on the flight, reliving the turbulent demise of the jumbo jet. He snapped out of it and back to consciousness just as the plane split into two and he was hurtling through the darkness. The beads of sweat flushed down his forehead and he gasped for air. The atmosphere was heavy going. It was hot and dry and the air was filled with little particles of microscopic sand which caught the back of his throat. The large carafe of water had come to his aid once more and soon he was much calmer and was able to focus on what he had come to accept as his current reality. The envelope was stuck shut and the blade on his utility belt came in handy. Michael chuckled to himself as he used the serrated edge of a military grade army knife as a letter opener. It only highlighted how much a three piece suit wearing office executive was such a fish out of water in a desert warzone. The letter had bold red capitals at the top and was followed by smaller black lettering. It was Arabian style text and Michael spent a short while assessing it, having no chance of deciphering its meaning. On the other side of the paper was a map, it was complete with directions to what looked like a concealed bunker at the final location. It was right in the middle of the barren desert. Michael stared long and hard at the small letters underneath the bunker's location. His eyes strained as he almost burned a hole in the paper, willing its meaning to jump out at him. Without warning the chest below him hummed and buzzed uncontrollably. It began to rattle and he felt it shift about violently beneath him. An overpowering urge to shut his eyes overcame him and it was followed by a blinding light. The pain was substantial, but he was beginning to cope with it better the more he was exposed to it. The light shone bright and the noise stopped allowing Michael to open his eyes. The words on the paper before him started to blur and reform. Beneath the maps destination the words read *"Official's Bunker"*. Turning over to the other side, all the lettering was now clear and legible. The red lettering at the top read *"TOP SECRET"*, Michael read the document in great detail, it was his mission. The document explained that he was to verify the bunkers location and then transmit the co-ordinates of

the bunker. Inside the envelope was a small black mobile phone.
Michael perused the phones cover, it was now clear that he was within
a few years of what he perceived to be 2012. It was not the most
modern equipment, but definitely within four or five years at most. It
had one number saved in it and Michael quickly turned it off to
conserve the battery and place it back in the envelope. At the bottom
of the letter it read *"FOR THE ATTENTION OF RAHEEM AL ZUHAIRI.
BURN AFTER READING"*. Michael studied the map again, realising its
importance to him, without it he would have no chance of finding his
way. He carefully folded it and with the mobile phone, he slipped
them both into his inside pocket. A rustling from the canvas veil
startled him and he approached *"Who's there?"* Deputy Gopher
appeared and greeted Michael with his trademark salute *"What are
you doing there?"*

"Nothing Sir.......do you require anything more Sir?"

"Not just now....have the men ready to leave in an hour"

"Yes Sir!" The gopher moved away and began to bark orders
at all the men who hurriedly prepared for the imminent departure.
Michael approached the chest and unlocked it with a small key which
was attached to his utility belt. He was surprised to find very little
within, just the sphere with the previous four segments protruding
from it, otherwise the chest was completely empty, and there wasn't
even a grain of sand. Michael stared at the sphere, wondering what it
had in store for him. His mind was filled with unanswered questions,
V.I.E.R.A, 324. He questioned the reality of it all and wondered
whether the sphere was making this whole adventure happen. Or was
he just trapped in a vivid and unescapable nightmare. He felt pain and
the sunlight on his face re-enforced the realism of his surroundings.
The sphere seemed to be the only constant which had some part to
play in every location he had been to so far. Spending a moment
reminiscing, he thought of where he had been, thought of Bernie
fondly and of course, Noritomo, who had been his undoubted saviour
while he cut his teeth in Japan. He thought of the difference of his
desperation to try and escape from that damned hospital bed with the
infuriating creaking door against his option of being able to leave
Agnieska and King whenever he chose, but he remained to help them.
Surely if this was all some sort of fantasy, then he would have no
problem in leaving Agnieska to the men and her fate. After all what
would it matter if the entire adventure had all been a dream? Michael
thought hard and decided that ultimately the adventure that he was

on, be it real or not, was more appealing than returning home to reality, which was colder than the mountains in Japan and emptier than the chest he stood staring blankly into. He removed the sphere which hummed quietly like a puppy glad to see its master and he slipped it into a small hessian sack which he found on the floor by the desk. The sphere and Michael's destiny had become entangled and it was becoming more powerful with every encounter. Or was it him who was becoming more attuned to its power? This time he needed no contact with it and the transference of its knowledge had been less stressful. His confidence was growing and he had become more confident that he was able to cope with the emotional and physical stresses which he was being subjected to. Brushing himself down, he prepared his mind for the next episode of his adventure until he was quickly washed with a wave of uncertainty *"Three Two Four?"* Michael said it aloud, what the hell was three two four, it had appeared all over the place. Flight numbers, Deposit Box and that envelope *"V.I.E.R.A 324"* Michael spoke aloud again. Nothing he could think of had any significance to that number. He was interrupted by Deputy Gopher again. An hour had passed in the blink of an eye, and whether he liked it or not it was time to move out *"Caravan primed and ready to move out Sir!"* In his deep thought Michael had forgotten to take a note of the co-ordinates from the map. He remembered at least that they were to head in a north-westerly direction *"Continue Northwest"*

"Same heading.....Yes Sir!" Michael grabbed his bag and stepped outside the Tent. A Humvee in a desert Khaki colour awaited him. Two armed guards set astride the open door. Michael entered the vehicle and the door was closed behind him. Deputy Gopher was instructing men to empty and pack up the tent onto the back of an accompanying transport truck. Pressing the button on the door, the bullet proof and black tinted window lowered and the sound of the two guards stiffening was instant *"Hey"*

"Yes Sir!" the closest guard nervously approached as Michael beckoned him nearer to the open window *"Go get Deputy Gopher"* the guard looked puzzled and Michael indicated to whom he was referring *"Captain Shafiq Sir?"* Michael nodded and the guard fetched him to the window *"I need a compass Shafiq"*. Shafiq swiftly produced a small plastic case and held it out towards him *"Yes Sir, have mine Sir"* Michael popped open the case and within was an orienteering compass, transparent on a thin Perspex base *"Thank you"*

"My pleasure Sir" The window slowly raised until it was completely shut and Michael set out the Map and Compass in the warmth and privacy of his personal transport. Northwest was O.K for now but that could change and he would have to be prepared. The journey was long and periodically Michael stopped the caravan and informed the lead vehicle of the adjusted heading, even if he had wanted to sleep the terrain would have made it impossible. The morning was well underway when the caravan reached its destination, It was a small rocky outpost in the middle of nowhere, there were a few crumbling buildings and it was long since deserted. Opening the door of the Humvee, he stepped outside. In the distance the mountains seemed like a thousand miles away. *"Shafiq….make camp for the night"* The miniature army burst into life, Michael was amazed at how much energy they had after a long night travelling, but they were probably used to the terrain and would have slept easily had they been permitted. The location matched the destination on the map and he checked he had not made a mistake. The area was desolate and the location was empty and felt unchartered. Before long Michael's makeshift home was rebuilt and he was feasting on various dried meats and breads. He consumed a considerable amount of wine, which was so fruity and light that he had not noticed how much he was drinking and he fell asleep for an hour. This time his head was empty, the long journey and the wine had knocked him out completely. Michael awoke as Shafiq entered the tent and loudly saluted *"Delivery of utmost importance Sir"* it was another envelope like the one from before *"That will be all Shafiq"* Shafiq exited the tent and Michael made sure this time that he had left him in privacy. The letter was in the same style as before and this time it gave more specific directions to the bunker's location. The instructions stated that Michael was to disband the troops and return them to base. He was to carry on to the destination with his trusted second in command. Again the communication was to be burned and the co-ordinates to be transmitted upon arrival at the bunkers entrance. The letter also stated that his final instructions would be communicated upon receipt of the co-ordinates. Michael removed the original letter and burned it from the flame of a candle which was propped on his desk, the smoke bellowed upwards and Michael watched the black particles of ash dance in the smoke before him. *"Shafiq"* Michael's right hand man appeared quickly and Michael issued him with the orders and he carried them out without hesitation. Before long the troops were nothing but a dust trail in the distance and Michael stood with only his hessian bag and a bottle of water. Shafiq was far more heavily laden

with various supplies, but stood resolute, strong and ready. *"O.K Shafiq, it's you and me now"*

"Sir, Yes Sir!" Michael had become sick of the constant arse kissing from Shafiq, but just went along with it as he thought it would have been a far greater task to re-program him. Michael headed to the most Easterly derelict building and Shafiq followed like a little lap dog. He stood with his back against the crumbling wall and began to pace, counting as he went. *".......123.......124......125"*

"O.K Shafiq, that's 125 paces east"

"Yes Sir!" Michael swivelled on the spot and faced South *"..........148..........149.........150. That's 150 paces south"*

"Sir 125 East, 150 South Sir"

"Good". Swivelling on the spot again, this time Michael faced South-East. The desert had grown cold and the wind had become far stronger making the piercing particles of sand become almost unbearable. The map had taken them through a maze of dunes and craggy rocks, the exhaustion was clear to see on Shafiq's face, although he always maintained a sturdy and obedient posture. *"......47.......48........49, and that's the last 49 steps southeast"* Shafiq struggled to speak in the blizzard of sand

"Sir.......125 East.......150............South and 49.........South-East.....Sir!" There was nothing of any significance to see and both men took shelter behind a nearby rock to catch their breath. After a while the wind calmed and the hot desert sun beat down on them. Michael's eye was caught by a glistening in the sand. It shone like metal *"Shafiq"*

"Yes Sir!" Michael pointed to the shiny object and Shafiq headed to it and returned to the rock *"It appears to be a length of chain Sir!"*

"Well go on then Shafiq" Shafiq returned to the chain and started to pull it with all his strength, Michael realised that his new command was going to his head and he joined with Shafiq and helped him to pull. The Chain revealed a large rectangular piece of steel which when pulled back in turn revealed a staircase which dropped deep under the desert. Both men stood and stared at the opening *"Will I investigate Sir?"*

"Carry on Shafiq" Michael's ease at adopting his new character was becoming enjoyable, if he ever got back home he thought he would have no problem at trying his hand at a career on the stage or at least join an amateur dramatics society. Shafiq disappeared down the stairs and Michael used the opportunity to transmit the co-ordinates of the bunker. *"Four bars? ….that's good"* the signal strength was considerable despite their location. The phone buzzed silently and soon a reply was with him *"Received, destroy all communications"* the mobile phone made a loud clicking noise and the display changed to a large number ten which was closely followed by an nine and then an eight, it was counting down, Michael tossed it far into the desert and watched as it flashed with a small flame and a small puff of smoke quickly rose and then vanished. *"All clear sir"* Shafiq had returned, none the wiser of the events of the past few minutes. *"A light Shafiq?"* Shafiq produced a box of matches *"Gather our things"* Michael stood and burned the second letter until nothing but ash remained as Shafiq collected up their belongings and they descended into the depths leaving the bleak and desolate desert behind. They pulled the chain at the opposite end until the metal plate clunked into its original position. The wind outside picked up and soon the entrance was disguised from any inquisitive yet unlikely passers-by. The descent was eerie and eventually they reached a corridor which was lit by industrial sized bulbs every ten or so metres. Eventually they reached a large iron door, it creaked and the noise echoed back and forth up the corridor they had just traversed. Michael looked at Shafiq with a concerned gaze and was met with the same unaffected expression, the little man's resolve was impressive. They were met by two armed guards *"Sir!"* They both saluted and relieved Shafiq of his bags *"This way sir"* Another long corridor was lined with crates down each of its walls and it led to another large iron door. Two more guards were on duty *"General Al Zuhairi"*

"Sir" the two guards opened the door and replaced the first two *"This way General"* A third long corridor led them to a central hub, there were LCD screens and people at computers, as well as uniformed officers discussing various tactics and battle plans displayed on the screens around them. Michael was led to a small room *"These are your quarters……..they await you in the debriefing room Sir?"* The two guards left and Shafiq began to unpack their things *"Prepare my things Shafiq, I will return soon"*

"Sir yes Sir!" Michael headed back to the central hub and he peered into a distant room through the window, it was filled with

111

important looking officials. He approached and entered the room and was met by a stony silence. *"General Raheem Al Zuhairi.........you finally made it"* the room filled with laughter and Michael joined in with the surprisingly jovial bunch. *"Good to see you"*

"Likewise" The officials, who all seemed to be of high rank greeted Michael as if they knew him well. *"O.K down to business"* At the head of the table a large moustachioed man began the debriefing *"Gentleman, the snare is set, the Americans are closing on him and it is now just a matter of time"* The statement was met by some appreciative groans and some mild applause. *"Once they have him and the celebrations begin in the west, only then will we emerge from this meagre cave and retake our country by force"* A rapturous applause began and Michael joined in so as not to arouse any suspicion. *"For months we have left General Al Zuhairi in the dark, and he has completed his mission with great leadership"* *"Here, here",* *"Well done"* Michael nodded with acknowledgement and respect to his peers and grew nervous as he began to understand the magnitude of his situation. *"General, over the last few months, you have blindly followed orders and not questioned what must have seemed odd at the very least, no?"*

"Agreed"

"You have been key to our survival, and the steps you have taken have been pivotal for the future of this great nation" At that point the door of the conference room opened and a soldier approached *"News report on CNN Sir"*

"On screen" The large LCD screen burst into life and soon the entire room was transfixed on the news report. *"Ladies and Gentlemen, we got him!"*

"Those were the words of US administrator Paul Bremer which was met by loud cheers from Iraqis in the audience" Michael broke out in a sweat and his throat felt like he was trying to swallow a pineapple whole while the report continued *"Saddam Hussein was found in a tiny cellar in a farmhouse about 15km south of his hometown Tikrit"* The room's tone was a sombre one now and the large moustachioed man spoke again *"Gentleman, he is a casualty of war, a war which led by him would have surely failed, Allah protect him"* the other officials nodded in reluctance acceptance. *"A US military spokesman, Major-General Raymond Odierno said 'The*

operation involving various combined US units was launched within 24 hours of receiving a tip off from a member of Saddam Hussein's Clan" The large moustachioed man grinned widely *"Gentleman, we have General Al Zuhairi to thank for that"* Again a rapturous applause. *"O.K, Saddam's capture has come quicker than we had anticipated, we will meet again in one hour to discuss the next stage. Gentlemen a toast"*. The men all lifted their glasses from the table and Michael mimicked them *"A New Stronger Iraq"* They toasted and Michael returned to his quarters. Sitting alone for a short spell, he contemplated the magnitude of what he was involved in. *"General Al Zuhairi Sir!"* Shafiq had returned and his abrupt entrance unsettled him *"What?*

"This is for you sir, it was delivered outside your door in your absence"

"By whom?"

"No-one Sir, it lay by the door"

"Thank you Shafiq, leave me"

"Yes Sir!" A black briefcase had arrived, and on it a small envelope, the case had a numerical lock on it. He opened the envelope and it contained a piece of paper with one sentence written upon it *"COUNT THE STEPS"* Michael said aloud *"Shafiq"* Michaels deputy came scurrying into the room again *"Sir yes Sir"*

"The paces Shafiq, what were the paces?"

"125 East, 150 South, 49 South-East Sir"

"O.K you're dismissed" Michael face widened with amazement *"I should have known"* He picked up the case and turned the three numerical discs until they read 324 and the clasp popped open. Inside was another mobile phone and it buzzed as soon as he lifted it. *"Mission complete, your reward has been transferred to the requested account, you have five minutes to evacuate"* The case also contained a pistol with a silencer which he grabbed and hid in his pocket. He grabbed the hessian bag and made his way towards the iron door, the guards did not question him and he passed through freely. He approached the Final iron door which led to the surface *"Open the door"*

"We cannot General Sir"

"No-one can leave sir"

"Open the door, or I will have you both shot"

"Sir Yes Sir!" The door opened and Michael directed the soldiers to pull the chain, revealing the desert above. The sun was blinding and soon he was back on the surface in the harsh desert heat. There was a distant roar and Michael turned to the two armed guards *"Close it........now!"* Michael pointed the pistol in their direction and they closed the hatch. *"Now come with me ....quickly"* the three men ran to a neighbouring rock for cover. The distant roar had become far closer to them and Michael was unsure of the safety of their position *"Further"* Michael encouraged the soldiers to come with him as he moved further from the entrance to the bunker. The noises from above were now visually apparent, it was a jet fighter speeding past in the clear blue sky. The missiles whistled as they plummeted towards the bunker and they sunk deep in the sand before a massive explosion sent soil and rock accompanied with a couple of tons of sand in every direction. The rocks plummeted all around the three men and Michael watched as one of the guards was smashed in the face by the debris, killing him instantly, The other soldier got up and ran off in a blind panic, Michael sat still and breathless waiting on the dust to settle. A shot rang out in the distance and slowly a rumble grew louder and louder. Michael stood and watched as a convoy of Western forces moved in on the bunker. The fleeing guard had made it as far as the oncoming force that had eliminated him without question. *"Another casualty of war"* Michael thought. How many deaths was he responsible for now? *"There's one over here"* Michael was grabbed and manhandled by a group of American soldiers. By this time the Attacking force had started to round up the survivors from the bunker and Michael was being dragged to join the dishevelled and maimed. *"Soldier, bring that one to me son"* A plump American Soldier with a shiny bald head and stylish desert sunshades intercepted Michael's delivery. *"In the truck"* Michael got thrown in the back of one of the many vehicles which had descended on the bunker *"Easy with him, he's one of the good guys"* The bald American looked Michael straight in the eye *"Well done soldier, the war on television is over, and thanks to you so is the real one......we can all go home now"* The American officer looked uneasy *"I'm sorry son, it's all gone, the city was destroyed. I have to inform you that you have been granted US or British Citizenship as recompense for you loss"* Michael realised that Raheem's family had been killed, but having no real connection and given the recent events was unmoved by the news. *"This I believe is*

114

for you" the Officer handed him a package which contained Raheem's personal belongings. *"They managed to save this for you........I'll leave you to your thoughts"* Michael perused the items and almost as if he was expecting it, was not surprised to find it wrapped in a piece of expensive silk, the fifth fragment. He rubbed his neck which was sore from the manhandling and took a deep breath. The sphere hummed and buzzed as it always did and Michael removed it from its bag, the pieces slotted together and fused into place just as the previous fragments had before. He took one last deep breath and the transition to the unknown commenced with still so many unanswered questions. V.I.E.R.A, 324. The horrors of war he had just experienced fell into insignificance. He had to find answers. He had to get home, wherever that was.

Chapter 9

I can see the pub from here

No light, no buzzing, no pain, Michael's eyes open and he is awake. The transportation is nothing like anything he has experienced so far. The feeling of disorientation completely gone in a matter of seconds and he feels as though he could have awoken in his own comfy bed at home. The comforting thoughts of home sent his mind spiralling deep into his memories of Kaitlin, Joseph and the beautiful life that he once knew and loved. The memories were replaced by an unwelcome but familiar feeling. He had the same feeling when Kaitlin and Joseph were still alive. Empty and distant, as if something was missing, an unidentified void that had to be filled. *"What could it be?"* He thought. Maybe the journey that he was being subjected to would hold the answer he was looking for. With every new environment, upon every bizarre and unexplained awakening, his thoughts slipped farther from home and he was gradually becoming unattached from his real life. The worrying thing was that he was beginning to be glad of it. The detachment served as a relief from what had become a sad and lonely existence. Michael cleared his mind and focused on his immediate surroundings. He was in darkness and lay still for a few moments until the silence was broken by a loud click followed by the sound of air escaping, the hissing continued for a few minutes and Michael watched as the top of the container began to move slowly away. He was in a coffin-like pod which had popped open. Light had begun to creep through the gaps and soon his ears were filled by a woman's voice. Michael sat up in his pod and listened *"You are awake, please remain still"* the voice was coming from all around him, but there was no–one to be seen. A small floating orb exited from a hole on the adjacent wall and slowly hovered across the room towards him. There was a small screen on its front, around four inches. A woman's face appeared, it was made up of blue lights, all the features of a human face but pixelated and computer generated. *"Please remain still"* Michael was unnerved by what he had seen so far and did not dare move. The hovering orb emanated a bright blue laser and scanned his face, vertically and then horizontally. *"Retinal scan complete…..please touch my face"* Michael remained still, not really sure what was being asked of him. *"DNA verification required, please touch my face"* Michael reached out towards the small screen touching his fingertip on the end of the blue nose. The orb flickered and made some bleeping noises *"DNA verification complete. BOSMA employee no 324. Designation: Danny Bryant, no foreign bodies detected"* The little orb backed off a few feet and continued *"Security clearance class one, please proceed to decontamination"* The hovering orb was obviously the physical representation of some sort of computer system and Michael wanted to know more *"Excuse me"* the little orb swiftly moved towards Michael *"Please state your designation"*

"What's a designation?"

"No access permitted until designation verification"

"You just done me"

"Please state your designation" Michael was quick to understand that he was dealing with a programmed computer system and he would have to communicate with it within its parameters. It may have had a human face but it was undoubtedly incapable of the nuances of human emotion or behaviour. *"Designation, employee 324"*. The orb whizzed and burred *"Verifying"*. It scanned him again *"BOSMA employee 324 Designation: Danny Bryant"*

"Where am I?"

"You are in the cryostasis wing, please proceed to decontamination"

"Can you answer some questions please?"

"Designation verified, state request"

"What is BOSMA?"

"BOSMA is an acronym. It stands for British Outer Space Mining Agency"

"Am I in outer space?"

"You are in the cryostasis wing, please proceed to decontamination"

"Is this a space ship?"

"You are on board the BOSMA Angel 9 mining and research vessel"

"No Shit?"

"No excrement detected, please proceed to decontamination"

"Wait, wait.....where is this vessel currently located?"

"BOSMA angel 9 mining and research vessel is currently in orbit around Europa"

"O.K, O.K what is Europa?"

"Europa is the sixth smallest moon of the planet Jupiter. Europa is made of silicate rock with an iron core, has an atmosphere of primarily oxygen and is covered in a layer of ice"

"O.K, that's enough"

"Please proceed to decontamination"

"This is sick"

"Please state your request" Michael was blown away by what he was hearing but took the opportunity to quiz the odd little machine while he could *"What year is it?"*

"The year is 2133 Earth standard"

"How long have I been out?"

"cryostasis has been active for 7 standard Earth years"

"Why am I here?"

"Employee 324, Designation: Danny Bryant, deep core miner"

"What do I mine for?"

"The iron core of Europa consists of 75% iron alloys, 10% gold alloys, 12 % precious stones and 3 % unknown material, please proceed to decontamination"

"Why do I need decontamination?"

"Protocol dictates after reanimation all personnel must go through decontamination"

"Can I come back and ask more questions?"

"LOIS access is available throughout Angel 9"

"Another acronym? What is LOIS?"

"LOIS is an acronym, is stands for Live On-board Integrated System. LOIS controls all systems on-board Angel 9 mining and research vessel, please proceed to decontamination"

"O.K lead the way to decontamination"

"Decontamination is located through the main exit"

"Thank you LOIS"

"You are welcome employee 324, have a nice day". Michael stood up and the cold glass floor sent a shiver through his body. The entire room and surrounding structure was made of the same thick, transparent glass. The main exit door opened and Michael walked through it into a small room and he was soon met by another voice echoing all around him just as LOIS had. This time the voice was far more serious sounding and was far more obviously computer generated, not quite as sophisticated as LOIS he thought. *"Remain still employee 324"* Michael complied and was quickly being engulfed in a gaseous vapour. The door slid shut behind him and without warning Michael began to float towards the centre of the room as the gravity was removed. He was now being guided across the room in mid-air levitating. He was systematically sprayed then dried in routine about half a dozen times until he was held in position, spread eagled in the centre of the chamber. All around him lasers began to flicker, they were not the friendly and inviting blue lasers which had come from LOIS, but a far more unnerving red. Michael felt a tingling sensation over his entire body as the red lasers danced around him for a few seconds. The lasers disappeared as quickly as they had come and Michael was lowered slowly to the deck below *"Decontamination complete, please report to the Storage facility, have a nice day"* Another door opened and Michael passed through it, feeling quite refreshed and wide awake. *"Welcome to the storage facility, state your designation"*

"324"

"Employee 324, Designation: Danny Bryant"

119

"LOIS"

"State your request"

"Why am I completely bald?"

"Protocol dictates all employees are subject to a laser shave to complete decontamination procedures"

"Explain laser shave?"

"Laser shaving uses small bursts of light to destroy the human hair at the follicle, this process eliminates all possible contamination"

"Will it grow back?"

"The follicle remains undamaged, hair regrowth is unaffected"

"Can I have a mirror?"

"Please look at my face" Michael peered into the screen and LOIS disappeared, replaced by a perfect reflective surface. Michael looked upon the face of a child, he must have been eighteen or nineteen at the most. He was as he thought, completely bald, not even any eyebrows had survived the laser shave. *"LOIS, what age am I?"* *"BOSMA records state Employee 324 is 17 years earth standard years"*

"So I was only 10 when I got on this ship?"

"That statement is correct"

"I thought the coma was a mind-fuck"

"State your request"

"Never mind" LOIS moved to an alcove on the wall and Michael followed closely behind her. *"Please input employee number"* The storage unit was within the alcove on the wall, Michael pressed the key pad which glowed with each touch on its surface, scanning his fingertips as he entered his number. The alcove beeped like a microwave and a box appeared with 324 written on its lid. Michael raised an eyebrow as he noticed just how much 324 had a part to play in this new place, surely he would find out its significance here, it was

everywhere. The box contained some basic items, some clothes still in a cellophane wrapper and a small cube with three buttons on it. Michael pressed the button which had a triangle symbol upon it, which he recognised as play. The cube transformed before his eyes into a small digital display screen. The picture blurred and then came into focus. It was a man, woman and a little boy who looked to be about 10 years old. *"Hi Son"*

"Hi Honey"

"Hey me"

"Daniel, not yet" Michael concentrated hard to what was being said, he had already noticed that the sphere was not within his belongings and wanted to make sure he did not miss any possible leads to its whereabouts. *"Well son, if you are watching this then it is 2133 now and you are at the other side of the solar system, me an your mum love you very much and I hope you can forgive us for sending you so far away. Life here on earth is really hard, we just wanted to give you the chance at a better life".* The video continued and Michael was in disbelief at what he was experiencing, nothing he had experienced yet had come anywhere close to this. *"LOIS"*

"State your request"

"Describe the planet Earth"

"Planet Earth 80% H2….."

"No, not its composition, what has happened in the last seven years?"

"Angel 9 database, historical entry. In 2126 the planet Earth was at the peak of the third race war, Human population decreased to a record low of 1.34 billion. Most of the planet's surface was not able to support life"

"Describe third race war LOIS"

"The third race war was a nuclear, biological and psychological conflict. The conflict was between Western Incorporated and the Afro-Chinese alliance"

"Describe Western Incorporated"

121

"Western Incorporated was a multinational company which dominated political and commercial interests on planet Earth since 2057 Earth standard year."

"Describe Afro-Chinese Alliance"

"The Afro-Chinese Alliance was the combination of the two single most powerful states on planet Earth. The Chinese Republic and the union of African states"

"Describe planet Earth today"

"File not found"

"LOIS, explain, how did the third race war end?"

"The third race war resulted in the annihilation of Planet Earth in Earth standard year 2130"

"So it's gone?"

"Planet Earth was destroyed by a cataclysmic nuclear explosion in Earth standard year 2130" Michael stood dumbfounded by what he was hearing, he got dressed almost automatically, staring into space as he contemplated the history lesson. *"LOIS"*

"State your request"

"Where is everyone else?"

"Angel 9 has a current active crew of 1"

"Me?"

"That is correct"

"Where are the rest of the crew?"

"They are no longer on board Angel 9" Michael started to breathe deeply and felt sick at the thought that he was alone in the middle of space, he struggled to remain upright when suddenly he was interrupted by a crackly voice which seemed to be coming from his new little hovering friend. *"Come in Angel 9........Angel 9 do you read me, this is Gabriel, come in"*

"LOIS who is this?"

"The Gabriel is the dedicated drilling ship from Angel 9"

"Answer them LOIS"

"The Gabriel has requested crew transmissions only, would you like me to patch you in?"

"Yes"

"Angel 9 do you read me"

"This is Angel 9 go ahead" Michael listened as a small crowd of people cheered with joy at the other side of the radio. *"Yes! It worked, who is this?"*

"Danny Bryant, employee 324"

"Shit! LOIS has reanimated a newbie"

"Listen 324, we need your help, we are stuck on the surface, I need you to hit the manual override" Michael frantically scanned his immediate area *"O.K, where is it?"*

"Oh use your brain newbie, ask LOIS"

"LOIS, where is the manual override for the Gabriel"

"The manual override is located on the main deck"

"Take me to it LOIS" Michael passed through another large glass door and LOIS led him to a console which had various dials and buttons all over it *"O.K newbie you're looking for the big green button.......do you see it?"* Michael spotted it straight away and reached out to press it *"O.K found it"*

"Press it now!"

"Done". In all the confusion Michael had not noticed the absolute beauty of the main deck. Everything was made of glass, the floor and the ceiling and the console with the big green button. Michael looked down below his feet through the glass at the surface of Europa, it was magnificent, like the surface of the moon but more clean and smooth. Michael likened it to an enormous spherical skating rink. On closer inspection he could see the surface was far more rugged and desolate, but no less beautiful. The Angel 9 was vast and seemed to be completely made from glass apart from an enormous

123

metal cylindrical rod which protruded from its base all the way down to the surface. Michael watched as a tiny spec in the distance grow larger as it made its way up the metal rod. It was the Gabriel ascending from the surface *"LOIS, who was that voice from the Gabriel?"*

"The Gabriel is being piloted by Captain Aliya Carson"

"She sounded hot"

"The temperature within the Gabriel is within normal parameters"

"Oh forget it LOIS" Michael chuckled to himself, LOIS was a machine, but was still able to make him laugh without meaning to. He turned to face the Airlock door which was part of the Main deck, just as it clunked loudly, hissed and began to open. The crew walked through and Michael stood in awe of the futuristic scene unfolding in front of him, he smiled as a woman in her thirties marched purposefully towards him. She had dark brown hair which was crop short around her neck and eyes which were as just as dark. Michael found her to be just a pretty as he had imagined, middle aged, maybe 33 he thought. *"Well done newbie"* He hesitated like a dumbstruck schoolboy

"Tha……..thank you C…Captain" Her attention then turned to LOIS

"LOIS"

"Yes Captain Carson, how may I be of assistance?"

"Did I not ask you to reanimate a senior officer?" *"All senior officers have at least 30 standard Earth days until reanimation can be initiated"* Captain Carson turned to face Michael *"Looks like I'm stuck with you kid"* She held out her hand and gripped Michael's firmly *"Captain Aliya Carson, welcome to the last human colony in the universe"* The Captain smiled and Michael contemplated her statement for a second then replied *"Is it really all gone?"*

"It certainly is kid, and we are in the market for a new property" The Captain grabbed a few items that she had placed on the deck while she spoke with him and started to move away *"Can I help?"*

"What's your name kid?"

"Danny Bryant"

"Think fast Danny Boy" The captain threw a couple of small rectangular satchels at Michael and he caught them, almost fumbling one to the floor *"Grab these sample packs and follow me, oh and call me Leese. Protocol died with the Human race, no matter what LOIS might tell you"* Following her like a lost puppy Michael was majorly unprepared for what was unfolding around him, none of his previous experiences could have prepared him for this. He was captivated by the surreal beauty of the ship and the alien world below. Leese and the crew had only strengthened his fascination to the point where he had completely forgotten that he had no idea where the sphere or the next fragment resided. *"LOIS, kit the newbie out with his gear"*

"Please state your request"

"God damn computer, what's your number Danny?"

"324"

"LOIS please provide employee 324 with his mining suit and plasma drilling equipment"

"Employee 324, Designation: Danny Bryant, please report to the cloakroom" Michael looked understandably lost and Leese smirked as she nodded towards another alcove as she unpacked a collection of weird and wonderful instruments from her pack *"Come on newbie, we don't get paid by the hour".* Michael moved into the larger alcove and was provided with a suit which matched the rest of the crew of the Gabriel. The crew consisted of three more, two middle aged men and a young boy about the same age as Danny. One of the men approached *"Right wee man, plasma drill training"* He was an enormous hulk of a man, and had obviously spent a lot of time growing and toning his upper body. His head was shaven and Michael felt dwarfed by his presence *"I'm Goth by the way"*

"Danny"

"Here goes Danny, listen up. Number one: Point it at the rocks. Number 2: Press the trigger, and number 3: Press the tractor button. It collects all the broken pieces of rock and transports them back to the Angel for processing" Michael smiled as Goth handed him the heavy power tool, he could not believe he was holding something

that could only have been described as a movie prop, the fact that it actually functioned worried him a bit. *"Sounds easy enough"*

"Oh, I forgot number 4, under no circumstances do you ever point the business end at another person"

"O.K"

"That one is real important". Michael was a bit shaken by that information and lowered the plasma drill immediately, the potential danger somewhat sapped his enthusiasm. *"Let's go and process these samples"* Michael followed Goth into another smaller room across the main deck from the airlock door. It was a processing plant. Varying sizes of space rock lay on a conveyor system and were being carried around the maze of belts while being scanned by a selection of coloured lasers which occasionally prompted robotic arms to remove the unsatisfactory lumps of rock. The conveyors terminated after a sharp climb into a large container. *"Try not to lose a finger wee man"* Goth sniggered. At the other side of the container was four slides where the freshly mined ores where deposited, the fourth slide deposited into a sealed container and Goth noticed Michael looking at it with extra interest. *"That's where the 3 % goes, no chances taken, could be anything you know? The separator pretty much does the job for us."*

"Do you find much stuff?" Goth shook his head, Michael could see his question had touched a nerve *"Listen kid, the stockpile of ores and stones is overloaded, there is nowhere to send it to"*

"So why keep mining?" Goth shook his head again, it was obvious he had asked himself the same question many times before *"Because the captain says so……..she spends every day and night searching the database for an inhabitable planet for us to colonise"* *"Nothing so far?"*

"No such luck……..all this, the jewels and gold, these are our bargaining chips, just in-case we find one which already has a tenant"

"Makes sense". Michael busied himself for a few moments, watching the little pieces of rock make their journey from black and worthless to wonderful coloured precious stones and metals. The process was fascinating to him and Goth's disinterest only reinforced Michael's understanding of how it must have been for him and the rest of the crew, stranded in deep space. *"Goth?"*

"What is it wee man?"

"Is it just the five of us?"

"Last I checked there are 328 of us in total, 4 of us awake, and then you. When........if we find a new home then the captain will wake the rest of from cryostasis"

"Don't they get older like me?"

"The majority are under thirty, apart from some of the commanding officers. Policy dictates that a skeleton crew should be maintained to allow maximum economising of the rations." Michael listened intently, it was like the plot of a movie to him and he couldn't help but be excited by every new nuance of the story unfolding. *"We have been out here for a long time now. Leese suggested we keep searching and when one of them reaches thirty, we reanimate them, can't have people live and die in a pod"* Michael shook his head in agreement. Goth had started to analyse a few fragments of rock when both him and Michael shuddered with fright as the high pitch shriek of Captain Carson reverberated around the glass structure of the ship. *"Yes! Goth, Sammy, get the others, get in here!"* Captain Carson was standing at the desk with the big green button. A visual display was being beamed from its centre, producing a three dimensional holographic representation of a planetary system. Captain Carson, flicked and moved the display with movements of her hands in mid-air. It was wondrous to watch and Michael stood with his mouth open like a bullfrog ready to catch some flies. It was like something straight from the set of a Hollywood movie and he was right there in the middle of it all. *"See this small moon here? "Yeah sure boss, come on tell us?"* Goth was eager to find out what the commotion was all about *"Goth.........it's M class"*

"No shit boss really?"

"I think it's the one" The other crew members looked nervous at the possibility and Michael was slightly perplexed that their reaction was not a more enthusiastic one. The youngest crew member plucked up the courage to ask the question on all their minds *"Captain?"*

"Spit it out Pat?"

"How long?"

"Only six months cryo at full speed" Sammy, the final crew member burst out in floods of tears *" Six months then out of this fuckin' place..........sir"* Captain Carson stood in front of the rest of the crew and prepped for an important speech. *"Well, crew of the BOSMA Angel 9 mining and research vessel. There is no definitive guarantee that the moon will be inhabitable, so as planned the final decision will come down to a vote. All those in favour of trying please show your hand"* Every member of the crew stuck their hand in the air instantly, Captain Carson looked at him with patient sincerity. Michael turned to look at the rest of the crew and they all stared at him with less than patient expressions. *"Oh sorry, me too"* He stuck his hand up into the air promptly and the groans of relief from the rest of the crew were instantaneous. *"Right prep for cryo. Goth, Sammy, check the power core, we need to make sure we have enough juice to get us there. Pat check all the pods, make sure the cryo's are tucked in for the journey."* Captain Carson looked at Michael and smiled, the joy at the prospect of the Angel's salvation was obvious to see on her face *"Newbie, you're with me on the bridge"* The captain shut down the visual display with a few flicks of the wrist and summoned a large rectangular glass platform which seemed to materialise on the floor behind the console. She jumped on and Michael followed. The platform transformed around them until a self-contained glass box enclosed them, and they began to ascend. They got higher and higher until they reached the deck head of the Angel 9. Michael perused his surroundings in awe of what he was witnessing. An uncountable amount of stars surrounded him, the spherical glass ceiling made for the best possible arena to view the wonders of deep space. Looking to the ground below, Michael's stomach turned inside out with vertigo. They were high. *"Yeah, forgot to say, don't look down"* The Captain chuckled to herself, obviously amused by the freshman's uneasiness. The glass box settled at a platform and Michael followed the captain as she moved onto the bridge. The design was much the same as the console that they had left down at deck level and she started to bring up various level indicators and status information on the visual display. *"O.K, you can help me program the journey into the Navcom, or at least you can keep me company"* Michael smiled realising that the captain was aware of his lack of usefulness, having had limited time on board. *"LOIS"*

"State your request"

"How are we looking? Run a full diagnostic"

128

"Processing...... BOSMA Angel 9 mining and research vessel is running at 99.9% engine efficiency"

"That's plenty"

"LOIS, Lay in a course to these co-ordinates"

"Processing........course set, awaiting initiation" Michael watched the captain as she buzzed around the console like a giddy schoolgirl. Her excitement was impossible to hide and she looked in complete control as she checked the ship's condition and prepared for their departure. Michael felt at ease in her company, she was in complete control of the situation and he was able to relax and let his mind soak up the fantastical surroundings. The penny dropped and Michael had a familiar feeling of dread come over him, the entire crew was going into cryostasis for six months and he still had no clue where the fragment or the sphere could be, he could not spend six months here, no matter how outstandingly beautiful it was. *"So when do we sleep Leese?"*

"As soon as everyone has finished their checks we can leave, I have to stay awake, just in-case the autopilot malfunctions"

"I'll keep you company if you like?"

"Don't be silly Danny, there's no need"

"But I just got up and you might need my help doing......stuff" Captain Carson grinned *"You know what kid, your pretty sharp"*

"Thank you sir"

Michael could see that the Captain was moved by his sentiment. She really did not want to spend the next six months on her own and Michael got the impression that his offer was exactly what she wanted and he was only too happy to make it, given his circumstance. The rest of the crew had been mining for years, six months rest would have been long overdue. *"LOIS"*

"State your request"

"I want to make a ship wide announcement"

"Initiating..........complete"

"Crew of BOSMA Angel 9 Mining and Research vessel, this is your captain speaking. The voyage to our new home will commence in T minus 10 Minutes. Please complete your final duties and proceed to the cryo facility. See you all in six months, sweet dreams." Michael could hear screams of joy and excitement coming from way below on the main deck. The captain and him joined in with the celebration and began to scream loud and stamp their feet. It was a rare happy moment for the crew and Michael allowed himself a moment of happiness, as he had managed to buy himself a reprieve from the six month long sleep. Surely that would give him plenty of time to locate his sphere and hunt out the next fragment, wherever it could be. The crew didn't mess about with pleasantries, they said their goodbyes and soon they were all fast asleep leaving Michael and the captain to their long shift. The Captain's face stretched and distorted as she let out the largest of tired yawns *"Danny, everything is on auto, so unless LOIS alerts you, you will be fine. I'm going to get my head down for a bit, O.K?"*

"No problem sir"

"Wake me straight away if there are any problems, goodnight". Michael spent the next few hours traversing the ship, investigating each room and searching for any clues as to where the sphere could be hiding. It had to be on-board somewhere or he was in for a long and frustrating visit. He searched high and low, stopping occasionally to take in the surreal environment. After an extensive search he was no closer to finding either of the missing parts. *"LOIS"*

"State your request"

"I'm looking for something"

"Please specify"

"Object, spherical, possibly made of glass"

"Processing......there are over ten thousand items on board which match the description given"

"The item has twelve holes, five holes are filled"

"Processing......no items on board match the description given" Michael huffed and puffed with disappointment and racked his brain for another possible direction of questioning. *"O.K LOIS"*

"State your request"

"Describe, Staff of fortune"

"Processing………There are seventeen entries in the ships records with reference to that specification"

"Staff of fortune, Japan"

"Processing………There is one entry which matches that specification"

"Read it LOIS"

"Processing…..The staff of fortune is a mythical object from ancient Japanese folklore"

"O.K LOIS, does it say what it was made of"

"Processing………That information is not recorded"

"Shit, shit, shit". Michael's patience was wearing thin, *"LOIS, describe 324"* *"Processing………324 is a numerical composition which consists of…."*

"No not that….LOIS, are there any entries which are not numerical, something significant or unusual"

"Processing…….there are no records with that specification" Michael was at a loss at what to do next, the sphere and the fragment could have been anywhere, LOIS could not help with a description of whatever 324 could have meant. He slumped on the console and let out an unsatisfied groan *"Unknown. State your request"*

"Ha, try this. LOIS specify unknown"

"Unknown is a word in the English language used to describe a material, knowledge, or identity that has no historical reference available" Michael sat up in his chair with a bit of purpose now. *"LOIS"*

"State your request"

"Is there any Unknown material on board Angel 9?"

"Processing…….There is a quantity of unknown material in separator chamber number 4, there are no other unknown materials

on Board BOSMA Angel 9 mining and research vessel" Michael was sparked into life and he headed straight to the conveyor room which he had been in earlier with Goth. Captain Carson lay fast asleep in a small bunk on the main deck, not wanting to be too far from the ships navigation controls. Michael sneaked passed being careful not to wake her. The separation chamber was sealed shut and had hazardous material signs emblazoned all over it. They were luminous and apparent that they were to be taken seriously. Michael peered through the viewing window and scanned the internals of chamber number four. A solitary object lay dormant at the base of the container, near its centre, it was fragment number six. *"Yes!"* Michael placed his hands into the large rubber gloves attached to the chambers solid exterior and reached inside. The fragment was just within reach and he picked it up, moving it to the exit chute. He let it go and it slid towards the exit tray. Before it had even stopped its descent, Michael swiped it from the tray and gripped it tightly in his hand. The feeling of relief was incredible, that little bit of control had been returned to him. This had to have been the most unobtainable fragment of the sphere he had to retrieve so far, mined from the core of a frozen moon at the other side of the galaxy and he now held it right here in his hands. *"Just the sphere now, where can you be?"* he said aloud *"LOIS"*

"State your request"

"Scan this"

"Processing......The object consists of the same material throughout, the material appears on no known database"

"Does this item match any others on board Angel 9"

"Processing......Negative it is unique"

"LOIS, run an analysis of the object and hazard a guess at its origin"

"Unable to comply, out with operating parameters ......incoming message, please proceed to the bridge"

"A message? Who from?"

"Employee 324: Danny Bryant does not have the required security clearance". Michael rushed to the bunk where the captain was out cold, she was covered in pieces of paper, some star charts and other documents. In her right hand she clasped a photograph. It was

a picture of her in far more womanly attire than the BOSMA Company issue uniform. She was standing alongside a man of similar age and a young boy around five years old. Michael drifted into thoughts of Joseph and immediately back, due to the urgency of the situation. *"Leese…..captain!"*

"Oh, what is it?" The captain groaned with disinterest.

"LOIS Explain"

"Incoming message, please proceed to the bridge" the Captain sprung to her feet

"A message? From who?"

"There is a ship on an intercept course, please proceed to the bridge to receive transmission" The captain headed straight to the bridge and Michael followed, upon arrival the captain barked her next instruction. *"LOIS, Message!"*

"The Transmission is audio only Captain………….Mining ship Angel 9, prepare to be boarded", in the deep darkness of space, the two remaining crew members watched through the glass hull as a small ship appeared, it was much smaller than the Angel and the Captain looked confused and somewhat concerned, she turned to Michael *"You recognise it?"*

"No sir"

"LOIS identify that vessel"

"Processing…..there are no records available for the specified vessel…we are being hailed captain"

"On screen LOIS"

"This transmission is audio only"

"Play it Damn it"

"Mining ship Angel 9, you have an unauthorised passenger on-board. Isolate him in airlock one and prepare to be boarded"

"Identify yourself, this is Captain Aliya Carson……."

"Our identity is irrelevant, comply with our demands or we will take our prisoner by force". The Captain had a confused look on her face and turned to Michael once more

"It's just us right?" Michael was sweating, he had to remain calm, he was Danny Bryant wasn't he? *"Yes Sir"*

"Prepare to be boarded"

"Oh shit, what the hell is happening here? Danny get down to the main deck, get your plasma drill, nobody boards my ship. Head to the airlock, that's the only way in" Michael and the captain headed down towards the console on the main deck and grabbed a couple of plasma drills on route *"Goth show you how to work one of these?"*

"Point and shoot?"

"Great, you're an expert, anything comes through that door.......well you know" The sweat was now dripping of Michael, who was this intruder? Surely it wasn't him they had come for. *"LOIS"*

"State your request captain"

"Perimeter defences, 4 foot wall, 15 metres from the airlock door, reinforced" Michael watched in amazement at the glass fortress that was materialising all around him, they were preparing for a siege and whatever came through the door would meet some tough defences in the form of Captain Carson. *"LOIS"*

"State your request captain"

"Turret nodes, 10 meter radius from this point, full spread". Nine little orbs appeared and circled Michael and the captain, just above head height. "LOIS, ready lasers"

"Lasers Primed". The airlock door opened and a solitary figure emerged. It was large in stature and looked strong. It was completely black from head to toe in a solid looking armour carrying what looked like a large assault rifle. *"LOIS fire"* The nine orbs began firing at the black figure and the lasers rebounded from him as if he was encased in a protective bubble. The figure stopped and a bright blue light began to emanate from its fingertips, it started to raise its right hand as the bright blue light grew larger by the second. The orbs fizzed and popped and fell to the deck, no longer a threat to the intruder. Captain Carson screamed like a soldier crossing the front line

134

and stood up in plain view of the figure and opened fire. The plasma drill exploded into life sending a large arc of superheated plasma towards it. The figure turned its hand to the arc and it stopped about 10 inches from its fingertips. The figure started to move towards the captain pushing the plasma arc backwards as it approached. Michael was frozen to the spot with fear, he had ran out of time and had to react. The intruder seemed hell bent on destroying everything in its path. Michael stood up and opened fire, only for the black figure to raise its other hand and hold his plasma arc in the same fashion, easily holding both Michael and the captain at bay. It continued towards the captain and removed her weapon from her. Its voice was electronic and emotionless *"You should be sleeping"* the captain fell to the ground lifeless and the black figure turned its attention to Michael. His arms grew heavier with the weight of the plasma drill, he could feel the beads of sweat drip down his forehead onto his face as the figure reached him. *"Goodnight 324".* Michael slumped to the deck just like the captain and was out cold. The black figure searched his lifeless body and removed the fragment, slipping it into a small opening on its armour suit. *"LOIS"*

"State your designation" the figure held up a finger to LOIS and touched the display right on the end of the nose *"Designation Verified. V.I.E.R.A software compatible"*

"LOIS"

"State your request"

"Display destination co-ordinates"

"Processing.....on-screen"

"Re-programme auto-pilot to these co-ordinates" the figure touched the screen again *"Processing....new co-ordinates set, adjusting course"* .Michael began to come round, he had taken a few bumps and bruises over the last while and his recuperation time was somewhat quicker as he grew accustomed to being mentally and physically battered. He reached for the plasma drill *"Ah.Ah.Ah"* The figure stood on the drill and pointed his finger in Michael's direction shaking its head in disapproval. With a flick of its finger and a little flash of the same bright blue light Michael was out cold once more. This time at the mercy of the black figure who reached down grabbed his ankle and dragged him towards the airlock.

Chapter 10

Lab rat

The engines hummed as the small ship moved off into the distance leaving Captain Carson and the rest of the crew of the Angel to whatever fate the black figure had left them with. Michael awoke on a cold slab and was unable to move in any direction. He was paralysed again, just like he was in the hospital. He tried to scream out but felt physically incapable of making anything other than a tame squeak. His head was held in place with a metal plate and Michael found his predicament even more unbearable than being in the coma. Being held down physically was somewhat more alarming. He was a prisoner. The ship was small inside and did not have the same majestic aura as Angel 9 with its completely glass composition. It was far more like what Michael would have guessed a space ship would have looked like. All Uniform metal panels, not unlike a military vehicle. If he did not already know he would have had no clue he was in outer space. The interior of the ship was not so blatantly futuristic. There was a small door which Michael presumed to be the bathroom. He could see the majority of the ship from his position. Beyond his feet he could just about make out the silhouette of the pilot who was sitting in the cockpit at the front end of the compartment. He was pressing buttons which were far more primitive looking than the visual display controls on the Angel. Michael could hear the pilot breathing heavily through the black mask which covered its face. He frantically squinted his eyes in every direction, trying to get a clue as to what was going on. There was a loud click, just like the handbrake of a car being released and Michael began to sit up from his horizontal position. He was still unable to move and was soon sitting upright. The black figure stood up from the cockpit and moved across the deck towards him. Michael was overcome with dread, the figure had shown such immense invulnerability on the Angel and it could have snapped Michael like a twig. As it moved into the light Michael looked upon it, able to see it up close and personal. It had no distinguishing features. The face was completely covered in a plastic mesh like fabric, serving only to make the imposing figure appear even more menacing. Michael tried his hardest to remain as calm as he possibly could, he was at its mercy and he felt his heart race as it lifted its arm and moved towards him. In its hand was a syringe which contained a bright blue liquid, which almost glowed with life, it was not a substance which Michael had ever seen before, swirling and sparkling within the glass tube. The Figure moved its hand towards his neck and his eyes remained transfixed on it. The syringe pierced the skin on his neck and Michael was powerless to stop the flow of the strange glowing liquid into his bloodstream. It did not take long to take effect and soon he began to feel a little drunk, getting more and more tired with every passing second. Trying to keep his eyes from closing, he felt like a long distance lorry driver who had missed his last pit stop. His eyes grew heavier as he watched the figure touch a keypad on the wall beside him. A Panel sprung open and a shelf protruded from the bulkhead. There was a machine of some sort which had lights and an alpha numerical digital display. Michael was on the limit of consciousness and just before he slipped into a drug induced state he noticed something that he could not believe he had overlooked. The machine was wired up to the sphere, each fragment had a probe attached to its end and each of the empty holes had coloured wires inserted in them. Michael was so confused, the drugs had almost knocked him out, only for the recognition of the sphere to keep him awake for a little longer. What was the black figure up to? Whom or what could it be? Michael feared it but could not help his desperation to understand what its role could have been. After all it was the only thing that had any real recognition of the sphere, everyone else was oblivious to its existence. Michael slipped away with a little echo of the final word from the figure *"Goodnight 324"*. Michael awoke and was surrounded by clean white walls. The room was empty and there was no sign of anything or anybody other than himself. His ears were filled with the sound of water trickling, it sounded just like the babbling stream which he had visited in the mountains of Japan. Shutting his eyes for a fraction of a second, Michael thought of Noritomo and feelings of genuine affection rushed through him, the old man was at the forefront of his thoughts as he opened his eyes only to find him standing a few feet in front of him. The room remained clinical and lifeless, only the two old friends stood together in its centre. *"Hello my son, you look tired"* Michael's head began to hurt with an unnatural pain, forcing him to wince and close his eyes. Upon opening them, he found that Noritomo had gone just as swiftly as he had appeared leaving him alone again. Michael was dazed and detached, although the potential benefits of his condition were not lost on him. Closing his eyes he thought hard about Kaitlin and Joseph and then opened his eyes. The smell was unmistakable, the aroma of charred meat filled his nostrils and he realised he was experiencing the same nightmare which he had been subjected to on the hospital bed. Little Joseph brushed passed his leg and rushed around the garden playing. He felt his touch and it felt so much more realistic than the ghostly appearance of Noritomo. The white room had this time been replaced with his back garden, just as he remembered it. Michael closed his eyes again and in a solitary blink he was returned to the white room. He tried to assess what was happening to him, he was unable to move and could only stand as an observer. Joseph had been able to touch him and Noritomo could speak to him but he was unable to interact with either of them. A familiar and somewhat welcome sound echoed all around him and Michael closed his eyes in anticipation. He was rewarded with a truly welcome sight. It was King who had barked and Michael never doubted for a second it was his brave and loyal friend. King stood a few feet from him, just as Noritomo had. He stood strong and proud, just as magnificent as he had remembered. Michael reached out to touch him, he was frozen to the spot and unable to interact. He longed so much just to pat his old friend who had played such an integral part in protecting him and Agnieska. The unnatural pain returned, forcing him to close his eyes once more. The process he was being subjected to seemed uniform and intentional, he was being put through a series of different scenarios and was experiencing some sort of hallucinogenic ordeal brought on by the bizarre blue liquid which the black figure injected into Danny Bryant's body. Michael was more accepting and at peace with what he was now being subjected to. Maybe it was another calming side effect of the blue drug or could it be that he was now become far more accepting of the unusual. He had experienced so much since the plane had plummeted to the icy depths of the ocean that he was now able to regulate his emotions far more easily. It was almost as if nothing had the ability to surprise him any longer. Whatever it was that he was forcibly being made a part of. He was now reliving some of his past experiences with the sphere. He was being reminded of a place he had been or a person he had met by a distinct smell or sound and in the blink of an eye was in the place which seemed as real as it had been. Michael remained unable to interact with any of the people or places and the process continued for a while longer until he slipped away into a deep and drug induced slumber. The process had taken its toll on his body and he had his fill of mental exercises for the moment. A sharp pin prick awoke him and Michael gasped for air just like he had seen people do in the movies when taking the first dramatic breath of resurrection after a near death experience. Above him stood the black figure, its entire body was covered in a mesh like material, not unlike the carbon fibre which expensive supercars were made of. Michael studied it, it was large and the carbon fibre suit accentuated a strong and muscular physique beneath. The rest of its body was streamlined and had very little paraphernalia other than a utility belt with various items which were currently indistinguishable to him. The assault rifle had also been removed and was nowhere to be seen and Michael wondered whether it had even been a weapon at all as the figure seemed more than capable of defending itself without the need of anything other than its hands. It had no problem incapacitating Captain Aliya and him back on Angel 9. The figures face was covered in the same carbon fibre but it did not have the same figure hugging effect that the body suit had, shielding his features and replacing them with an unnerving blank expression. It had a slightly rounded face plate and above it on the forehead area was a little solid metal plaque which had previously had something written on it. The writing had been scored off with a series of vertical scratches. A great deal of care had been taken to ensure that whatever had been written was removed permanently. Michael attempted to move his body again and then to speak, but just like before he was immobilised. He watched as the figure moved away from his side and approached the sphere which was still wired up to the machine. It began to remove probes and reattach them. Michael's eyes hurt as he was constantly squinting from his lying position to get a look at what was happening. The figure seemed familiar with the sphere and was keeping track of data on a little screen which was monitoring the spheres output. Michael had no idea what the figure's intentions had been and he yearned for some sort of communication with it. Frightening as it was, it was the first being he had encountered that had any awareness of his double life and Michael was desperate for some answers. Maybe his captor could enlighten him with exactly what the whole journey was all about. His immobility enraged him and he could feel his heart racing as his temper broke. Simultaneously the readings on the display screen which the figure was working on started to spike and it turned to face him almost robotically. It moved to the adjacent bulkhead and spoke into a little aperture *"Tricilate five millilitres"*. A small vial popped from the aperture and the figure removed it and moved towards Michael. This time the injection had an instant effect and Michael's heart rate lowered immediately. The feelings of frustration and rage soon left him and he lay silent and calm. The figure had given him a narcotic or relaxant of some sort and Michael felt much more at ease and a little bit giddy as well. The figure returned to the sphere and was studying it with great interest and Michael was far less concerned due to the new substance circulating his blood stream. A few moments later the figure approached and revealed another syringe which was filled with the same blue liquid as before. It flowed into Michael's bloodstream and before long he stood alone in the white room. A voice echoed around the room, just as King's bark had and Michael recognised him immediately. He knew what he had to do and shut his eyes with excited expectancy. *"Alright Dickhead?"* It was Bernie, he was standing at the bar in the Crown and Michael watched as the little pub materialised all around him *"Go on then boss"* Bernie encouraged Michael to drink a pint of Lager which lay on the bar in front of him and just as he did Michael felt the palm of his left hand tingle with pins and needles. Within a few seconds the life had returned to it. Michael reached out towards the pint glass and gripped it firmly. The moisture on the glass was so realistic and the temperature was so perfect. The remainder of Michael's body had remained static and was able just to lift the glass towards his face. The flavour was so refreshing and he savoured every drop. If this was a dream, then they certainly knew how to pull a pint in the land of nod he thought. Michael tilted his head back as he swallowed and shut his eyes. Within an instant he stood alone once more in the white room. He was ready for it this time, he was wise to what the figure was inflicting on him. His captor was monitoring him as he was being put through a series of tests on his senses and now it seemed his motor skills were being put through their paces. Michael shut his eyes and thought hard of Kaitlin and Joseph once more, he opened his eyes and he stood unchanged in the silent white room. It seemed that he could not affect the experience as easily as he had presumed. He was unable to direct his thoughts and emerge in whatever location he had desired. A wind blew through the white room and he could feel the sharp sting of microscopic particles hitting his face. He closed his eyes instinctively to protect them and when he opened them he stood alone, this time in the bleak burning desert. A sandstorm was in full swing all around him and he recognised the distant hum of the allied jets encroaching on his position. A tingling sensation shot through his entire body and he began to run in fear of the imminent air strike on his position, he got faster and faster until far in the distance behind him a large cloud of smoke bellowed up into the sky. Michael turned and watched as it began to settle to the desert floor sending a dust cloud hurtling towards him. The dust surrounded him and he shut his eyes once more. Michael awoke on the slab and gasped for a desperate breath once more. The figure stood over him once more and for the first time it spoke to him *"Who are you?"* The figure stood with a small touchpad in hand, ready to note any reactions to his questions *"Let me out of this, who are you?"* A sharp electrical shock was administered to Michael's head. The pain was excruciating and he screamed out in agony until it stopped. *"Answer the question, who are you?"* Michael did not dare refuse his captors wish. He had so many questions of his own and wanted to find out any information which would hopefully help to lead him home. But in this instance he simply answered to avoid another burst from the electric shock *"Danny Bryant"* the slab hummed and Michael was again electrocuted causing him to writhe under the intense pain. *"Response not acceptable, who are you?"* Michael wriggled to try and free himself and remained silent. The figure was by no means a friend to him and the thought of revealing his true identity to it seemed like a bad idea. After a few moments the slab hummed and the electricity rushed through his body with the same violent ferocity getting more and more intense with each burst. Michael wept uncontrollably, the pain was too much for him to handle and yet again he was met with the same emotionless response from the figure. *"Answer the question, who are you?"* He was broken and whimpered his real name *"Michael"*

   "Excellent, full name?"

   "Michael Cameron"

   "Now we are getting somewhere" The figure moved away and started working on the sphere, Michael's body was completely exhausted and he struggled to lift his arms after the torture he had endured *"Who are you? What is happening to me?"* The figure approached the aperture in the bulkhead again *"Tricilate thirty millilitres"* the figure administered the dose and Michael was instantly pain free. This time he was a little more than giddy, he was smashed and began to giggle like a drunken teenager. *"Sleep now 324"* The figure flicked his finger towards him and he drifted off into a calm and relaxing sleep. The dreams this time were uninspiring and unaffected by outside intervention. Michael awoke from what felt like a long and comfortable sleep. The ship was rocking from side to side and the figure was up front in the cockpit. The noise of a large engine roared from beyond the bulkhead *"Come on, come on!"* The Figure shouted aloud as he spun dials and pressed buttons frantically within the cockpit. Michael lay as he had been for the entire trip lifeless and incapable of movement. A loud announcement was transmitted across the ship, crackling with interference *"You are in violation......, surrender and prepare to be boarded"* The figure it seemed had befallen the same fate that it had enforced on the angel. A much larger ship had caught them in a tractor beam and was preparing to

141

board. *"Come on!"* The Figure struggled with his controls until the ships computer interrupted *"Tractor beam disengaged"*

"Excellent, engage light drive" The small ship shot off at an incredible speed, Michael watched through the cockpit as the little spots of light from distant stars changed into elongated white lines of light as the ship accelerated to what was for him a previously unexperienced speed. The ship's hull rumbled and creaked under the pressure until it slowed to a stop and the little ship floated silent and alone in the darkness of deep space. The figure unclipped his harness and rushed to the sphere to monitor it. Michael watched and was far more intrigued by the figure than he had been so far. Who could it be? Was it a man? A woman? Neither? What did it want with him? Who was it running from? Michael's mind rushed with a million questions and the figure lifted its head from the sphere and turned to face him *"These are all questions of which you already know the answers"* Michael's eyes widened and he wished he could have spoken to the figure and got some answers, but it moved back to the sphere and ignored him. He thought about what had just happened. The figure was using some sort of telepathic ability he thought. How else would it have known what he was thinking? Michael tried to think about the things that he wanted answers to. He focused on the sphere and the fragments. The figure remained unresponsive. Michael cleared his mind and thought about the figure directly and tried to question its intentions. The black face turned to face him and spoke again *"Clever, very clever, goodnight 324"*. With a flick of its finger the figure sent Michael to sleep once again and returned to work with the sphere while he slipped into a comfortable and uneventful slumber. The familiar sound of the sphere woke him and he could see that it was now unshackled from the probes and wires. The figure was now standing above him and administering a white creamy substance to his temples, hands and feet. The feeling was soothing, the cream was being applied to the electric shock contact points. The figure moved away and picked up the sphere along with the fragment which Michael had found in the unknown materials chamber on the Angel. The figure placed them both within a canvas bag, approached Michael and spoke again. *"Do not wake the captain, it is time to move on"* Michael listened intently, the figure spoke of Captain Carson and it seemed that it intended on returning him to the Angel. *"Do not fail me, I will be watching, who are you?"*

"Michael Cameron" He replied this time in an instant, knowing the possible repercussions of an incorrect reply to his captor.

The figure reached out and injected Michael, putting him to sleep for a final time. Michael heard a faint whisper as he drifted away *"You are 324"* The figure unshackled Michaels lifeless body and threw him over its shoulder, grabbing the canvas bag in the process. It moved swiftly across the ship's deck and approached the airlock. The doors slid open with a hydraulic hissing and the figure entered the airlock with the doors closing behind it. After about ten seconds or so the opposite airlock doors opened and the figure carried Michael across the glass deck of the Angel and placed him in the same spot from where he had picked him up before. The captain lay lifeless, not moving since their departure. *"LOIS"* the figure summoned the on board system and began to instruct it with new orders. *"Display Destination Co-Ordinates"*

> *"Processing……..On screen"*
>
> *"Delete"*
>
> *"Processing"*
>
> *"Display previous co-ordinates"*
>
> *"Processing…..On screen"*
>
> *"Re-initiate"*
>
> *"Processing…….Co-Ordinates set, course changed".* The

figure moved away and then stopped for a moment on the deck of the angel. It scanned the area for a moment, after a final glance in Michael's direction it headed for the airlock. The little ship burst into life again and vanished into deep space leaving the Angel and its crew in the same condition as when they had first encountered each other. *"Employee 324………..Employee 324 please respond"*

"I'm O.K LOIS". The little orb moved away from Michael and towards the Captain, attempting to wake her *"LOIS stop"* Michael shouted across at LOIS in panic, he remembered what the figure had said to him. *"Do not wake her…..I will be watching"*

> *"State request"*
>
> *"The Captain is sleeping"*
>
> *"State request"*

"Allow the Captain to wake naturally"

"Request confirmed" LOIS floated off and carried out whatever duties it had been assigned. Michael sneaked passed the Captain and made his way up to the bridge. He grabbed the canvas and kept it near to him. *"LOIS"*

"State Request"

"What is the ship's destination?"

"Unknown M class planet"

"How much cryosleep till destination?"

"It will take 6 months cryosleep until destination is reached". Michael realised that the destination had been re-instated and rested on the console for a while, contemplating what he had just been through. The figure was powerful and brutal. It had put him through an intense torturous experience while he was on board the little ship. It seemed to be robotic and devoid of any emotion. Michael wondered just how much it must have known about the sphere. It must have been extensive as it spent hours analysing it and monitoring Michael's reactions to it. The experience in the white room also had to serve some sort of purpose. He was put through a series of tests which assessed his responses and interactions with each person and environment that he was integrated with. Michael deliberated for a while as to why the figure had carried out such a bizarre collection of examinations. The most puzzling thing, was why the figure took such a big risk to capture him and put him through a disturbing ordeal only to leave him in the dark as to its intentions. It was a complete mystery to him. The journey he had been on had been incredibly mysterious and continuously left Michael feeling lost and confused. This latest episode had only sent him way back to the start of working out just what on earth was going on *"What on earth?"* He chuckled aloud *"Wherever it is!"* Michael spent a while longer resting and trying to understand any little snippet of information he had absorbed. The figure it seemed was also being hunted by an even bigger fish, who was it? They had only just escaped and made it back to the angel. The figure had to be some sort of outlaw or criminal, it had the scored plate on its head which signifies that in some way it was trying to remove an enforced designation. Michael also questioned why the figure had returned him to the Angel and provided him with the sphere and the fragment, it had a vested interest in him. What it could be was as elusive as

everything else. The ship had been rerouted to the planet of the crew's possible salvation which contradicted the cold and emotionless being he encountered. It seemed to care about their arrival at their new home which displayed a degree of compassion. *"LOIS"*

    "State your request"

    "I'm hungry"

    "The ships store has a full supply of nutritional supplements" Michael was starving and he made his way down to the main deck. He laid out a table and prepared himself a meal from the alcove in the glass bulkhead. The food was all synthesised, but it did resemble and taste like the real thing to a certain extent. *"LOIS"*

    "State your request"

    "Is there any beer?"

    "The ships stores are stocked with 17 types of beer". Michael approached the alcove and finished off the meal with a six pack which he sat down on the table. It was a brand which he had never encountered before. He poured a large glass and slurped it down, he was reminded of the lager from the weird dream in the white room. They both tasted just as real as each other. The meat from the roast chicken which he prepared was succulent and juicy and Michael sat staring at it for a while. His encounter with the black figure had made him start to question reality again. It had tortured him and forced him to reveal his true identity, it must have known so much about what was going on. Michael found himself conflicted, although the figure had treated him appallingly, it was the only being which he had encountered that could have answered the many questions that he had buzzing through his mind. There was one question that he had not asked himself in a long time *"When can I go home?"* Michael was flooded with guilt, he thought of his life at home with Kaitlin and Joseph and how he now seemed to forget those more and more often. Taking a bite from a fresh green apple, he had a brainwave. *"LOIS"*

    "State your request"

    "Historical records, Earth"

    "Please specify"

    "Kaitlin Cameron, born 13 January 1981"

"There are 397 records with that specification"

"Husband Michael Cameron, Son Joseph Cameron" Michael gave his and Joseph's date of birth to LOIS and sat waiting for the results staring into the vast openness of space. He could not believe how accustomed he had become to the bizarre and unusual surroundings he found himself in. He was in the future, thousands of miles from earth which no longer existed and had arrived here from Iraq via Japan with a few other stops in between. The figure had made him reveal he was not Danny Bryant and was somewhat satisfied when he revealed his true identity. The captor must have had a reason for what it had done but it was beyond his imaginative capability to fathom what it could have been. LOIS interrupted his daydream *"File not found"* Michael screwed up his brow with confusion. *"LOIS, is the file lost? Did it ever exist?"*

"Unable to acknowledge, file not found" Michael angrily threw his apple and it bounced around the glass floor of the main deck. *"Oh well, here we go again".* He stood up from the console and removed the fragment and the sphere, he had one final look around the Angel and could not help but be impressed with what was a sight he would likely never have the chance to see again. Captain Carson lay peacefully sleeping and he was content that they were all going to be fine and make it to their new home. He could focus on pushing onwards in the hope of making it home himself. He slipped the piece into place and it attached with the usual hum and buzz that it always did. Michael slipped slowly off to the light and this time felt no passage of time or any pain, he shut his eyes for a second and unlike before he was not engulfed and taken. He had initiated the transportation. He opened his eyes a moment later and he felt stronger and more focused than he had done in years. The hot sun beat down on him and he could tell he was moving at a considerable speed. *"Look out"* A woman's voice rung out and before Michael could react he was struck clean on the face by a low lying branch and sent flying from the back of his speedy transportation. Dazed and sore, Michael squinted to see the approaching figure. It was a magnificent horse, a beautiful steed and upon it an even more beautiful woman. Her hair was long and dark and she had a beautiful light brown hue to her skin. She leaned out and reached for Michael's hand, helping him to his feet. *"The camp is only a couple of miles over that ridge, jump on, let's go"* Michael climbed onto the back of the horse and fell off immediately, landing on his feet. *"Come on, we need to hurry"* He jumped up again and used his spurs from his boots to grip the horses

146

saddle. The pieces started to join together in his mind and he painted a picture in his head. He wore spurs on his boots and upon his head a dark brown Stetson *"I'm a cowboy!"*

"Yeah, well I'm an Indian and this horse ain't big enough for the both of us" Michael laughed and the woman smiled back at him, she was truly a site to behold, beautiful he thought. *"Let's go cowboy"* the woman laughed and with a loud *"Yaaaaah!"* Sending the horse towards the ridge in the distance, at a thunderous speed. Michael gripped his companion tightly as she guided the horse through the rocky terrain. The scenery was unbelievable and the sun had just begun to disappear behind the distant mountains casting a dusty brown and orange tone across the evening sky. He took another gulp of fresh country air. The exertions of his experience on the Angel had tired him out and along with the heat from the horse and his companion he slipped softly off to sleep. It was another place in another time once again, no idea, no explanations given, but he slept soundly finally free of the fear of the black figure, for the time being at least.

Chapter 11

Sophie

The soft and warm touch of lips touching his woke Michael. He was lying comfortable and this awakening had been the most pleasurable he had experienced. Upon him lay his latest companion, about six inches from his face she gazed longingly into his eyes, she was beautiful he thought. Her Long ebony hair had vanished and it was now abundantly clear to him that she was not the American Indian he presumed her to be. That revelation was bolstered by a uniform line which ran along her forehead where the makeup stopped and the considerably paler real life skin tone was revealed. Her eyes were the brightest of blue. They sparkled like a cluster of crystals around her pupils. Her hair was in fact light brown and had been cleverly hidden beneath her exotic facade. *"You O.K?"* Michael listened as she opened her perfectly formed, glossy lip and spoke to him. Her accent was a surprise to him, it was a soft and polite English. The sound of her voice only helped to further enhance his attraction to her. *"Hello? Anybody home?"* Snapping out of his trance he answered

>*"Great..........I'm great"*

>*"You regretting coming?"*

>*"No........No.....not at all"*

>*"It's great to have you all to myself for a change"* The woman kissed him passionately and Michael moved away initially, feeling uncomfortable as he was partaking in what he considered infidelity. He soon was overcome with desire and reciprocated. Before long clothes began to fly off in all directions, Michael's pulse shot up and he began to pant heavily as the beautiful woman pressed her semi naked body against his. It had been so long since he had been intimate with anyone. Kaitlin had become increasingly distant and they had spent most nights in different wings of the Cameron mansion which they had expensively furnished as the empire grew and the relationship faltered. With thoughts of Kaitlin fresh in his mind, Michael started to struggle and she stopped abruptly and backed off with a concerned look on her face. *"What's wrong Stuart?"* Michael registered his new designation, glad to have found out relatively quickly this time. *"I thought you wanted this?"* Michael did not know where to look, how

he could explain the truth to the obviously hurt woman who lay before him he thought *"Listen, you really are beautiful and I really want to, but I'm still in love with the memory of my dead wife from another plane of existence"* there is no way he could have even begun to explain. It was a completely bizarre situation to be in and Michael quickly thought of a significantly more generic excuse. After all he did not want to hurt the woman's feelings. Michael plucked up the courage and just before he spoke she cut him off *"I thought you were going to leave that bitch?"* Stunned Michael remained silent. *"You said this was it, I left Tom three months ago"* Michael panicked and took a random stab in the dark, *"I have left her"*

"I mean completely, move out, sign the fuckin' papers"

"O.K, O.K, I'm sorry" The woman stood up and Michael scanned her from head to toe from where he lay. She was quite petite, not even five feet tall, but her body was perfectly formed and Michael struggled to contain his ogling. The restraint that he showed was significant, every atom in his body was attracted to her, he had not felt so captivated by a woman since he first gazed upon Kaitlin. The woman started to get changed into her costume again and Michael lay in silence watching as the transformation from English rose to Pocahontas transpired before his eyes. Michael had had some rough times recently and some incredibly awkward moments while trying to decipher his identity and role in each of the places he had visited. It was typical that the most challenging interaction would have been with a relationship with a woman. Reattaching her long black wig, she flicked the hair back and turned to face him, adopting a provocative stance *"Listen up cowboy, its decision time O.K?"* Michael was completely at her mercy, she was stunning and he had no defence from her womanly charms. *"It's either her or me?"* The woman pirouetted and displayed like a peacock just exactly what she had to offer. The saliva in his mouth overloaded as he tried to contain his desire to grab hold of her. *"The hunt starts in a half an hour, I'm off for a drink."* The woman turned and moved to leave their abode, which had up until now been completely overlooked by Michael. It was a small log cabin, with all the available amenities of a small apartment. It was now certified that he was not in the Wild West where he had first thought he had materialised. One thing for sure was that if the Hollywood movies where anything to go by, Men of the old west did not have relationship problems like the one which Michael was experiencing. Checking around the cabin for more clues, Michael stumbled across two suitcases which put him in no doubt that he was

149

in a far more familiar decade. He trawled through the cases and buried deep at the bottom of what he presumed was Stuart's case was the sphere. Removing it, Michael was glad he had it in his possession so quickly and easily this time. He sat watching the swirls of blue light traverse the black glassy orb for a little while, wondering just what it was and whether or not he would ever find out exactly what its purpose could be. The holes were now half filled, six remaining and six filled and sealed in place with the fragments from everywhere that he had been so far. His mind filled with thoughts of the places and people he had visited until he came out of his temporary daze and returned the sphere safely to the bottom of the case. Within a small zipped pocket on the reverse side of the case front was a wallet. The bank card read *"STUART MATHIESON"*. There was also a business card which was emblazoned with a company logo *"WTL COMMUNICATIONS…….MANCHESTER BRANCH……….GENERAL MANAGER: STUART MATHIESON"* the card had a telephone number and various other contact details. Within the wallet was a small flap which Michael turned to reveal a photograph. It was a couple, a man and woman. The man was the typical executive type, a ridiculous fake tan. Michael immediately recognised him as the sort he worked with at the office who had the golf membership, but spent the day sitting in the lounge with the laptop and mobile phone headset in the ear. Unfortunately it was a stereotype that he had become accustomed too, a necessary unwelcome perk of being a successful businessman. The woman in the picture was what could only have been described as a trophy wife. She had bleach blond hair and was just as orange in colour as her partner. She had large and almost certainly fake breasts and was dripping from head to toe in gold and diamond jewellery. Michael dropped the wallet and commenced a fact finding hunt through his current companion's suitcase, It was filled with far more dainty items of clothing, including some tiny underwear which he quickly moved to one side as he felt his pulse began to increase again. A small vanity case was neatly packed at the corner of the case and Michael lifted it carefully, purposefully trying to stop the flimsy clip from opening and spilling the contents all over the floor. Within the little case was a collection of makeup and accompanying utensils for application. He was only after one thing and he located it underneath the other contents, contained within the little velour bag. Removing the tiny mirror from its protective bag, Michael raised it up to his face, and inspected the shell which he inhabited. *"Oh my god! … Cheese factor ten!"* Michael grimaced as he examined the perfectly trimmed facial hair upon a lovely shade of orange. He was indeed the person from the photograph and the thought that he had to complete his search for the seventh fragment while inhabiting such a body made him cringe. *"What on earth does she see in him?"* He said aloud. Upon further inspection he realised that he still had on the same costume as he had the night before minus the boots and the Stetson. His outfit was all over the place and it required some serious attention to bring himself back into some sort of order, especially after the roll in the hay which had helped to partially remove his jeans and shirt. The mirror slipped smoothly back into the little velour case and Michael returned it carefully to the case. Sitting on the edge of their bunk, he slipped on the boots, complete with blunted novelty spurs and found himself drifting again. He wondered when it would all be coming to an end, there was still no indication as to why he was on this seemingly unending journey. With every new transportation he was subjected too, and each body which he was held within he grew increasingly more distant. He felt it would not be long until he started to forget his real life altogether. The temptation that he felt was intense and he would have liked nothing more than to give into desire and fulfil his manly needs. The only thing that held him back was a nagging feeling of guilt and that if he was to partake in any intimacy with this woman it would only strengthen his feelings of disengagement from Kaitlin and Joseph. Yet again he came to the same conclusion as he always did. There was only one thing for it. He had to keep moving forward, unite the twelve fragments and see where the sphere took him next. In the absence of any other logical reasoning, Michael had no other choice than to be left to the mercy of whatever lives he was forced to be a part of. His thoughts turned to the black figure and he gulped with fear as he remembered his experience with it. He contemplated whether his time on board the Angel was just another episode on his way to rebuilding the sphere. It was like no other place he had been before and seemed to be much more attached to the mystery of 324. The figure could have answered so many of his questions, had it not been so domineering and uncommunicative. As usual the decision was made for him, he had to just keep going, blind to his destination with no other alternative available to him. Unite the twelve, complete the sphere and be left powerless to the outcome. Michael came back to his more localised predicament. How long could he inhabit the body of Stuart Mathieson? He could certainly think of worse ways to see out the rest of his days, than with this beautiful woman. *"What's her name?"* He said aloud. Michael searched the case and found an identification card on a lanyard with the same company logo written on it. She was stony faced like you had to be in an official photograph.

151

It did not take away from her attractiveness and Michael could not help but feel drawn to her. He gazed upon her blue eyes in awe at her immense beauty. *"Sophie….."* *"That's not very professional"* Sophie snuck up on him and snatched the badge from his hand *"Oh sorry ………..Sophie"* She closed over the case and turned to face him

"Well Cowboy?" Michael knew exactly what she was getting at. The ultimatum was made clear to him and without a pause he gave his reply; *"You"*. Sophie pounced at him and he allowed her to lavish him with a long and sensual kiss, this time with no retraction. The decision was made in his mind, he wasn't in his actual body, and so it wasn't cheating, was it? And in any case if he was to be stuck here for the foreseeable he might as well enjoy what little pleasures came his way. For all he knew he may have ended up in another warzone or any far less desirable location. *"O.K , let's go enjoy ourselves, the hunt is starting"* Sophie grabbed Michael's hand and dragged him through the door of the cabin, he reached for his Stetson and stuck it on his head, beginning to get much more relaxed with his new persona. His memories were becoming fainter with every passing minute that he spent being mesmerized by her charms. Sophie was beautiful, intriguing and exciting and she felt more genuine than anyone that he had encountered so far. Noritomo, Bernie and little Agnieska were all important to him, he had made real connections with them all, but this woman was just so perfect, he was completely captivated by every aspect of her physicality and her personality. It was almost as if she had been custom built to match every one of his desires. A bespoke model, she was perfect and Michael was completely under her spell. Outside the cabin, there was a party in full swing and it appeared that Stuart and Sophie were not the only attendees in fancy dress. The light was just beginning to fade and he determined that it must have been late afternoon. The terrain was a small forest which had been kitted out with temporary tents and toilets, as well as two large diesel generators on the back of matching pick-up trucks which appeared to be powering the cabins. The ground was marked with the signs that this area was used on a regular basis. In the centre of the makeshift camp was a main socialising area which was populated by a random mix of revellers all adorning a vast array of fancy dress. Marilyn Monroe hobbled past them wearing the most unsuitable of heels for the ground surface. She was closely followed by a man in a gorilla suit, he carried the head under his arm and both him and Marilyn were swigging bottles of beer and giggling with each other. Around the Campfire in the centre of the socialising area, a crowd had started to

assemble and Michael followed Sophie and joined the rest. Marilyn and the Gorilla were joined by Abraham Lincoln who was deep in debate about the current strength of the US Dollar with two oriental men who had come as Captain Kirk and Spock from Star Trek. They also swigged away at their alcoholic beverage of choice and everyone seemed to be in good spirits. A slightly overweight man in a sparkly white jumpsuit, stood up on a large tree stump near the centre of the opening. He had on large golden rimmed sun glasses and slick wig with large sideburns. *"Ladies and Gentlemen, attention please"* the crowd grew silent. *"Welcome to the third annual WTL Communications staff hootenanny"* a loud cheer and applause broke out for a few seconds and then the crowd focused on the speaker for his next announcement. *"My name is Elvis Arron Presley and I will be your host this evening"* the host struck a typical Elvis Presley style pose and swung his hips while simultaneously shouting *"Ah, thank you very much"*. The crowd erupted into laughter and Michael joined in, he was loving it. The idea of just letting go was too tempting and he carried on without a care. He was going to have some fun and try and forget everything for a while. The announcer continued *"O.K everyone, you have been put into teams of six, no cheating! The first team to find the lost jewels of Cleopatra and return them wins........3......2.....1......Go!"* Another enormous cheer erupted and the crowd split up into their teams of six and started to move off. Michael remained still and soon his team descended upon him. Marilyn and The gorilla man joined him along with Abraham Lincoln and to Michael's delight the superb Sophie. The final team member joined them a few minutes later, he was on a mobile phone and was arguing with what Michael had presumed to be his wife, having experience of a similar type of conversation with Kaitlin. The man was also incredibly drunk and it was clear that his presence was making the rest of the group uncomfortable. *"Listen Karen, I don't give two flying fucks about your mother"* the five team members all looked around at each other and the atmosphere was growing unbearably intense in anticipation of what this new member would bring to the team. *"You know what Karen, fuck her and fuck you too"*. The man hastily hung up and turned to face the rest of the group, he was dressed like a vampire, probably Dracula Michael thought. The Man looked at Michael and then turned his attention to Sophie, He looked her over from head to toe with a sneer that only a drunken man is capable off. *"Fuck me, alright hen?"* The hairs on Michael's neck stiffened and instinctively he stepped forwards towards him *"Hey Dracula, mind the language in front of the ladies eh?"* The man scowled with dissatisfaction and he pushed his face right up into Michael's *"And what are you going to do about it Nancy boy?"* The blow was quick and devastating. Michael had reacted and his heart pounded with adrenaline. The vampire fell to the dirt and was soon drinking his own blood which was leaking from his freshly pounded nostrils. The anger and jealous rage overcame Michael and he moved towards the man again. *"Stuart leave him"* Sophie's voice cut through Michaels rage like a peaceful and soothing injection of Valium and he stopped in his tracks instantly at her command. Her hold over him was incredible. Dracula picked himself up from the dirt and the rest of the team stood silent, awaiting his next move. *"Stick your stupid hunt, I'm off to get the necklace and throw it in the fuckin' river"* The vampire moved away into the darkness of the woods shouting obscenities as he went. *"It's in the cave anyway, that's where it's been the last four years, fuckin' stupid hunt"*. The man dressed as Abraham Lincoln approached Michael and in character removed his top hat and congratulated him, *"Well done sir, a fine strike indeed"*

"He deserved that, what an arsehole" The gorilla also felt the need to comment and shook Michael's hand. *"He is right though, it's in the cave"* Marilyn directed her comment towards Sophie who was in a world completely of her own, somewhat beaming with the glow of a saved damsel in distress. *"No point in us doing this hunt then?"* Sophie had pointed out the obvious and the rest of the team agreed. *"Meet us back at the fire in an hour, someone will have found it by then"*. The group split and headed off their separate ways. Sophie and Michael headed back towards their Cabin. The cabin was warm and the maid had been and cleared up the mess and made the bed which Sophie jumped on as soon as they entered and grabbed Michael, dragging him onto the bed beside her. *"Come here you"* She kissed him even more intensely than before and barely stopped for a gasp of air. *"My hero!"* She giggled, smiled and leaned over to the bedside lamp, dimming the light. Michael watched on as she stood at the bedside and started to remove her clothes slowly. His heart raced like it had when he first encountered a naked female, when he was a young acne covered virgin schoolboy. He was a gibbering wreck, brought on by the most amazing and shapely figure being gradually revealed before him. Sophie kneeled down on the bed before him and started to undress him, this time there was no hesitation and his desire had blocked out any feeling of guilt which may still have lingered. Before long her naked warm skin touched his and Michael took long, slow breaths inhaling the sweet smell which emanated from her. She

smelled as good as she looked. Michael closed his eyes and soaked up every touch and movement of her body. How could one person be so perfect he thought, she had everything, the right look, she spoke the right words, and she even smelt the right way. He was beaten, nothing could stop him from going down the path which he was taking. For now Michael Cameron was gone and Stuart Mathieson's life was far more appealing. The next hour passed, and for the first time in so long, the hour actually seemed to pass in real time. So much time had been lost in confusion. This hour had passed just right, maybe even longer. Every second was intense and spectacular. Michael lay gazing at the light brown locks of hair and for the time being had forgotten all about Kaitlin and Joseph. *"Sophie"* she stirred and wriggles but did not wake *"Sophie"* Sophie pushed her body close into Michael's and gripped his hand in hers *"I know let's go…..do we have too?"* *"Yeah, let's get drunk"* Michael laughed and poured them both a glass of the complimentary wine which had appeared in an ice bucket on the bedside table. The pair laughed and giggled while they got dressed and then headed back to the fireside to meet with the others. The crowd had already started to replenish and soon they were all back, minus a few who had either fell asleep drunk or simply given up on the hunt. Elvis returned as master of ceremonies *"Ladies and Gentlemen……it appears we have a problem"*. A confused grumble of voices rippled through the crowd until Elvis continued pointing in the direction of the two oriental men from before *"Captain Kirk and Spock were the first to reach the cave, only to find that the necklace of Cleopatra had already gone……so own up, who is the spoilsport?"* By this time Marilyn and the gorilla were completely drunk and the gorilla was not shy at immediately fingering the culprit *"It was that Dracula prick"*

"Johnny, Language" Marilyn quickly scolded the gorilla for his words, having seen what had happened the last time someone used colourful language in front of the ladies. *"He was drunk and said he was going to throw it in the river"* Sophie explained. The crowd was again rippled with localised conversation *"O.K everyone, keep it down."* Elvis quietened the crowd and then issued instructions, *"We need to split up and search for him……it's dark now and if he is drunk he might get lost in the woods"*. The party atmosphere was all but a distant memory now and the revellers split up and began to search the area in twos. Sophie and Michael headed towards the river and held hands, sauntering along smiling and being pretty pleased with themselves. The river was shallow and was quite well lit under the little floodlights

which were attached to a small wooden bridge which crossed to the other side. They moved to the bridge and stood peering over the side as the shallow water trickled over the smooth pebbles on the river bed. *"I wonder where that clown is"*

"You really got him a cracker" the pair sniggered like a couple of lovesick teenagers and Michael moves his arm over her shoulders pulling her close to his body. They both stared into the water below, snuggled together to keep warm. The transparency of the running water began to fill with an increasingly more cloudy mixture. At first the change seemed unimportant until the fluid became far more viscous. Sophie let out a panicked shriek. The river had now started to flow red with the blood of a body lying face down just upstream. *"Look, there is someone in the river Sophie"* Michael jumped off the bridge and sprinted up the river bank towards the body. The long black cloak was the only give away to its identity. *"It's him isn't it?"* Sophie was sheepish and clung to Michael like a frightened child *"I think so, looks like his costume"*

"What's wrong? We heard a scream" Captain Kirk and Spock had now joined them having been alerted by Sophie's scream *"Shit, it's him isn't it?"* the smaller of the two oriental men spoke first, he had come as Spock while his considerably taller companion came as kirk, they seemed friendly and the larger of the two joined the conversation *"We should go get Elvis"* Kirk made a good point and they all agreed that they would wait while he headed back to get the master of ceremonies. *"Wonder what happened, did you move him?"*

"No we never touched him" Michael explained. Sophie and Spock spoke in perfect unison as they highlighted something that none of them had considered *"What if he's not dead?"*

"Quick help me then" Michael beckoned Spock to assist him and they attempted to turn him over. *"He weighs a ton!"* Both men pushed and pulled until eventually the lifeless carcass of Dracula was lying face up with his injuries on show for all to see. Sophie let out a horrified squeak *"Oh, that's horrible, what is it?"* She turned her face into Michael's chest to hide her view from what was a grotesque sight. There was a large wound on the chest and his white shirt was soaked in blood, it was fresh and dark, like red wine. *"Yeah, what is that?"* Spock pointed at the wound on his chest and tried to ascertain what was protruding from the freshly cut flesh. The body was in such a mess it was difficult to tell what was costume, flesh or stabbing

156

implement. *"O.K. O.K, step back, give me some space"* Elvis had returned and tried to take charge of the situation. A crowd had started to collect, having heard of the demise of Dracula *"Well it looks like we have a winner"* Elvis pointed to the murder weapon sticking from Dracula's chest. *"It's Cleo's jewel"*. Elvis moved in closer to the victim and reached for the necklace attached to the jewel. *"Wait!"* Sophie stopped him just before he touched it. *"You can't touch that, not till the police get here"*

"He's dead, not going to make much difference now is it?" The crowd erupted into concerned chatter amongst themselves until someone with an unusually similar sense of control *"This looks like no accident people, there could be serious consequences for tampering with a murder scene"* Lincoln's comments sent a ripple of panic through the crowd, although his words were measured and sensible, he had highlighted that a murder had been committed which sent them even further into a chaotic rabble which forced Elvis to interject once more. *"O.K everyone, try and remain calm please. Lincoln is correct in what he says, I will call the sheriff now. He is at least three hours away"*. More outbursts of concerned panic shot through the revellers as their isolation was made far more apparent. A shout came out from the back of the crowd *"So that means that one of us here did this then?"* The crowd then descended into mass panic at the realisation that they had a killer in their midst *"Everybody, shut up!"* Elvis had completely lost his professionalism and was reduced to shouting, to try and keep the crowd calm and focused. *"For all we know, he could have tripped and fell onto it, we will take turns to guard the body until the Sherriff arrives. No one is to wander off, stay indoors if possible."* Most of the crowd concurred with Elvis's suggestion, but there was one person who took it upon himself to add more fuel to the out of control fire that had started to rage in the revellers frightened minds. *"So, tell me again? A man dressed like a vampire accidently trips in a river and stakes himself through the heart?"* Johnny the gorilla made a good point, it was at any stretch of the imagination pretty far-fetched. Elvis studied the body in more detail *"Looks like he smashed his nose on the fall"*. Sophie gripped Michael's hand, realising how the broken nose could have made him look. Johnny the gorilla spoke out again, *"Nah, that's when 'The Suntan Kid' cracked him for his cheek"*. The latest revelation sent accusatory whispers through the crowd this time and Michael could feel the eyes beginning to peer at him suspiciously. Elvis interjected *"O.K calm down, please everyone. Until the sheriff arrives we need to remain calm and not start pointing*

157

the finger at anyone. I will take the first watch with the cowboy, the rest of you return to your cabins, lock your doors and remain inside until you are sent for". The crowd slowly began to dissipate, *"The sheriff's office has a register we provide when we booked, so they have everyone's home address, no-one is to leave".* Sophie kissed Michael softly and he felt her tears against his skin, *"Be careful"*

"Come with us" Marilyn ushered Sophie to join Johnny and her

"Good, Sophie, go with them, I'll be fine" Michael tried to remain as calm as he could under the circumstances. Soon he stood alone with the King himself. Conversation was few and far between with his watch partner and time seemed to drag on. Suddenly the heavens opened and a heavy downpour soaked Michael, Elvis and the unfortunate vampire. The blood on the chest began to wash away in the river, helped on by the battering rain. The necklace was now far easier to make out, it was small triangular jewels set in a thick band of gold like metal. Michael knew it was not the real thing as it had that cheap costume look to it. The main pendant which was stuck deep in the deceased chest was of far more interest to Michael. It was tubular and about four or five inches long, glowing with a light and sparkly blue glisten, soaked by a mixture of rain, river and diluted blood. It was the seventh fragment and its appearance brought Michael out of the love induced trance that Sophie had put him under. He had been completely lost in his role play as Stuart Mathieson that he had completely forgotten his far more pressing task at hand. Sophie would have to wait, and who cared how this poor individual had met his death, he had the next piece of the puzzle sticking out of his chest and Michael needed it. *"How long till the Sherriff gets here?"* *"Still two and a half hours"* Elvis sighed as he informed Michael of the long wait they still had ahead of them. Another half an hour passed and soon the waiting pair were replaced by the next watch. Lincoln returned with another of the party goers who had since disrobed and returned to his everyday attire. Lincoln it seemed had really gotten into his role and stood before them, still with beard and hat. *"Go get some sleep if you can, me and Abe will take over."* Elvis seemed glad at being relieved

"O.K stay awake though, and guard him and the necklace". He pointed at the now far clearer injury and headed off into the woods towards the cabins. Michael headed back, listening to their replacements as he went. *"Wow man, that's nasty Abe"*

"Indeed it is" Abraham's voice faded out as he walked off and was replaced by another *"Happy Birthday to you, Happy Birthday to you"* Michael could just make out the silhouette of Marilyn through the thin curtains of a cabin a few feet from Sophie and his. It looked as if Johnny the Gorilla was being treated to his own private show. Michael watched for a few seconds and decided to leave them too it. The cabin door swung open and was dark and silent. Sophie had obviously been the unwanted third wheel and retired to her own cabin. She lay upon the bed sleeping and Michael sat and watched her for a while. Her chest rose and fell with every breath that she took and Michael looked upon her with the same burning desire as before. What was it about her that he could not resist? He had an almost addicted attraction to her and unusually he felt no remorse or guilt for what he had done with her. Removing the little mirror from Sophie's bag, he gazed upon the face he had quite happily accepted as his for the past few hours I *"The Suntan Kid"* Michael sniggered and tossed the mirror down. The tanned, alien face had made his mind up for him, yet again he knew what had to be done. He had to return to the body take the fragment and move on. That would be seven of the twelve, one step closer to some answers. Surely that had to be the best course of action. Sophie stirred and Michael screwed his face up with fear that he had woken her. Saying goodbye would have been really hard, she was wonderful and he had a genuine desire not to leave her behind. The sound of her voice would only have put another stumbling block in front of his need to get on with his primary goal. He reached into the depths of his Stuart's case and grabbed the sphere, it buzzed and swirled with light as it always did upon his touch and he slipped silently out the cabin door avoiding a final look at the beautiful Sophie. He walked from the cabin and tried to put her to the back of his mind. The crime scene was unusually silent and it looked as if Lincoln and his partner had abandoned their post. Michael scanned the area and rushed to the bridge, the fragment was gone, it had been prised from the now almost completely blood soaked victim. Michael stood with his hands on the bridge side, gripping the wood until his fingers almost bled with frustration. He turned and started to head back towards the camp, he would have to wake Elvis and let him know what he had found. A rustling came from the darkened trees just a few metres from Dracula's corpse. Michael was on his guard *"Who's there?"* The rustling stopped instantly and Michael's attention was now completely focused *"I can hear you in there"* There was no answer and Michael turned to face where the noise had originated. He began to walk towards the trees. The floodlights from the bridge just about

penetrated them, allowing him to see the first few feet into the cover. His foot caught on a root sticking out from the ground and sent him tumbling to the forest floor. The darkness had now engulfed him as the light from the bridge was no longer of any help. Michael's eyes refocused as he found his way to his feet, his hand had landed in a sticky substance and he rubbed them together to try and remove it. Michael scanned the ground below him, now being able to see the tree root with more detail. It was in-fact a foot, one of four. It was the freshly slaughtered bodies of the latest watch. Lincoln and his mate had been slit precisely from ear to ear and the newly opened wounds had provided the sticky substance which was now all over him. The bushes rustled and Michael was pounced at by a far more lively body. *"Another nosy one eh?"* The person sounded familiar and swiped at Michael with a large serrated knife which he jumped backwards to avoid *"First that arsehole ruins my event and then fuckin' Lincoln, too smart for his own good that one. And him, well he's just the unfortunate witness"* Michael backed off as Elvis made random swipes in his direction *"But you, you're just a nosy bastard, I've never liked nosy bastards"* Michael could hear the maniacal breathing and psychotic rage building in his attacker's voice. He took his chance and turned, running towards the camp. Elvis followed him closely, swiping frantically at his back, trying to cut him down. Around his neck hung the Fragment, it shone in the light of the moon and swung from side to side. A small tuft of grass wrong footed Michael and his ankle doubled over on itself and he crashed to the ground. He was in agony and was now incapable of escape. Towering over him, Elvis raised the knife high above his head, he smirked with pleasure as he thrust the blade deep into Michael's belly, twisting the blade and laughing with joy. The pain was sore upon entry but his body numbed almost instantly and he felt strangely at peace. *"No!"* Sophie screamed with anguish as she witnessed Michael's attack, she had approached from the darkness of the wood and swung a large metal spade towards the back of Elvis's head, caving his skull on impact and killing him instantly. Sophie dropped the spade and tended to Michael immediately *"Don't, move, stay with me"* Michael felt warm and fuzzy, he could not speak even if he wanted to and was fading fast. His vision blurred and soon Sophie was nothing but a mixture of colour with a vague outline. Sophie reached into Michael's canvas bag and removed the sphere, she seemed to be familiar with it. Placing the sphere upon his chest she quickly snapped the fragment from Elvis's neck. Stroking Michael's face and kissing his forehead, she slipped the fragment into place. The light engulfed them and Michael struggled to remain conscious, his

160

limited vision focused on Sophie's every move. She leaned over him and began to whisper in his ear *"Unite the twelve…..and don't forget me 324"*

Chapter 12

High Stakes and No Brakes

The transportation felt like the single blink of his eye. Michael's vision returned a few seconds before his hearing. Before him was a vast surface which was covered in green material. The sense of touch came back to the palms of his hands and he pressed his fingers into the soft felt fabric on the table in front of him. He was surrounded by people. They were all sitting evenly spaced around him and were different in age gender and general appearance. A little old lady sat to his immediate left, she wore thin rimmed spectacles, and they were square in shape with a string attached to the end of the legs which were hanging around her neck. The old lady's hair was like a big ball of candy floss, bouffant white, with a pink or purple tint through it. The smell of sticky, sweet hairspray filled his nostrils. On the old lady's left was a man, he was large and she was dwarfed by him while she sat in his shadow. He wore a black satin shirt with a silver lining and he had the thickest of moustaches which created an archway over his mouth which he periodically lifted a large cigar up to and blew large puffs of smoke up and over the rim of his white Stetson. Time seemed to slow as Michael scanned each individual in turn, he had not yet fully engaged with his surroundings. The table was round and the group consisted of six people in total. The soft green felt under his fingertips was accompanied by chips, cards and a selection of beverages along with a few ashtrays. He had landed smack bang in the middle of a poker game. The sounds from all around him were constant and varied, there was the chatter of many voices, he was in a very public place, there was music being blared out from speakers throughout the area and the slot machines clicked and rang bells like the rumblings of machinery on a factory shop floor. Michael tried to soak up as much of his new locale as possible before he was interrupted *"25"*, one of the six attempted to gain Michael's attention *"25?"*. It was the dealer, she must have been in her early twenties and had dark brown hair, neatly brushed into a business like pony tail. She wore a blindingly white blouse and her demeanour was professional as you would expect from a croupier. *"You in or what?"* The man sitting next to the large cigar smoking man had lost patience with Michael's lack of action. *"Leave the kid alone, he's thinking"* interrupted the large man *"Take your time son, could be your last hand"*. The impatient man took far less interest in his physical appearance, he had all the hall marks of a man who gambled not only with money but with his very existence. He wore jeans and an old worn t-shirt, his fingernails were filled with dirt and he lit one cigarette after another which had resulted in two fingers on his hand being almost brown in colour with nicotine. He stared at Michael and his unnerving glare encouraged him to pick up his cards and have a look. They all had two cards each which no one else at the table was allowed to see. On the table in the middle in front of the dealer there were three more cards face up. Michael recognised the game immediately, he had played "Texas Hold-Em" a few times before with a few of the men that he worked with at the office. He raised his cards and looked at them, he had a three of spades and a nine of diamonds. The three cards on the table consisted of a queen of diamonds, a four of clubs and a six of diamonds. The object of the game was to get the best possible hand from their own two cards and the community cards on the table. Michael looked towards the dealer *"How much?"*

"25 sir" the impatient man barked in his direction again

"How many times? 25!" Michael picked up his chips and threw them down on the table. The impatient man sighed to signal his relief that his wait was over and turned his gaze immediately to the little old lady. As the game moved around the table, Michael was able to see the rest of the group free from the impatience of the nicotine stained timekeeper. There were two more people, the first left of the dealer was an oriental woman, she must have been in her forties and had the look of someone who had spent many a night sat at a table playing cards. She had lots of jewellery on and wore a pair of diamond encrusted shades which covered half her face, obviously an important part of her poker uniform. The oriental woman sat still and silent and stared at a fixed point on the table, appearing sometimes to be completely devoid of emotion or personality. Ideal for a poker player Michael thought. The final member of the group was an Afro-American male in his late twenties, he had a massive pile of chips in comparison to everyone else's. At a nearby table, two girls kept waving and smiling at him, they were both really slim and pretty and Michael could recognise gold-diggers when he seen them. The man was a *'Player'* and reminded Michael of the hip – hop stereotypes he had watched on music channels back home. *"250 kid"* The large cowboy reminded Michael to play, 250 was a lot, counting his chips he noticed that another community card had appeared on the table and it was another diamond. Michael's interest was now captured and he gave the game the due attention it deserved, he only needed one more diamond for a flush. *"All in"* Michael pushed all his chips to the centre of the table, it was about 450 chips. *"Flush draw, he wants a*

163

diamond" The impatient man liked Michael's decisiveness. The game moved around the table with all the players folding until only Michael and the *"Player"* remained *"450?"* He stacked his chips and fiddled with them, while trying to work out if Michael was bluffing with an icy stare *"Call"* The player turned his cards and produced two queens, he had three of a kind, and only a diamond could save Michael now. The dealer turned the last card, it was a two of spades *"No luck kid".* The big pile of chips on the table got even bigger as Michael's last chips were added to it. Michael stood up from his table and moved to a stool at a nearby slot machine, the other players, still focused on their game did not even bat an eyelid at his departure. The casino was enormous and bells ringing from slot machines filled the room, waitresses scurried around delivering drinks to patrons happy to throw their money away on the varied games of chance and luck. Michael scanned the casino floor until he spotted a sign for the gents. He stood up and made his way across the casino floor, not stopping until he was safely locked inside one of the cubicles. Emptying his pockets, he placed all the items on the cistern block. A bunch of keys of varying shapes and sizes, a wallet packed full with notes. There must have been thousands of dollars *"U.S again"* he whispered. There was no bag, no sphere and no fragment. The only other item was a small metal tin, it was yellowish in colour, like brass or a similar metal. Upon it was two words *"Bobby's Shit!"* The tin popped open and the aroma of the sweet smelling contents wafted up Michael's nose. It was obvious to him what it was, he remembered partaking in some recreational dope smoking when he was a lot younger. The toilets main door swung open and Michael quickly packed away the contents of his pockets and sat in silence. The sound of the man relieving himself rung out as he splashed against the ceramic urinal. It was followed by the systematic use of the sink and then the hand dryer. Soon he was on his own again. Michael stroked his head and sighed, he was tired and just wanted to go home. Sitting for about ten minutes, he thought of Kaitlin and Joseph, he missed them so much. He knew that even if he seen this through to the end and he was returned home, it would be a sad and lonely existence that he was returning too. *"Hope"* Michael spoke aloud *"A second chance"* Again he spoke and rose to his feet, he had to believe that he was experiencing some sort of test from a higher power which would reward him in some way for re-uniting the sphere with all its missing parts. Just keep going he thought, there were 12 slots in the sphere and he had already gotten seven of them, maybe he could see them again. He opened the cubicle door and let out a yelp of fright as he was met by the steely stare of a young man, he was black and in his late teens or early twenties with a red baseball cap, jeans and a black canvas bomber jacket. He stared at Michael with an uncomfortable expression on his face and he stared back at him, both still and stiff as boards. Michael decided to break the ice *"Scuse' me"*. The youth copied his facial expressions and moved as if to mimic him, and then the penny dropped. Michael laughed long and hard, there was no youth, the cubicle that he had been in was facing the mirrors which spanned the height of the room. He was staring at his own reflection. He chuckled to himself, thinking of why he was not used to his cohabitation by now. The door swung open again and the large cowboy entered the bathroom. Michael's heart skipped a beat again, he was on edge, still startled by his reflection. The latest patron of rest rooms entered like a bull in a china shop and Michael almost fell down the toilet as he shouted gruffly through the cubicle door. *"Hey Kid. You ready for the next hand?"*

"Yeah, sure" Michael exited the cubicle and proceeded to wash and dry his hands, giving the impression that he had just utilised the toilet in the normal fashion, rather than unveil the truth that he had used it as a refuge while he determined his current supernatural predicament. Michael left the bathroom, closely followed by the cowboy, they sat down in their previous positions and the dealer commenced shuffling the cards on the table. The old woman sipped from a small crystal glass and Michael watched as a drop of the mahogany liquid rolled down her chin and plummeted to the green felt. Michael averted his gaze as the old lady lifted her head to check and see whether anyone had noticed her little accident. She rubbed the mark for a few seconds until it evaporated. The dealer looked in Michael's direction and raised her eyebrow with expectancy. *"$500 dollar entry sir?"* Michael searched his person and produced a wallet. He removed five crisp $100 bills and placed them on the table. The impatient man's eyes were transfixed on Michael's wallet and he quickly shut it and returned it to his pocket. Michael moved to push the bills towards the dealer and was interrupted by a faint buzzing, it was not the sphere and it was a few seconds before he noticed the muffled vibration from his jacket pocket. Michael reached into his jacket and removed a mobile phone, the impatient man let out a groan of disapproval and Michael glanced to the dealer who nodded her head, allowing him the time to take the call *"Two minutes sir"*

"Thank you, sorry everyone" The impatient man let out an exaggerated sigh and lit another cigarette, adding to his already disgustingly stained fingers. The player had sat quietly until this point

and stood up from the table and headed to the bathroom. Michael looked at the display on the mobile and it read "Kung Fu". He held it up to his ear and pressed the little green telephone below the screen *"Sup bro?"*

"Hello, who is it?" Michael answered sheepishly

"It's me bro………………..Fu?"

"O.K what's up?" Michael tried to leave his answers as open ended as he could, after all his current mission's parameters had not yet been specified and the person on the other side of the phone could have been the key to finding the sphere and the next fragment. *"What you mean, what's up?"* The few moments' awkward silence felt like an age and he struggled to find another nonspecific response. *"I'm outside bro, oh man, are you wasted?"* *"No…….no, I'll be right out"*

"Cool, hurry up" The phone clicked and the voice was replaced by the dull tone of a dead line. Michael approached the table *"Sorry…..I'm out"*

"No problem, thank you sir" The dealer was professional and courteous, quickly cleaning away his space at the table. The other players glanced towards him bidding him farewell with a collection of nods and smiles. The impatient man sat counting his chips and never acknowledged his departure at all. Michael headed for the main exit and was stopped on his way by the Player who was returning from the bathroom *"That you boosting?"*

"Yeah, home time"

"We never got much time to talk, you know?" Michael was confused by the sudden onslaught of interaction from the Player, he had been so uncommunicative so far and Michael stood staring blankly at him. *"Karina………..Yo Karina, bring my jacket"* One of the players scantily clad entourage stood up and hitched her skirt down as it rode close to revealing a little too much leg and gingerly walked towards them. She was a little drunk and the player smirked at Michael as she struggled in her enormous heels. Reaching into his jacket, he revealed a small card, the size of a credit card and handed it Michael. *"Your call man…..later"* The player put his hand around the shoulders of the girl and swaggered off like a stereotypical pimp. Michael had likened her to a concubine of an old English king or a person of similar status, she seemed to dote on every one of his words and Michael sensed an element of fear in her. The player carried himself like someone who expected this sort of behaviour from his company. The business card read *"Cartel productions, Las Vegas, Kris Cartel, 555-38-324"* Michael's eyes widened with realisation, was it another sign or purely a coincidental phone number. He slipped into deep thought, considering

166

the complicated mystery of the ever re occurring 324. Its significance was still a mystery to him and he gazed at the card in his hand until he was awoken by a firm punch to his upper arm *"What you doing punk? You are wasted bro! Come on let's go"* The assailant was about the same age as Michael's current shell, he was white and kind of scruffy looking. He wore a green army style jacket and blue denims. His hair was shoulder length, brown and greasy looking. Michael followed him out the main door and they headed to a car park, not far from the entrance. The vehicle's lock clicked open, accompanied by the lights flashing in unison. The remote locking had served as an indication as to Michael's destination and he headed to the now opened station wagon. It was old and had seen better days, definitely in the budget range. Both of them entered and closed the doors behind them. Michael was in the passenger's seat. *"You got my shit?"* Michael remembered the little tin he had investigated while in the casino bathroom and removed it from his jacket *"Yes! Thanks man"*. The man reached and grabbed the tin from Michael's hand, he planted a big kiss on its surface *"I thought I'd lost it, had this for years"*

"No problem Bobby". Michael took a stab at his name, after all it was obviously his tin. *"You sure you're all right man? Call me Fu for fucks sake, you know I hate Bobby. It's not like I call you Stephen"*

"O.K Fu, Sorry" Fu removed the contents of the tin and Michael watched as he rapidly assembled the various components into a well-practised and perfect little joint. He rolled the window down and tilted his seat back slightly. Lifting the lighter to his mouth he took a deliberately long and heavy drag. The smoke billowed out from his mouth and soon the cockpit of the station wagon was filled with a creamy, hot smoke. The smell was not unpleasant and he watched as Fu sucked back another enormous inhalation *"So what was he like?"*

"Who?"

"Cartel man, who do you think?"

"Oh right yeah, he gave me this" Michael reached over and handed the card to Fu which he had received from the player. *"And.......?"* Fu beckoned Michael to be a bit more descriptive on the events which had taken place in the casino. *"Well............... I lost a flush draw"*

"Fuck the poker bro, come on Chuck, what is happening?" Michael was taken aback by his name. He would have thought a black American teenager would have had a far less white name. Chuck was so typically Caucasian. *"He said It was my call........think he wants me to call him"* Michael was trying to seem as in control as he could.

"Excellent buddy, this could be the break we are looking for" Michael smiled and tried to share the excitement for the as yet unknown. Fu was visibly buzzing from the news "Fu and Chuck living the dream man" He started up the station wagon and after around three attempts it spluttered into life. He passed the joint to Michael who looked upon it with caution and temptation at the same time. He took it from Fu's hand, not wanting to seem any more unusual than he already had. "Let's go to the Lock up then bro"

"Let's go then…Fu" Fu smiled, struggling to contain his beaming grin, he was obviously really happy about whatever was unfolding. Michael looked at the smouldering joint in his hand and raised it up to his lips. It was hot and he inhaled slow and steady, so as not to burn his throat. The flavour was sweet and woody. The microscopic particles of ash and fibre tickled the back of his throat, forcing his body to instinctively react. He spluttered and coughed until the irritation subsided "Yeah bro, it's good shit?" Michael nodded and smiled at Fu. The second drag was far easier to handle as he was sure not to make the same mistake twice. He blew the smoke out in a long and measured puff, and then passed the joint back to Fu, who accepted it gladly. Michael's face felt odd and he experienced hot and cold rushes through his body. The lights from other cars and buildings flashed all around him as he stared out the window. He watched as single stationary bulbs elongated into long comet like splashes of colour. He was stoned and was experiencing the visual and auditory after effects. Fu was talking at great speed about something that was incomprehensible in Michael's current state and he sat silently as he drove them to yet another unknown destination. His eyes blinked regularly as he tried to refocus on his companion. The joint had gone straight to his head and he shut his eyes in an effort to stop the wooziness. Michael passed out and was soon engrossed in a vivid and captivating dream. He was stood in a room and was surrounded by uniformed men. They all had their backs to him and they were dressed in exactly the same bright red overalls. The men all had the same haircut and seemed to stand devoid of personality like a row of zombies. At the far end of the room was a tinted window. Michael's attention was drawn to it and he stared intently, trying to decipher what was behind it. He could just make out the silhouette of two people. Their features where not clear, but he could tell that it was a man and a woman. The men in the red overalls started to chant in perfect timing as they moved forward as if on a conveyor belt in a factory. They shifted away from Michael's position. A large gap in the floor opened up before them revealing a bottomless and lifeless pit of darkness. A klaxon sounded and the first row of men plummeted down the gap into the nothingness. They were followed by the next row and the process continued, consuming and reproducing them in an eternal cycle. Michael began to move forward, taking his place among the ranks of the red simpletons. He reached the front row and he felt his stomach churn as he dangled precariously over the edge. Behind him the men had continued to pile up and Michael was sent plummeting through the darkness into oblivion. *"Chuck…..Chuck….!"* Michael awoke, slumped in the same place he had fell asleep *"Man, you are such a lightweight"*

"How long was I out?"

"Just a few minutes man, let's get in" Michael rubbed his eyes and stretched his face out, he was a little more grounded than before his sleep. The odd dream stuck in his mind as he exited the station wagon. Fu reached for a garage door and pulled it upwards, rolling the shutter on its rails, only to pull it down behind after they were both safely inside. The garage was quite large and Michael perused its contents, quickly ascertaining that whoever owned the garage, they must have spent a considerable amount of time there. There was a variety of paraphernalia connected with the recreational smoking of marijuana. There were a few sofas and couches which had throws over them, in an attempt to disguise they had definitely passed their best. The walls were plastered with lots of posters. One side was covered in musical artists from almost every genre imaginable. The opposite wall was homage to the martial arts, a display of all the famous champions of past and present. The famous hard men were accompanied by the infamous also. A large poster featuring Mike Tyson in a typically menacing pose caught Michael's eye until he was distracted by the glaringly obvious centre piece of the shrine. There were two posters of equal size, which had no others encroaching on them unlike the rest of the wall space. These two seemed to have a special importance to the occupants. Michael perused them for a little longer and he soon realised what he was staring at. A white male, bulging with muscle and loosely maintained facial hair looked back at him. The Bottom of the poster had been carefully written upon with indelible black ink *"Chuck Norris: Legend"*. The second poster was an equally macho representation of Bruce Lee and was similarly inscribed *"Bruce Lee: Kung Fu Master"* Fu joined Michael and stood alongside him, staring at their heroes who they and had adopted their pet names from. *"We should get the gear ready Chuck"* Michael nodded in agreement and followed Fu through the back of the Garage and out a small access door. They crossed a small back yard and approached a

169

wooden trapdoor, horizontal at ground level. It was difficult to make out through the overgrown garden. Fu unlocked the large iron padlock and the trapdoor rose slowly upwards. It was on a spring which creaked slightly as it ascended, reminding Michael of the annoying hospital door. After descending around a dozen stairs, Fu produced another key and unlocked a larger door which carried far more weight, intended to protect whatever lay beyond it. They were now in darkness and Michael grew anxious, not knowing where he was being taken too. The joint had also heightened his paranoia. The door swung open under its own weight and Michael was almost knocked on his backside by the overpowering aroma of marijuana. The cellar was vast, it must have been at least fifteen metre squared and every spare bit of floor space was completely covered with plants. They were about five feet high and all sparkled with tiny glistening crystals. Michael knew immediately what he had walked into, It was a cannabis farm, but on an enormous scale. *"Never get sick of looking at it eh?"* Fu had seen Michael's astounded reaction and had surmised that he was just looking upon the plants with the same feeling of great pride that he felt himself and not that he was actually dumbfounded with fresh amazement. Michael followed Fu through a long corridor lined with the narcotic shrubbery and they reached a small office like area at the other side. There was a small desk with a computer on it and it was surrounded by bags of fertiliser which were piled almost as high as the ceiling. *"O.K then, call him"*

      "What will I say?"

      "We agreed tomorrow at 11:30, right?"

      "O.K" Michael reached into his pocket and removed his mobile phone, he was ready to make a call to the man who he now knew as Kris Cartel. *"What you doing? You're fucking losing it man?"* Michael stopped what he was doing and looked at Fu, puzzled by his interjection. *"Don't use your own phone man, these guys are heavy dudes remember, the disposable one is in the drawer"* Fu looked concerned at Michaels lack of understanding, Cartel must have been a dangerous man. He reached into the drawer and pulled his hand back after a painful snap of static electricity shot through his fingertip. *"Whoa man, I heard that"* Fu smiled in an obvious attempt to put this friend at ease. Michael peered into the drawer again, this time wary of any further unwelcome surprises. It was packed full of debris of a particular type. Lighters and empty cigarette paper packets were mixed with chocolate bar wrappers. Michael had come to realise that Chuck and Fu were involved in far more than just a recreational smoke. A little basic mobile phone lay side by side with a tin which was almost

identical to the one from before. This time the tin read *"Stephen's shit"* Michael lifted the phone and the tin and left them on the desk. *"Good idea, your turn"* Michael panicked at the thought of the outcome of his attempts to build the next joint. *"I'll phone, you do it"*

    "Yeah sure thing boss, I'm using your shit though" Fu sniggered and opened the tin. It was almost identical in content. *"You still got this old thing"* Michael watched as Fu removed the eighth fragment from the tin. It had lost some of its lustre due to the dustiness it was covered in from the contents of the tin. The mobile phone crashed to the floor and Michael held his hand out, urging Fu to hand it over *"Don't fret bro, I'll look after it. Make the call"*. Michael contained his desire to grab it from him and picked up the mobile. He started to dial the number from the card *"21 and still got a lucky stone, ha pussy"* Michael smiled back at Fu, glad in the knowledge that he had no idea just how important it was to him. *"Yeah?"* The voice on the other side of the line answered abruptly. *"It's Stephen from earlier"*

       "Yeah?"

       "Tomorrow at 11:30 cool?"

       "Meet me at the scrapyard"

    "Cool" The line cut off and a dead tone filled Michael's ears once again *"Give"* Michael pointed to his lucky stone. *"Here you go man, you really are getting weirder"* Both guys laughed and Michael gripped the fragment tightly in his hand. He slipped it into his inside pocket to keep it safe. He was fifty percent through now, just the sphere to locate. *"O.K bro, we need to get started"* Fu stood up and headed back to the main room with all the plants *"No smoke till were done, then we get smashed? Deal?"* Michael agreed and stood awaiting his next instruction, Fu it seemed had taken a lot more to do with the plants and Michael was happy to labour to him as long as it got him to the sphere. Fu handed him a pair of small garden clippers, the type used for pruning a hedge or small tree along with a handful of heavy black refuge sacks. *"O.K you start there and we will meet in the middle"* Fu disappeared behind the forest of weed and started to fiddle with an old stereo. Before long the cellar was filled up with the sound of music that Michael was unfamiliar with, but he tapped his foot along with it and found himself enjoying it. He approached the first plant and snipped of a large bud on a leafy stalk and placed it in the bag. *"Fu!"*

       "What's up man?"

       "Just the buds?"

"Yeah bro, we will process the rest later, Just the good stuff for Cartel" Michael removed the first snipping and cut it clean at the stalk, leaving just the thick sticky bud. The next few hours were spent harvesting the illegal crop. By the end of the night they had accumulated ten packed sacks. Both Michael and Fu reeked of it. They were both speckled with tiny particles of green leaf, through their hair and all over the cellar. It took around another hour of hard work to clean up the floor space. *"At last"* Michael sighed and Fu acknowledged their joint effort with a high five *"Dooby?"*

"Why not" Michael had got a taste for it. He might as well, he was not going to fail a drug test. That was Chuck's problem. The pair moved back to the office area and Fu picked up the joint from before *"Glad I rolled this earlier"* He lit and passed it to Michael straight away. He savoured the thick and creamy white smoke and soon they were both wasted again. The hours seemed to disappear and they spent the night giggling and listening to music. Fu produced a small acoustic guitar and they sang songs as well as having highly charged conversations about music, martial arts, war and religion. The grass had really helped Michael to relax and he once again had become consumed by his current persona. The veil he was so used to wearing to hide his true being had been lifted monetarily. *"Fu?"* Fu was nearly asleep. He slumped in his chair with his eyes barely opened *"Sup bro?"*

"Is this real?"

"What you saying bro?"

"I mean, are we real? Do you know who I am?"

"Ha, ha bro, you're wasted" Fu struggled to reply and slurred his words before he drifted off to sleep and Michael was left to sit with his own thoughts. Whatever was happening to him, it looked as if Fu was oblivious to it, just like mostly everyone he had encountered. He sat for a while looking at the fragment and deliberating on the events of his visit. Sitting up quickly, Michael was sobered by a memory of Sophie which popped into the forefront of his mind. She knew. Fu is oblivious, but Sophie knew, she had to. Michael remembered how he was incapacitated and she used the sphere to save him. Who could she have been? Michael went over the details in his mind again. Sophie, the black figure. They were more than just another character in his exploits, and in both their cases he did not get the chance to quiz them. He made a decision to try and stay more aware of the unusual and not miss an opportunity again. Fu was out cold and Michael envied his capacity to be able to fall asleep in an upright position. He grabbed the tin and attempted to build another. Hoping it would knock him out and let him get to sleep for a few hours at least. The

skill had long since abandoned him and he took a little pipe which Fu and he had used earlier. Filling up the chamber he inhaled vigorously. It felt like a blink of an eye when he was being woken by the smell of fresh coffee *"Hey Chuck..........coffee"* Fu was awake and was already into the morning's proceedings. Michael's head throbbed and his throat was sore and dry. *"Big day ahead bro, drink this"* the coffee was too hot, but it was a welcome change to the awful taste he had in his mouth. *"What time is it?"*

      "11:05"

      "What!"

      "Don't worry, I've packed the shit"

      "Good"

      "Finish your coffee, I'll get you outside" Fu threw Michael the keys to the cellar and headed out to the station wagon. He finished his coffee and stood up, stretching and groaning simultaneously. He dusted himself down and pulled on his baseball cap which had fallen to the floor. *"Here goes nothing"*. He headed out to the station wagon. Fu stood waiting for him, smoking, what this time appeared to be a cigarette. He must have been keeping straight for the upcoming transaction him. *"Let's go then"* They jumped into the car and headed for the docks. The journey was over quickly and soon they approached the solid metal gates of the scrapyard. Michael noticed the isolated location *"Bit remote eh?"*

      "This is where Cartel does most of his business, must be safe" Fu put the engine in neutral and two large men in black suits and sunglasses stepped out from behind the towering layers of scrapped vehicles which surrounded them and approached the driver's side window. Pointing to a small shed with a large SUV with blacked out windows parked alongside it, they indicated for Fu to park up. Fu rolled down the window and the man spoke. *"You Steve?"*

      "Yup"

      "Go upstairs, boss is waiting" Michael looked at Fu, who was now visibly nervous, but still attempted to reassure his friend. *"Go on bro, I'll wait for you here"* Michael nodded in agreement and left the station wagon, he crossed the path of the men who looked upon him with distrust. The office was at the top of a flight of wooden stairs which Michael climbed and opened the office door. *"Come in"* Cartel stood and watched from the window as Fu backed the station wagon into the shed. The office was unusual. From the outside it looked like a basic log cabin, inside was a different story. It was kitted out like a penthouse apartment. Rugs, lights, complete with an enormous fish tank which was loaded with brightly coloured tropical specimens. They

danced around the central piece in the tank which was a large rock filled with many little holes that had bubbles emanating from them. It was topped with a black glasslike object which shone and sparkled almost as much as the fish. Michael's eyes met with the sphere and the tank rattled. Cartel rushed across the office towards the tank *"You feel that?"*

"Feel what?" Michael shook his head knowing all too well where the vibration had come from. The sphere this time had pride of place in a drug dealers pet project, that he had shown a great deal of concern for. Obtaining it could prove to be quite tricky this time. Cartel turned to look at him, and then strutted around the office like a peacock, obviously proud of his gangster image, purposefully trying to exert his authority. *"Stevie, Stevie, Stevie"* He paced the room and made Michael feel uneasy. He sat at his large oak desk and stared at him for a few moments *"How much for the Grass?"* Michael's heart sank. That detail was never discussed and he tried to bluff his way through. *"Usual?"*

"Usual? How about, I give you one of these?" Cartel removed a black semi-automatic pistol from his desk drawer and pointed it straight at Michael. He raised his hands immediately and was overcome with panic as the adrenalin pulsed through his body. The blast from the pistol was deafening and it caught him sending him to the ground in a bloody heap. Cartel approached the window and signalled his men below. He placed the gun on the desk and stepped over Michael's bloody body as he made his way down to the yard. Fu's face was bloodied and raw. He was kneeling with his hands tied behind his back. Cartel punched him into the ground with a series of heavy blows and then instructed his subordinates to lift him back to his feet. Michael's ear rung with agony and he slowly lifted himself to his feet. He approached the desk and perched on the end. The bullet had just grazed his head and he reached up to feel the damage, he was missing the top part of his ear and the pain was insufferable. The fish tank gargled and a large bubble of air ascended to the top of the water, which diverted Michael's attention to it. It was time to leave he thought. Fu screamed from the pier side and Michael moved silently to the window. The men were beating him badly. Michael moved quickly, he approached the tank and with an almighty push he sent it crashing to the floor. The rug was now covered in a frantic collection of flipping fish. Michael grabbed the sphere and snapped off some of the artificial rock which it had been set in. He headed out the door of the office and down the wooden steps as stealthily as he could. He slipped between the towers of scrap until he reached some cover and

174

took a quick peek at his targets. Michael took aim and fired a few shots, he watched as the man beating Fu slumped dead to the floor. Cartel dived into the shed and crouched between the other man and the station wagon. *"You're a dead man"* Cartel shouted over at Michael who was quick to respond *"And you need to learn how to shoot"* Cartel pushed one of his minions into the firing line *"Kill him, fool"* Michael popped up again and the man dropped after two bullets blasted through his chest. Fu coughed and groaned in pain *"What you going to do now?"* Cartel goaded him, while remaining hidden, aware of the possibility for him to share his colleague's fate. *"We just want to go, let us leave and you will never see us again"*. A few uncomfortable moments passed and Fu spluttered and coughed continuously. *"O.K, I can live with that, take the Escalade"* Cartel remained hidden and threw his keys towards Michael and they landed near his feet. Michael checked first then jumped into the driver's seat, keeping his gun pointed in Cartels direction the whole time. *"Fu, come on!"* Fu stumbled to his feet and climbed into the passenger side, shutting the door behind him. Michael dropped the pistol, slipped the shifter into drive and sped off. *"Thanks man, I thought you were dead"*

"No problem bro, we need a hospital" The escalade accelerated out onto the main road and Michael turned, barely missing the oncoming traffic. He put his foot down, accelerating down the main drag. *"Where is it Fu?"* Fu was getting increasingly light headed and struggled to reply *"Straight on bro"* the upcoming traffic lights changed to red and Michael slammed his foot down on the brake lever. There was no effect and the escalade shot through the red light. A loud horn sounded, it came from a massive rig which was smashed into the side of the escalade as it flew into the junction without warning. Michael's flashbacks were so vivid and frightening. He relived the horror of the crash in a few seconds as he and Fu were tossed around the cockpit of the SUV. Michael struggled to see through the blood streaming down his face. He wiped them and managed to open them enough to be met by the lifeless stare of Fu's corpse staring back at him. His body was mangled and contorted and Michael vomited without control at the grotesque sight of his friend's demise. He could not tell where the dashboard stopped and Fu began. He reached into the foot well where he had placed the sphere and it was not there. He felt around for a bit and realised what he had done. The sphere was lodged under the brake lever and had caused the accident. Michael screamed out in anguish after realising what he had done. Fu was dead and it was his fault. Michael wept and his eyes where filled with a mixture of salty water and thick fresh blood. The

sphere was stuck fast and Michael could not dislodge it as he grew weaker by the second, he reached down and clicked the eighth fragment into place. Immediately the pain subsided and he was engulfed in light. As he drifted off he listened to a distant voice, it wasn't Joseph or Kaitlin, and in fact it wasn't any voice he had heard so far. Although the words were all the more puzzling *"Wow, that was the best yet.........awesome!"*

Chapter 13

Fight Club

Michael opened his eyes and quickly shut them as the bright tungsten filament of an unsheathed light bulb pierced them painfully. His eyes filled with water and he could still see the imprinted image of the bulb when he shut them. The bulb was centralised on the ceiling and it dangled unspectacularly, occasionally flickering and dimming Michael's surroundings. There was no shade and the ceiling was faded white, dim and rather unimpressive. As his blurred vision subsided, Michael sat up from the horizontal position he had arrived in. The room was sparsely furnished and the bunk he rose from creaked horribly at his slightest of movements. The bunk was rusted and quite old and had a mattress which consisted of a simple wire mesh covered with a thin fabric matt. The opposite wall had a small stainless steel sink which had simple fixings. A single cold tap donned the tiny little sink and it appeared to have been well used as it had long lost its chrome effect finish. Standing up, Michael moved to the sink, his body cracked in several places, probably a result of sleeping on the feeble excuse for a bed. He turned the tap and the water trickled out at first until it settled. The pipework feeding the tap vibrated and echoed all around him, the noise faded into the distance and Michael could hear the echo faintly for what felt like an age. The structure was far bigger than the small room in which he found himself. The freezing cold water was a huge relief and he repeatedly splashed it on his face. Touching his face, Michael verified his gender, he had a bristly beard with at least a few months' worth of growth. It would have taking Michael Cameron a few months to grow one this length. The facial hair was not manicured and had been left to sprout naturally. The atmosphere was humid and Michael likened it to the evenings spent with his family on holiday in Spain in the middle of summer making him presume that it must have been the middle of summer. His body was moist with an uncomfortable layer of grimy sweat and the basic and well-worn underpants he was wearing were the only item of clothing he had on. After splashing more water on his face, Michael investigated the remaining contents of the room. The most obvious feature which he had overlooked indicated his current whereabouts. Solid black, painted steel bars reached from ceiling to roof on the wall directly behind where he had laid his head. The only other item within the room helped Michael to piece the location puzzle together. A tiny stainless steel toilet pan was set into the wall, floating about two feet from the floor. *"Well this is new"* He said aloud. The silence was broken when a klaxon sounded followed by a voice blasting over a speaker system. The announcement was muffled by crackling, the speaker system had seen better days. Everything he had seen so far in this place appeared to have passed its use by date. *"This is your first call, two minutes until inspection"* The klaxon sounded again and repeated the same announcement. Michael grabbed a bright yellow set of overalls which had been discarded in a heap next to his bunk and quickly pulled them on. An electronic buzz caught his attention and the cell door began to slowly move forward a couple of inches and then slide open automatically. Michael popped his head through the opening and watched as a long line of men in yellow boiler suits hurriedly exited their cells and stood to attention, still and silent. The block was enormous, rectangular in shape and Michael could see it was three levels high. On the ceiling was a large skylight which spanned the entire length of the block. Michael shielded his from the bright sun as it beat through the skylight, cooking the occupants of what was now obviously some sort of penitentiary. The men had all moved into position until all but one inmate stood outside his cell. The cell next to Michael's was stony silent. Michael had moved out and mimicked the behaviour of the others, so as to appear natural and well versed in the routine. The men were almost identical, if it was not for the variance in race and age, they could have been a collection of clones Michael thought. All standing upright and in unison wearing the identical yellow overalls. *"Morning Inspection commencing"*. The announcement had encouraged the inmates to stiffen their stance. Michael followed suit almost straining his neck trying to keep the same standard as the others. Peering over the edge of the third floor landing, Michael could see through the fenced barrier to the ground floor. A large iron door swung open and a group of suited men entered. One of them carried a clip board and they made their way across the block floor towards the first flight of stairs which allowed access to the three floors of the jail block. He watched on with interest and leaned out towards the railing to get a better view. A muted whisper alerted him and he turned to face the inmate from the cell next to his *"Hey, get back"* The man from the next cell was panicked and tried not to be seen moving or speaking. He stood as stiff as a board and spoke without making any eye contact *"You're crazy man, get in line"* Michael withdrew and fell back into formation. *"Two weeks, you should know better by now"* Michael turned his head and looked towards the man *"Jesus, and he still looks"* Michael snapped his

178

head back into position, the man's fear was far too obvious to ignore. He had seen too much recently which alerted him to possible mistreatment from his incarcerators. The crowd of suited men had made it to the second floor of the block and were walking the length of the block checking each of the inmates as they went. The clip board that the man carried was now more visible and Michael noticed that it was in fact a type of tablet computer. The operator flicked his finger over its surface and was accessing data which was too far away to be decipherable. They covered the entire second floor and made their way to the stairwell once more. The group consisted of the man with the tablet and two stocky armed guards, who carried some sort of baton on their belts. They were large and muscle bound and looked as if they were able to handle themselves. The remaining three men in the group followed behind, simply viewing the activities. They were smartly dressed and it was clear they were in the higher echelons of the organisation. They occasionally stopped at a particular cell and discussed the occupant in more detail. Michael likened it to three judges who were assessing which cow to award the blue rosette at a county fair. They were all dressed similarly, each with a black shirt. The most distinguishable difference was the ties they wore. Each had on a plain coloured one. Red, yellow and blue. The group made their way up to the third floor and worked their way across the landing towards Michael's position. Standing still, Michael heeded his neighbours warning and tried not to divert their attention to him. The man who wore the Yellow tie took centre stage and began to tell the others about something in great detail. Again it was out with Michael's earshot, but he dare not turn and look while they had been so close. The man with red tie interrupted the detailed description and spoke over his colleague *"Where is twenty five?"* The little man with the clipboard beckoned the guards to check the cell next to Michaels for the missing inmate, which prompted the man in the yellow tie to break the silence *"He is probably sleeping………he had a late night"* The man in the Yellow tie sniggered nervously as he awaited the outcome of the cell search, the two other suited men joined him in a muted chuckle, both with smug looks upon their faces and Michael noticed their delight that their host on the yellow floor had failed to produce a flawless visitation. The man with the clipboard emerged from the cell and was met with an impatient grunt from the man in the yellow tie *"Well man, where is he?"* He was sheepish and very reluctant to reply, Michael could almost smell the fear on him. *"Parker, I asked you a question?"*

179

"You should come and see Mr Cochrane" Cochrane entered the cell and a few minutes passed until they emerged. *"Twenty five won't be joining us this morning gentlemen"* The two men grinned, beaming with pleasure watching their yellow counterpart squirm as he proceeded to give them a more detailed description of what was going on. *"And more so, I need to apologise to you Mr Burbank, twenty five will not be joining you on the second floor"* the man with the blue tie nodded in acknowledgement. The man with the red tie laughed loud and hard *"Seems you dodged a bullet there Burbank."* Michael was amazed at their lack of compassion and glanced slightly in their direction, catching the man in the red tie's eye for a second. *"Cochrane, you need to get your house in order that one just looked at me".* The rage was easy to see in Cochrane's face. Michael could see the blood vessels on his face gradually filling up until he was as red as his counterpart's tie. Cochrane stood in front of him and screamed right into his face. Small particles of spittle landed on him and Michael struggled to remain calm. He showed enough restraint so as not to add any further fuel to the fire. *"How dare you look upon Mr Babcock, you know the rules. Guards!"* Removing their batons, the guards began to beat Michael around the head and body. The men watched on with no remorse and seemed to pay great attention to whether or not Michael could handle the beating *"O.K. O.K."* Cochrane stopped the onslaught and Michael struggled to remain conscious, *"Spark him".* The guards switched a small button on the bottom of their batons and they flashed into life. A blue bolt of electricity flowed from the base to the tip and a ring of bright light settled around the tip of the baton. They both touched Michael simultaneously and he shuddered for a few seconds until he passed out. *"O.K., shift this piece of crap out of my sight"* Cochrane turned to the others, *"I can only apologise Mr Babcock"*

"Not at all Mr Cochrane, comes with the job, up here on the third floor" Burbank interrupted *"Best weeding out the weaklings, bit of pain though.......for you I mean"* Burbank and Babcock chuckled again and Cochrane snapped back, *"Don't worry, he'll be ready, you'll have your replacement"*

"Good that's the spirit Cochrane" Babcock smiled and he began to walk away with Burbank. *"Mr Babcock!"* Cochrane shouted after him as he walked away *"We are going to need a replacement for twenty five"*

"See parker, he has the holo-roster"

"Thank you Mr Babcock", Cochrane stood and watched as Michael's body was dragged across the cell block floor towards the stairwell and he shouted on Parker; *"Parker, out here"*

"Yes sir, Mr Cochrane sir?"

"When they drop him off at the A.CT room, get them back to clear out twenty five's cell. Get the holo-roster also, we need a replacement"

"Yes Mr Cochrane sir"

"And Parker, no more duds, we can't afford another one to pop and show me up again"

"Yes sir". Cochrane walked off and Parker busied himself, talking to his tablet. *"Holo-roster"*. The tablet bleeped and responded

"Specify level"

"Entry level, yellow"

"Please wait". A few seconds passed and the device sprung into life, projecting a three dimensional image from its screen. It was the image of a man, a new inmate to be precise and it rotated three hundred and sixty degrees on its axis. It revolved as if it stood on the turntable of an old record player. Different statistics appeared and disappeared. Parker spent a short while perusing about a dozen candidates. *"Availability?"* The tablet responded immediately *"Available for immediate dispatch from penitentiary seventeen"*

"Confirm"

"Specify location"

"Replacement, penitentiary one, main block, floor three, cell twenty five"

"That location is currently occupied", Parker got annoyed and lightly bashed his fist against the side of the device. *"Replacement! Penitentiary one, main block, floor three, cell twenty five is deceased!"*

"Please wait". Parker tapped his finger impatiently on the side of the tablet *"Replacement confirmed"*. Parker sighed and slid the tablet under his arm. The guards returned and carried the corpse from the cell towards the stairwell *"straight to incineration"* *"O.K boss"* the

181

guards carried out their duty and Parker moved off towards the stairwell. *"Wake up idiot"* A bucket of freezing cold water splashed all over Michael. He lay on a hard and cold concrete floor and he ached all over from his beating *"Get up Chris, have you not had enough yet?"* Michael's eyes focused on his rude awakener, it was the inmate from before *"You really don't learn do you?"* Michael tried to ignore the pain and answered him

    "Where am I?"

    "Exactly where you deserve to be for your stupidity. Two days in the Shitbox"

    "Shitbox?" Hoping the inmate would elaborate, Michael just stood and stared at him blankly. *"Well, it's a tiny little box room and there is nowhere to take a shit, you do the math"* Michael continued to look suitably perplexed *"Oh forget it, you're in the hole, you know solitary?"*

    "O.K. O.K. I'm a little woozy"

    "A Little? Come on let's get out of here, it stinks" Michael climbed through the tiny opening and the light hurt his eyes. *"Shower quick and then straight to the A.C.T room, looks like it's your turn"* Michael had so many questions, but did not want to further arouse his fellow inmates suspicions or the suspicions of the two guards from before, who had now approached *"Move it"* they pushed Michael and led him to the shower block *"Two minutes"*. Michael had hardly covered his body in the relaxing warm water when he was forcibly removed and shunted down another corridor until he reached a room with a closed door. *"Nice knowing you, get in"* The guards opened the door and threw Michael inside. A man in a lab coat with long white wiry hair greeted him; *"Ah yellow, floor three, cell twenty four, welcome to the advanced combat training facility. "* Michael stepped back, surprised by the enthusiastic and eccentric façade of the man. *"Don't look so frightened, in here we look after you. No one wants a lame racehorse"* The room was filled with all sorts of equipment. Treadmills and various other fitness gadgets. In the corner of the room was a dedicated medical station and there was a small basic kitchen area with a table and two cheap plastic chairs. *"You must be hungry, go ahead sit, eat"* Michael sat and a young man approached the table, he did not utter a word and furnished the table with an array of fruits and vegetables and some plain boiled chicken. Michael ate furiously.

It felt like he had not eaten for days. The wiry haired scientist type continued *"Your system should be purged of any of the toxins from the crap they give you on the wing. Hungry Eh?"*

"What's going on?"

"Surely they never hit you that hard" The man held a small device up at Michael's skull and moved it around, he bit his bottom lip as he deliberated his findings *"Nope, no damage, I suppose a little recap should be O.K."*

"I'm Dr Anderson, this is the A.C.T room" Michael interrupted

"Advanced Combat Training?"

"That's right.........good!" The doctor looked relieved that Michael was responding adequately. *"You have been chosen to represent yellow. In two days you will contest with a representative from level 2, blue"*

"O.K.?" Michael looked at the doctor eagerly, hoping for more information *"Fighting?"* The doctor scanned his skull again and continued *"If you defeat him, you will take his place on the blue level, and receive the appropriate benefits.........no definitely no damage......... and If you're lucky in six months, maybe a year you will get a shot at the reds".* The doctor stopped scanning him and looked at him puzzled *"No physical damage, yet a complete loss of memory, weird"*

"I'll be fine, just tired and hungry" Michael distracted the doctor from his train of thought *"Any water?"* The doctor smiled excitedly

"Ha, *much better than water, in here you get this instead. Solution one, only available in penitentiary one"* The doctor handed Michael a bottle of fluorescent blue liquid and he recognised its glow immediately, it had the same bizarre glow that the sphere had when it came in contact with a missing fragment. The solution flickered just like the syringe which the black figure had injected into his neck on board the ship. Michael never hesitated and drank a large gulp, it tasted like the freshest and cleanest water he had ever had but surprisingly had no unusual effect on him, which disappointed him, being hopeful for some sort of supernatural boost from the odd blue liquid. *"That's it, get it down you, got a few of them to get through over the next few days"* The doctor moved away and shouted back at him without turning around *"Give your meal time to settle and then meet me at the cylinder, servo will get you everything you need"*. As if on command the silent young man appeared at Michael's side, he was devoid of any awareness and seemed to stare aimlessly into space *"You Servo?"* The little man nodded and a long stringy drop of fresh drool dripped from his lip until it hit the floor *"You O.K?"* Servo did not reply and Michael tried to engage him again *"Can you get me my things?"* Servo nodded in agreement and headed off. Michael spent the time awaiting Servo's return surveying his surroundings. He had become so engrossed in his latest existence that he had not given a second thought to getting home. He pushed the thoughts to the back of his mind once more. He had a mission to complete. There were still four fragments to reunite and he had to remain hopeful that they would take him back to some sort of coherent reality where Michael Cameron existed, free of a symbiotic partnership. He hoped above all, that he would be returned to an alternative reality, one where he could be with those who he missed and loved so much. He was losing a grip on their memory with every new location that he surfaced and concentrating on uniting the twelve for the moment was at least serving as a welcome distraction from his own guilt. Servo returned with a few items and laid them on the table. A pair of strong looking boots and some clothes. There was a pair of gloves with no fingers and reinforced knuckles. Some trousers and a short sleeved upper garment. They were both similarly reinforced, a bit like the protective gear a motorcyclist would wear. The final item was a headset. It had an attachment for the ear and a mouthpiece. Michael placed it over his head and clipped it securely in place with the strap which fastened under his chin. On top of the headset was a tiny little camera lens. *"That everything?"* Servo nodded and raised his hand, pointing to an archway which led to another part of the room *"This way?"* Servo nodded again. Michael headed in the direction of the archway and was startled by his assistants first word *"Drink"* Servo handed him his solution one and he took another large swig. With every drop he seemed to be growing in confidence and energy *"What's in this stuff then?"* Servo stared aimlessly into nothingness and Michael felt a bit uneasy with the lack of personality or emotion that he had shown so far *"Thanks anyway Servo"*

 "Drink" Servo uttered the same monotone grunt and raised his hand pointing to the archway once again. The other side of the archway was filled with monitors and panels, displaying charts and other complicated data. In the centre of the cylindrical room stood an

enormous machine. It was in the shape of a man sitting in a large steel chair. The doctor approached as he continued to scan the awesome example of engineering before him. It was a mass of cogs and pistons. Hydraulic hoses ran from one section to the next. Michael likened it to the central nervous system of a human body, linking all the limbs together. It was at this point that he realised that the machine was missing one important part and he couldn't resist asking. *"Where's its head?"*

"Drink up.......in fact what is your name?" Michael struggled for a second, the inmate had mentioned it earlier. He relaxed as the memory came back *"Chris"*

"O.K. Chris, drink up, all will be revealed" Michael downed the remainder of his bottle. He could the feel the hairs on his neck stand on end and this time was flushed with a massive jolt of adrenalin. *"Aha, getting a belt off the good stuff I see"*

"What the hell is this stuff?"

"The one and the only, Solution One, now jump in before it starts to wear off" Michael turned to face the machine and it burst into life. The cogs spun and the pistons moved in and out, hissing and blowing gasses in every direction. The torso of the machine opened up like a rib cage being split up the middle and the arms and legs split open at their centres. The entire machine moved slightly towards him and then dropped to the floor in front of him. *"Come on then Chris, two days is nothing you know"* The doctor encouraged Michael to Enter the Machine. Hesitating for a second he backed off until a massive rush of adrenalin overcame him and he pounced eagerly into the small carbon fibre seat at the machines core. *"O.K good luck, first run shouldn't be too painful"*. Michael's heart skipped a beat hearing the doctor's comment. *"Pain?"*

"Oh well too late now" The doctor smiled and proceeded to press some buttons that made the machine burst into life. Michael tried to yell through the whirrs and clanks of the cogs and pistons. The machine swallowed his entire body clamping his limbs into place until only his head was visible sitting perfectly in position, where the machine's missing head should have been. *"Not like you've got much choice, you are a prisoner after all"* Michael could only just make the doctors last comment over the noise. He was then completely drowned out as the mechanical whirring of a large head piece silenced

185

all other noises. The large head piece settled on Michael's skull and he felt a familiar and almost comforting buzzing noise. He would have recognised it anywhere. Two metal rods with flat cylindrical discs protruded from either side of the head piece and rested on his temples. They were cold and squeezed his head firmly so as to hold him in place. A visor dropped in front of his eyes. The lens was transparent and he could still see the doctor at work on the floor below him *"O.K, head piece in position, subject seems in good health"* Michael couldn't see it but it was nearby, he could feel it. The sphere was integrated into the headpiece of the machine and its presence was unmistakable. Some static rung in his ear *"Chris, can you hear me"* *"Yeah I'm here, what's this on my head?"* The doctor laughed.

"Well that's the question on everyone's lips, I've learned not to ask. It doesn't bode well for those who ask too many questions, just ask poor Servo" Michael could just make out Servo, who was cowering behind a filing cabinet in the corner of the room. He was fearful of the machine's power or it was the sphere that he feared *"O.K. Chris, here we go"* The doctor removed a chain from around his neck and opened a small glass box on the control console he was working at. There was a small cylindrical hole and he placed a small glowing piece of black glass into the hole and Michael throbbed all over with the same familiar feeling as the fragment was inserted. This time it felt amplified a thousand times and his body physically vibrated. The visor change from transparent to black and displayed a countdown sequence from five to zero. *"Can you hear me?"*

"I hear you"

"What a rush eh? O.K, A.C.T stage one. Muscle refinement and endurance enhancer" Michael listened intently but was baffled by the purpose of the machine so far. His senses were cut off from the outside world and his body and mind was focused purely on what was being displayed on the visor. *"O.K Chris can you see the river?"* Michael watched as a crude representation of a river appeared before his eyes. The visual display was old fashioned and pixelated. *"Some river"*

"Hey don't diss. the program, it does the job, anyway concentrate". Michael felt his body relax and his anxiety eased off a bit *"O.K. Swim".* He felt his body plummet until the screen changed to the start line of a race. A traffic light starting system counted down red then amber then green *"Swim!"* The doctor screamed in Michael's

ear and this was enough to kick him into gear, he moved his arms and legs and simulated swimming. The movements were quite realistic and before long he had got himself into a decent rhythm. The visual display showed a distance, time and position. He was currently sixth. *"That's more like it Chris, see you in three hours"* Michaels enthusiasm was stunted at the thought of three pixelated hours of enforced exercise. After a half an hour he started to weaken until he spotted the blocky feet of the computer generated fifth place swimmer. The hairs on his neck stood up at the sight of his opponent and he was overcome with a massive kick of adrenalin once again. The Muscles in his arms and legs recuperated rapidly and he took off again at a blistering pace. Soon the fifth place opponent was a distant spec behind him and he was quickly closing down on the fourth placed swimmer. Each physical barrier was now easy to overcome by the right application of adrenalin and determination. The last swimmer approached and Michael swung his arms and legs with added determination. The virtual character on the visual display started to blur as Michael's speed overtook the capability of the system. The Finish line came and went and the visor returned to its previous transparent state. *"Chris"* The doctor yelled with concern.

"I'm O.K, what's wrong?"

"Unbelievable, he is still alive!" Michael was confused, it was supposed to be three hours hard slog, but had felt like a leisurely dip in the local swimming pool. The doctor was clearly concerned *"Doc, everything O.K?"*

"Unusually it would seem so Chris, you should be dead"

"I feel great"

"You have been swimming on the maximum setting for twelve hours, the machine went crazy and no matter what , I could not get it to let you go" The doctor laughed nervously *"How do you feel? No Pain? No headache?"*

"I'm a bit thirsty"

"Servo, Solution one now" Servo nodded and the doctor flicked a few switches bringing the machine to the ground. The cogs and pistons whirred and turned, opening up the legs and arms. The rib cage split like it had before and ejected Michael, sending him crashing to the floor. Michael lifted his head and glanced over to Doctor

Anderson. The look on the doctor's face was one of absolute fear *"What's wrong Doctor?"*

"Eh no, nothing prisoner" Servo approached Michael and grunted again

"Drink". Michael sat up and reached over to take the bottle and stopped before taking it from Servo, Distracted by the tiny little bottle he was being handed. He shook his head, his eyesight was not functioning correctly, and even Servo seemed unusually small. Michael perused his arm, it was bulging with veins, and his hand was enormous. Nothing was smaller and his eyes were functioning normally. Michael was enormous. His Arm had at least trebled in size, as had his entire body. *"Drink"* Servo was completely unaffected by the occurrence and simply insisted that Michael drink his Solution One. Michael looked at the doctor *"I take it this is a first"*

"Oh god yes, no one has ever lasted even three hours in accelerated growth"

"What now?"

"Go and rest, I need to make some phone calls" Michael moved to the kitchen and squeezed into one of the now tiny plastic chairs and took a drink from the tiny bottle. The doctor slipped back into the cylinder and ushered Servo to follow him. Michael watched on from the kitchen. The doctor kept popping his head through the archway while on the telephone. He was watching Michael with more concern than curiosity and it had begun to unsettle him. He finished off another bottle of Solution One and stood up. The chair was now stuck to his rear end and he pulled at its metal legs to remove it. The chair popped off and fell to the floor, now just a useless lump of broken plastic and twisted metal. It was completely destroyed. His strength was unfathomable, almost superhuman. The clang of the chair hitting the ground had alerted the Doctor who had come running to see what had happened. He glanced at the chair and his eyes widened with amazement *"Sorry Doc"*

"No, No, no … no problem, just an old chair" the doctors uneasiness was obvious to Michael, he was fearful of him *"So what did they say"*

"I'm sorry who?"

188

"The phone call?"

"Ah yes, they are coming down to see you now"

"Who?"

"The overseers of course....Mr Babcock, Burbank and Cochrane" The doctor busied himself nervously *"Servo, prepare the observation room"* Servo nodded and disappeared into the background. *"So what's the deal then doctor? Am I ready to fight?"* The doctor continued busying himself and tried not to make any eye contact. *"Your condition is unprecedented Chris, It may not be fair to put you in with another inmate"*

"What will happen to me then?" The doctor ignored Michaels question *"Doc?"*

"They will be here soon Chris, let's see what they have to say" the doctor moved towards the archway and turned to face Michael *"This way please"* Michael manoeuvred his hulking body towards the archway and moved through it into the cylinder. A small door at its rear opened and Servo was scurrying in and out. *"In the observation chamber please Chris"* Michael looked around the Cylinder as he passed through into the chamber, it was unchanged but smelled strongly of bleach. The doctor had been cleaning before the dignitaries arrived. The Machine stood dormant and lifeless as the doctor stood at the chamber entrance awaiting Michael's attendance. He ducked down to clear the frame of the door and entered a small and clinical looking room. There was a cabinet on the wall with bottles of solution one locked in it. There was a slab in the centre of the room which resembled an operating table *"Please sit Chris"* Michael sat on the slab and noticed there was a glass viewing window about fifteen feet above the floor. The room dimmed and he could hear the shuffling of bodies as they entered the room. The viewing window was tinted and the occupants were obscured from his vision, *"Is this thing on?"* Michael could hear the noise of someone fiddling with a microphone. *"We can hear you sir"* The doctor alerted the viewing party *"O.K. Anderson, show us"* Servo entered pushing a trolley with a selection of materials on it. The doctor handed Michael a thick metal bar *"Straight to the big stuff doctor?"* said a voice from the viewing room

"No point with the other materials Sir, look at the size of him" Michael took the metal bar and twisted it in his hands until it cracked

and splinters of metal shot all over the room. The doctor ducked, cowering in the corner of the room. Servo stood unmoved and quite oblivious to the potential danger *"Impressive, how is his resistance doctor?"*

"It would seem he is extremely resistant to superficial damage and pain sir"

"Show us" The doctor lifted a large sledgehammer from the utensils and looked at Michael sheepishly. He swung the hammer with all his might towards his head and Michael raised his hand to protect his face. The hammer shattered throwing shrapnel everywhere again. A Large piece of shrapnel hurtled across the room and struck Servo on the lower leg, shattering his leg and he collapsed in agony. Michael jumped to his feet and rushed to aid him immediately *"Leave him inmate, he is nothing but a turnip, one of the doctor's failed experiments"* Michael could feel the rage begin to build within him. The viewing party had shown no remorse. They had no care for Servo and almost took pleasure in what they had just witnessed. He placed Servo on the slab and turned to face the doctor *"Calm down Chris, I'll go get a med pack"* the doctor darted out the door and the hydraulic hiss of the solid chamber door came down at his back. *"Well doctor it would seem you are right, he is too dangerous"* The doctor watched on through the small glass window in the door *"We all agree then, termination? O.K. Parker Read it"*

"Inmate Chris Temple, yellow floor three, cell twenty four, for crimes against humanity and the state, you are hereby sentenced to death" Michael listened as his fate was decided from the viewing room above. Some small holes opened at the base of the walls around the room. A black gaseous smoke emerged and soon began to choke him and the suffering Servo. The visibility was becoming impossible and Michael began pounding on the door. He hardly dented it and the doctor took a step back watching on as his subjects suffocated. *"Chris"* a voice from the smoke grabbed his attention

"Who's there? Servo is that you?" Michael approached the slab and for the first time Servo looked him straight in the eye with a degree of a conscious mind. He held out his hand and offered him a small key, *"Drink"*. Michael turned immediately to the cabinet and unlocked the Solution One, He drank three bottles in quick succession and then was half way through a fourth when the solution's effects

completely overcame him. A distressed shout came over the speaker system *"Parker initiate block wide shut down"*

"Yes Sir" a loud siren rang out and the sound of heavy steel doors slamming down rung out all around the facility. Michael approached the door and peered through the little window. The doctor had vanished. With one swift Jab the door flew across the cylinder smashing into the dormant machine. Michael gently lifted Servo and placed him on the floor of the Cylinder, free from the gas. Servo looked him straight in the eye, not fearful of the hulking beast before him and with his last breath uttered a few words *"No more"* As servo slumped to his death in Michael's arms the rage overtook him and he headed back to the chamber to fulfil his saviours dying wish. He ripped the operating slab from its plinth and launched it through the air towards the viewing room. The slab smashed through and crushed two of the occupants. Mr Babcock lay still and lifeless and it was now hard to separate his red tie from his blood stained shirt. *"Surely we can work this out inmate?"* Mr Burbank lay unable to move with the slab on his legs, the rage was now in control and he grasped his head in one hand squeezing until it exploded like a ripe blood orange. Drops of dark purple blood and other pieces of matter from Burbank's brain dripped down and settled on his clean blue tie. Michael turned to Parker and stared at him for a few seconds. The beige trousers he wore became a darker brown as they filled with urine. Cochrane cowered in the corner and Michael reached out and lifted him by the scruff of the neck. He carried him down to the chamber, Parker was rooted to the spot and Michael uttered one word to him *"Run"* Parker never hesitated and took his chance to escape. The cylinder was in lockdown and Michael stood central near the machine. *"Doctor?"* There was no reply *"Doctor, you see Cochrane?"* Michael held Cochrane at arm's length *"Bring it to me or this is you"* Michael ripped Cochrane limb from limb like a child with a spider. The rage was uncontrollable and he felt himself enjoying the retribution unmoved by the horror of what he was engaging in. *"O.K. O.K. I'm here"* The Doctor popped his head from inside a small cupboard and then slowly approached him *"I'm just doing my job you know"*

"Give it to me"

"It's this you want isn't it?" The doctor held out the fragment with the chain still attached around his neck. Michael pounced and dragged him across the floor by the chain. *"What is it?"* The doctor choked and struggled to reply

"You tell me, it seems to like you"

"No bullshit, now tell me. Where did it come from?"

    "I honestly don't know" Michael gripped the chain and it started to penetrate the skin around the doctors neck *"I'm telling the truth"* Michael looked over at Servo's lifeless body and back at the doctor *"Wrong answer"* Michael pulled the fragment and the chain ripped through the skin and bone sending the doctors head and body in different directions. Michael stood for a few seconds while the rage was still rushing through his body. *"O.K calm it, it's time to go"* he spoke aloud to calm his nerves and turned to the machine smashing it to pieces. He gently lifted the sphere from the wreckage, snapped the fragment from its chain and slipped it into place. He had seen and done the unthinkable in this place and it was time to move on. With his family a distant and fading echo. He was becoming more detached from his goal, blindly submitting to his emotional desires, sexual and now it seemed his thirst for brutality had been truly satisfied. Perhaps the sphere had completely consumed him, would he ever find his true self again. The light engulfed him and as he slipped away he heard another whisper *"Wonder what's next?"*

Chapter 14

Fake Plastic Trees

"Wonder what's next?" The voice repeated over in Michaels head. It was the voice of an excited youth, a young man, no more than seventeen he thought. His voice was eager with anticipation. Was he listening to his own subconscious? Internally assessing just where he would be propelled to for the tenth instalment of his unexplained adventure? The sickly taste of salt water touched his lips and he awoke with his face buried in wet sand. The heat from the sun cooked his back as he lay exposed to the elements. The sound of waves splashing onto the beach around him and the distant squawking of some sea birds was enough to wake him fully. He sat up and stared out into the vast ocean before him. It was spectacular and was one of the few times during his long journey that he was able to relax and appreciate a magnificent and beautiful sight. The water was crystal clear, inviting and the temptation to run into the surf overcame him. Diving in he swam a few yards under the water before surfacing. The temperature was perfect, not cold at all and he floated around on his back a bit, the sand under his feet was soft and golden, he must have been somewhere very exotic he thought. Kaitlin and Joseph were lost to the deepest recesses of his memory and Michael was now fully focused on living in the moment. Taking advantage of the beautiful surroundings that he was taking full advantage of. The last few locales he had faded from his mind and similarly fade to a distant memory and they had let him indulge in with some of his basic desires. Sophie had helped him with the most basic of carnal desires and he had no problem with letting his hair down while he had visited the unfortunate Fu. More concerning was the pleasure he had taken from his most recent stint in prison. He was glad to be free of violent thoughts and was happy to bathe in a far more innocent indulgence. He walked through the shallows until he reached the beach, schools of multi colours fish darted between his legs. This place was undoubtedly the most welcoming of anywhere he had been yet. The view from the water could have been taken from a holiday brochure. Palm trees hung lazily, dotted along the shore front, almost as if they had been placed carefully in each position to create a serene and picture, perfect, paradise. The back of the beach was lined with a small forest area and at both sides curled away from view. Michael was on an island and he decided that he would start walking the beach to find some clues as to his current whereabouts. On his way around the

shore he investigated his latest body. He was in no rush, this place was idyllic, no gangsters, loud machines or guns. It was just a calming and quiet environment, which was long overdue. Michael's feet were bare and really hairy, the new legs were also uncovered to the knees. A pair of olive green fabric shorts covered the rest of his lower body. Soaked with sea water and heavily tattered around the edges. Michael's upper body was similarly shabby looking. A thin cotton polo shirt with matching tattered edges finished off the outfit. Reaching for his face he checked his features. He was not a young man, his skin was wrinkled and felt dry with over exposure to the sun. His most distinctive feature was the long white beard which he was able to see by squinting towards his feet. Michael chuckled to himself *"Hobo chic!"* The beach front was a stereotypical desert island scene and was littered with drift wood and mini rock pools filled with seaweed and small crustaceans which scurried for cover as Michael's shadow passed over the water's surface. The sand seemed to go on forever and his legs grew weary. The body he inhabited was thin and he felt some niggles of pain from his stomach, he was hungry and exhausted. As the sun beat down on him, he grew increasingly more tired and stumbled to the sand. He lay spread eagled and gasping for breath. The bright sun obscured his vision. In the distance the outline of a small building started to take shape. Concentrating he tried to force his eyes to focus more. It was definitely a small shack of some sort, hidden between a small collection of palm trees. Michael struggled to his feet and soldiered on. The sight of some possible refuge from the sun had given him the motivation to push his battered body one more time. He grabbed the framework of the doorway with both hands. It was a welcome relief to have something upright to lean his weight upon. The shack was constructed of various random materials, which looked to have been salvaged from the beach. Large perished pieces of drift wood and rusty iron sheets had been wedged into the sand. Old worn rope secured the pieces together and the surrounding trees had been utilised as vertical stiffeners. Whoever had lived in the shack, they had worked on it extensively, ensuring it retained its structural integrity. A small makeshift bunk lay uninhabited, tucked away in a corner, safe from the elements. The only other furniture was a large wooden crate which was being used as a desk. It had a collection of smaller items strewn across its surface. The walls of the shack surrounding him were covered in snippets of newspapers and magazines and a small plastic box finished of the interior décor. It was blue and had a large rock on its lid. Michael stumbled through the shack door and the relief brought by the shade was incredible. He scanned the crate for water, his lips had begun to crack, splitting from a combination of the dry sand, salt and blistering heat of the sun. Lifting the rock from the lid of the plastic box, he let out a groan of pain as his already weary biceps struggled with its weight. The box was similar to the rest of the shack and was filled with an assortment of items. There was a smaller box which was surrounded by a collection of packets and little boxes. There were soups and tins of boiled veg. The box had been packed carefully and Michael surmised that it was a collection of important items. Hidden at the bottom was one bottle. It was half filled and the colour of its contents was obscured by its green glass. One thing was for sure, it was not water. Michael took a deep breath and popped the cork which sent a small burst of dust into the air as the ancient particles were displaced. He was parched, whatever it was, it was liquid and he took a large swig. The wine was cheap and nasty, not like the fine ones he had grown accustomed to back home. Michael's throat relaxed at first, the moisture was well accepted. Then the harsh, dry and viscous liquid made him cough like an amateur attempting his first strong whiskey. He sat down on the bunk and wheezed for a few minutes. The sun beat down and Michael felt he was beginning to cook from the heat. The shade from the direct sun was welcome but the shack had begun to absorb all the strength of the midday sun. The crate was littered with lots of paper drawings. They were not artistic, more like diagrammatic sketches accompanied with numbers in the corner of each sketch. Michael flicked through them, skimming past most of the bundle with no interest in their content. They were all irrelevant to him as he had no clue as to their meaning or their current significance. He spent the time in the shade sorting through as much of the shack's contents as he could. He was searching for some meaning amongst all the crisp, dry paperwork and the rag and bone man style collection of paraphernalia. The sun dipped beyond the distant ocean horizon and the sky was filled with an orange and pink tone. Michael moved outside and watched on in awe as the sky seemed to transform almost as if someone somewhere had flicked a switch which had signalled the correct time of day to change the scenery. A cold wind blew in from the sea and it caught him unawares. *"Time for a fire"*. He grabbed some dry sticks and ripped the dry wiry husks from some nearby coconuts which had fallen to the sand and set about starting a little fire. His mind wandered and soon Michael was reminded of his little friend who had started her own fire with such ease. His time with Agnieska had been such an emotional part of his journey but now seemed so distant and insignificant. The flames were now burning

195

bright and high, little snaps and cracks rung out as air escaped from the burning material. He surrounded the flames in a little circle of stones and cracked a bigger rock upon one of the coconuts, staring out into the dark ocean as he sipped its cool contents. The body he inhabited was tired and old and by now Michael surmised that he must have been there for a long time. The newspaper clippings had yellowed like the pages of an old book. The shack itself had stood for such a long time that it had begun to mould into its surroundings, giving the impression that it was part of the natural terrain. Michael grabbed the blue box from the shack and lifted it, ready to carry it to the fireside. A silver flash caught his eye, there was something else buried beneath the thin covering of sand below the box. Michael carried the box to the fireside and hurried back to investigate. A deep breath followed by a blast of air from his lungs almost made his old and frail shell pass out, but it was enough to clear the sand from what appeared to be the top of another box. It took about ten minutes to dig it out and Michael dragged it to the fireside along with the other one. Tired from his exertions, he finished off his coconut water and cracked open another with no problem. If anything, this journey had turned him into a far more resourceful person. He sat and panted for a few moments and stared at the box while he caught his breath *"I know you're in there"* Michael spoke to the box like it was going to answer him, it had to be the sphere or even the next fragment he thought. Struggling to his feet, the campsite had now become dark, lit only by the fading light of the fire. Moving towards the box, Michael looked up into the night sky and sighed, surely after all he had had to endure up until now this it would just be a simple and hassle free re-unification. A loud crack rang out all around, as the clouds clattered high above him. The heavens had opened and a storm was heading his way fast. Michael swiftly headed for the box with increased urgency, he let out a yelp of pain as he stubbed his toe on a protruding tree root sending him crashing to the ground. It felt like slow motion as he descended towards the now far cooler sandy beach. His head cracked a small rock, enough to knock him out cold.

"Daddy?"……………………Daddy?"

"What is it Joseph? Daddy's busy" the voices where the only life in the blackness which surrounded him. Michael felt awake, but there was nothing to indicate where he was. *"Daddy…………Daddy?"* Little Joseph's voice this time had a disconcerting tone. He was whimpering and sounded frightened *"Don't worry wee man, Daddy's here"* Michael listened to a conversation between his son and himself, he was disconnected from them, purely listening to a past

conversation which must have been buried deep in his psyche. The darkness all around him was constant and consuming until a distant dot of light shot towards him. Michael now stood in the darkness over the lifeless body of his latest cohabiter. Blood had spilled down the rock and had begun to coagulate in the soft golden sand. The darkness of the dream completely engulfed him, with only the body and the two boxes given a physical form. *"Open the box, sweetheart",* Michael knew the voice anywhere, it was Kaitlin but she was nowhere to be seen. *"Open the box and come home, we miss you".* Michael stared at the carcass below him and his heart almost stopped with fright as the eyes suddenly opened and the mouth moved, miming Kaitlin's words as her voice rang in his ears *"Open the box, nearly there"* Kaitlin's voice was comforting, but the vessel which it had been transmitted through had made him feel sick. The darkness consumed everything once again until it was interrupted by the sound of robotic marching. Something was approaching relentlessly and Michael grew increasingly uneasy until once more he found himself looking upon a scene surrounded by bleak nothingness. Upon a familiar slab lay little Joseph. He was strapped into it, just as Michael had been while he was aboard the black figure's ship. The figure emerged from the darkness and approached the sphere which was wired up as it had been before. The figure worked on the sphere and little Joseph lay still as Michael was helpless to intervene. An enforced voyeur of the proceedings. Little Joseph turned his head and much like the bloodied carcass had and spoke to him *"Open the box Daddy"* The black figure laughed maniacally and Michael's gaze was forcibly drawn to its face . The black mesh mask began to retract into the helmet, revealing the face from underneath. The face behind the mask was Joseph. He snarled and insisted aggressively. *"Open the box! Open the box! Open the box!"* Michael looked towards the slab, Joseph had been replaced with Agnieska who after a few moments changed to the face of Fu. The face of the figure and the body on the slab began to flicker frantically between various people. Noritomo stood over the flight attendant who had been sucked out into the night sky during the accident. They were replaced by Al Zuhairi standing over the lifeless body of Captain Carson. Everyone he had encountered seemed to appear for a few seconds and then disappear mixed in with the faces of people from his real life. And then the darkness fell once more. The two faces, the slab and everything else had gone and Michael stood alone in the darkness accompanied only with an eerie chanting. All the voices of the people who had appeared before him chanted in unison. *"Open the box"* Over and over, getting louder and louder until one voice

197

broke through *"He's not ready leave him"* The soft and angelic sound of her voice was the most soothing tone he could have hoped for *"I don't care, leave him, he can handle it, I know he can"* Sophie's voice was so perfectly attuned and Michael stood doting on every utterance of her words. Sophie was replaced by the sound of another voice that he had not heard before. *"We should cut it short now, before it kills him."*

    "Sophie! I was lucky to make it"

    "I said leave him, he is so close" Sophie sounded pained but resolute in her opinion. *"O.K you're the boss, one last push 324"* Michaels whole body tingled with electricity and he gasped a large intake of breath, closely followed by a mouthful of sand and rain water. The storm was in full swing by now and the fire had long been extinguished. Michael lay bloodied and cold, he struggled to his feet and dragged the two boxes back to the shack. He placed a few empty cans and bottles as well as an old steel pan outside to collect as much of the rainwater as he could. The dream he had just experienced played on his mind. The journey he was on was already a wholly bizarre affair, but the dream had proven all the more surreal. Michael contemplated the paradigm of a dream within a dream and rubbed his head. He was forcing his already fragile mind into an even more confused state than usual. *"Open the box"* He said aloud. He reached towards the now completely saturated wooden chest, it clicked open on two hinges and the lid flicked back. The contents were surprising but Michael was becoming all the more accepting of the unusual, even so the contents still raised an eyebrow. The wooden chest was filled with sand which surrounded a singular glass bottle at its middle. Within the bottle was a little roll of paper. The Stereotypical message in a bottle confused him, it was all so staged and unnatural. He pondered the reasoning as to why someone would bury a note in a bottle, in a chest full of sand and then in turn bury the box it was contained within. The fabrication of the scenario played on his mind, no locale he had encountered so far had been so contrived and 'Hollywood'. None the less there was no point in attempting to question the unquestionable and he hastily popped the cork and removed the paper. It was old and very brittle. Michael unfurled it carefully. The writing on it was written in black ink and if he could have given the font a title I would have been called 'Pirate no1' or 'Ye Olde Helvetica' The inscription was even more bizarre *"Follow the Turtle"* Michael looked at the paper and wracked his brain for an explanation, his face grew increasingly more scarlet as his temper built up and eventually broke as he launched the bottle exclaiming *"What*

does it all mean?". The bottle smashed into pieces on a rock just bedside the campsite which was now beginning to dry off as the storm suddenly stopped, just as rapidly as the sun had set earlier. *"This place isn't right"* Michael was becoming ever more frustrated with his surroundings, nothing seemed to be real. For him that was quite a thought to have, but the entire visit so far had just been the unusual followed by some more unusual. Michael spent the next short while going through all the clippings of paper. He determined that they were all attempts at solutions to various puzzles and activities. The sketches and numbers seemed to be the work of a person who had been studying them for some time. It was probably himself he thought. At the bottom of the pile was a tiny little book, no bigger than a few inches square. It was bound together with elastic bands. Opening it, he perused it contents. It was a miniature version of all the paperwork which he had been looking through. On the last page was an instructive list.

  1. *Pack supplies.*
  2. *Remember me!*

Michael thought about what the second instruction could have meant and then realised it was in reference to the book itself

  3. *Wait till moonlight*
  4. *Open the box*

Michael sat on the end of the bunk and felt like crying, yet more half-truths and unanswered questions. What was he supposed to do now? *"Moonlight?"* He gazed outside at the brightly lit sky, it was pretty impressive and the beach looked again like a perfectly manufactured movie set. He had no idea what to do, so he simply started to follow the instructions set out in the tiny book. He grabbed a few bottles that were now filled with the collected rain water and sealed them with their corks, he tied them onto a length of string along with some of the tins and packets inside a little plastic carrier bag. He noticed a small tin from within the blue box which that had gone overlooked, due to the discovery of the hidden chest and picked it up. It made a heavy clunk as the contents of the tin shifted and he smiled instantly *"I knew you were here somewhere"* The tin popped open and just as he suspected the tenth fragment slid out into his hand. It was mounted on a neck chain, just as the Doctor's had been back in the Cylinder. He placed it around his neck and slung his make shift back pack over his shoulder. He gripped the little book in his hand, being sure to keep it close. It probably would be of importance to him *"O.K Moonlight"* Michael walked outside the shack and gazed at the perfectly formed moon, it was so bright, clear and mesmerising. *"Open the box? O.K, I think I've*

done that". He sat on the sand, lit only by the large moon above
"What does it all mean?" 'Follow the Turtle?' Ah! Who Knows?"
Disheartened he slumped to the sand and lay still in the quiet of the
darkened beach. The sound of the waves gently lapping to the shore
was the only disturbance to the absolute deathly silence that
surrounded him. The silence prevailed for around a half an hour and
Michael's eyes grew heavy and he was just about to slip away again
when the silence was broken by the prehistoric groan of an animal
which was no further than a couple of yards from his position. Michael
darted for cover behind the roots of the palm trees and peered over
towards the direction of the new sound. The loud screech was like and
air horn which was muted underneath water and must have been
produced by a beast of a great size. Another almighty groan rung out
and Michael struggled to make out where it was coming from. He
crawled slowly along the sand until he got a better view. It was an
enormous leatherback turtle and it had been laying its eggs into a large
sand pit which it had hollowed out. Michael approached slowly and
realised the moonlight was not enough for him to see the beast in all
its glory , so he darted back to the camp and quickly lit a small torch he
made from coconut husks and a charred branch from the fire. He
moved back towards the turtle, now far less fearful having determined
the origin of the blood curdling screeches. The turtle was enormous,
coated with algae and a few large green barnacles. It was very old and
long travelled. Michael watched it, in great appreciation for its
majesty and even started to assist it as it began to fill the pit with sand
having finished laying the last of what looked like hundreds of eggs.
Michael sprung to his feet as the great beast moved towards the
beach. With every rotation of its massive flippers it moved a few more
inches towards the water's edge. He panicked, Follow the Turtle it had
said. He grabbed the book from his waistband, where he had placed it
for safe keeping. He held his torch up to it, being careful not to burn it.
"Phase 1: Keep me dry and hold on till the dive". The turtle moved
towards the water's edge and Michael hurriedly read the instructions.
There was a diagram of a sea bed with a 27 in the top corner. A Dotted
line showed a descent from the surface to a cross on the sea bed.
Michael was perplexed at how staged it all seemed to be, He felt he
was part of a treasure hunt on a cheesy game show. Everything was
planned and predetermined he thought. A Loud splash was twinned
with another beastly groan from the turtle and she set sail into the
distance, moving far easier in her natural habitat. Michael put the
little book between his teeth and swam out to meet her. He leaned on
her back. The turtle did not even flinch under the extra weight. The

water was warm and soon Michael was surrounded by nothing but the vast ocean. The moon shone to the reef below and the corals glistened under its intense glow. The turtle hissed as it took a long deep gulp of air before it started it descent to the sea floor. It was too late for the little book and Michael tried to conceal it in his shorts as best he could. He took a deep breath and followed the turtle into the depths. He began to run out of breath as the turtle reached the bottom and displaced the silt on the sea bed. The sand settled and Michael darted quickly for the surface as he ran out of air. The turtle disappeared into the murky depths and he treaded water wondering what on earth he would do next. In the darkness below a light shone from where the silt had been uncovered, Michael took another breath and dived down towards it. It was a bright Red LED and was part of a metal door underneath the sand. Another bizarre addition to the already messed up locale. It was alien to the idyllic terrain around it. Upon it was a keypad, numbered like a telephone and a small handle. Michael reached out and pressed the 2 followed by the 7 and pulled on the handle. The hatch opened and Michael was pulled through it like a spider down a plughole. The chamber was just big enough to hold him and it began to drain slowly. Michaels head cleared the water line and he sucked in a desperate gasp of oxygen and spluttered as some water got caught in his airways. The Chamber emptied of sea water and another hatch opened below Michael, he held on for a second and then let himself drop to the solid floor below. It was a long corridor and the floor was lit along its sides, not unlike a commercial airliner. The little book was soaked through and the ink had started to run, he peeled the pages back carefully and read as much as he could "Phase 2: Nine Litres, share it" Michael moved along the corridor until he reached another large metal door, on the floor next to it lay a large bottle filled with liquid. The bottle had a large number nine and incremental markings on its side and the door had the same handle as the hatch had on the sea bed. On the door front there were three tubes which could contain liquid, each of them could hold five litres and were marked with a gauge on their side. He struggled to lift the nine litre container and his weak body strained as he filled the first one up to the three litre level. He continued to share the liquid equally between the three tubes as he had been instructed. He waited for some sort of indication as to his next move but nothing came and he grew ever more impatient. The little book was quickly losing its usefulness as the ink continued to run from its pages. The diagram was difficult to decipher and he could just make out the three tubes. The number in the corner had now been completely lost. The tubes had all but completely gone other than the centre tube which had shown a smaller amount within the tube. Michael turned a small tap on the bottom centre of the tube and the liquid began to trickle back into the nine litre container. He waited again and kicked the large container in frustration at the inactivity. The book was now beyond comprehension and Michael sat on the floor of the corridor while he assessed his options. Studying the metal door and the cheap plastic of the tubes. He realised this was no desert island. What was going on? He seemed to be thinking that more and more. The artificial make up of this place was so different than everywhere he had been so far and he felt uneasy with the feeling he was being directed. The dream he had, left him feeling violated, the faces and voices were so real yet the way he had experienced them was so abnormal and freakish. *"324?"* He spoke aloud, yet again the constancy of those three little numbers drove him mad with wonder, and what they could mean. Although the sphere and the mystery of 324 had plagued his every thought, they had also provided him with a little hope that there would be a meaning explained to him at the end of the chaos he was being subjected too. Michael sprung to his feet *"I'm a dick!"* Picking up the nine litre container he poured two litres into the centre tube and the last remaining litre into the third tube. He pointed and spoke aloud systematically; *"three litres, two litres, four litres".* The door clunked as it unlocked and swung open. Michael shook his head as he realised just how obvious it had been. 324 was the answer that he desired, it seemed to be involved in everything, but in this case it was quite literally the answer he needed. Drinking one of the bottles of water, he studied the surroundings within the next room, the metal door swung under its own momentum and shut behind him, closing him in. The latest chamber was much bigger and was lit periodically throughout with lanterns high up on the surrounding walls, placed into little alcoves. The flames where green and lit a pyramid structure which stood in the middle of the chamber. Standing at its base, Michael had an unsettling feeling that he was being watched, he removed the little book and opened it *"Final Phase"* He could just make out its title but that's where the books usefulness came to came to a soggy end. The rest of the writing had been completely ruined by the salt water. The pyramid was synthetic, made of blocks of black and silver material constructed in the traditional fashion, first done by the Egyptians. There was no doubt to Michael that the pyramid and the chamber itself were not quite as old. It was very much plastic and modern. At the four corners of the pyramid, staffs protruded from the floor and at the top of each staff was a mirror which pointed towards

202

the centre of the structure. Michael scaled the pyramid, investigating as he went. There were four mirrors at the corner of every level, totalling twelve. He soon reached the summit and was met by a flame. A torch protruded from the final block of the pyramid and it glowed with the same green coloured flame as the surrounding lights in the chamber. Michael removed the torch from its position and it left a small gaping hole where it had been placed. Michael realised exactly what was missing from the aperture. He took the fragment from around his neck and slipped it into the hole, it fitted perfectly. Nothing happened and Michael pulled at the chain. It was stuck fast. He panicked as he realised how easily he had offered up the fragment without any concern to the possible outcome. Michael turned and headed to the base of the pyramid to get a better view and decide upon his next move. The mirrors flickered as he made his way passed them. Inspecting the four staffs in more detail he had noticed that one of the four at the bottom did not have a mirror like the others. In its place it had a plain black metal disc. Michael pulled at it and it removed quite easily, just as the torch had. The disc left a small cylindrical aperture like before *"Let there be light!"* Michael joked as he raised the torch and placed it in the slot. Beams of green light shot off in every direction, reflecting from one mirror to another until one solitary beam of green light rested on the fragment at the summit. The beams of green light crisscrossed each other like a neon spider's web and Michael smiled, impressed by the futuristic light show. The fragment glowed brighter and brighter until a thick beam of blue light emanated from it and engulfed him. He was tingling with the familiar electricity that he had now grown to appreciate. The blue light of the sphere signified something solid for him to keep focused upon. It helped him to remain resolute on his quest to achieve his goal whatever it may be and it helped stop him from losing his mind in the maze of new people and places. With every person he met or place he experienced came an assault on his emotional state. For something that was so mysterious and unexplained it had been the only thing for a long time that was simple and uncomplicated to him. Unite the Twelve. Forget and move on. After a few seconds the Pyramid split at its base and a doorway appeared. The door swung open and simultaneously the light faded. Michael's body stopped tingling and he collapsed in a heap. Concerned for the fragment he got to his feet and scaled the pyramid to retrieve it. He felt invigorated and the old body he inhabited was refreshed. The fragment had popped back out from the opening and he slipped it over his neck. The doorway remained opened and he made his way back down towards it. He walked through the opening and was met with exactly what he had desired. Upon a grand and ornate plinth the sphere glowed bright with the previous nine fragments all in place. Michael gripped the fragment in his hand and moved towards the sphere. He wanted out of here, this place was a little odd to say the least and he was sticking by his earlier mantra; *"Don't question the unquestionable".* Michael moved to lift his arm to the take the sphere and was overcome by a huge weight which had frozen him to the spot. His body felt like it weight a ton and his feet were stuck fast to the floor. He tired quickly as he tried to free himself. The hairs on his neck stood on end as he heard the rhythmic beat of approaching footsteps. The green lanterns cast the shadow of the approaching intruder who had now approached from behind. He stood powerless, unable to turn and face his visitor. The footsteps stopped and a black glove reached and removed the fragment from Michael's hand. The intruder moved before him and his worst fear was realised. The black figure had returned. Michael watched on as it collected the sphere and placed it in a small black case along with the tenth fragment. *"Hey! You! Who the hell are you?"* The figure ignored him as it had before *"Hey You! I'm talking to you, what the fuckin' hell are you?"* The Figure turned to Michael and tilted its head like an inquisitive dog as it looked at him. *"Tut, tut, tut, you look tired 324".* Michael screamed out as the figure reached out to touch his face *"No, wait who are….."* With a flick of its finger Michael was once more in the company and at the mercy of the sinister black menace.

Chapter 15

Oh no not you again

The slab was hard and cold and Michael lay restricted and unable to move just as he had before. The scene was all too familiar. He could feel a constant subtle vibration reverberate throughout the ship's structure and in turn through his captive body. The ship's engines were running. He screwed up his attempting to take in the immediate surroundings and determined that it was indeed the black figure's ship which he had the unfortunate pleasure of previously visiting. Glancing past his feet, Michael noticed that the sphere was once more positioned just beyond them and was wired up in much the same fashion as before. He could just make out the cockpit and his captor. Sitting in the flight chair, pressing various buttons, busying himself controlling the ship. Without warning an intense stabbing pain shot through his head and he let out a scream in reaction to the agonising pain he was enduring. It was a constant and excruciating, forcing him to keep his eyes firmly shut as he uncontrollably tensed up. A sharp prick on his neck was followed by relaxed relief and Michael felt the same pleasurable wooziness that the fluorescent blue liquid had shown him before. He soon passed out and once again found himself in the empty white room. *"Welcome 324"* An unfamiliar voice spoke to him. It was the same indistinguishable one that he had heard while he lay bloodied on the beach. *"Who's there?"* There was no reply and Michael again spoke out, in hope of a reply *"Who are you?"*

"Do not worry Michael" A cool sensation rippled over the surface of Michael's skin as the sound of Sophie's voice instantly calmed him. *"Sophie?"*

"That's right Michael, it's Sophie, be calm"

"Where am I?" The room grew silent, he blinked and then opened his eyes. Upon opening them he was met by a stunning sight. He sat peacefully by the river in the mountains where he had first encountered Noritomo. He looked around, soaking up the instantly generated tranquillity. Blinking again, his eyes were met by those of Sophie's who appeared beside him on the pebbles by the river. She was as stunningly beautiful as he remembered her. Her soft lips touched his cheek sending his heart into a quickened pace. It pulsed now with a renewed vigour. *"How is it possible, how can you be here?"* Sophie stroked his face with the back of her hand and replied *"Where*

is here my love?" Michael was lost in the mesmerising beauty of her eyes and he sat still as she moved towards him. Sophie leaned in and kissed him on the lips, the texture of her skin, the warmth and the taste were all exactly as he would have wished and had come to expect from her. He shut his eyes instinctively and when he opened them he lay still in his bunk within cell twenty four of penitentiary one. Another voice stirred his attention. *"Drink"* Servo pushed a bottle of solution one into his face and Michael took the bottle *"Drink".* The solution was exactly the flavour he had remembered, and just as he had experienced while in the penitentiary he was overcome with a feeling of intense rage. The rage culminated in another sharp pain in his head which forced him to close his eyes. The unrecognised voice spoke again *"We need to pull it"*

       "Leave him, he is fine" Sophie replied.

       "I tell you, he is going to pop"

       "He has made it this far, keep it running" the voice which accompanied Sophie's seemed concerned. Whatever it was they were witnessing, it sounded to Michael that it was putting him in some sort of danger. Sophie was obviously adamant that they continue and reassured her companion. *"He's stronger than you were, I'm pretty sure we can pull him out intact".* Michael listened intently to the pair's conversation. Surely he could learn something as they deliberated over his fate. *"O.K bring him back"* Sophie sounded authoritative and after a little burst of the same pain in his head, Michael was back standing in the white room. *"Welcome back 324"*

       "Who is this? Is that you Sophie?" Michael waited for an answer and was relieved to hear her voice again *"I'm here too Michael, try and relax"* *"Sophie, what is happening to me? Who is that with you? How do you know my real name?"* Sophie was stern with her response *"Relax and stay calm please Michael, it's very important"* Michael felt the same little prick on his neck and it was followed by him slipping into another drug induced state. The white room was empty, apart from a table in the centre which Michael now stood over. Observing its contents he noticed it held the sphere which was glowing brightly, almost alive with light and power as it always did. It was disconnected from the ten fragments which he had collected so far, they lay uniformly on the table beside it. The table was Perspex and transparent and the fragments where placed in a little rack with twelve slots, two being left vacant. *"Michael? Can you hear me?"* Sophie spoke aloud and he answered calmly, still feeling the effects of the blue drug. *"I hear you, Sophie"*

206

"Do you know where you are?" Michael chuckled like a drunk teenager and replied

"Hell no"

"That's good Michael, now what do you see?"

"It's mine" there was a momentary pause and Sophie spoke again *"What is it Michael, what is yours?"* Michael snapped angrily *"I don't know what it is, but it's mine!"* Silence fell again and then Michael was unsettled by the unfamiliar voice *"Michael".* Michael interrupted *"Who the fuck are you? Where's Sophie?"*

"Relax Michael" Sophie interrupted and administered him with another shot of the blue drug which relaxed him instantly. *"Michael"*

"Yeah, I'm still here Mr?"

"Michael, who I am, is not important, what I know is" Michael was woozy and incapable of partaking in a heated discussion, so he played along. *"O.K I'm listening"*

"What do you see?"

"I see the thing, the thing that takes me places"

"Good, what is the thing Michael?"

"I don't know, it's mine"

"O.K that's good". The questions were vague and Michael answered them almost robotically with the fluorescent blue drug helping the conversation to flow. Michael could hear Sophie and her companion move around him as silence fell and he awaited the next line of questioning. The background noise changed to excited rustling and Michael could sense that there was some sort of commotion ensuing. *"Shit Sophie, they found us, how did they find us?"* Sophie responded with a concerned tone to her voice which made Michael sober up quickly. *"We need to abort and put him under, if they get him, then it's over"* Michael stood patiently in the white room, now fully aware and desperate to understand what he was hearing *"Sophie, what is it?"*

"Michael, can you hear us?"

"Yes, what is happening?"

"Nothing to worry about, just keep going. We have to leave you for now" Michael could not let her go, without some answers" *Tell me what is happening, what am I doing? When can I go home?"* Sophie's companion cut him off

"No time for this 324"

"What the hell does this 324 mean?"

"O.K Sophie, less than a minute" The as yet unidentified companion sounded reasonably concerned. The light in the white

207

room started to flicker and Michael could hear some pops and crackles in his ear which accompanied the strobe like effect of the lighting *"Michael.....I'm losing him"*

"Sophie?.....Sophie? Oh shit, are you there?" Michael's breathing grew more rapid by the second as he contemplated being left alone again. *"Michael...............Mich.........if you can hear me..............you are 324, unite the twel....."* Michael had heard enough to understand what he had to do. He approached the sphere and started to reunite the fragments and listened as little snippets of dialogue continued to filter into the white room. *"We need to go now, quickly 324"* the other voice sounded desperate and encouraged Michael to complete the task as quickly as possible. He slotted the ninth fragment into place and the sphere left its stationary position and levitated above his head gradually glowing brighter and brighter. Michael reached out towards it with the tenth fragment and the entire white room flickered in unison with the sphere. A blue flash emanated from the sphere as he clicked the tenth fragment into place and the bright light surrounded him, paralysing him and engaging him into the transportation sequence. Michael could hear the blast of weaponry and Sophie's voice grew more distant by the millisecond. Her screams continued to fade until he slipped into dark silence, unaware as to whether the tenth fragment had been fully reunited. Michael's eyes opened and they required several wipes with the back of his hand to remove the thick deposits of sleep which had built up in their corners. His body was the same old and tired one he had inhabited on the beach. Sitting up from his sleeping position, it did not take him long to assess his surroundings, as they were small and scarcely decorated. It seemed he had materialised in another cell, quite unlike the one in the penitentiary. The walls and ceilings were made of solid black glass and he had been lying on a glass bunk in the centre of the room. A light on the ceiling was getting gradually brighter and Michael watched with interest as it was not an ordinary bulb. The entire ceiling was increasing in brightness until the room was sufficiently lit. He stood up from the slab and danced uncomfortably as the icy cold glass floor made him shiver. The room could only have been ten feet square and there was no obvious entrance or exit. On one of the walls were three circular discs which were set under a couple of inches of the black glass. Each of them had a different symbol. After studying the three discs for a few minutes, it was a language which he was not familiar, he could not even have hazarded a guess. It was a style of writing that he had never came across, even in his line of work. Michael sighed as he realised that once again he was fumbling in the dark. He turned his

208

back to the discs and leaned wearily on the wall. Michaels shoulder touched the glass at the middle disc and at the opposite wall a small opening appeared, closely followed by a shelf containing a small metal box. Michael approached and removed the box, laying it on the glass slab from where he had woken. The box was quite warm to the touch and consisted of two halves, a base and a lid. The aroma was so inviting, it smelled like a Sunday roast but unfortunately it did not look like one. A solid square shaped block filled one half of the container which had been split up the middle. The block was a brown and black colouring and it lay in about 10mm of a liquid which was the same drab colour. In the other half of the tray were two blocks of equal size. Both the blocks were half the size of the first and one of them was green and the other one white. They were not accompanied by a liquid. Michael determined that it was some sort of food and for the first time in what felt like an age he thought of home. Kaitlin made a killer of a Sunday roast and both Joseph and he would look forward until such a time that they could afford all the required ingredients to make the special treat for the family. He strained his eyes as he tried to picture their faces in his mind. They were so blurry and almost completely eradicated. Had the strong aroma from the food not stirred his memories, he may not have thought of them at all. Kaitlin was so strong willed and he remembered her being such an independent woman. He squeezed his eyes tightly together as he tried his utmost to bring a vision of her into his head. Her face was slightly blurred and it would disappear being quickly replaced by another face. A far more recent and captivating individual. His eyes opened quickly as he became wracked with guilt. He had tried his utmost to bring Kaitlin to the forefront of his mind. Only for the feelings of love and desire that he had for her to conjure up an image of Sophie. She was so Beautiful and mysterious , and it seemed no matter how unexplained or sinister her involvement in all this was, he could not get her out of his mind. Michael removed a utensil which was attached to the underside of the lid of the container. *"Ha, a Spork!"* He said aloud as he inspected the quirky piece of multi-cutlery. He used the serrated side of the Spork to carve a piece from the large block of food and lifted it up to his mouth. The aroma was reminiscent of real hearty homemade gravy. Thick with the fat of the animal from which it had been made. The consistency was quite a different sensation all together. It was a combination of dry and crunchy parts about the size of garden peas and a moist jelly which was coagulated around them *"Cat food!"* Michael continued to eat the meaty part of his meal. The aroma was intensely attractive which made the crunchy cat food a little easier to digest. The other two cubes where now as disconcerting as they were intriguing. *"Meat and two veg then"* He said. Michael cleaned of the edge of his Spork with his tongue and chopped a piece of the green cube. He smiled with satisfaction upon realisation that he had guessed correctly. It tasted of fresh green vegetables He cut into it the white cube and placed a large slice in his mouth. He braced himself for a buttery and starchy mashed potato. The flavour was so overpowering and Michael gagged as he spat it back into the container. It was not potato, it was in fact dessert. *"Yuck! Vanilla"* Michael had always hated the taste and even the sickly sweet smell. He pushed the container away from himself in disgust, and approached the three discs on the wall. He pushed the one on the left without hesitation and a tubular container appeared in the alcove, which he popped the lid of. It was water and he gulped it, quickly removing the unwanted flavour from his mouth. The third disc intrigued him even more. He pressed his hand to the wall and another alcove opened in the corner of the room. It was a tear drop shape and had a small six holed drain at its base. It was quite obvious to him, what its function was and he was soon relieving himself. The urine splashed against the side of the glass and it rang like a constant muted bell. He leaned his hand on the wall above the urinal, physically tired by the evacuation of the old man's bladder. He sat on the end of the slab and supped from the water container. There was no clear indication as to the purpose of the room. It was clear he was being held there as there was no exit. Michael began to feel drowsy and likened the feeling to the blue drug of which he was now becoming a regular user. A voice spoke to him *"Lie on the slab 324"* Michael followed his instructions hypnotically, the food or water must have had something in it he thought. He was powerless to do anything other and obey. *"That's it sleep now".* The voice was unfamiliar, it was not the voice which had partnered Sophie from before, it was new and sounded business like. There was certainly no intimacy in its tone. He lay on the slab and passed out only hearing whispers of what was happening around him. *"We should just terminate it"*

"Terminate it? You any idea how much one of these costs? We need to replace it with a brand new one if we shut it down"

"I know, I know, but imagine if they had got to it? If it gets out?"

"Don't worry, that's why we are here"

"So do we just wipe it?"

"No we need to keep as much as we can or the user will notice the glitches, O.K concentrate, slip in Japan"

210

"But Japan was fine"

"We need to do it in order, try and listen and learn something"

"O.K sorry, I'm just nervous"

"First time eh? O.K put them in one by one, we need to remove the infected files"

"O.K that's the upload in progress, it will take a few hours to purge all the files affected by the illegal access, fancy some lunch?" A loud hiss and a clunk of glass on glass signalled that Michael was alone again. He remained still on the slab and very drowsy, he had heard enough from the two men who had just left to send his imagination into overdrive. Were they talking about him? What were they purging? Michael's head spun with drug induced confusion and he struggled to keep conscious until a piercing ring in his ear made his entire body jolt with pain. It was followed by the crackle of interference "Michael? Michael can you hear me?" Struggling to remain awake, he focused on the sound of Sophie's voice. "Michael you need to wake up, snap out of it" Sophie's voice kept breaking up and Michael tried to answer her "Sophie.....where are you?"

"We are in the next room, you need to get up" Michael could hear her instructions but had no way of carrying them out. His body was numb with whatever the two men had used to incapacitate him. "O.K do it, it's our last chance"

"You're the boss" Sophie's companion was with her in the next room and he spoke to Michael "O.K 324 this is going to hurt a little" Michael lay helpless and braced himself as his entire body began to vibrate violently. He lay convulsing and his limbs darted erratically in every direction. A sudden jolt of electricity travelled through his body and he sat up from the slab. He was naked and the old man's body looked even more limp and pathetic than it had with his clothes on. His entire body was covered with pads with wires coming from them, at the base of the slab laid the sphere. It was similarly wired up like it had been on the black figure's ship. "Michael.......get up, you need to get out of there" Michael was reinvigorated and he leapt from the slab and removed all the pads from his body. His ragged shorts and polo shirt were on the floor and he quickly pulled them on. "Michael get up......you need to get out of there"

"I'm up, where are you?" Michael searched the room, but there was no obvious exit, the glass door which the two men had left through was now hidden from his sight. The sphere was still wired up and he pulled at them to release it. The centre piece of the sphere was placed upon a small square dock and Michael attempted to remove it unsuccessfully. It was stuck fast and he strained for a few more moments until he shielded his eyes from a bright spark of molten glass which exploded from the corner of the wall with the alcoves in it. The glass popped as it began to melt and a small blob of molten glass landed on his arm making him squeal like a stuck pig. The wall began to glow with a deep orange colour and a small bubbling line of glass formed as it moved from the ceiling to the floor. Michael watched on aware that whatever was on the other side of the glass had decided it was coming for him. The molten line continued at a steady pace and Michael ran to the sphere again, furiously trying to remove it from its base, it would not budge. The glass was now glowing brightly, and it now covered most of the wall. The molten line had almost made it back to the point where it had originally started, creating a large man sized rectangle cut out. Michael stood in fear, unable to dislodge the sphere and watched as the block of molten glass tilted towards him and crashed to the floor. The room had filled with the smoky fumes of the melting glass and Michael waved his hands to try and clear some of the smoke. *"Sophie, is that you?"* Stepping through the newly forged doorway, the black figure towered over Michael and he stood rooted to the spot in desperate fear. The black mesh mask which covered its face moved closer and Michael cowered with fear, having seen first-hand what it was capable of *"Back off him!"*

"Sophie, is that you?" Michael opened his eyes and once again he breathed easier

"What the hell is going on?"

"Not the time for a summary, we need to get out of here"

"What are you doing with that thing?" Michael nodded towards the black figure that had now backed off and was standing awaiting instruction *"There is no time Michael, trust me"* Sophie held out her hand and helped Michael to his feet. She turned to the black figure and issued instructions *"Pack it up, carefully"* the black figure removed the sphere from its plinth with ease, it packed it in a silver case along with the ten fragments. It closed the case and stood to attention awaiting Sophie's next order. *"Come this way Michael, we need to leave now"*

"Where?"

"Enough questions, let's go" There was a serious urgency to her voice and he followed her through the opening in the wall. The black figure followed and they made their way into another cell, exactly the same as Michael's. The opposite wall had the same hole cut from it and they pushed through into a third cell. *"Where now?"*

"Stand back Michael" The black figure moved to the opposite wall and raised its arm. The same blue light which Michael had witnessed on the Angel beamed from its finger and it began to cut through the glass. Michel turned and looked at Sophie. She was dressed fully in black and her hair was tied tightly in a ponytail. She looked nervous and kept checking the display on her wristwatch, which was large and seemed far more complex than a simple time piece. *"Move it"* She shouted at the figure who replied in a familiar voice. *"As quick as I can boss".* It was the voice of her companion from before who was the figure in black. Michael was surprised even though he had never seen the face to match the voice *"Sophie, who is he?"*

"Give it time Michael, let us get out of here first"

"O.K, O.K" Michael was desperate for any little snippet of information and had to stop himself from continually probing Sophie with questions. After all she was busy saving him. The figure finished cutting out the block and it too fell to the floor. It held out his hand and helped Sophie through the opening into the next compartment. It then turned to Michael and held out its hand. He hesitated and then accepted its offer of assistance. It lifted him through the opening and he gagged at the change in atmosphere. The new compartment was a long service corridor, filled with pipes and the floor was covered with metal gratings. The air was filled with various fumes and was humid with stale moisture. *"Close it up"* Sophie directed the figure, who lifted the glass block back into place and started to reseal it. *"Quickly, they will notice he is gone soon"*

"Someone please tell me what the fuck is going on" Michael's exasperation was now uncontrollable and Sophie ignored him this time. The figure finished sealing the glass and they moved on quickly. They had accelerated into a quick sprint and Michael struggled to keep up with Sophie who was rocketing down the service corridor. They reached a dead end and Sophie held her hand out towards the figure who produced a small keypad with a digital display *"We need to open this airlock"*

"What airlock?" Michael could see nothing around him, just pipes and bulkhead. The black figure pointed to the deck head, where a small hatch was visible about fifteen metres above them. *"O.K I'm going up"* Sophie climbed onto the figures shoulders and shimmied up a vertical pipe. She soon reached the hatch and attached the pad to the large iron hinge. She pressed a combination of buttons on the pad and a digital display came to life. A timer started to countdown from 25 seconds. She quickly climbed back down and the three took shelter behind a large pipe spool which shielded them from the impending

213

blast. The display reached zero and the pad exploded, blowing the hinge clean off. Sending the hatch to the deck below. *"O.K quickly"* The figure lifted Sophie back to the hatch and she shimmied up the pipe and out through it. Michael followed and Sophie reached down and helped him up through the opening. The figure barely fitted through and they both helped it until they emerged standing in a vast hangar. It was long, empty and was lit throughout by large floodlights. At the far end was a small ship and Sophie began to run towards it shouting back as she went. *"Come on then"* Michael was slow again and the figure lifted him from behind and headed after Sophie with him on its shoulders. The figure who had seemed so menacing was now proving to be a useful ally and Michael spoke to it as it carried him *"So, what's your story then?"* It remained silent and Michael was persistent, bordering on rude. *"Hey you"* the figure replied and infuriated Michael even more

       "Sophie will make things clear, for now we must escape this place"

       "But who are we running from?" Sophie dropped her head from the loading bay doors and looked at Michael with a serious glare "No point talking to him, he won't tell you nothing, now get in here" The black figure lowered him to the floor and Michael looked at him, for some sort of reaction, but true to form he was met with a lifeless black mask, bereft of expression. *"Get on board"* the figure spoke and pointed to the loading bay doors. Michael climbed the small ramp and entered the ship. The sweat began to ripple over his body at the shock of what he had walked into. It was the same ship, where the figure had held him and tortured him. Michael backed off towards the loading bay. Sophie approached him, noticing the fear in his eyes. *"It's O.K Michael...Don't worry"*

       "Who the hell are you people?"

       "Michael calm down, let me help you" Sophie got closer and he backed off until he was running down the ramp towards the hanger. He was sweating and overcome with panic, questioning the motives of Sophie and the black figure. Why would they torture him? Why won't they tell him anything? *"Michael come back"* Sophie chased him down the ramp *"They are coming for you!"* Michael screamed with anguish back at her

       "Who? Who is coming for me?" The black figure placed his hand on Michael's shoulder and he turned to face him *"They are coming"* The figure pointed towards the hangar doors and Michael looked on as the enormous hangar doors lifted to reveal around fifty bodies marching in unison. They were all dressed in black and Michael

could just make out the enormous firearms which they carried. *"Quick, I will stall them!"* The figure bent on one knee and pointed both hands towards the oncoming hoard of soldiers. A bright blue ball grew from each hand and it retracted its arms like two enormous powerful pistons firing the blue balls of light simultaneously towards them. Michael watched in awe as the front row of soldiers scattered like bowling pins. Sophie grabbed him by the arm and pulled him on board, he never resisted being too mesmerised by the figure's immense power. *"Michael"* Sophie attempted to grab his attention. He shook his head and focused on her. *"I know it is a lot to take, but please just trust me"* he could hear the sincerity in her voice and he nodded in agreement. *"I need to fire her up, stay out of sight"* Sophie moved towards the cockpit and began prepping the ship for ignition. Michael was so amazed by the figure and he moved to the loading bay doors and peered around to catch a glimpse. He watched as legion after legion of soldiers filled the hangar. The black figure was firing an array of weaponry at the small army. It all originated from the blue light. Grenades, Machine gun fire, were included in a multitude of various weaponry. *"Michael, get inside now"* Sophie shouted angrily and he obeyed and re-entered the ship *"Get in your chair, we are leaving"* She pointed to the slab, where he had spent a considerable amount of time previously. It was in its upright position. *"No way, I'm not getting in that again"* He backed off and looked at her with defiance. *"Trust me?"* He could see she was beginning to lose her patience with him and he reluctantly sat on the slab. She pressed some buttons in the cockpit and two seat belts crossed over his head, locking him in place. The ships engine burst into life and Sophie manoeuvred it into position. *"What about him?"*

　　　"Just sit tight Michael" A loudspeaker sounded out from the ships exterior and Sophie spoke into it. "We need a way out of here" Michael looked out the loading bay doors and could just make out the carnage below. The figure was holding off the onslaught of attacking soldiers. They all wore masks, not unlike the figure himself but he was much larger and far more powerful. It dispatched one soldier after another with ease and swivelled on the spot and pointed both arms towards the nearest bulkhead and Sophie acknowledged. *"Roger that"* the figure placed both hands in front of its chest and bowed its head for a moment. Bullets and missiles bounced off and rebounded back at its attackers. It was so strong and seemed indestructible. Separating his hands slowly, the figure began to create a large singular ball of blue light which was bigger than anything it had conjured so far. With an almighty roar it launched it towards the bulkhead and it blew a hole in

the side of the hangar. Pulling soldiers out into the dark vacuum of space. The black figure fell to the deck of the hangar, visibly fatigued by its work. *"Hold on"* Sophie shouted across the loudspeaker *"O.K here I come"* The small ship positioned itself over the body of black figure and he crawled towards the loading bay doors, slowly making his way inside. The ramp retracted, dragging his exhausted body into the ship's hold. *"What's wrong with him?"*

"That last blast it drained him, he's weakened" The loading bay doors creaked as they started to close over and just as they were about to close fully, Michael heard the fast moving wiz of a projectile passing through the air. *"No!"* Sophie shrieked *"Auto Pilot"* She unclipped her belt and ran to the loading bay. The black figure lay still and Sophie used all her might to flip him over onto his back. *"Not now, not after all this"*

"Sophie, let me out, let me help" Michael struggled to get out from his chair.

"No Michael stay there." She had difficulty speaking through her tears and Michael tried again to persuade her *"Please, I want to help, he saved my life"* The black figure stirred and spoke with some of his remaining breath. *"Let him see my love"*

"Release safety harness" The belts unfastened and shot back to their holder. Michael jumped from the slab and approached Sophie who was holding the black figure in her arms. She was sobbing uncontrollably. Michael noticed the pool of blood which had accumulated on the deck around his head and shoulders. *"Who is he?"* Sophie looked upon the masked face of the figure before she replied, as if she was gaining his permission to speak *"My love, you know what you must do"* Sophie nodded in agreement and sobbed heavily. *"Do not fret my love, 324 is strong".* Michael listened intently and his heart beat like it never had done before, bursting with anticipation of a long overdue explanation. *"Michael, come closer"* The figure beckoned Michael towards his mask and he approached, tingling all over with nervous excitement. *"You must protect it, they must never get it, it's your only way out"* The figure groaned and Sophie embraced him softly, she was only too aware that his moments of life were down to their last few. *"Listen to Sophie, she will guide you".* The Figure's mask exhausted some pressurised gas from its sides and the black mesh material started to retract slowly upwards into the mask. Michael took a deep breath and waited for his full face to be revealed. He gazed upon the now chalky complexion of the dying black figure. The eyes were familiar, the nose too. Michael tried to remember where he had seen the face before. It had been such a long and confused journey

216

and he had met so many new people. He remembered all the bodies which he had inhabited and eliminated them one by one until the figure spoke to him and he realised who the man that lay dying before him was. *"What's the matter Michael, not recognise your own face?"* Michael grew short of breath and began to hyperventilate. He backed off and Sophie moved closer to the figure and kissed him softly. *"Goodbye my love".* The figure smiled back at Sophie and chuckled as he uttered his last words *"Ha, don't forget to wipe".* Sophie screamed in anguish as he passed and Michael was now pressed up against the bulkhead in shock. The black figure was him, not any of the bodies which he had inhabited, not a hideous alien or mindless soldier. It was now all so clear and unmistakable to him. The black figure was Michael Cameron. The realisation was already too much for him to handle. Michael wretched and his two and a half cubes of diner were soon splattered all over the deck of the ship. Sophie stood up from the figure and turned to face him, she wiped her eyes and walked passed him towards the cockpit.

"Sophie?"

"Not now 324, stand back from him". By now the auto pilot had taken the ship through the blast hole and was making its way through space to whatever destination was programmed into the ship's computer. *"I said step back you fool"* Michael backed out of the way and watched as Sophie brought down a force field and blocked the entrance to the loading bay where the lifeless figure now lay. *"Goodbye my love"* Sophie pushed another button and the loading bay doors opened, sucking the black figure out into space. The doors shut and she silently returned to the cockpit. Michael approached her with caution, she was fragile. *"Yeah, it was you"*

"But how can that be?" He could not help but quiz her, even at this emotionally charged time. *"Well I suppose you need to know soon en……"* The ship rocked with a massive blast from outside and a loud voice drowned them out *"You are in violation….."* *"Fuck your violation"* Sophie flicked a switch which muted the attackers warning and returned fire *"What's happening Sophie?"*

"Time to run again, get in your seat"

"But what were you going to say?"

"You heard what he said, listen to Sophie, now get in your god damn chair" Michael sat in the slab and the seat belts secured him in place again. *"O.K light drive on-line, hold on"* Another loud blast hit the ship *"Shit, shit, shit!"*

"What's wrong Sophie, can I help?"

217

"They've taken out the light drive", we're going nowhere" Sophie jumped from the cockpit and moved towards him hurriedly "Or at least I'm going nowhere" She started to flip switches and press buttons around him. "It's all down to you now 324, you must finish the task you have been given" the slab repositioned him in the horizontal position. Sophie opened the silver case and began to replace the ten fragments into the centre piece of the sphere until only the tenth piece remained. "You must do the last piece". The ship shunted fiercely in one direction and started moving slowly towards the other ship. "They have us in a tractor, you need to go now Michael"

"What about you?"

"Too late for me now, don't worry you will see me again. I will see one of you or you will see one of me"

"What does that mean?"

"Unite the twelve 324, for now you will forget him" Sophie Chuckled "Don't forget to wipe!" A blast from a weapon shot past Sophie as the ship was boarded

"Freeze, you are in violation…" The voice faded and Michael looked deep into her eyes for what felt like the final time. All outside noise was muted while he listened to her final instruction. "When it ends, remember, Question the Unquestionable" Sophie grabbed the tenth fragment and put it in his hand, pushing it into the slot together. The light engulfed him and Sophie faded away with her voice drifting to silence. The light faded and Michael awoke. The transportation had seemed longer and more arduous than the last few. He stretched out and groaned loudly. "O.K, what have we got now? That island was a bit weird". Awake and unaware of his ordeal on the ship, he remembered only the pyramid. Sophie had remembered to wipe.

Chapter 16

Daughter of the moon

The bed was lavishly ordained with ornate cushions and pillows and Michael lay outstretched focusing on the impressive drapes which hung magnificently around the room. A single silk sheet covered his body and was more than enough insulation as the temperature was humid and uncomfortable. A little tinkle of a small bell rang for a few seconds until at the far side of the room beyond the bottom end of the bed, one of the drapes began to flutter. An entourage of people snaked their way into the room and assembled like a military unit at Michael's bedside. There were twelve of them in total and they were all women, dressed in the same attire. The bottom half of their legs were bare to the knee, showing off the exotic bronze skin which was smooth and blemish free. The upper part of the legs were tightly wrapped in a white fabric, it was intentionally crumpled in design and was folded over itself with the cut running diagonally up from each knee until both sides of the fabric met in the middle, revealing a little more leg and sitting like a mid-length skirt. A brightly coloured belt made with many different coloured beads encircled their tiny waistlines and lengths of beads dangled down the front, creating a colourful addition to the white fabric. The belt also cleverly doubled as a disguise for the joint in the makeshift skirt. Their upper bodies were adorned somewhat differently. Michael was engrossed in the study of their torsos. A double banded sash made from beads which were carved from what appeared to be green glass-like pebbles barely covered their breasts. The item crossed their fronts like a saltire and seemed to sufficiently hold everything in place. They all stood with heads bowed and never glanced in Michael's direction. Their hair was thick, dark and shiny, and had the appearance that they constantly maintained it, to protect its lustre. Each of the women had their hair rolled into a tight bun on top of their heads, held in place with a cylindrical rod which looked like a knitting needle. The first attendant raised her head and approached the bedside, carefully trying not to make eye contact with him. She was of eastern appearance, or possibly north African and Michael likened her complexion to that of some of the beautiful Indian woman that he had seen in ancient paintings hung around the various galleries he had travelled to with his job. Her eyebrows were dark and manicured, rising slightly as they travelled outwards towards her temples. Her eyes were sparkly white and they were even more intense due to the black make up which was expertly drawn around their perimeter, making them appear to be bigger. They matched the extra-long dark eyelashes which appeared to be natural, thick and sturdy. The iris surrounding the pupil was magnificent, it was a golden colour, a dark yellowy amber which was as unusual as it was captivatingly beautiful. The girl bowed and held out a fabric cloth in both arms, beckoning Michael to pick it up. Having not moved yet, he groaned heavily as if he had been out for days, unable to remember that his body had endured another exhausting episode. He stretched his hand towards the offering and noticed the intricate pattern which was detailed on the skin of his arm. A large tribal design covered most of the arm and it was incredibly detailed. There was minimal hair on the forearm and a feeling of uneasiness began to overcome him as he inspected the remainder of it. The nails were perfect and the bone structure was slim and smooth to the touch. Michael pulled the sheet back and the soft silk slipped over his body *"Oh shit! Not again"* The first girl coughed nervously and attempted to avoid gazing in Michael's direction. He had been deposited in the body of a woman once again. This time the body in question had a far healthier disposition than his previous feminine incarnation. He too had the lovely light chestnut skin and his four limbs had the same lavishly decorated symbolism. Michael, now a little panicked by the revelation stared down upon his chest. This woman whoever she was of some importance. Her body was decorated with great care and her breasts sat firm and appeared flawless. Urged on by his obvious nakedness, Michael reached out for the fabric offering and soon realised it was an item of clothing. It was an all in one and he pulled it over his head like a poncho. The garment had a fixed head piece which slotted over his head, encapsulating his entire skull. It left only a small rectangular slit to allow him to see. The twelve girls then burst into life and the first girl looked upon Michael and began to speak, Michael was dressed and it was clear that the girl felt far more comfortable with interaction. *"Good morning My Madokht"*. She was undoubtedly speaking a foreign tongue, but Michael had become so attuned with the sphere that he understood her instantly and replied *"Good Morning"*

"Please, eat now my Madokht". The girl pointed to a large wooden table which the others had just about finished filling with a vast array of pots and bowls. It was covered in every type of fruit Michael had ever seen and some exotic ones which were new to him. The surface of the table was completely covered in a selection of breads, meats and refreshments. Michael approached the table and

220

sat down. The twelve girls backed off from the table and stood attentively in formation once again. The food was delicious and he spared no time in getting stuck in. The little bell tingled softly again and the girls robotically dropped to one knee, still with heads bowed. The ringing increased in volume and seemed to be approaching. From the same break in the drapes a small man entered. He was dressed in a black gown with golden lace sewn into the seams. He wore an enormous head dress, it looked like a half dozen exotic birds deconstructed and reattached, overly bright and packed full of colourful feathers. The man carried a little bell which he continued to ring until he stopped and spoke aloud. *"His Majesty.........King Kamal"*. A massive brute of a man entered through the drapes, he was at least six foot six and had long dark hair with a large beard. The beard and the hair had been arranged so as to give him a large pleat at the back and two smaller ones which covered each side of his face. His demeanour remained emotionless and Michael found himself in Awe of his presence. The massive man carried a scimitar, which looked well used and had certainly not been for decoration he thought. The little man with the feather hat changed the rhythm of the bell which had signalled the girls to get up silently and leave. The little man left, looking top heavy, leaving Michael alone with his visitor. He sat silently, patiently awaiting any information to hopefully explain his latest predicament. The man stood staring away from Michael and he spoke to him in a subdued and somewhat harsh tone *"You have eaten already Madokht?"* Michael was ready to answer and was cut off abruptly *"This outrageous behaviour I will forgive due to the occasion"* The man approached the opposite end of the table and sat down. He began to eat and Michael joined him, remaining silent. Michael munched on a bread roll which was soft and fresh. *"Well Madokht, have you prepared for today's ceremony?"*

"Yes, I have" Michael answered him, in fear of what his reaction may have been this time, as usual he had no idea where he was or what his role could have been. *"Your insolence is unacceptable, you should address me in the proper fashion!"* Michael was at a loss , so sat in silence once again *"Yes I have Majesty, if we are to be married then you will have to learn to behave in the correct manner Madokht"* the man angrily ripped a bread roll in half with his teeth and supped from a large clay carafe before he continued *"Today is the wedding of my youngest brother to that eastern whore he has been bewitched by"*. Michael listened intently as his breakfast companion continued his rant. *"As he will never be king, I can accept this, for the*

time being". Michael's silence was for once not as uncomfortable as it had been in previous locales. It would seem that the woman he inhabited did not have much chance at conversation while around this man anyway. *"Make yourself ready, and do not shame me with your lack of respect today"* The man stood and clapped his hands together which resulted in the entourage returning swiftly to the room led by the little man in the feather hat. *"Madokht",* Michael looked towards him awaiting the next burst from his vile tongue, *"Remember your respect, punishment is one tradition that I will make sure is not lost in this house"* the massive man left the room and was followed by the little man who exclaimed *"His Majesty King Kamal"* as they left, while ringing his little bell. Michael breathed easier and continued with his breakfast, eating small bits and pieces. A meal was such a luxury in the recent weeks. He sat and struggled to think of the few occasions where he had eaten anything. The places he had been and the opportunities he had to eat had been both rare and in most cases impractical. The body he inhabited was in prime physical condition. Had he inherited the appetite of this woman as well as her body and predicament? Michael's deliberation only proved to remind him of the debacle he found himself in again. He sat and thought of the last place he had been, which was so calculated and prepared. The setting had been so fabricated and set his mind racing as to what its purpose could have been. Japan was so real, cold mountain air, medieval and believable. The time spent as the poor unfortunate coma victim was an experience which he had nothing to compare with. But it was a genuine shock to the senses and he had no problem in believing that he was truly trapped within the poor soul's lifeless body. The angel was so futuristic and he remembered it like he was watching a movie, with star ships and planets surrounding him. It was a truly fantastical situation, but again Michael had no problem in believing that he was really there, a part of Captain Carson's crew. Hoping with the rest of them, that they would find a new home. Then it was there. The black figure. Michael's eyes widened as he remembered the cold and dead look that the black mask provided. He was in no doubt of its true existence. A shiver ran down the tanned and perfectly formed back of the woman which he now possessed. His daydream continued and his thoughts drifted back to the island. It was so manufactured in style and the beach was perfect with the sea water at the ideal temperature. The weather had been the first signifier that he had noticed something was off. It seemed to be so unpredictable and sporadic all the time, but to such an extent that the unpredictability was the thing that had made it so staged, not unlike the turning on and

222

off of a tap or the flicking of a switch. Everything about the last habitation had been bizarre. Puzzles, pyramids and turtles. Michael shook his head in disbelief at what he was thinking. *"Madokht, are you O.K?"* The hand maiden from before awoke him from his daydream *"Yes, I am fine. Give me a moment"* The hand maiden backed off and waited silently for her next instruction. Michael drifted off again *"How did I get here?"* Michael struggled to remember how he had finished in the pyramid. Normally the transportation sequence was so vivid and vibrant. He could not remember utilising the fragment at all. His memory had deserted him on this occasion. He was dragged back to reality again by the comforting sound of a little boy's voice filling the room as he sprinted full pelt across the floor waving a wooden sword and giggling as he went. He had no clothes on his bottom half and was being chased by two servant girls who were having just as much fun trying to catch and dress him. Michal closed his eyes and there he stood clear as day in front of him in the darkness. Still a little boy as he always remembered him, pure and unspoiled by the lack lustre upbringing that a large bank balance and limited family time together would eventually ruin. He felt the tears build up in his eyes. He had forgotten his son. He had become so obsessed by the sphere and his mission to reunite it with its missing parts that he had given little thought to why he was bothering to complete the task in which he had been entrusted. It felt like years since he had heard his voice and felt the soft warm kiss of Kaitlin's lips on his. A solitary tear ran down his face and soon the hand maiden approached to offer her assistance. *"I am fine"*, Michael stood up and moved towards where the little boy was playing, he caught sight of her approaching and backed off, hiding behind the legs of one of the servants who stood still bowing. *"Do not be afraid"*. The boy winced at the sound of his voice and cowered with fear. Michael turned to his hand maiden, *"What is he afraid of?"*

"Madokht, it is your attire"

"Then take it off!"

"But Madokht..." Before the hand maiden had a chance, Michael removed the head dress and gave the little boy a beaming smile. *"What is your name?"* The boy approached *"My name is Kamiri, I am the Queen's son"* Michael thought for a second

"The Queen who will marry the King's brother?"

"Yes, who are you?"

223

"I am Madokht"

"Are you to marry King Kamal? He is very big"

"That is right, although I agree he is big and a bit mean too".
They both giggled and Michael took some light relief from the
normality of having a conversation with a child who was unshackled by
the burdens which accompanied adulthood. *"Madokht please!"* The
hand maiden thrust the headdress towards him with a look of
concerned urgency on her face and Michael reinstated it. *"Goodbye
Madokht".* The little boy raced off and was closely followed by the two
servant girls again. *"Goodbye son"* Michael replied with thoughts of
little Joseph fresh in his mind. The Hand maiden approached again,
"Will Madokht be praising the moon this morning?" Michael had
absolutely no idea what she meant and agreed with a solitary nod.
The entourage burst into life and before he knew it Michael stood fully
adorned in a white fabric gown which had multiple layers of fine cloth
covered in detailed patterns. It was interwoven with gold and silver
threads. The head dress was removed and was replaced with a thin
veil which done the same job, leaving only his eyes visible. *"The altar
lies ready Madokht"* the hand maiden gestured towards the opening
and Michael passed through the drapes into a long thin corridor. He
dragged his new attire down the long corridor, physically hampered by
the amount of layers until he reached an opening at the other end. He
passed through another set of drapes and was soon standing alone in a
small chapel. None of his entourage had followed. The room was
scarcely decorated, but what was there was obviously of high
importance. The altar was carved with incredible skill and
workmanship. It spanned the width of the room and seemed to be
illustrating a story on its front. It was constructed of a white marble
which glistened under the light from the two braziers which hung from
the ceiling in each of the corners above the altar. Michael leaned in to
take a closer look and let out a yelp in panic as a man's voice spoke
from behind him. *"The work is astonishing is it not?"* The man was
younger than the king and far more attractive. It would seem that the
exotic beauty that Michael had gained was not limited to the women
in this region. His hair was dark and flowing. His jawline was firm and
sturdy. Michael thought how it would take an almighty crack to
disturb it from its set position. Unlike the woman, his eyes were a
sparkling green colour, like Japanese jade. *"Do you look forward to the
wedding festivities Madokht?"* He bowed slightly as he used Michael's
adoptive name *"Which one?"*

224

"Of course, yours will come in due course, I mean today's Madokht?" Michael nodded and returned to the carving *"You look upon it, as if you have never seen it before Madokht, it is beautiful"* Michael nodded in agreement

"Describe it for me"

"Madokht, I am sure you know it so well" Michael could tell that the exotic visitor desired the body he inhabited and had decided to use his newly obtained feminine charm to gain some explanation of the altar inscriptions. He fluttered his eyelids and smiled with an obviously flirtatious attempt to woo him, which was blatant even through his veil. *"It would please me"* The man looked around and peered through the entrance.

"O.K but we must be quick, if my brother caught me here…" He leaned down and stretched over his shoulder and described the first image on the altar. It was a full moon which cast its light over a cradle with a man standing by it *"That is Adjuk, he is standing over a new born baby deep in the desert; she is the daughter of the moon"*. The Man smiled enthusiastically and continued. The next depiction was a war scene, many great men and horses locked in a great struggle, above them a blazing sun. *"This is the eternal war of the Kings, two peoples locked in battle for eternity"* The man looked sad at the mention of it

"And what do they fight for?"

"Power, fame, glory, but mostly for riches buried deep in the mountains" The man pointed to the next depiction which was a mountain scene with slaves working a mine at the bottom. *"It was said that whoever found the fabled jewel of kings would end the eternal war once and for all"*. The next carving was of a mine worker handing a large jewel to the king *"That is King Kamar, he worked the slaves night and day until one day a farm boy found the jewel and presented him with it in return for his freedom"*. Michael listened intently hoping for some clue as to his involvement in all this. The jewel in question was looking like a real candidate for the next fragment. The next carving showed an older man and a pretty young woman standing before the King. *"King Kamar promised to stop the war if Adjuk would promise him a wedding to the daughter of the moon. Adjuk was wise and knew the power his child possessed and allowed the wedding to continue."* Michael listened with great

225

interest, the story was fascinating. The man pressed his back closer against him as he pointed to the next carving *"On the night of the wedding, King Kamar presented her with the jewel of kings. Unbeknown to him the daughter of the moon knew of the other who had actually found the jewel"* Michael whispered

"The farm boy"

"She refused the jewel and the king reacted angrily. The daughter of the moon saw the king for the evil man he was and held out her hand to him" the final carving showed the girl with the jewel inside her heart. The two joined as one. *"The daughter of the Moon, her as powerful as the gods themselves joins with the jewel of the Kings and King Kamar is transformed into the true finder of the jewel before the watching crowd. Together they ruled in peace for a thousand generations".* Michael studied the altar for a while longer *"It is an old fairy story Madokht"* Michael nodded silently. *"It is central to my vows I will take today and has been the bond which keeps our people at peace for many years".* Michael saw an opportunity *"Do you use the jewel of kings?"*

"It is a symbol of our unity and I suppose there is a chance I could turn into a simple farm boy, Madokht". The man laughed and Michael joined him, so as to not seem ignorant or even simple. The draped entrance rippled as King Kamal strode in *"What is the meaning of this little brother? The day of your wedding and you crave the attentions of your King's future wife?"* Michael could see the anger on the King's face and similarly the fear on the face of his younger sibling and spoke out. *"We were discussing today's events your Majesty"* The King's eyes turned to Michael's and grew angrier. He raised his hand to strike him and as his hand travelled towards his face, it was stopped short as his brother intercepted. *"Kamal, no".* The King turned to his brother and slapped him firmly across his face. *"You foolish clown Kinra, have you no respect for your King? If this was not such an important day for this kingdom, you would be spending it in the sewers with the rats".* Kinra was red in the face with anger *"I would spend a thousand days with the rats than another spent here with you!"* King Kamal laughed

"Your wish is my command, after today you can go and live with the vermin from the east" The king turned to face Michael, *"I will deal with you later".* He turned and marched off arrogantly *"Bring the sewer rat with you".* Two guards grabbed Kinra and dragged him off

226

leaving Michael on his own again. Michael stared blankly at the altar. The jewel of kings had to be the next fragment and he would find out for sure at the wedding *"Now where is the sphere?"* He searched the entire chapel and found nothing. The drapes opened again and the hand maiden entered, *"Has Madokht praised?"*

"Yes Madokht has praised"

"Please come we must prepare". Michael followed the entourage back to the bedroom and they began to fuss over him again. This time the proceedings seemed to last forever and a few hours passed of titivation and over indulgence. A dull repetitive thud repeated in the distance, followed by a loud burst of a distance horn. The drapes parted at the other side of the room. *"The king approaches your quarters Madokht, should we prepare the viewing spot?"* Michael agreed blindly, still captivated by the repetitive thud and horn blowing. The drapes were drawn and two large wooden thrones were placed in the veranda which looked out far into the distance. The landscape was scorched by the hot sun, but seemed immense and filled with little pockets of civilisation. The buildings looked as if they had been moulded from the sand itself, yellow, baked and for the most part crumbling. A long narrow pass led up to the main gates of the palace which had been decked out ceremoniously. The royal armies were in full regalia and in strict formations. It was a much a show of strength as it was a mark of respect for the oncoming caravan. Michael stood before the smaller of the two thrones and gazed in wonder at the sight before him. If this experience had given him anything, the scenery was outstanding and it was a privilege to gaze upon it. The little bell rang out and the entourage stood to attention and soon the little man entered and Michael sniggered upon seeing his attire. The exploding bird hat from before had been replaced by something even more ridiculous. It was much the same design but was twice as large and he struggled to keep it upright as he made his announcement. *"Ahem, his majesty King Kamal!"* The King entered and was also kitted out in a flamboyant and clearly uncomfortable outfit. *"I am surprised you are not sitting already"* Michael remained focused on the world outside. The king was clearly spoiling for a fight which he knew he would be best to avoid. *"Here she comes, scab covered eastern dog, ha".* The king laughed at his own insult *"Bring me wine!"* The entourage came to his side with a selection which he grabbed and downed *"More, bring me more wine"* Michael sipped a small glass, to keep his wits about him, would surely be sensible. The approaching caravan was now far louder and the repetitive thud was that of a pair of elephants who

227

were marching side by side. Across their backs was a large cane structure which held the royal party. Michael could just make out three figures within. The elephants were followed by some horses drawing a couple of wagons and a few camels accompanied by around 50 servants who followed on foot. *"Look, she brings her own servants, I bet each of them has a sword",* the caravan approached the main gate and the trumpeter let out a loud blast to signal their arrival. From the back of the greeting party a white horse darted towards the main gate with his sword held at head height. He reached the gate and the trumpeter blew again at full blast. The rider sheathed his sword dramatically and signalled the gates to be opened *"Well done brother, at least he has done this without a stumble"* the King gulped more wine and turned his attention to Michael, he was clearly drunk now. *"This little affair this evening will be nothing more than a child's birthday celebration in comparison to when we are married. The land will not see the likes for another ten generations".* Michael remained focused on the proceedings as the caravan slowly entered into the palace grounds, *"Do you not hear me Madokht?"*

   "Of course my King"

   "You watch him with more interest, am I not your betrothed, am I not good enough?" Michael could hear the anger building in his voice again *"Of course my King"*

   "You answer because you have to, soon he will be gone and you will have no distractions" the king stood up and staggered. *"I take my leave of you, until tonight"*

   "Yes my King" The king left and headed for the corridor, *"Hand maidens, prepare this chamber for two for this evening, I plan to use it".* Michael's attention was grabbed, he did not mean what he thought he meant. If so he had little time to find the sphere and the fragment or he could be experiencing an event which would surely rival anything he had yet encountered. His body was that of a woman, but Michael Cameron was very much a man and unless he could do something soon. His mind could be violated in an unthinkable fashion. The night passed in a flash and before long the moon was full in the sky. Michael watched over the palace grounds from his vantage point. It had been prepared for the wedding which was now less than an hour away. Tables lined each end of the courtyard and were adorned with uncountable amounts of food and drink. An army of servants buzzed around like worker bees in a hive, making sure that the royal family

228

had everything they could possibly need to ensure a hassle free celebration took place. He watched on as a small party of servants approached the small stage which had been erected for the ceremony. The servants produced what looked like thousands of clay pots and soon the entire stage was covered, making it look like a field of Multi Coloured flowers. There was barely enough room left for the bride and groom *"Madokht....Madokht!"* Michael was startled by the voice of little Kamiri *"Hello, what is it little man?"*

"Do you know what I know?"

"Ha, I do not, what do you know?" Michael kneeled down to the little boy's level and smiled as he explained his news *"Your name is Madokht and my mother says it means"* Another voice broke through that of Kamiri's *"Your mother says you should not run off"* A middle aged but very beautiful woman entered the room. *"Forgive me Madokht"*

"It is no problem, Kamiri, is welcome"

"Thank you for your kindness" the woman wore a sapphire blue garment, it was interwoven with fine silk and jewels. She was no servant and Michael was intrigued by her

"I am Kamiri's mother, it is an honour to meet you, your grace"

"Please my name is Madokht, come in, sit down". The woman's eyes widened with excitement *"If it would please her grace"* The two sat for around fifteen minutes and made idle chit chat, or as close to it as Michael could manage. *"So, the ceremony, how does it proceed?"* The woman looked slightly perplexed

"As it has for centuries your grace, the bride presents the groom with the moon, he then presents her with the jewel of the Kings. Which as you know is the real symbol of her true love. The jewel unites with the symbol of the moon and the happy couple bathe in its light spending eternity together."

"Who keeps the two parts?" Again the woman seemed surprised at Michael's ignorance *"Are you not familiar with this? It has not changed for some time your grace"* *"Humour me, it is nice to hear a new voice"* The woman smiled and Michael was content that he had her eating from his hand now. *"My people keep the symbol of the*

moon and traditionally provide the brides for your kingdom, who provide the willing suitor, although King Kamal in his case has chosen a native bride in yourself. Your royal family keep the jewel of Kings until the wedding is upon us". The Woman stood and called Kamiri to her side *"Come Kamiri, the time is upon us, I beg your leave your grace, I can only hope that your King will treat you with the same respect that his brother has treated me"* Michael nodded with respect and as their eyes met a knowing look came over the woman's face. She was aware of the reputation of the King. She backed out of the room and bowed as she left *"Your grace".* Alone again Michael had an idea what he had to do. The two wedding symbols had to be the sphere and the fragment. He just had to attend the wedding and obtain the two fragments *"Easy"* he said aloud

"What is easy Madokht? forgive me it is not my place" A hand maiden had approached and Michael put her at ease *"Do not worry, it is fine, I speak of nothing"* the Maiden looked relieved *"We must take our seats now Madokht"* Michael followed his entourage down through the dimly lit passageways and stairwells of the old sandstone palace until they emerged in the courtyard. The congregation stood to attention upon his arrival and they were in silence for a few seconds while the little man made yet another announcement. It was all very ceremonial and culminated in *"Your future queen, Princess Madokht".* This was met with rapturous applause and Michael was overawed by the adulation he was receiving. He smiled and waved and could not help but feel rather silly knowing that these people were currently worshipping a suburban archaeologist, office jockey. He took his seat which was next to the King's empty one. A few moments passed and the little man prepared himself for another announcement, King Kamal was arriving shortly. The announcement never came and the little man signalled the trumpeters to allow proceedings to begin. The King it seemed had become somewhat indisposed for the time being. Michael watched as a group of six horses trotted down the aisle which was created by the split in the long tables of guests. At the front was Kinra. He wore a bright green suit with white and gold and a simple but elegant head piece. He dismounted and climbed on stage to rapturous applause from the guests. Michael watched on as he reached inside his shirt and removed the jewel of Kings, holding it high for all to see. It was the next fragment, just as he had predicted and Michael exhaled loudly with relief. He was half way to getting out of here and was ready to start the final chase. This was the eleventh fragment, just one to go

230

after this. Michael soon snapped out of his excitement as he realised he had not yet found the sphere. The sounds of tribal drums filled the air and a troop of scantily clad exotic ladies began to dance their way down the aisle towards Kinra. They were followed by a small wooden box being carried at head height by six enormous men wearing nothing but lion cloth style pants. The box was draped by thin curtains all around to mask the interior from outside eyes. The six men lifted it onto the stage. The moonlight shone brightly upon it and it had been strategically placed to utilise the lunar glow. Kinra kneeled next to it and held the jewel out in offering. The box began to ruffle and shake and from the top the fabric which covered it began to raise until it cloaked the sphere perched on the top of a long golden staff which raised from it. The moon cast its light in perfect alignment with the sphere which was as glorious as Michael had seen it to date. The fabric fell to the floor and a perfect shadow was cast over the stage. The audience celebrated with a prolonged and enthusiastic applause. Michael grinned uncontrollably, he now had a way out of here. He continued to watch proceedings and soon the betrothed moved across the stage towards each other and reached out to touch hands. Almost perfectly timed a loud crash or crockery disturbed the beautiful moment. It was the King, he was completely drunk, staggered towards the bride and groom and shouted incomprehensibly. Then he spoke. *"Brother, how is it you start without your King to witness your happy day?"*

"Your majesty, you are a little drunk" Kinra tried to remain calm

"I am the King, and what if I am drunk" The bride interjected

"King Kamal, it is our wedding day"

"Ah yes, my little brother is too marry yet another eastern whore" the audience gasped with horror at the disrespect shown towards the bride and the visiting guests began to rise from their seats and shout angrily towards the stage, the men reaching for their swords. Kinra noticed this and addressed them, *"My brother, the King is not well, please be seated, I will deal with him"* the King turned angrily towards Kinra

"I will deal with you brother, you are nothing but an insignificant farm boy" He drew his sword and attempted to attack him. The audience grew angrier and soon chants rang out around the

231

courtyard. *"The King is dead, The King is dead"* Kinra seized his moment and plunged his scimitar deep into the belly of his older brother which was met with gasps of disbelief and closely followed by rapturous applause. The little man removed his ridiculous head dress and stood up from the body of the king. *"The King is Dead, Long live King Kinra"* the applause subsided and Kinra spoke aloud *"We have a wedding to finish"* the crowd went wild once more and various servants removed the corpse of the quickly forgotten king. They covered the mess left with flowers and barrels of wine. Kinra offered the fragment to his bride to be, she put up her hand and refused to take it. The crowd gasped again with disbelief. The woman spoke. *"Today is the Third full moon on the second day of the fourth month. It has been foreseen by the wise elders of the east. King Kinra has rid us of a long and painful burden and it is my duty to reward him with a gift worthy of any King.* "Madokht, please join us" The Crowd gasped as Michael made his way to the happy couple. *King Kinra is fair and handsome, a match well superior to myself, I know his heart lies with another and so it shall be."* Michael approached and the woman bowed and joined his hand with Kinra's which was met with a loud roar from the crowd. Kinra's smile beamed and his delight was obvious to see. The woman presented Michael with the sphere and he smiled and nodded reverently. Inside he could have screamed out with joy at the ease in which he received it. Kinra kneeled and offered him the fragment. *"Not too bad for a farm boy?"* Michael smiled back at him and took the fragment *"Madokht"* Michael turned to face the woman *"Kamiri wants to tell you his news now"* The little boy approached and whispered in his ear and he smiled back at him. He pushed the fragment into place and the light engulfed them all. Kamiri's words echoed all around him as the transportation took place. *"Madokht, the Daughter of the Moon"*

Chapter 17

The honour is all mine

"If you would like to follow me this way, the tour continues in the ancient civilisation exhibit" A bespectacled lady is the first thing that comes into focus as Michael comes around. She is middle aged with dyed blonde hair and is wearing a matching blouse and skirt. She appeared to be a guide who was showing a group of people around. Michael smiled as he looked at the little hat which she was wearing. "Tour Guide" was written upon it. He thought the last few weeks would have been far easier if everyone he had met had their designation on a handy piece of headwear. He was in a foyer in an old and expensive looking building. The floor was marble and the doorways were lined with thick polished oak. There were small glass display cases and marble plinths which housed random artefacts. Michael was certainly not unfamiliar with this territory. He spent a few moments taking in the surroundings, it was indeed a museum, but he never recognised it as one in which he had been in before. The small group started to move off and he noticed just how much taller everyone else was. His head was flung backward as some forward momentum kicked in. Disorientated, Michael searched his new body, his hands were older than a child's which eliminated that possibility immediately. His vision was blurred quite badly and he struggled to make out anything that he didn't hold right up to his face. Fumbling around his lower body, his hands were met with cold steel. It seemed to be everywhere. The steel was symmetrical on either side of his torso and were tubular with rubber fixings attached at the front ends. Michael screwed his eyes to try and gain focus on the alien object. He could just make out its chrome and black colouring, but was being dazzled by the bright light reflecting from the highly polished marble floor. Relying on his other senses, Michael could hear a repetitive ticking which seemed to be related to the forward motion. It was accompanied with a flicker of light, both sound and vision harmonising with each other much like the workings of a primitive movie camera, light and noise accompanying each other in perfect synchronisation. *"Excuse me sir?"* Michael heard the voice of another woman which seemed to halt his forward motion as she spoke, sending his head forward this time and bringing the sound and light show to an abrupt end. *"Oh thank you, he's forever dropping them"*

"No problem sir, have a nice day" Michael listened hard, at least his hearing seemed to function correctly. It was a man who

spoke to the lady, she seemed very proper and professional and Michael guessed that she also worked within the museum. *"Here I am, carting you about and you can't even see anything, Sorry"* A pair of large gold rimmed spectacles were thrust into Michael's face and he took them from the man. As he placed them on his face the transformation from blurred confusion to ordinary visibility was instantaneous. The glasses were thick, a good 6 or 7 millimetres. Michael rescanned his new shell and was immediately sent into a state of panic. It was a wheelchair and before him stood an elderly man, at least in his late fifties. Upon further inspection his initial panic was replaced by the realisation that this part of his journey could be the most challenging to date. As with no legs below the knee would surely struggle to cope with the challenges that he met, if they were to be similar to his previous obstacles. *"Hello there, can you see me now buddy?"* The man stood before Michael awaiting a response. He was still dumbfounded and unable to speak at the thought of what he had to come. *"Logan?"* The old man's face was friendly looking, a light stubble and very rosy cheeks. He was also carrying a bit of extra weight. He wore a green New York Jets baseball cap which covered a head of short dark hair which had started to go considerably silver on the sides. *"You alright buddy, Logan?"* Michael snapped out of it and acknowledged the man

"Fine, sorry just a bit dizzy"

"No wonder without your super goggles" the man laughed and returned to the back of the chair. *"Let's go quick and catch the up with the others"* Michael's head was thrown back as the man sped off down the lobby and into a darkened room. The group had congregated and was listening to the tour guide who stopped to greet them as they entered.

"Logan and Derek, we thought we had lost you"

"Sorry, carry on" Derek spoke out and the tour guide continued *"As I was saying, there are many displays in the ancient civilisation section of the museum, please feel free to peruse them for the next half hour, we will be opening to the general public at 9 am"*. Derek pushed Michael around the exhibition room and stopped at a display which had a board indicating it was Ancient Japan. There was a beautiful samurai sword and the head wear of a samurai warrior, along with a few other artefacts. At the rear of the display was an illustration which looked very old and Michael leaned in to have a closer look. It depicted a samurai warrior standing at the top of a heap of his slain enemies. He held a small wooden staff above his head which emanated light from its top end. *"Is it?"* Michael muttered

"Is what Logan?" Derek looked on as Michael scrutinised the display with great interest. *"Oh look Logan, here is some information on the glass"* Michael snapped instantly

"Read it"

"O.K jeez!"

"It says, 'An ancient Japanese Samurai's sword and helmet, undated, the scene depicted is of a mythological warrior who defeated all before him to claim the Staff of Fortune'"

"Does it say anything else?"

"No Buddy, you O.K?" Michael ignored Derek's concern and continued scanning the exhibit. *"O.K, let's move on, we only have a few mins then we need to get across town to meet Calvin"* Derek began to push the chair and headed to the exhibit just beside the exit. *"O.K buddy, Persian kingdoms this one says, remember we only have five minutes"* Michael again was captivated by the exhibit and was engrossed in the glaring similarities to what he had experienced. Some clay pots and scraps of material were accompanied by another perfectly preserved item. He was sure it was the little man's feather hat. Michael almost fell out of his chair as he leaned in for a better look. *"What does this one say?"*

"O.K let see, last one remember" Michael nodded and he could not help to convey his impatience *"Come on Derek"*

"This elaborate head dress was worn by the aide of a Persian King. It is said that it was worn during his Marriage to Madokht, the mythical Daughter of the Moon". Michael's jaw dropped, what was this place? It was like a chronicle of his adventure. He had to see more. *"Sorry Logan, we need to go now"*

"But I need to see all the displays"

"Don't be silly, your brother will be waiting for you"

"I don't care, take me back now!" Derek had already started to wheel Michael through the lobby and was heading back to the main exit *"Logan, that's terrible, it's your brother, I promise we will come back before we head home O.K?"* Michael, with no other choice sat back in his chair and let out a big sigh. He was powerless to stop Derek and could only hope he would be true to his word and bring him back later. *"What time will we be coming back Derek?"*

"Jeez the display is not going to disappear, you have not seen Calvin in over a year"

"O.K, but please bring me back today"

"You have my word, you big nerd" Derek laughed and pushed Michael into the street and whistled for a cab. The driver helped them into the car and placed the wheelchair into the trunk. *"O.K where to?"*

"We need to be at the WTC for Eight Thirty"

"Hold on to your hats" The driver sped off and headed for their destination. Before Michael even had a chance to catch his breath, he was being lifted back to his chair and parked on the pavement. The building before him stretched high into the sky above and he felt dwarfed by the masses of iron and glass. He sat and stared at its immense size until his brain realised he had seen the building somewhere else. Before him stood the structure of the World Trade Centre in New York City. The Iconic buildings stood proud and tall before him and he was dazzled by a truly iconic vista *"WTC. That's it buddy and its south tower for us, we need to hurry, we said we would meet Calvin at eight thirty remember."* Derek wheeled him up and through the entrance. Michael was in complete awe at his surroundings. Never did he think that he would be inside the building which was destroyed during the most notorious terrorist attack in the history of the world. *"Hold the elevator"* Derek hollered at a woman who looked decidedly miffed that she had to cope with the extra weight of Michael's wheelchair. *"Thank you"* Michael said sarcastically, having seen her reaction. She winced with embarrassment. *"Logan! Derek!"* Derek held the doors opened and a smartly dressed man in his early thirties rushed in. *"8:32, that's not bad little brother"* Calvin leaned down and embraced Michael. He squeezed him vigorously and Michael could tell he was happy to see him. Calvin moved to Derek and greeted him also. *"You're looking well Logan"* Michael remained silent as his eyes were fixed on the lady who was standing by the elevator buttons, she was now blatantly fuming at having to wait so long. Calvin saw Logan and Derek's expressions and turned to face the woman. She recognised him immediately and spoke with a large grin *"Which floor, Sir?"*

"73 please, sorry to keep you"

"Oh no problem at all sir" The woman stood, bursting with embarrassment and Calvin turned to face the others sniggering and both Derek and Michael could not help but join in like playful schoolboys. *"I've missed you bro"*. The elevator bell rang as it reached its desired floor. *"O.K that's the first one out the way, only one more to go"*

"I forgot about the elevators Calvin, how can you do this every day?"

"You get used to it after a while" Michael listened to Calvin and Derek discuss the internal layout of the south tower. In order to reach his office, they had to take two separate elevators. The first was the one which they just alighted from which took them straight to the

44th floor which was known as a sky lobby. *"From here you can access all floors up to level 77"* Calvin explained *"That's 8:40, I need to be in a meeting for fifteen minutes at 09:30 then we will hit the town O.K?"* Michael was numb by his presence in this place. He felt like he was a passenger on a ghost ship and for the time being was happy being pushed around allowing him to get acclimatised with his infamous surroundings. The second elevator opened and it was packed. There was no room for the three of them, never mind Michael's extra baggage. *"Tell you what, I'll nick up to my office, I will meet you back here in five minutes……with your present"* Calvin winked and the elevator doors shut. *"Good to see him, eh Logan?"*

> *"It is yeah"*
>
> *"You O.K, you've been a bit weird this morning?"*
>
> *"I'm fine, just a little tired"*
>
> *"We will get out of here and get a beer soon?"*
>
> *"Sounds good"* Derek could tell Michael was distant and tried

to reassure him with the promise of fresh air and a cold beer. A whistling sound grew louder and louder until it turned into a rumble which was closely followed by a deafening explosion. Michael sat up in his chair and looked around. The people waiting for the elevators all stopped for a second and then carried on with their conversations, discussing the possibilities of the disturbance quite calmly. *"What's today Derek?"*

> *"It's Tuesday, I think"*
>
> *"No not the day, the date"* Michael uttered the words in

unison with Derek

> *"11th September"*
>
> *"If you know why ask me, I think you just try and wind me up*

sometimes"

> *"Shut up, we need to get Calvin now"*
>
> *"He'll be back in a minute, what's wrong with you?"* The lift

bell rang and the doors opened. A mad rush of frantic passengers pushed through the doors and headed for the stairwell *"What's going on?"* Derek quizzed the people who passed him like he was invisible all desperate to vacate the building as quick as they could. Michael had pulled himself into the lift and pressed the button heading for the 73rd floor, *"Wait for me".* Derek slipped through the doors as they closed *"What the hell is going on"*

> *"A plane has hit the tower, we need to get to Calvin and get*

out" *"A plane, are you high again?"*

> *"Trust me Derek, we need to get out of here"* Derek could see

the real fear on Michael's face and had worriedly noticed his weird

237

behaviour. He was worried his friend was losing his mind, so played along *"O.K let's go get Calvin"* Michael heard the doubt in Derek's voice and hoped that by some chance Derek was right and he was losing his mind as the reality of the situation was unthinkable. The lift took what felt like an age to get to the 73rd floor and Derek pushed through the crowd of people all rushing to get into the elevator that they were trying to vacate. *"Jeez, these people look pretty scared Logan"* Derek looked at Michael and raised a concerned eyebrow, now thinking that his companion's prediction could actually be feasible. *"Excuse me, what is going on"* Derek asked a tearful woman as she rushed passed, not stopping to give her explanation *"There is a big hole in the North tower, nobody knows why?"*

   "Hey you better get the cripple out of here" Shouted another man

   "Thanks, I think"

   "Hear that Logan? Cripple, cheeky……" Michael interrupted

   "Come on Derek, we need to get to Calvin" Derek pushed through the crowd until they reached Calvin's office. It was really large and reminded Michael of his own back home. The exterior wall was glass from floor to ceiling and Calvin stood with both hands on the glass staring at the gaping hole on the side of the North Tower. *"Jesus Christ Almighty, what the hell happened Calvin"* Derek asked. Calvin turned to face the pair with tears streaming down his face. He robotically handed a small box to Michael *"Happy birthday bro"* he turned back to the window and looked out *"Calvin, what happened?"*

   "A jet went straight into the tower, boom, I've never seen anything like it" Michael could not wait any longer *"Calvin, we need to leave now"* Derek looked upon Michael with a fearful expression *"How did you know?"*

   "What do you mean know?" Calvin added. Michael's patience was wearing thin.

   "I overheard the people in the lobby, let's go"

   "That's weird, I never, you were the first to mention a plane" Michael blew up, he had had enough deliberating *"Come on you fucking idiots, everyone is evacuating, let's go now!"* The realisation finally came to them and they both prepared to leave.

   "I just need my laptop" Calvin moved back to his desk. *"And I'm taking a picture, two seconds"*. Michael was just about to start screaming at the pair again when the same distant whistle grew louder and was followed by a second far louder explosion. Michael was thrown from his chair and a large concrete block smashed through the ceiling crushing it like it was made of putty. He turned to check for the

others and found that Derek had succumbed to the same fate as his chair. Lifeless he lay face up with his eyes open, but they were devoid of any cognition, he was dead for sure. Calvin let out a scream, he was somewhere in the thick dust and smoke. Michael crawled, following the sound of his screams until he found him. He was pinned to the ground by more fallen debris and reinforced steel rod had pierced through his leg, skewering him to the floor. He screamed again in agony. *"I can't move it Calvin!"* Michael could hardly hold himself up and attempted to push the debris from him, but it was stuck fast. Calvin smiled at him *"I love you little bro"* Michaels heart swelled as he witnessed the face of a man who had accepted his fate *"I hope you like your gift, it's rare"* Michael smiled back at him, not wanting to make his final moments any more distressing, if that was possible. *"Open it bro"* Michael took the small box from the pocket of the hoodie he was wearing and slipped it open. *"How did you know?"*

"Hey it's an unexplained oddity, just like you" Michael peered upon the final fragment and it glowed momentarily through the thick dust and smoke. It was set in gold and attached to a chain. The box had a little shiny brass plate which read. *"For Logan, one of a kind"* Michael slipped the chain around his neck and reached out to grasp Calvin's outstretched hand. A loud crack sounded above them and masses of rubble fell from the ceiling, showering the brothers with even more debris. A small piece of concrete cracked Michael on the back of the skull. The dust and smoke caught the back of his throat and his nose filled with particles of cement and paint until he passed out on the floor of the office, helpless with no control over his fate. *"Hey there pal?"* Michael's eyes were thick with dust and he struggled to open them. As the slowly opened he could just make out the silhouette of a man leaning over him *"You alright wee man?"* He was large and powerful looking man with a neatly shaven haircut and Michael choked on the dust in his throat as he responded *"I…….think so"*

"You're lucky I even noticed you. I just seen a flicker from your chain which made me come and look"

"Calvin?"

"Sorry pal, looks like you and me are the only two left alive on this floor" Michael peered through the limited visibility at his two companions, he could not make out their faces as the air was too thick with airborne particles and a film of dust had already started to settle on their corpses. *"No time to waste, let's get going"* The man started to move debris from around Michael and reached out to grab him *"O.K ready?"* Michael nodded and he pulled him out and sat him upright

against a pillar of concrete which had landed next to them. *"Looks like your wheels are out of commission wee man?"* Michael was a little more aware, now that he was free and focused on the accent of his saviour. It was instantly recognisable *"Ah, said wheels are passed their best eh?"* The man smiled and they both chuckled. *"On my back then……..can't keep calling ye wee man"*

"I'm Logan"

"Righty oh, let's go Logan". He picked him up and Michael held on with his arms around his shoulders. *"So what do I call you?"*

"Name's Gordie, nice to meet you……ha ha" they sniggered as he spoke, the circumstances were anything but nice. *"So where about in Scotland are you from?"* The man's accent was undeniable and Michael was intrigued by the possible other dimensional connection. *"Very good, most of the locals think I'm Irish, Paisley, you know it?"* Michael knew it well, it wasn't far from him at all. He stopped short of creating a difficult situation by explaining his connection. *"I've heard of it"*

"Shite hole, glad to be out of there" The conversation continued as the man climbed and moved debris from their path. He headed towards the elevators. The 73rd floor was now deserted and Michael could hear distant sirens constantly ringing in his ears. *"So what brings you to New York Gordie?"*

"If I told you, I'd have to kill you" Gordie laughed and continued, *"No, I'm a squaddie, just back from operations, needed a break from it, you know?"* Michael took a large breath trying to avoid as much dust as he could. He was relieved that Gordie was a trained soldier. If anyone could get them out, he seemed like the ideal candidate. *"You come for a break and end up in this shit!"*

"Tell me about it, O.K the lifts are just up here" Gordie pushed a final broken object from their path and they approached the elevators that they had emerged from previously. *"The lifts are either fucked or too busy"* Gordie placed Michael on the ground and grabbed a discarded bottle of water which lay among the debris. He took a swig and passed it to Michael, who was glad to clear the chalk and grit from his mouth. The few seconds rest only caused more chaos in his mind. Flashes of news coverage from his first experience of 911 filled his thoughts. He had forgotten that they had limited time to get out before the south tower was reduced to a mangled piece of glass, rock and steel. *"We need to go now Gordie" "Try and chill wee man, if we sit tight the fire brigade will be here to get us out"* a cold chill ran through him as he remembered the fire men who never hesitated in entering the building and had no doubt unknowingly signed their own

death certificates. Gordie assessed the area and took another sip of the bottled water. Michael had no choice he stared at Gordie and decided to lay his cards on the table. *"Gordie?"*

"What's up wee….Logan?"

"I have to tell you something and you will probably think I am off my head" Gordie could see the honesty in Michael's eyes and he sat down next to him to try and comfort him.

"What's up pal?"

"I have seen this before, I dreamt all this, the crash, meeting you"

"Away ye go and don't talk pish" Gordie moved as if to stand up again and Michael gripped his arm tightly which drew his attention back. *"I know I sound crazy, but if we do not go now, we are both going to die"* This time Gordie's attention was obtained and he gulped with fear as he could hear the seriousness in Michael's voice *"So in this dream, what happens?"* Michael braced himself

"The tower comes down"

"Fuck off, no chance, these things are solid" Gordie stood up and paced back and forth for a few seconds *"The whole thing comes down? And in this dream, what do we do?"* Michael was startled by the question, what should they do? He was forced to think fast. *"Don't know, it just goes dark"* Gordie face wrinkled with disapproval

"O.K I'm not having that, stairs it is" Gordie picked up Michael and he clung to his back again. He pushed open the door to the stairwell and headed down for the next level. The first few floors were deserted and they made excellent time passing through them heading towards street level. Conversation was at a premium as Gordie regulated his breathing. He jogged down the stairs, sometimes three and four at a time. The heat in the building was immense and sweat build up all over Michael's body his hands grew moister with every flight of stairs passed until he lost his grip and his hands split sending him crashing to the ground. Gordie stumbled forward as the change in weight threw him off balance. Michael hit the central platform between levels and bounced towards the edge of the next flight of stairs unable to slow himself. He was headed for a certain fatal tumble. He slipped form the edge and fell of the first step letting out a cry of anguish as he began to plummet. The large muscular arm of Gordie reached out and grabbed him *"Whooooah! Where are you going wee man?"* Michael shut his eyes and shook his head, so grateful that yet again he had been plucked from certain death by his personal Samaritan. *"Come on"* Gordie pulled him up towards safety, and just like before he lost his grip as his sweaty palm slipped from his

241

grip. The building was sweltering hot and the unavoidable exercise was making the moisture build up even more prolific. Michael swung his other arm around and grabbed the thin cotton t-shirt that Gordie was wearing. In a panic, Gordie threw himself backwards, dragging both of them to safety. Michael ripped the sleeve clean of Gordie's t-shirt in the process. Both men lay face up panting and exhausted. Gordie started to giggle uncontrollably, Michael turned to him and asked him what was wrong. *"I can believe after all this, you nearly got killed because of your B.O"* Michael laughed and retorted

"Hey, you're just as sweaty" they both laughed and Michael stopped abruptly as he focused on Gordie's sweat and dirt covered Bicep. He had a tattoo which was coloured in red, white and blue. It was three little parachutes, a red, blue and white one. Each of them carried a number. *"Oh my tat, Para's, best in the fuckin' world, none of your American shite"* Gordie sniggered again *"Is that your division? 324?"*

"Sort of, was kind of a covert squad if you know what I mean" Gordie winked and Michael could see that he was uncomfortable discussing it any further *"Anyway, if you are the fuckin' oracle, we better get a move on"*. Gordie picked up Michael again and they headed off down the stairs. Michael was deep in thought. The final fragment was secured around his neck. If Gordie could get then back to street level, he would need to get back to the museum and search the exhibition for the sphere, It had to be somewhere within that building. The heat grew steadily more uncomfortable until the noise of people shouting and moaning filled the air. *"Looks like we caught up with the crowd"* Gordie sighed as he pushed the first few people aside. They were irate at first, thinking a queue jumper had skipped their place. Michael looked at their faces and noticed the variance in moods which was on display. Some looked so very sad, while others looked impatient. Many were frantically trying to get a reception on their cell phones. The first few floors were O.K. The evacuating crowd could see that the condition of Michael merited his fast track through the crowd. Gordie and Michael continually thanked them as they allowed their quick passage. Some even assisted in whatever way they could. Gordie was a fit man, but even he grew tired as they embarked on yet another jam packed flight of stairs. He pushed through until a large man in his forties blocked their path, *"Excuse me pal"* the man never turned around and Gordie tried to squeeze passed him only for him to step in his way *"Excuse us please"* Michael added. *"Wait in line, like the rest of us"*. There was an uneasy silence in the crowd until a little old lady spoke out, *"Let them through"*. Another man spoke out

"Yeah, stop being a douchebag". Michael laughed to himself 'Douchebag' what an Americanism. The man stepped aside reluctantly. The pressure from the crowd around him had made him crack and give in. Michael and Gordie moved off until the man decided to try and get the last word. *"Yeah on you go, probably picked up the cripple to get through the crowd"* Gordie stopped dead in his tracks and Michael could feel his heart beat even stronger than it had been. *"Here hold him"* Michael was passed to another man who did not hesitate to take him, having noticed the rage in Gordie's eyes. He walked up to the man and stopped around eighteen inches from his face *"You want to apologise to my friend ya fuckin' arsehole?"* The man looked uneasy but stood firm and tried to appear unaffected by Gordie's request. *"Oh, we might have known another Irish immigrant prick".* Without and warning or hesitation, Gordie unleashed his head and butted the man clean on the nose. He stood for a few seconds and then his eyes rolled back into their sockets and he crashed to the floor in an unconscious heap. The crowd let out a cheer and those in the direct vicinity backed off and smiled nervously *"I'll fuckin' Irish ye, I'm fae paisley"* Gordie grabbed Michael and put him on his back again. The people parted like Moses at the red sea. The pair made their way through each level, getting increasingly cramped as they went until eventually they made it to the foyer. The scene was manic. Emergency services buzzed around like ants in an ant farm, oblivious to Michael and Gordie. They made their way to the main doors and Michael turned back and watched the people who were all so unaware of their impending fate. A large clock in the foyer read "9:56 A.M". The street outside was just as manic, but the breath of fresh air was really welcome. A nearby ambulance driver jumped from his cab and signalled the pair towards him. *"I have a chair in the back"*

"Cheers pal" Gordie said and he placed Michael in his new wheels.

"They are taking refuge in St Paul's" the driver pointed to a little chapel not far from their current position. *"O.K"* Gordie started to wheel Michael towards the church when they were both deafened by a loud crack *"No way"* Gordie exclaimed as he turned and watched as the South tower crumbled and started to fall to the city streets below. Gordie ran towards the church and Michael struggled to stay in his chair. Screaming rang out all around them and policemen shouted at people to take cover. Although some stood precariously close mesmerised by the unbelievable sight that was occurring. The rumble was long and constant and Gordie soon realised the church was too far. Just as the cloud of dust and rubble got within metres of them, he

243

threw open the back of a van and tossed Michael in closing the doors behind them. The fragment glowed a little and Gordie looked at it with intrigued concern. The dust cloud hit the van and it swayed like an old barn caught in a hurricane. Debris bounced of the sides and left visible dents on the inside. Both Michael and Gordie held their breath with fear. One final piece of flying debris, rattled the sidewall of the van, flipping it onto its side. They both tumbled over and Gordie was quick to check on Michael. *"You O.K pal?"*

> *"I think so, you?"* Gordie remained silent and then spoke
> *"So this dream of yours, what happens next?"*
> *"I told you, it went dark"*
> *"Bullshit wee man, what's going on?"*
> *"You would not believe me if I told you"*
> *"Today I would believe anything, so spill it, what's next?"*
> *"The North tower".* Gordie's face dropped and he stood up

and kicked the van doors open *"Long have I got?"* Michael frowned

> *"You're not going out there"*
> *"How fuckin' long wee man?"*
> *"Half an hour tops, maybe?"*
> *"Get to the chapel, someone will help you there"*
> *"Where are you going?"*
> *"Half an hour is half an hour wee man"*, see you at the

chapel. Gordie disappeared into the dust and Michael could just make out his chair which unbelievably had survived the cloud with minimal damage. He pulled it towards the van door and positioned it to jump from the back of the van. He ripped a piece of the sleeve from his hoodie and made a makeshift mask to protect himself from the dust cloud. Visibility was almost non-existent and he lowered himself into his chair. The fragment glowed as he sat down and then reverted back to its original state. He started to move of towards the general direction of the chapel and his large spectacles proved an ideal protection from the atmosphere, helping him to make the most of the limited visibility. He weaved in and out of debris until it was clear that he had no idea which way he was going. The fragment was dark and lifeless. Michael spun on the spot and the fragment flickered slightly, he moved off in that direction and the light grew in intensity. He was blind in the cloud of dust and the fragment carried him through the darkness like a torch through an ancient underground cavern. He followed the light until he reached the doors of St Paul's Chapel which he banged his fist hard upon. The door opened and he was dragged in with the door slammed behind him *"Hello my son, are you hurt?"*

244

"No father" Michael was greeted by an elderly priest with small square rimmed spectacles and the whitest short wiry hair. An identical crack rang out all around them and a fireman burst through the chapel doors and the priest closed them behind him. *"The North tower has just went, don't go outside"* The fireman's face was covered in dust and Michael could hardly make out his features *"Father this man has asked for his last rites"*. The fireman carried an elderly gentleman whose face was caked in blood and dirt. He had a large steel spike through his torso. *"Put him over there my son"*. The fireman sat him down and watched as the priest inspected his wounds. "He is too far gone father"

"I see that now my son, please comfort him, I need a few things" Michael watched as the priest approached the tabernacle behind the altar and opened it with a large golden key. The fragment glowed much brighter and Michael's eyes were drawn to the contents of the holy locker. There it was, all intact missing the one final piece that he had in his possession. The priest removed it and lay it on the altar as he grabbed the various items required to perform the dying man's last rights. While they were distracted Michael approached the altar and slipped the sphere into his lap. *"This is it"* he whispered to himself *"Time to go home"*. He was now oblivious to the catastrophic and unbelievable scenes around him. To Michael the reunification of the twelve fragment was of far greater importance. He slid the final fragment into position and shut his eyes hoping that this would be everything that he had been waiting for and that little Joseph and Kaitlin would be awaiting his return. The Light engulfed him and silence fell. Only for a faint voice to whisper some final words *"Unite the twelve and remember; Question the Unquestionable"*.

Chapter 18

Welcome Home Daddy

"Good morning, you're listening to three two…." Michael reached out and clicked the radio off, only too aware of the annoyance that it regularly presented. As he came around from his slumber, the light began to fill the room and he pulled the duvet up and over his head and snuggled in tight. He had no intention of moving today. *"Michael! Michael!"* Sitting up his eyes focused on a familiar face. *"What are you doing?"* She asked

"I was sleeping!"

"Ha ha, very funny, Joseph is in the next room getting changed for school, why is your alarm switched off?" Michael let out an enormous yawn *"You know I can't stand that clown on the breakfast show, plus I had a really weird night's sleep".* Kaitlin frowned and Michael knew that she was sceptical about his explanation. *"So what was so weird about this dream that it merits another sicky?"*

"I really am exhausted sweetheart, I feel like I've been battered all night" Kaitlin grabbed her long dirty blond hair and tied it up in a neat bun on top of her head. She glared at Michael with a mischievous look-in her eye. *"Well bad dreams or not, it's time to get up and get back to reality"* She stood up and with one quick move she swiped the duvet from the bed, leaving a half-naked Michael chitterling from the cold air. Bouncing up to his feet he chased her around the room and she giggled uncontrollably as he grabbed and wrestled her to the bed *"Ya wee shite ye"*

"Michael, not so loud" Michael laughed and pinned her to the bed so she could not escape and began to kiss her all over her face, uttering the obscenity in between each kiss*" Shite, shite, shite"* Kaitlin laughed and wriggles uncontrollably until Michael stopped and she broke free. Kaitlin had noticed the dead and distant look in his eyes as he sat upright and gazed into nothingness *"Michael? What's wrong?"* Michael shook his head as she uttered the words and turned to look into her eyes. *"Just had major Deja-Vu"*

"Oh I hate that" Michael looked at Kaitlin as she stood up from the bed and started to tidy some clothes and other things that had accumulated on the bedroom floor. There was something about her today; he couldn't quite put his finger on what it could be. She looked the same and smelled the same, but there was something different, something missing *"You O.K sweetheart?"* Kaitlin asked again as she noticed that Michael had slipped into another trance like state.

246

"I don't know, I just feel a bit weird this morning, I'll be fine" Michael swung around to the edge of the bed and placed his feet on the floor. Kaitlin opened the blinds and a blast of light beamed through the window forcing him to close his eyes. The light frightened him and his heart began to pound in his chest and he was soon sweating heavily from his brow. His breathing became quicker and he felt extremely anxious. *"Michael, what the hell is it?"* He struggled to gasp enough air to muster a reply *"Shut.......The...... Blinds"* Kaitlin shut the blinds and rushed to his side. *"You're burning up are you in pain?"* Michael's breathing slowed and he relaxed a little *"The light, it really freaked me out, it was so bright, surrounding me"*. Kaitlin picked up the phone which was on the bedside table *"I'm calling the doctors surgery"*

"It's O.K don't bother, I feel better now"

"No, you're not right Michael"

"I'll be O.K once I'm up, I'm just over tired". Kaitlin replaced the receiver and returned to his side placing her hand on his forehead. *"You're not as warm now, are you sure you can go in today?"*

"I'll be fine" Kaitlin agreed reluctantly and moved to the bedside dressing table, she picked up her watch. *"Oh shit, its half eight, we're going to be late again"* Michael jumped to his feet and threw on his uniform as Kaitlin scurried off to the next room to check on Joseph *"Jo-Jo, where are you?"* She yelled and the response came quickly.

"Eating my cereal mummy" Michael listened as Kaitlin issued instructions to little Joseph, ensuring he would be ready to leave in five minutes. *"I'm already ready Freddie"* he laughed. Kaitlin rushed back to the bedroom. *"At least one of us is organised!"* Before long the unusual awakening that he had experienced that morning was a distant memory and Michael had moved through the house and was out in the car waving goodbye to Kaitlin with Joseph strapped in and they were on their way to school. *"You O.K daddy?"* Michael was startled again as he sat at the traffic lights daydreaming, *"I'm fine wee man, just a little tired that's all"* Little Joseph smiled a big tooth filled grin and returned to his comic. The traffic lights changed and their journey continued. Michael glanced in the rear view mirror at his son. Just like with Kaitlin before, he felt uneasy. He still looked the same as always with his long black hair. But Michael sensed a difference. Whether it was with little Joseph or himself he was unsure. Something just did not feel right. As he drifted in and out of his subconscious thoughts, he had slowed to a snail's pace. A vehicle had come right up to his tail and was flashing its lights angrily at Michael's lack of progress. The vehicle roared as it sped to overtake him and Michael

247

was transfixed on the vehicle and its driver. The man waved his hands angrily and mouthed a suitable insult in his direction. He remained mesmerised by them and instinctively raised his hand to apologise. The bright red sports car sped off into the distance and soon only the outline of the heavy set, skin headed driver was no longer visible. Little Joseph had sat up and was watching on with great interest *"Wow, did you hear that daddy? Do you know that big man?"* Michael searched his memory, not only did the man seem really familiar, but the car was so vivid and significant to him. *"I don't think so son"* Michael shook his head and muttered *"Deja-Vu?"*

"What's deshavoo Daddy?" Michael laughed

"Nothing wee man, we better get a move on" Michael sped up and before long they had made it to the school. Little Joseph jumped from the car and headed up the path towards the entrance. Michael spotted that he had left his comic book on the back seat of the car and shouted out the window after him *"Hey Spidey, you forgot something?"* Michael waved the comic book in the air and Joseph came scurrying back for it *"Thanks daddy. But remember, I'm on Batman now!"* Joseph pointed to the comic and Michael stared at the front cover blankly. *"But it's school time, so I'm Bruce just now"* little Joseph winked at his daddy and ran off with the comic book in hand. Michael waved as little Joseph disappeared through the main door. He started the engine and headed to the traffic lights which were stuck on red. He was still drifting in and out of deep contemplation. *"Even Batman seems familiar? Oh my brain is fried"* he chuckled to himself and drove off as the lights changed. He parked up as he always did outside the museum. He was detached from his surroundings and drifted through reception passed Pat who sat in his usual position without even acknowledging him. To be fair he never even noticed the oversized menace. He headed straight for the service elevator *"Woooah, Cameron you're late"* The sound of Pat's voice penetrated his ears, like the wail of a street cat and he stopped and turned to face him. *"Trying to sneak in are we?"*

"No Pat, I'm busting for a piss" Michael rushed off using his visit to the bathroom as the perfect excuse to escape Pat who was shouting after him as he went. *"That delivery is here, get it sorted".* Michael waved back in recognition and escaped into the lift descending to the darkness of the museum basement. There was indeed a large delivery and Michael sat in his little office and began to read the itinerary which was attached to the side of one of the crates in a little transparent plastic envelope. The delivery contained various antiquities and Michael had seen it all before. He continued reading

until one particular item caught his eye. It read *'Category: Unspecified, Origin: Unspecified, Era: Unspecified (Carbon free).'* He took a note of the catalogue number and hunted through the crates. This item intrigued him, he was drawn to it and he searched through the items thoroughly until he dug it out. It was a relatively small crate and he pulled it to one side and began to prise it open. The lid popped off unexpectedly and dropped towards the floor. Michael reached out to grab the lid and it froze in mid-air. He too was frozen to the spot and was powerless to move as a bright light grew ever stronger, emanating from the contents of the box. He began to feel dizzy and disorientated and within seconds he passed out while frozen in his upright position. Voices echoed all around him *".........too badly damaged.............neural pathways are like scrambled eggs".*

"..........full wipe.............move him to phase two..............if it's the same again, then we'll pull it" another voice spoke.

"..............I'll prep another just in case............"

"Beep, beep, beep, beep, beep" Michael remained stationary and the alarm clicked as Kaitlin switched it off and stood over him as he snored heavily. She nudged him *"Michael, you're going to be late".* He pulled the duvet over his head *"Your loss I'm off to the salon".* The door slammed and Michael sprung to life, he jumped out of bed and began to get ready, his smart suit, shirt and tie fitted comfortably and he muttered away to himself as he got changed. *"Stupid Bitch, sick of her crap"* He moved to the bedroom window and watched as Kaitlin moved his car out of her way and then sped off towards the salon. He watched on as some commotion ensued across the street. A few men in boiler suits were emptying a van, carrying various items around the back of a neighbour's house. He stood and watched for a few minutes gradually getting into his suit until without warning a voice attracted his attention *"Yooo Hooo!"*

"Oh shit" He muttered. Michael was so engrossed in watching the workmen that he had let his guard down and had been spotted by his neighbour, who was now waving and beckoning him down to her *"Hi Mrs Wallace".* Michael forced a neighbourly smile and headed downstairs; He grabbed his briefcase and locked the front door behind him. Mrs Wallace had made her way across the street and was now headed straight for him.

"Morning Michael, off to the office?"

"Same as ever Mrs Wallace"

"Now come on Michael, Irene, call me Irene" Michael smiled and nodded as she continued in a vain attempt to engage in idle chit chat. *"Bloody Poles, can't get an honest day's work out of them"* Mrs

Wallace gestured towards the migrant workers who she had employed to build her conservatory. Michael neglected to react to the suburban racism that Mrs Wallace had deemed worthy of the neighbourly chin wag. *"Nothing new happening with you then Michael?"*

"You know Mrs Wallace, just the same old dusty artefacts" Mrs Wallace's frustration was only too apparent as she could tell Michael was intentionally avoiding her blatant attempts at poking her nose where it did not belong. The central locking system of Michael's car clicked open and he hurriedly opened the door, placing his briefcase on the passenger seat and hanging his suit jacket on the little coat hook on the rear door. He waved politely at Mrs Wallace and started his engine. She was still not finished with him yet and was still mouthing the next instalment of her one way conversation, drowned out by the sound of the vehicle revving. Michael put the window down slightly and shouted over her *"Goodbye Mrs Wallace."* He moved into the street and glanced in the rear view mirror at her. She waved back, choosing to ignore the obvious cold shoulder that Michael had presented her and moved across the street, barking more instructions at the workmen. *"Mrs Bucket, eat your heart out"* he chuckled and flicked on the radio.

"Waltzing Matilda….Waltzing Matilda……You go waltzing Matilda with me" Michael sang along with a song he knew really well. His mother had always loved Rod Stewart and through association he had inherited a great appreciation also. *"News update coming soon, but first here's Sharon with the traffic update"* Michael clicked the radio off and pulled up outside the museum. His space was empty and he carefully reversed into it. The enormous glass doors whirred as they opened automatically on his approach. *"Morning Mr Cameron"*

"Morning Eddie, you good today?"

"I'm great Mr Cameron, and you?" Michael leaned in to Eddie and was about to speak when Eddie beat him to it *"Same shit, different day, eh sir?"* Michael hesitated for a second and then laughed aloud as he headed for the elevator. *"You have a good day Mr Cameron"* Eddie shouted after him and Michael waved at his old friend. Eddie always had a knack of making him smile. The elevator journey was quiet, he was only accompanied by one other, and who remained oblivious to his presence. The elevator bell rang and he headed down the corridor towards his office. The door swung open and Carol stood in front of him with a cup of steaming hot coffee. *"Morning Sir, here's your coffee"*

"Morning Carol, thank you very much" Carol buzzed around the office and Michael watched, something was different about her

250

today *"Carol?"* She spun around and her hair followed soon after, reminiscent of one of the cheesy shampoo adverts which infuriated him and Kaitlin always complained were unrealistic and ridiculous. It was a mass of red hair, curly and full of volume. *"Ah it's your hair, nice colour".* Carol looked confused

"What do you mean sir?"

"Your hair, you've had it done…..it's nice" Carol looked back at him with a hint of confused concern, *"But Mr Cameron, I always have my hair like this"* Michael stared back at her, awaiting the punch line *"I'm not kidding sir, it's always like this, it's my hair, I should know"*

"Of course Carol, I'm sorry, for a minute there I was sure your hair had changed" Carol looked a little uncomfortable and continued with her duties *"Well sir, it's nice of you to take an interest"* Michael smiled and chuckled

"Even if it is imaginary?"

"Yes sir, even so" Carol laughed and Michael left the reception area and entered his office. The large glass desk was polished with a glossy sheen and Michael sat his case upon it and slumped into his chair. The door opened and Carol popped her head in, *"Expert at 11:30, Distribution 2 p.m and the board are on their way"*

"O.K Carol, thanks" The board meeting was the usual run of the mill agenda, which overran as it always did and soon Michael was thanking the expert and her aide for their time. Carol popped her head in again *"You have a break before the distribution meeting, do you want me to double check these numbers?"*

"No Carol, take an early lunch, I need a breather"

"Yes Sir, Thank you" Carol disappeared quickly before Michael could rescind the offer of the extended lunch break. Michael stood at the window and stared out into the vast openness, he could just make out the noises from the street below through the solid glass panes. The sky seemed to get brighter with each passing second and Michael focused on the bellowing smoke from the top of a distant stack. The smoke was thick, dark grey and creamy. Michael felt uneasy as he watched the smoke change direction in the wind and almost engulf a neighbouring building. Beads of sweat built up on his forehead and he soon found himself in a state of panic. His throat tightened almost as if he was being starved of oxygen and then without warning he collapsed to the floor with no feeling in his legs. The smoke in the distance had now completely engulfed the top of another building. Making it appear to be on fire. The bright sun reflected back from the buildings glass exterior and he screwed up his eyes as he tried to determine whether it was actually on fire. His

throat tightened further and the feeling in his legs remained absent. He shut his eyes momentarily and slipped away, helpless and confused. The sound of a telephone ringing brought him round. Michael stood from the carpet and had a quick check, his legs were working again and his breathing had returned to normal. The chimney in the distance burned a solitary tower of smoke, without encroaching on the surrounding buildings. Michael breathed easily *"Must have fainted, I'm working too hard"*. The phone continued to ring until the automated message kicked in. Carol had left for her early lunch and was not available to answer for him *"You have reached the office of Michael Cameron, please leave a message after the tone, thank you"* Carol's professional message was followed by a far more abrupt and aggravated Kaitlin *"Carol, get him to call me ASAP, it's the god damn school...."* Michael rushed and picked it up *"Kaitlin it's me, what's up?"*

"Where's Carol?"

"Oh, I've locked her in the stationary cupboard, what's the big issue?"

"Hilarious as always" Kaitlin showed no interest in his attempts at humour. *"We need to go to the school, something's happened"*

"That wee arsehole, what's he done?" Kaitlin sighed and replied

"I don't know, maybe he's won pupil of the year, they wouldn't say"

"So go deal with it then!" Kaitlin reacted angrily to Michael's request

"Yeah I'll go, you sit on your arse as usual"

"Kaitlin, I'm really busy you know"

"And I just sit about with my finger up my arse all day? Anyway, tough shit, they have asked for both of us" Michael groaned as he realised his attendance was not debateable

"Oh, what has he done now? I'll pick you up in twenty minutes"

"Right, twenty minutes, don't be late" Kaitlin slammed the phone down and Michael listened to the dead line for a few seconds and stared blankly at the desk before him, His reflection was quite obscured by the bright sun bouncing back off the glass table top. *"Why do I even bother with this shit?"* He snatched a small note pad and left Carol a message, alerting her of the afternoon's agenda change. Ensuring that she knew to free up his diary for the rest of the day. The journey to Joseph's school was silent and awkward. Neither Michael nor Kaitlin had anything positive to say, so they decided to remain

quiet and avoid yet another blazing row. The car came to a halt outside the school and they both made their way inside. They never spoke a word to each other, both consciously aware that they had appearances to keep while they were on show for the upper classes. Two policemen passed them as they approached the headmaster's office which made them both turn and look at each other nervously. Worried that Joseph may have been in more serious trouble than first anticipated *"Mr Cameron, Mrs Cameron, this way please"* A middle aged man greeted them and beckoned them to follow him. Michael looked at Kaitlin with a confused look. Who was this man? The man had perfectly sculpted hair, which had numerous helpings of gel or mousse. Too much for a grown man, Michael had determined. He could not take his eyes off him for a moment even though he had never met him before, he felt like he had encountered him previously. He focused on him and could not help but be drawn to the ridiculous orange tan the he had. The fake tan paired with the large diamante earing made it impossible for Michael to be surprised as to how someone with his appearance held such a high position within a private school. *"Who is this character?"* He whispered to Kaitlin *"Shh!"* Kaitlin cut him off just as the man ushered them into the headmaster's office. Michael sat opposite the headmaster's chair with Kaitlin in a matching leather bound chair. A boy with a shaved head sat facing towards the window, he was flicking a lighter open and closed in his hand. The office door closed and to Michael's amazement, the tanned man returned and sat opposite him in the head masters chair *"Mr, Mrs Cameron, about Joseph"* Michael interrupted *"Excuse me, but when will the headmaster arrive?"*

"Pardon me Mr Cameron?" The man seemed insulted. *"Is he unwell? Otherwise engaged?"* Kaitlin looked at Michael scornfully and the man replied once again *"Mr Cameron, I have been the headmaster at St Cuthbert's for going on 3 years now"* Michael's head began to grow fuzzy and he slowly began to lose focus as the headmaster continued to explain his position. He started to sweat heavily, just as he had in the office that morning *"I need some air!"* He sprung from his chair and rushed out the office. He darted down the corridor and swung the main doors. He tried to calm himself, sitting on a small brick wall, breathing deeply *"I don't remember him being………"* He said aloud to himself *"I would have remembered him"* Again out aloud. A few pupils had noticed his bizarre behaviour and were watching him sit ranting away to himself. Michael stood from his sitting position and returned to the car where he put the air conditioning on full blast and sat with his head in his hands. He was so hot, what was happening to

him? He was sitting alone for what felt like a few seconds when the sound of car doors opening made him jump. Kaitlin and Joseph had returned. *"I can't believe you just left me in there to deal with this, what the hell is wrong with you?"* Michael breathed deeply and tried to remain calm.

"I don't feel right"

"What happened?" Kaitlin sighed *"Oh so now you care.......go on Joseph tell your dad what's wrong"* Joseph sat silent and disinterested *"You see that........he doesn't even care"* Kaitlin was on the verge of tears and Michael tried to remedy the situation *"O.K it doesn't matter what has happened, we will sort it out, let's just go home"* The journey home was calm and none of the three tried to engage each other. Kaitlin and Joseph had fallen asleep or at least were pretending to be to avoid a conversation. Michael pulled up outside a little roadside café and woke his family *"Fancy something to eat?"* Neither replied, but both left the car and headed inside. Michael felt an overwhelming urge to make the effort and mend the cracks which were tearing his family apart. They all sat and ate for a long while and before long were engaged in an in-depth political discussion about their future. It was decided that the time for change was upon them and they promised each other that from that day forth they would all make far more effort to improve their family life. The second part of the journey was full of enthusiastic and hopeful thoughts. They giggled and carried on like they had not done since Joseph was a little boy. They sang along to songs on the radio and a particular song had Joseph dancing from side to side on the back seat of the car. Michael's arms and legs locked in position *"That song, what was it?"* Joseph danced and sang along *"U can't touch this".* Michael sweated heavily once more and slammed on the brakes, stopping dead in the middle of the road. *"Michael what's wrong?"* Kaitlin's fear was impossible to hide as she watched on as Michael breathed uncontrollably with sweat dripping from the edge of his nose. *"Dad.......Mum call an ambulance"* Michael let out an almighty scream of pain as a bright light engulfed him and pierced his eyes like two daggers through his skull. He was out cold and the next voice he heard was one which he recognised and welcomed *"Michael....Michael"*

"Soph...."

"Don't speak, you're in hospital" Michael's eyes focused on Kaitlin's, she stood over him and gently stroked his face. She was a welcome sight, but not a match to the voice he had just heard. The woman in his dream had gone by another name which now eluded him as the dream dissipated as his body awoke from its deep sleep. *"What*

254

happened to me?" "The doctor said you had a seizure, not a big one, but you have to take time off and take it easy"

"Are you and Joseph O.K?" Kaitlin smiled and looked longingly into Michael's eyes "We are fine"

"And the car?"

"Don't worry about that, I got us here, everybody is safe" The overwhelming sense of relief was intense as he felt he had in some way survived a potentially cataclysmic event. He did not know what it was or why he felt so lucky "What a weird day honey?" Kaitlin smiled again "I know sweetheart, everything from now on is going to be perfect, I promise" A few days passed which turned into weeks. Kaitlin took the time off work and Joseph was given permission to remain at home while his father recovered. They spent the time rebuilding their life and before long, a far more loving and stable home life had been created. It was summertime and Michael stood outside with the midday sun beaming down on his face. A few months had passed since the hospital visit and he had no recurrence of any of the symptoms. Michael started to fire up the barbecue and before long guests had started to arrive. The Cameron household was a hive of activity. Joseph had benefitted from time they had spent rebuilding their relationship and had left the private school and enrolled in the local comprehensive, excelling at his schoolwork. Michael gave him a wave and a big toothy smile as he watched on while he frolicked and laughed with a few of his friends who had come for the barbecue. One of which was a girl who he had been seeing for a while now. "Hey there handsome" Kaitlin approached from behind and threw her arms around him "What will I make for the veggie?" Michael pointed to Joseph's female companion

"I got some of those fake sausages........and it's Agnieska not the veggie" Kaitlin giggled and continued preparing the table which had the food on it for the guests. Michael looked over at the kids enjoying themselves and smiled. "Agnieska, that's a nice name eh?" "She's a nice girl Michael" Kaitlin added. The evening came and went and Michael sat on the front step of the house and watched as Joseph seen Agnieska to her taxi and waved her off. He skipped up the drive towards him "Alright son? You get her away all right?"

"Yeah dad, she'll text when she gets up the road, like you asked"

"You like her then?"

"Yeah she's pretty cool"

"Good stuff son, on you go and give your mum a hand to tidy up" Joseph skipped off to help his mother and Michael sipped his beer

255

and sat in silence watching the night pass by, bringing yet another perfect day to its end. The wind picked up and before long he moved inside. Kaitlin was packing some of the leftover food into Tupperware and she stretched letting out a groan, tired from the evening's activities. *"You tired honey?"*

"Been a long day"

"Is the wee man in bed?"

"Yeah he's long gone…..I'm going to join him" Kaitlin kissed him and headed off to bed. *"I'm just going to watch a bit of telly"*

"O.K, don't stay up too late" Michael sat down on the couch and the room was dimly lit by the television. He flicked through the channels, briefly stopping to take in snippets of each programme. *"Late night news, with me Angela Pregiya"* Michael tuned in to the news while supping another beer, by this time he was a little drunk and concentrated hard to hear the report. *"Now more on the Chinese mining accident, the Kung Lao mining company have today confirmed reports that a mining accident occurred early yesterday morning. They report that they are still unsure as to the cause which has left a number of workers unaccounted for. So far the number of missing men is at three hundred and twenty four"* *"Poor bastards"* Michael muttered to himself as he flicked the remote to the next station. *"The west indies have fallen apart and it looks like the Indians final score of three hundred and twenty four all out will be enough to clinch the series"* Michael sat up and flicked the channels back and forth *"Well that's a bit weird"* he muttered *"Beer, beer, beer"* Michael staggered and headed to the fridge, he grabbed another bottle and headed back to the couch. Flicking the remote once more, he put on the game show channel. It was the price is right, not the old version from when he was a teenager, but some z list celebrity's revamped and half as good version. *"O.K Karen you are saying £402 and Jennifer you are saying £436, the actual price of the four items is"* A suitably dramatic pause and musical jingle, typical of the genre played as the eager contestants waited for the answer. Michael had begun to fall asleep; the beer was working on him. His eyes closed just as the presenter announced the correct answer *"£324, Karen is tonight's winner"* Michaels eyes opened wide, the coincidence had now become far more unlikely *"Three times"* He said aloud. He changed the channels and was met with more of the same. The prices on the shopping channel were all some variant of 324. The dating channel's telephone numbers all ended in 324. Michael grabbed a newspaper from the table. The headline read in bold black lettering *"Hello 324"* The pages seemed to have nothing on them other than threes, twos and fours. Michael opened the fridge

256

and grabbed a can of coke, he quickly opened it and drank a large gulp. He held it up to his face all the writing was changing before his eyes *"three, two, four, three, two, four, three, two, four"*. He ran to the bathroom and doused his face with cold water. He lifted his head to look in the mirror and was met by a large numerical scar on his forehead. It was as if he had been branded like a cow, a large 324. He shut his eyes and let out a shriek *"Michael, Michael"* Kaitlin shook him quite roughly. *"Wake up you're on the couch"* he sat upright in his chair, with beer still in hand. The television was reporting the late night news. *"Come to bed……and no more cheese before sleepy time"*

   "O.K Honey" Michael was still quite shaken from the dream and tuned into the TV for one final time *"The Kung Lao mining company have reported that they are still unsure….."* Michael watched intently, awaiting the figure quoted by the news reporter *"…….so far the number of missing miners is at two hundred and thirty four"* Michael relaxed and shook his head, surprised how much a silly dream had affected him. Brushing his teeth, Michael checked his forehead in the mirror, it was brand free. He switched out the light and headed to bed, he snuck in quietly trying not to wake Kaitlin who was already wide awake and awaiting him. *"I thought you would never come to bed"*. She slipped her body on top of Michael's and began to kiss him passionately. Their bodies entwined and they had become fully immersed in each other. Michael's heart beat faster and faster, he soon begun to feel overpowered by the emotions invoked by the love making. Kaitlin writhed uncontrollably on top of him, yelping with pleasure at every little burst of motion. Michael got more and more claustrophobic, the pleasure had turned to blind panic and he shut his eyes hoping to refocus on a usually enjoyable experience. Opening his eyes, he shut them again immediately. In disbelief at what he had seen. *"Kaitlin?"* Michael quizzed the woman who was straddled over him. Her hair was darker, her skin was darker. *"Kaitlin?"* He opened his eyes again and seen that it was Kaitlin and the light was playing tricks on him. The Love making had now reached a climactic stage and Michael could feel his body tingle under the intense pleasure he was experiencing. Kaitlin let out a few loud yelps and Michael retaliated with stronger and more forceful thrusts. His eyes remained shut as he concentrated hard. Kaitlin let out an ecstatic roar *"Thrreeeeeee"* Michael by this time was passed the point of no return, a dozen wild horses couldn't have pulled him off. Kaitlin let out another loud roar *"Twooooooooooo"* Michael noticed the odd second bizarre outburst and opened his eyes. Kaitlin was gone, it was the dark haired woman, she was intensely beautiful and Michael was completely captivated as

she let out the final roar *"Fooooouurrrrr!"* Michael was engulfed in light and lost consciousness immediately.

Michael lay on a stainless steel rack unable to move or even see, his hearing was muffled and incoherent whispers echoed inside his head *"He, is coming around"*

"Don't touch him, he needs to surface on his own" He felt like an empty shell, Devoid of any feeling. He was in some sort of state of existence, he had no idea whether he was alive or dead, awake or asleep. The world seemed to be out with the reaches of his conscious mind. Someone was there, someone or something. He could hear their whispers. A woman. *"He's been in for so long, do you think he knows I'm here?"* She sounded distressed and desperate. Michael was lost, floating around in some sort of incomplete plain of existence, his mind was fragmented and disconnected from any sort of reality. Was he Michael Cameron? Or was he back on the unexplained journey which had taken over his life. The last few months with Kaitlin and Joseph was everything he had hoped for. A second chance taken. But now lying here, disconnected from the life he had accepted, he thought just how easily it could have all been fabricated like everywhere else he had been. Why now lying here did all the memories become so easily accessible? His mind took him from the Japanese Mountains, to London, America, Iraq. He drifted through each locale like a ghost. Silent and incapable of interaction. The experiences that he took part in were no longer a locked chest buried deep in his mind. He floated around out with the confines of his mortal shell, able to inspect and analyse each detail with a simple thought or memory. *"He's lost in there......I'm going to start the process".*

"O.K you're the boss, we need to be quick" Michael was plummeted in darkness, he fell for what felt like an eternity, in complete silence with downwards motion being the only physical sensation. *"Quick, he's almost gone"*

"Initialising". Michael was engulfed in the Light that he had become so accustomed to. And shut his eyes, just like he had on every single locale as he engaged in his mission to unite the twelve. The downwards motion ceased and he opened his eyes. He stood alone in the middle of nowhere. The terrain was bleak and a long straight road was the only piece of decoration as far as the eye could see. Michael checked out himself, He was himself this time, Michael Cameron. No shoes and wearing a hospital bed gown. Two tiny dots of light shone

out in the distance and gradually got bigger and bigger as the approaching vehicle homed in on his position. The horn started to blare and the driver waved excitedly. The car skidded to a halt a few feet from Michael and he watched as the driver popped open the door and turned to face him. *"What's up Dickhead?"*

"Bernie, what are you doing here?"

"Question is; what are you doing here Alfie my son, or should I say Michael?" Michael stood lost for words and Bernie approached him with outstretched arms and gave him a brisk and reassuring hug. *"Time we got you up to speed, let's go, I'll drive, if that's all right?"* Bernie laughed and jumped into the driver seat of the beautiful red Porsche 911 Targa. *"Come on then what are you waiting for"*

"I'm waiting for an explanation Bernie?"

"Listen Mate, that's why I'm here, one step at a time" Bernie opened the passenger door and signalled for him to enter. He sat down and pushed the bed gown down between his knees. *"Time for Michael Cameron to meet his maker"* Bernie put his foot down and the Porsche shot off at an incredible rate. The stars in the night sky flew past and within seconds their locale had completely changed. *"O.K, this is where I let you off, it's been emotional"*

"What, where are you going?"

"Michael, where I am going doesn't matter. I'm not real" Bernie raised his hand and clicked his fingers and in an instant he and the Porsche had disappeared and Michael stood in a busy industrialised zone, surrounded by warehouses. His attire had completely changed, he was now in a navy blue boiler suit and noticed a multitude of others walking in unison towards an open door in one of the large warehouses. Michael joined the queue and headed towards one of the doors. A hand rested on his shoulder and he turned quickly, on edge and pretty shook up. He was met with another familiar face. It was Fu, he also had on the blue overalls and was heading for the warehouse entrance. *"Don't worry bro, no-one can hurt you here"*

"Where is here Fu?"

"Keep going, not long now" The pair walked on until Michael passed through the door way and the interior was transformed into a busy factory floor. He was standing at an assembly line and large glass capsules were passing down, various electronic and steel fixtures were being attached to them. The factory floor was enormous, to the extent that he could not see the far off wall. A large display screen was up high on the wall which read *"V.I.E.R.A Corporation 336,987,324 units sold to date"*. Michael recognised the acronym, he looked all over the place, there seemed to be finished units being produced

every few seconds. He walked towards the end of the production line to see the final product. It was a glass chamber which was sealed in a steel structure. There were various cables which were unattached, presumably from linkage at the unit's destination. Another worker stood with his back to Michael and scanned each of the units as they passed, an electronic beep sounded much like a supermarket. *"Excuse me, can you tell me what these are for?"*

"Well Michael, that is the burning question is it not" The man turned to face him, It was Noritomo and he too was adorned in factory blue. *"Noritomo, my friend"* Noritomo grimaced with a look uncharacteristic of the old man for whom he had care for. *"Ah still not ready I see! Move it along"* Noritomo clicked his fingers just as Bernie had and Michael was instantly transported. He stood atop an enormous building in the centre of a city scape, it dwarfed all others for miles around and Michael held onto the ledge, fearful of the drop. He could hear the flapping of what sounded like a flag and looked around for some sort of clue as to where it was coming from. The flapping grew louder. But still no sign of its origin. *"Just like the gulf, watch your dome wee man"* Michael turned and dived out the way as a Parachutist just missed him and landed on the rooftop beside him. *"Alright wee man?"*

"Gordie?"

"Who else is gonnae make an entrance like that?" Michael watched as Gordie unhooked his parachute and approached him, he gave him a powerful handshake and a big smile. *"Well, in case you've not guessed by now, I'm not real either?"*

"That seems to be a recurring theme" Michael had noticed that everyone was different, they looked the same, but their function had changed somewhat. Gordie was there standing right in front of him, but he was a messenger of some sort, trying to communicate an as yet unexplained plot line. *"Turn round wee man"* Michael turned around and behind him, built up on stilts like the Hollywood sign was an enormous company logo in bright blue neon lights. *'V.I.E.R.A'.* *"O.K, now I'm guessing this has a big part to play"* *"Jesus, that wee man's quick"* Gordie laughed as Michael stated the obvious. No one he had met so far was real? *"Gordie, am I real?"*

"Now you're asking the right questions, see you later wee man" Gordie snapped his fingers and Michael was transported to a fresh new area. He was sitting in the passenger seat of a police car and he was accompanied by a police officer who was driving at a crazy speed. *"Shit were, going to lose him, take out his tires Michael!"* Michael had no control over his body this time, the body acted by its

261

own volition and he just happened to be able to view the situation through its eyes. He watched as his body reached for his gun and could not release it. He slipped off his seat belt and pulled the gun from its holster. Leaning out the window he fired off two shots and the rear passenger side tire exploded sending the assailants car tumbling down the road. The body sat back down and the police car screamed to a halt. Both officers left the vehicle and approached the wrecked car. *"Looks like they've both had it boss."* Michael approached the passenger door of the upturned vehicle and pulled it open. *"Rookie, no!"* The warning from his partner was too late. A single shot rang out and the body fell to the ground in an unconscious heap. The other police officer clicked his fingers and Michael now lay in the back of an ambulance with two paramedics over him. *"O.K call it, TOD 18:43".* The paramedic approached to close his eyes and stopped short. It was little Agnieska smiling from ear to ear. *"So yes, you are real Michael, dead but real, but that unfortunately is only the beginning".* Agnieska clicked her fingers and Michael found himself standing at the side of a grave amongst a grieving congregation. He was back in his hospital gown and seemed to be invisible to the other mourners. He did not recognise any of them at all. A woman stood right at the front and placed a single red rose on the coffin, she wore a black veil which hid her from view. Michael stood and watched as the mourners left in dribs and drabs until only the woman remained. She lifted her veil, it was Sophie, she did not acknowledge him at all and he approached her only to be sent tumbling into the open grave. He passed through the coffin like a ghost, only to find that it was empty. He jumped up with fear and turned to face her again. She did not look at him and clicked her fingers. Michael found himself back within a facility, bodies were lined up on individual slabs as far as the eye could see. They all seemed to be under some sort of medical observation and Michael approached the nearest one. He was being kept alive, his face was covered with a cloth like fabric to hide the grotesque mess which lay underneath. *"Unimaginable is it not?"* Michael was approached by King Kamal, dressed in all his glory *"What are they doing?"*

"Is it not obvious Michael Cameron, they are keeping him alive, or should I say, they are keeping the dead alive". Michael listened to the King who was now far easier to get along with. *"Is this me?"*

"Your body is weak but your mind is still in there somewhere"

"O.K, enough with the preparation, just tell me the truth, I'm ready" The king clicked his fingers and disappeared and Michael found

himself standing alone in the white room again. Before him a figure began to materialise. *"Sophie? Is that you?"*

"Hello Michael, I've been waiting for you" Sophie stood before him in all her glory. As beautiful as he remembered her. *"Please tell me you're real?"*

"What you see before you is not real, I am a just construct of your unconscious mind implanted by me, out there in the real world" Michael listened intently to Sophie, he was finally getting some answers. *"Although what you see before you is an accurate representation of me, Sophie Cameron. Well I'm a few years older now"*

"Tell me everything Sophie, am I dead?"

"You're supposed to be dead, I thought you were dead along with everyone else, apart from the corporation". Michael was engrossed in the truth, at last he might actually be able to get some rest. *"Come with me, I will show you. Touch my hand"* Michael reached out and touched Sophie's hand and they were both engulfed in the light. They re-emerged in a highly populated shopping mall. They both wore generic clothing which seemed to fit in nicely with the rest of the shoppers. *"This is the Chicago Outer City Commercialised Zone, or COMOZ for short, it is one of many of the same type which are owned by a single corporation. The V.I.E.R.A Corporation"* Michael noticed how far advanced everything looked and struggled to comprehend exactly where or when he was. *"When is it Sophie?"*

"Oh sorry, of course. Michael, it is not 2012, in fact it is nowhere near that time any more, it is much further along, 2431 to be exact"

"But my life, my family the museum?" Sophie frowned and looked a little hurt

"Come with me" Michael followed Sophie as she walked through the crowd and made her way to a large and busy venue in the mall. *"V.I.E.R.A own it all, every shop, every manufacturer, every food outlet, they are truly global and have every government in the world in the palm of their hand due to this"* Sophie pointed to the sign above the entrance to the shop. '12' it was a large number 12 above the entrance and upon entering there were a multitude of booths throughout the entire shop floor *"This is how they started out, with 12. It is the singular most popular consumer product in the history of the known universe, the V.I.E.R.A Corporation have built an empire off the back of it"* Michael watched as people entered and left the booths, people of varying ages, genders and creeds. It seemed to have a mass appeal. *"This has to do with the sphere?"* Sophie smiled *"The sphere?*

Such a generic name you gave it. To you it was the sphere to all these people it is the satisfaction and glorification of uniting it that brings the appeal, and to them it is simply called 12" Michael was blown away by what surrounded him. *"Shall we?"* Sophie directed him to one of the booths and they entered and stood at the back watching a consumer interact with 12. *"Listen carefully now, this is the geeky part. The user pays for their experience in stages. First they attend a briefing where they determine which package is most suitable, In terms of age and affordability. A credit check is carried out and the first payment is requested. The player can chose to directly control the hero or simply give him or her certain characteristics and watch the story unfold for themselves. They have a maximum of twelve resurrections for their character and can chose from hundreds of thousands of scenarios from Ancient Japan to top model"* Michael started to get a little on edge and Sophie drew it in a little. *"Alright Michael stay calm"*

"How can I stay calm, I'm nothing but a fuckin' computer game"

"Oh you are so much more than that, come with me" Michael touched her hand and they were whisked off to another area. They were now in a massive facility which was filled with thousands of the glass tubes which he and Fu had watched being created. *"The COMOZ is the public face of V.I.E.R.A, this is where the real stuff happens. Ask yourself what is more attractive than being able to control an actual living breathing individual, he reacts and behaves in a completely natural and non-programmed sense. This is why everyone is so hooked".* Michael began to try and build a picture, he understood the intricacies of what Sophie was explaining but failed to see how he fitted into all of it. Sophie approached one of the glass tubes and took Michael by the hand. A tear filled her eye and dripped down her cheek. *"3 years ago, you were taken from me, some trigger happy hood........we were going to start trying for a baby"* Sophie sobbed for a few seconds and then wiped her eyes clean. *"Michael, this is you"* Michael looked into the glass chamber and was met by his own face staring back at him, eyes closed and wired up to the innards of the glass tube. Only his face was on show and the rest of him was encased in the familiar armoured suit of the black figure. *"So I'm dead then?"*

"V.I.E.R.A own everything Michael, The own the food we eat, the shoes we wear, they own the living and they own the dead, You were dead until V.I.E.R.A decided otherwise."

"So I'm alive then?"

"Come with Me" Michael followed Sophie and listened to her as she explained as best she could. *"See him"* she pointed at one of

the glass tubes. *"He is number 1, this is number 2, 3, 4 all the way up till number 12"*

"So they are all me?"

"Touch my hand Michael". Again they were transported to another area where a single glass tube lay in the centre of a small chamber. *"This is you, the other twelve are simply shells, created by V.I.E.R.A for the purposes of the game, clones if you will"*

"And I'm alive in there?"

"V.I.E.R.A snatch you within hours of your death and the resuscitate you, no one knows how they do it. They keep you alive and extract matter from your living brain. They create 12 doppelgangers which they then use in each of the levels of 12. At the end of each level they terminate the clone and move onto the next." Michael sat down on the floor in disbelief, his heart sank *"So Kaitlin and little Joseph, they don't exist?"*

"They are your home program, they are created in order to keep the host brain active, while the game progresses, they give you a nice normal, but not perfect existence so as to trick your brain into conforming"

"I know they are not real but it makes me sad that I won't see them again"

"That is the power of V.I.E.R.A, the end user and the host are both completely unaware of the truth. You are locked in a subliminal fantasy world and the end user does not even know that you exist, only a few of us know the truth"

"So how were you able to visit me when I was under?"

"In order for 12 to work, it requires a fully functioning brain which V.I.E.R.A clone. But they are unable to clone emotion and that is why the host is kept alive. Their living minds are transferred to each of the clones to allow the user to have as real an experience as possible, the clue is in the name Michael"

"I don't understand, explain it to me?"

"V.I.E.R.A it's an Acronym Michael. Virtual Interactive Emotional Response Apparatus" Michael stood in wonder and looked upon the body within the chamber. Everything was piecing together now, he was indeed a puppet, being used against his will.

"So how do we get me out of this?"

"That's the difficult part, no one has ever gotten out alive, we managed to reanimate your first clone"

"The Black Figure"

"That's right, after we got him resuscitated we were able to hack the system and send him into help, that's how I got in as well"

"So he is just a clone?" Sophie looked angry

"He was much more than that, we programmed him to be just like you" Michael could feel her pain, the black figure death had hit her hard. A crackle was followed by an outside voice *"Sophie, we need to move it along, I think they are on to us?"*

"Who is that?"

"That is your saviour, I just hope you get to meet him, lesson over for now Michael. O.K Travis take me out" Michael panicked and screamed out at Sophie,

"Where are you going Sophie?"

"I'm no good to you in here Michael"

"What should I do?"

"Sit tight I'll be able to talk you, I love you Michael Cameron, see you on the other side?"

"But Sophie what about 324, what does that mean?" Sophie dematerialised before his eyes and Michael cursed at his own stupidity, he had been bombarded with so much glorious information that he had completely forgot to ask the question that had been plaguing his mind for so long. What is 324? The locale disintegrated all around him and Michael was stood back in the white room once more. *"O.K Michael, can you hear me?"*

"Yeah I can hear you Sophie, are you out already?"

"For me it's easy, I've only been under less than an hour, you've been in for considerably longer, so it's not quite so easy" Michael stood eager to get on with it, it was time to go home, somewhere he could not even remember being before. But anything was better than what he had just learned. *"O.K Michael this is going to hurt a little, close your eyes"* Michael closed his eyes and the piercing pain in his skull returned with a vengeance. He opened them and he stood on the 73rd floor. *"Michael, we need you to sever the link from the twelfth clone."*

"O.K what do I do?"

"This is going to sound crazy but you have to kill it, there is no other way of transferring the part of your subconscious back to your body. The Actual clone is already dead, it is just the emotional attachment that you are terminating, O.K?" Michael was completely freaked out by the concept, he felt alive and kicking, and although he knew he was not actually there. The pain itself would still be real enough to him *"O.K let's do this?"* Michael approached Calvin's office window and threw a chair at it, after the third attempt it smashed through and he felt the wind blow accompanied by a distant whistle. *"Here goes nothing"* Michael ran at the window full pelt and launched

himself through the opening. The wind threw him around like a paper plane until his body cracked the solid concrete below, he screamed and opened his eyes, he was now back in the white room again. *"Good Michael, that seems to have done the trick, O.K 11 more to go"*

"What I have to kill myself 11 more times"

"I know it's hard Michael, there is no other way". Each of the places he visited he came up with the easiest way to end his life, the levels with guns proved to be the easiest. Next was Persia where Michael materialised in the chapel with The King and his little brother. Michael went through the process of listening to Kinra explain the carving and when the King arrived he pounced on Kinra and kissed him passionately. The King became incredibly angry and plunged his sword through Madokht's heart, before finishing off his little brother. When Michael reached the Island he simply swam out into the dark ocean and kept going until his arms could not carry him anymore and he slipped into the darkest depths succumbing to the water as it filled his lungs. Michael rematerialized in the log cabin. This time there was no Sophie to tend to his wound and send him on the next locale and he expired by the same wound he had from the first visit. Michael materialised in the prison and walked out the cell door, just as he had when he first arrived. He climbed up onto the railing and stood arms outstretched and plummeted considerably less than his first suicide, but it was enough to ensure he got the job done. The next four levels were ended with the quick blast of a pistol or rifle. Alfie Charles lay on the bed with blood soaking into the bed sheets. The Iraq sand grew more moist than usual as it soaked up the brains of General Al Zuhairi. A slight movement to the left ensured that the player's bullet made a far more deadly connection. Kings yelping was hard to bear as the irradiated woman ended her life deep in the wastelands of Eastern Europe. Sophie was clever to ensure that she did not reanimate Michael within the Coma victim and chose to wait until he was walking through the station. A long walk across the tracks taking in some Beautiful weather was the prelude to his final act as he was dragged under the wheels of a large diesel locomotive. Young Danny had the most spectacular end of them all, they were all asleep, and he locked himself inside the airlock. He waited a few minutes and ordered LOIS to open the outer hull door and he was sucked into space, imploding within the most beautiful of surroundings. That just left one final location to deal with. Noritomo and Japan. Sophie placed him in just as the tournament was beginning and Michael played his part, enjoying it now having the benefit of hindsight. He awaited the final attack by the treacherous opponent and sidestepped him advance. He

avoided the fatal blow from the first visit and sliced his head clean off. Michael then kneeled on the dirt and raised his sword and spoke a final sentence *"Time to go home, Unite the twelve".* He thrust his sword through his own heart, this time expiring far quicker and rematerializing back within the white room. *"Michael, can you hear me?"*

"I'm Here Sophie, Did it work?"

"Still a bit to go yet Michael, hold on" Michael waited around 15 minutes and periodically asked whether they were ready yet until Sophie finally gave the nod. *"O.K Michael we are going to try and pull you out, don't do nothing, it's all down to us at this end now."*

"O.K, I'm ready"

"I love you Michael Cameron"

"I love you too Sophie"

"O.K Travis, start it up" Michael felt his body travelling at a hundred miles an hour, he was all over the place. Memories of all the places he had been as well as the faces of everyone he met flashed before his eyes until darkness. There was nothing to stimulate his senses at all. No light, sound, no hot or cold. Michael felt conscious but lay in doubt of the success of the procedure. Was this it was he dead? He was buoyed by a distant sound. He listened as hard as he could until he made out a faint voice. He managed to open his eyes just a touch and noticed the condition of the room which he was revived in. The building looked old and barely liveable *"O.K Travis keep him sedated, the longer we let him recover, the better chance of survival"* It was Sophie's voice and she was directing people, Michael could just make out some shadows of people bustling around him. *"Quick we only have a minute till they reach us, get him in the back of the van, we need to get him to a safe house"*

"I can't believe we got him out Sophie"

"I know, I can only hope he likes what he sees when he wakes" Sophie leaned in and gave Michael a little kiss on the forehead. *"It's O.K my love, nearly there, one more big push to the finish line. Travis take him out"* A few men surrounded him and a loud hiss was followed by the glass exterior of the chamber he was in slowly lifting towards the ceiling. Michael was bundled onto a trolley and lifted towards the back of a van. His vision returned a bit more and he watched Sophie as he was moved. She was blurry and Michael noticed that her clothes seemed well worn. He looked beyond her to the glass chamber he was removed from and could just make at a black metal plaque with silver writing on it "V.I.E.R.A 324" The shutter came down and Travis directed the driver *"O.K safe house, quick now he is very*

weak" Sophie stood alone in the room and stared into the empty chamber. A young man dressed like a soldier approached and spoke to her *"Do you think he will understand Captain?"*

"We need him soldier, whether he understands is irrelevant, if he doesn't then he will have to go against his will like 323 and all the others before him. We just have to hope his mind can handle it".

16646269R00151

Printed in Great Britain
by Amazon